Little Girl Lost

BOOK 1

ILISE DORSKY

Ilise Dorsky

7/23/2022

PAGE PUBLISHING, INC.
Conneaut Lake, PA

First originally published by Page Publishing 2021

ISBN 978-1-6624-3654-3 (pbk)
ISBN 978-1-6624-3655-0 (digital)

Printed in the United States of America

For Sam
Not only did you save my life
but you saved countless others.
You are the love of my life and the
constant beacon we all use to find
our way back home.

Chapter 1

It started out as a normal Long Island day. Little did I know my world, the world, and the life I thought I had was about to come to a crashing halt.

To paint a picture of my life thus far, I was a suburban wife. My husband at the time owned his own business, so his hours were pretty much his own. I had two children, a daughter and a son. He was the stepparent. Life, for all intents and purposes, was okay—or so I thought. Sure, we had our problems, but who didn't? Yes, on occasion, he lost his temper, and it could get pretty ugly, but it was always aimed at me. It was manageable. The good far outweighed the bad. After all, we had a nice house, everything we wanted, and we were providing a good life for my kids. My daughter was, at this point, an aspiring actress/model with magazine spreads, runway shows, and acting gigs on her resume. My son played on various sports teams and excelled in many areas of his life. So if there was an occasional fight at home, I did my best to keep things in check.

It was winter, and life was pretty normal until I discovered that my beautiful, perfect daughter was hooked on pain pills. Back in 2011, that wasn't as prevalent as it is today. I was horrified, scared, sad but mostly in shock. At this point, I had no idea what to do, whom to call, or basically anything else. So I did the only thing I knew how to do. I researched everything I could on the Internet and started making calls. I called all of my local drug rehabs only to be asked what her insurance was. I was shocked to realize that drug rehabs are insurance based. That this world we live in cares more about the financial aspect of things than the health and welfare of our loved ones. On with my search. I finally found a facility that took our insurance, one that sounded positive. Now I had to persuade my daughter to go.

Unfortunately, she was over eighteen, and according to the law, she was considered an adult. Never mind that she was not clear thinking; never mind that she was a full-blown pill addict. She was over eighteen and an adult.

Okay, so after three days of begging, pleading, and threatening, she finally agreed to go. Now I had to call the facility back and hope that they still had a bed. You see, unless your loved one is ready to go at that moment, they don't hold the bed. Thankfully, one was still available, so off we went. It is such a delicate thing to arrange—you only have a small window of time to persuade your addict to go. The facility only holds the bed for a short amount of time. Anything can change in an instant. But off we went, an hour's drive to what I thought was our salvation. Little did I know. Once we arrived at the facility, my daughter was immediately taken away from me and brought to the back for intake. I was relegated to the waiting room with the other family members. Waiting…waiting for what? At this point, I didn't know. As I sat there not sure whether to cry, scream, or be sick, I started to think, *How did we get here? What did I do wrong? How could this be happening to us?* I sat with my own thoughts, trying not to make myself crazy. I tried to focus on the conversations swirling around me. I finally heard my name being called. I jumped up, grabbed my daughter's bags, and followed a nondescript person down a long, dreary hallway. I thought I was being brought to see my daughter, but I was wrong. I was ushered into an office with a woman sitting behind a desk. She told me to have a seat, and then she proceeded to go over my insurance, my out-of-pocket cost, and lastly, how long my insurance company would cover my daughter's stay. As I came to find out, insurance companies only pay for a specific amount of time. Not nearly long enough. Once papers were signed, checks written, and a list of do's and don'ts passed to me, I was escorted back to the waiting room, where I continued to wait to see my daughter. Once again, I was called into an office. A different one this time. This one had a long table and a rather stern looking young man. I was instructed to place my daughter's bags on the table and to have a seat. To my horror, this young man went through everything in her bags. I was given armloads of things to take back. When we were done, I was again taken back to the waiting room. At this point, the director told me I was free to leave. Leave? Leave? What about my daughter? Didn't I get to see her before I left? Hug her goodbye, wish her luck anything? I was told no. It was easier this way. *Easier for whom?* I wondered.

I was told she would be able to call me in a few days—a few days for fifteen minutes. I had to wait a few days? An eternity. I was escorted out, arms full of clothing, heart full of dread. I remember hearing the click of the door locking behind me. Was it locking to keep them in or us out? I walked to my car, every step harder than the last. I got into my car and immediately started to sob. I cried for my daughter, for my family, and for myself. What did I do wrong as a mother? How had I failed her? I wouldn't get those answers till many years later. The next few days were a blur of sadness. I felt alone and lost. After all, I was the mother of two, and one was missing. My son was spending a lot of time in his room—time doing things that he didn't want me a part of. I counted the days then the minutes until that first phone call. It finally came at three o'clock on Friday. She sounded distant and sad. She kept apologizing to me. We cried together on the phone. She said she felt good. She told me that the next day was family visiting day and could I please come. Of course I would be there—anything for her. Right at the fifteen-minute mark, she said that she had to hang up. We said "I love you" to each other, and I promised to see her the next day.

Bright and early on Saturday morning, I hit the road. Much too early for my visit but I wanted to make sure I was there on time. I was by myself for the visit as my son did not want to go and I was going through a divorce. We had been separated for months by now and just had to go thru the legalities. It was better this way; after all, I didn't want to share my time with her. I pulled up to the facility and found that the parking lot was pretty full. I hadn't realized that there were going to be other people. I walked in, signed in, and took a seat. I didn't know what to expect. I can tell you that what happened next was a shock. We were all ushered into a big room like an auditorium and asked to take seats. We were then addressed as a group. We were given some rules for when we saw our loved ones. Then a speaker came in and introduced herself. She told us she was an addict in recovery. She had been an active drug user for many years but at this point had been in recovery for ten years. She went on to explain addiction to us and how it not only affects the individual but also how it affects the family as a whole. How it is a disease and how hard it is to escape. After listening to her for almost an hour, she told us to look around the room. We were then told that out of the fifty-plus people in that room, only 1 percent would not be back in treatment. Only 1 percent—I was certain that we were that 1 percent.

Chapter 2

F inally, it was time to see Molly. I felt like it had been years instead of days. I waited and watched as other families were reunited. I waited and waited. Would she come? She had asked me to be here. Had she changed her mind? Was she still angry at me for bringing her here? Finally, I saw her. She was in the doorway, hesitant to walk into the room. My eyes immediately filled with tears. I held them back; I would not cry. This was going to be a happy visit. As Molly walked toward me, I thought, *She doesn't belong here. She doesn't fit in. She belongs at home with me.* As soon as she was close enough, I grabbed her in my arms and hugged her. She felt thin and fragile. But oh so familiar. I remembered the many times I held her before. Molly broke the embrace and took my hand and led me to a sofa. We sat down and I immediately peppered her with questions. Are you eating? sleeping? Did you make friends? She took her time answering me, almost as if she was measuring her words. Measuring what she was going to tell me. She told me that she had been really sick those first few days. She thought she was going to die. The facility she was in did a medical detox, but it wasn't very good, she said. She started feeling better and was able to start to participate in the different groups. She told me about her days. She had therapy twice a day once in a group setting and once alone. The rest of the groups consisted of art therapy, meditation, yoga, and self-reflection. They also had speakers come in to speak about their experiences, their time in recovery, their successes and failures. And yes, there were failures. Molly and I talked about lots of things that first day, but mostly, we just sat holding hands, each of us lost in our own thoughts. Before long, a counselor came in to let us know that our time had come to an end. I could not believe that the day was over, but it was. Molly walked me as far as she could and then stood in the doorway, watching me go. I left with a heavy heart, part of me hopeful but a larger part of me sad, sad for the little girl she was and sad at the thought of leaving her again. I waved and I drove away, watching as she became a dot on the horizon.

Now to begin the long drive home, lost in my own thoughts and regrets. I thought back to the early days where my biggest worry was getting my kids to their various activities. Who could have ever known that this was the road that we would travel? I was overcome with emotions, so much so that I did what I thought was the responsible thing to do—I pulled over onto the side of the road. I put my head on the steering wheel and wept. Great, big, soul-crushing sobs. I cried until I was weak, until I had no more tears. As I picked up my head to dry off my face, I heard a tap on my car window. What now? I wondered.

I turned my head to look, and there he stood—a police officer. I wondered what was going on. I was parked on the shoulder of the road, not obstructing traffic, so what could it be? As I rolled down my window, the office shined his light into my car. He asked me if I was okay. I wanted to say no. That I would never be okay again, but I said yes—I was fine, just tired, so I had stopped for a few minutes.

He looked at me with a little skepticism, trying to decide, I guess, if I was believable or not. Doubt won, and he asked me for my license and registration. Well, I knew where my license was, but since I was in a rental car, I wasn't sure where the registration was. After several minutes of fumbling around looking for it, I found it. I handed him both and waited. After several minutes, he came back to my car; he asked me to get out of the car. *Really? Come on now.* He asked me to walk toe to toe, to extend my arms out and to touch my nose with my fingertips. What? Come on. I did all that was asked. Once done, he told me that I was free to get back into my car. He then apologized and said he needed to make sure that I hadn't been drinking. "After all," he said, "not too many people park on the shoulder of a semi busy road." I thanked him for his concern and went on my way.

By the time I got home, I was exhausted. Emotionally drained, I hardly had the strength to get out of my car. I sat there, looking around at the other homes on my quiet tree lines street and wondered how many other families were going through some kind of turmoil. I finally got out of my car and walked into my house. I was greeted by complete and total silence. A silence so deep and profound that it was suffocating me. I immediately turned on the TV, lights, and the radio. I needed the chaos to keep me from thinking. I called out to Luke, my fifteen-year-old son, and was met with silence. I realized that I was alone. I had no idea where my son was. I went into the kitchen to check for a note. There wasn't one. There was, however, the mail. I thumbed through it and saw an official-looking letter. I held it for a moment before opening it. It was my final divorce decree. Instead of feeling sad, I was somewhat relieved. It was finally over and one less thing for me to have to think about. It was a good thing. I had far too many other things to worry about.

As I was sitting there thinking, the phone rang. It was Luke. He told me he was out, not to worry he would be home early. We hung up without him even asking me how my visit with Molly went. A few hours later, Luke came home. He was oddly quiet; he spent just a few minutes talking to me. He finally asked me how his sister was. I told her she was okay; she was adjusting. He leaned down and kissed me good night and went to his room. I heard his door close and then silence.

The rest of my week went by pretty uneventfully. I went to work with a smile on my face, hoping no one could guess my shameful secret. You see, at the time, I felt shame, again being plagued by the question "What did I do wrong?" Each night, I came home from work to an empty house, no Luke, no Molly, just quiet. I was sad and lonely. The only high point of my week was my fifteen-minute conversation with Molly. Fifteen minutes on Wednesday evenings. Wednesday, it seemed, was my day. I sat by the phone an hour before our call time. I wanted to make sure I was ready. Sure enough, at exactly 6:00 p.m., the phone rang, and there she was, sounding almost like herself. She asked me how I was. How was I? At that moment, I was filled with happiness and hope. She told me how her week was going and what she was doing. I told her what was going on at home, making sure to keep things light and positive. And again, fifteen minutes was over far too soon. We once again said "I love you," and I promised to see her again on Saturday, and then she was gone. I continued to sit there for what seemed like an eternity, thinking about everything we said and more importantly, everything we didn't say. I was exhausted and went right to bed. That night I had a dreamless sleep—much better than the impending nightmares that were waiting for me in the nights to come.

On Saturday, I was up once again bright and early to begin getting ready for my drive to see Molly. I packed up the things she asked for and went to find Luke. He was in his room listening to music. I told him we were going to be leaving in about an hour. He looked at me with what appeared to be sadness and said, "Mom, I am not going with you."

"You're not? Why? Why don't you want to see your sister?"

He didn't really have much more of an answer than "I just don't want to go."

To say I was disappointed would be an understatement. I was heartsick. So into my car I went once again with only my thoughts to keep me company. The drive was long, but the scenery was lovely, and as I neared the facility, my heart racing, I was pulled over by a police officer. What? In all my years driving, I had never been pulled over, but now in the span of a week, I was about to have my second encounter. As he approached my car, I reached for my license and registration. I knew where it was this time. I rolled my window down and asked him what I did wrong. He told me that I had made an illegal turn. I didn't and told him so. Nevertheless, he wrote me a ticket. I took it and drove away. I didn't want to be late for my visit.

Again, I pulled into the somewhat crowded parking lot. I walked in and waited. We again had a speaker; this time it was a young man. He couldn't have been more than twenty-four or twenty-five years old. He spoke of his addiction and how he started by smoking pot and graduated to heroin. I was shocked. Heroin—now that was really bad. I silently gave thanks that my daughter "only" abused pills. When he was done, the director spoke to us. She spoke about meetings for us and how we should get a sponsor. Someone whom we could talk to in those dark lonely days yet to come. And then she told us that next Wednesday, there would be a meeting at the facility that she encouraged us to attend. I thought about it, thinking, *No, I won't be going.* But then I realized it was another chance to see Molly, so much better than the weekly phone call I would receive. I would go if for only that reason. Then I waited again, waited for Molly to join me. Once again, she was one of the last to come into the room. I wondered why this was and was going to ask her, but I got distracted by the friend she was introducing me to. Her name was Julie and she was nineteen. She wasn't expecting any visitors, she told me; her parents had pretty much given up on her. This was her third rehab, and they were tired of doing this. I thought that was so sad. How could parents give up like that? When Molly hugged me, she whispered, "Please, Mom, can Julie stay? She is lonely." What could I say?

My brain screamed, *No, no, no.* I wanted to selfishly spend every minute with Molly alone. But my heart said, *Yes, of course. How could we leave this child alone?*

We went outside, found a spot to sit to enjoy the sun. I asked Julie to tell me a little bit about herself. She lived in a small town in Pennsylvania. She got into drugs because her boyfriend at the time was using them. When he broke up with her, she started using more to numb the pain. She overdosed, and her mom found her. She spent two days in the hospital before being sent to her first rehab. After completing the thirty-day program she was back home. After two weeks at home, she started using again. When her parents found out, they sent her to stay with her grandmother. When that didn't work, they sent her back to rehab. Another stint and another relapse. Now she was here. Her parents made sure that she understood that this time was the last time.

I felt sad for this lost child. I could not imagine the heartache and pain her mom and dad felt or how much they went through to get to this point. I asked them both if they were eating, sleeping, working in their groups. Both told me that things were going good. They were learning a lot. The food was okay—not great but okay. I asked them if they wanted me to run to the deli for sandwiches or something else, and they both smiled as they nodded. So off I went, a little reluctant to cut into my visit but at the same time happy to be offering something. Once back, I sat with Molly and Julie as they enjoyed their sandwiches. After they were done, Julie thanked me and then excused herself. Perhaps she sensed that I needed some alone time with Molly. When she was gone, I turned my attention to Molly and asked, "How are you really doing?"

She broke down crying, telling me she was lonely. She missed me and her brother. Missed being home, her bed, her friends, her life. As I sat there soothing her, I thought about her life too, thought about how she had gotten here and that this was just a detour—that she would be back on track in no time. Before I knew it, it was time to say goodbye. But this time, I told her I would be back in just a few days. I would see her on Wednesday after my meeting. This time, the drive wasn't as bad maybe because I'd done it before, or maybe it was because I knew that in just a few days, I would be seeing her again. Either way, I was glad my trip home was uneventful.

Chapter 3

Again, when I arrived home, Luke was out. I started feeling a little nagging in the back of my mind. I couldn't quite put my finger on it yet. As I peered into my refrigerator, looking for a little something to eat, I realized I had not been to the grocery store in at least a week, maybe more. So back into the car I went, heading to my local supermarket. As I pushed my cart from isle to isle somewhat aimlessly, I thought I heard someone call my name. "Brenda, Brenda, is that you?" I stopped and turned around to see who was calling me, dreading to see who it was, hoping it wasn't someone who was going to ask me questions that I was not prepared to answer. I was astonished to see standing right in front of me Sam. Sam had been my crush all through high school. The boy whose name I used to scribble on my notebook. Sam who was my friend but never any more than that. Sam, who was now standing in my supermarket calling my name. As I looked at him, I was instantly transported back thirty-plus years, forgetting for a minute everything that was happening in my life. I asked him what he was doing in my neck of the woods.

His answer was simple. "I am buying groceries." Why hadn't we run into each other before? Different schedules? Or maybe it just wasn't time yet. In any event, here we were. Of course. we made the usual small talk: "You look great." "How have you been?" "What have you been doing since we last saw each other?" After what seemed like a few minutes but was actually an hour, we said our goodbyes. As I was leaving, Sam stopped me and said we should exchange numbers. "Let's stay in touch." Funny how things work. I was at the lowest point in my life, and in walks Sam, a ray of sun in my otherwise gloomy day. I finished my shopping with a hint of a smile and headed home.

This time, when I walked in, Luke was in the kitchen looking for food. As I was setting the bags down, he was rummaging through them, trying to decide what he wanted to eat. I told him that I would make dinner. He said that he would. So I agreed to let him cook for us; it was nice to be able to spend this time with him. Watching him move around getting pots and pans, opening and closing draws and cabinets. When he was finished cooking, we sat down and enjoyed dinner. The conversation was light; he told me he was doing well in school, not too much homework. I told him about my visit with Molly and of meeting her friend Julie. Before long dinner was over. I told him that since he cooked, I would clean up. He agreed and said good night.

The rest of the weekend I spent trying to catch up on some paperwork. I also tried to read and relax. I avoided talking to anyone on the phone; I didn't want to answer any questions from concerned friends. Monday came, and it was back to work. I kept to my routine as best as possible. I felt it was the only thing keeping me sane.

On Wednesday morning, I told Luke that I wouldn't be home after work, that I was driving out to Molly's rehab to go to a meeting there. I invited him to come, but as usual, he declined. I left work early so I could be on the road before any possible traffic, and as usual, I was there early. I waited in my car until I saw other cars pull in. Once the parking lot was half-full, I got out and walked in. This gathering was different from the usual Saturday visitors' day. A lot of the people there seemed to know each other. I was to find out that this was a weekly support group meeting for loved ones of addicts. I took a seat and waited for the meeting to begin. I had no idea what to expect. But believe me, I was nowhere near prepared for what I was about to experience.

We all sat in a circle, about twenty of us. A young woman who seemed to be conducting the meeting asked us to go around and introduce ourselves, first names only and who we were there for. It started with Sally. Her son was an addict, had been for five years. She was still hanging on, but her husband was not. Next was Joan. Her daughter was an alcoholic; she was also a single mom, so Joan was now raising her three grandchildren. She was exhausted every day. Next was John. His wife seemed to like heroin more than she liked him. He didn't know how much longer he could hold the family together.

Then it was my turn. "Hi, my name is Brenda, and my daughter is Molly. She is addicted to pills. This is my first time dealing with addiction."

As I was finishing up, a woman dashed in, apologizing for being late, for interrupting the meeting. "You see," she said, "I just left the hospital. my son Eric overdosed again. He is on life support this time. I wanted to say goodbye. I told him it was okay to go. To leave this world and go on to the next to find the peace he was so desperately looking for."

I sat there in stunned silence. How could any mother say goodbye to their child? How could she tell him it was okay to go? I was to find out many years later when our paths crossed again. I saw her speak and heard her story from beginning to end and finally understood. But that night, all I felt was deep sorrow for her and her son. We continued to go around the room, introducing ourselves. When we were done, the young woman introduced herself. Her name was Beth, and her dad was an addict. She explained that addiction does not discriminate. It hits every age, every race, everyone. She told us how addiction makes us, the family feel shame. We isolate. We don't tell our families, our friends, anyone. We feel the stigma of addiction, but we shouldn't we should seek support, we should get a sponsor join a support group something, anything to help us feel less alone. She told us that if any of us wanted her number, she would be glad to give it out. I sat there and listened, sure that I would need none of that. After all, we were that 1 percent. After the meeting was over, I had a chance to see Molly. She looked good. We talked for a while, and then I asked her about her friend Julie. "Oh, Mom, she said Julie's insurance ran out and she had to leave. Her mom had a change of heart and picked her up to bring her home. Julie promised to keep in touch. I met her mom and she gave me a hug and thanked me for being such a good friend."

After about an hour, I was told I had to leave. We said our good-byes, and off I went. This time leaving wasn't so bad. I knew I would be back on Saturday. About fifteen minutes into my car ride home, I received a call; it was Sam. He was calling to say hi and to see how I was doing. Surprisingly, I was in an upbeat mood. My visit with Molly had gone well, and now this phone call combined with that equaled happy. We chatted for a few minutes, and then he invited me over for coffee and catch up. I hesitated a minute, wondering to myself what I was prepared to share. Before I realized what was happening, I agreed, and we set the day and time. Friday night at eight o'clock.

The next two days flew by at work. I alternated between being excited and nervous. My nerves won out. On my drive there, I almost turned around twice, but I kept on going, showing up about thirty minutes late. As I pulled up, Sam was waiting at the door. He showed me in; I sensed that he was as nervous as I was. He asked me if I would like a tour of his house. Of course I did; from the outside, the house looked beautiful. He took me around, showing me everything; there was great pride in his voice as we went from room to room. The house was just beautiful. We finally settled down on the sofa in his living room. He asked me if I wanted coffee or wine. Wine of course. I was so nervous I needed something to help me calm down.

After taking a few sips, I was ready to play catch up. We took turns filling each other in on the lives we had led since high school. Sam, it seemed, had a very high-powered position in the police department, had been married before but never had kids. Although he always wanted them, it was just never in the cards. I told him that I too had been married before. It hadn't worked out either, but I did have kids, two of them. Both doing well. I tried to move past that subject as quickly as possible. I wasn't ready to talk about that whole situation not yet, maybe not ever.

There was a certain ease with the rest of our conversation. It really didn't seem as if much time passed, but in reality, it had been years, many years. Time was flying by, and I was starting to think I should be going. Just as I was about to get up to get ready to leave, I heard my phone ring. I excused myself and walked into his kitchen. I didn't recognize the number, but I picked it up anyway. "Hello? Hello? Is anyone there?"

I was not prepared for what I heard next. "Mom," I heard a voice say and then sobs, sobs so loud I could barely hear anything else.

My heart started racing. I was having trouble concentrating, breathing, standing. "Molly, Molly, what is it? Are you okay? Please," I begged her, "please talk to me."

After what seemed like an eternity, she started talking. Her speech was garbled and rapid; I could barely understand her. I pleaded with her to calm down, telling her I couldn't help her if I couldn't understand her.

After about five minutes of hearing her cry, someone else's voice was on the phone. The woman introduced herself as Sheila; she was one of the nighttime counselors. She apologized to me for scaring me. She explained that Molly had just received a call; it was from Julie's mom. Julie had overdosed earlier in the day, and this time, they couldn't save her. She died a little while ago. As I listened to Sheila talking, I flashed back to that sweet girl I had met just a week ago. She looked happy and positive. How could this have happened? She finally put Molly back on the phone.

"Oh, honey, I am so, so sorry. Can you ask your counselor if I can come there now? I want to be there for you." As a mother, it's our job to protect our children to keep them from being hurt. Here I was miles away from her, completely helpless. She told me that I couldn't come, that it would have to wait until the next day. After a few more minutes, we had to hang up. I told her that I loved her, and I promised her I would see her the next day.

After we hung up, I continued to sit there, lost in my thoughts. I wasn't sure how long I sat there, but I was aware of a hand on my shoulder. I looked up into the kind, warm eyes of Sam. He asked me if I was all right. If everything was all right. I can't really explain what happened next, but before I knew it, I was telling him everything, telling him about Molly, about what was going on, and what had just happened. Everything just came spilling out; I was powerless to stop it. He just sat there listening; I couldn't read his expression. I had no idea what he was thinking. More importantly, I had no idea why I was telling him any of this. Maybe it was because I needed to talk to someone, maybe it was because he was so kind, or maybe just maybe I was losing my mind. Whatever the reason, I was relieved when I was done. I felt like a giant weight was lifted off my chest. I could breathe again.

After what seemed like an eternity, he looked at me and asked, "What can I do?" I couldn't begin to describe how I felt. It was a relief to share this burden with someone. Maybe this is what Beth was speaking about when she told us we needed some kind of support system. Whatever it was, I was happy to have someone in my corner. As far as what Sam could do to help me, I told him that just being there to listen was enough. After a few more minutes, I got up and told him I had to leave. I was emotionally exhausted from the night and had a long day ahead of me. He walked me to the door rather hesitantly and said goodbye. He asked me to call him when I got home. I promised I would and left.

The drive home was a blur. I was thankful that we only lived a short drive apart. As I pulled into my driveway, I noticed that there wasn't a light on in my house. I walked in, calling out, "Luke? Luke are you home?" I was met with silence, so I walked up to his room. His door was closed, so I gently pushed it open. There he lay sleeping. I looked at him for a few minutes, wishing he was up so we could talk. I closed the door and walked to my room. Once inside, I called Sam to let him know I was home. We spoke for just a minute as I was tired and wanted to compose my thoughts for the next day.

Chapter 4

Saturday morning came very quickly. I got out of bed reluctantly. I was exhausted I hardly slept at all. All I kept seeing was Julie's smiling face. I couldn't begin to imagine what her family was going through. I got ready quickly and poked my head into Luke's room for a quick goodbye, only to discover that he was gone already. I went into the kitchen to see a note—one line. "Mom, I will be gone for most of the day. Love, L." As I stood there looking at the note, I realized that he was gone a lot lately. I chalked it up to Molly being gone and him not really knowing how to handle things.

Off again I went, heading to see Molly, not really sure what was in store for me once I got there. Once I pulled up, I went through the familiar routine. I found my way to what had become "my seat." I watched as the room filled up and a speaker stepped in. She introduced herself as Nancy, an alcoholic in recovery for four years. She went on to tell us about Julie and what had happened. Some people, including myself, wept softly, while others shook their heads in disbelief. She went on to explain how this was affecting the "clients." Some, like my daughter Molly, were taking it very hard, crying, talking, then more crying. Others were very quiet and withdrawn. There was no right or wrong way to handle this kind of situation. It just made everyone that much more aware of how fast things could change. Nancy went on to explain that when we saw our loved ones, we should just listen to them to try to console without saying too much She didn't really say much more as she realized that we were eager to see our loved ones.

I proceeded to the visiting area, slightly nervous at the prospect of seeing Molly. I waited. In she walked, much paler and thinner than she had looked only two days ago. Was that possible? I wondered. As soon as she saw me, she rushed over and threw herself into my arms, sobbing so hard that her whole body shook. All I could do was hold her and try to comfort her. I had no words that could even begin to touch her pain. Once she calmed down a bit, she took my hand and led me to a sofa. We sat, and she began to talk. Evidently, she received a call on Friday evening from Julie's mom letting her know what had happened. She didn't want Molly to wonder why Julie stopped calling her. She wanted Molly to find out from her and to have the support she needed to process this. She told her what had happened. Molly did not share the story with me that day. She was taking it very hard for many reasons—Julie was her friend and the first person she knew who died from drugs. She talked some more, going on about love and loss about being scared and about life in general. I mostly just sat there holding her hand and listening. When she was done, she just looked at me, staring to see what my reaction would be. I had no words. I just hugged her the way I use to hug her when she was little. We sat there side by side, both lost in our own thoughts. After a while, a woman walked up to us and introduced herself to me. Her name was Ann, and she was Molly's main counselor. She had wanted to meet me and perhaps get a chance to talk. Would this be a good time? she asked. I sat there for a second or two. I wanted to talk to her, but I didn't want it to cut into my visit. As if reading my thoughts, Ann assured me that it wouldn't take more than fifteen minutes. Molly encouraged me to go talk to her. She said that she would be fine; she was going to rest for a bit anyway.

So off we went. I followed Ann to her office. I took a seat and waited. Ann started talking to me about Molly and her progress thus far. She told me that Molly was working really hard on her recovery and on her step work. Step work I asked, what is that? Ann explained that addicts in recovery work a twelve-step program. Each step takes time. The steps can take as long as a year to complete, but it is very important to work and complete them. Molly had also found a sponsor that she was working with, someone who was also in recovery but had several years of clean time. She went on to ask me if I had made arrangements for Molly's continued care.

"Yes," I said. "When she is done here, she is coming home. She is going back to her life, and we are going to continue on."

Ann looked at me with a sad smile. "If only it could be that simple. Unfortunately, it doesn't work like that. If Molly goes back to the 'same people, same places, and same things,' she will be right back here. She will have a better chance of recovery long term if she stays in a program longer than the thirty days that this program and your insurance allows."

I sat there trying to absorb everything Ann was telling me. *Molly not come home? Go somewhere else? Where?* I asked Ann if she had spoken to Molly about any of this.

"Yes, I have," she said. "I spoke to her one on one and in group. Molly believes that she will be ready to go home when she is done here. We disagree strongly, but it is up to you."

"Up to me," I said.

"Yes," Ann said. "If you want Molly to succeed, you need to do your part."

I needed to be ready to take a hard line and tell her she needed to continue with treatment. What a lot to take in. I needed time to think. I asked her if I could call her in a few days.

"Yes," she said. "Of course. Give it thought—it's an important decision to make. One you should believe in."

We finished up, and I went to find Molly. She was sitting in her room, staring off into space. When she realized I was there, she started to cry. She told me that she had been crying all day and could not seem to stop. I hugged her and told her that it was okay to cry, to be sad. All I seemed to be able to do was hold her. We spent a very somber visiting day that Saturday, one that I would not easily forget. Before long, it was time to say our goodbyes. Leaving was very difficult that day. She promised to call me. We hugged again and off I went.

The drive home was exhausting. All I could think about was my conversation with Ann. What was the right thing to do? I had never been in a position like this. Usually I had some kind of direction. This time, nothing.

When I got home, Luke was there with his girlfriend, Stacy. I hadn't seen Stacy in a while, so I didn't really know what she knew about Molly. I was to find out that she knew it all. Molly and Stacy were close; after all, Luke and Stacy had been together a few years by then, so Stacy was a part of the family at this point. She hugged me and told me how sorry she was for me and for Molly. I sat down and told them everything Ann had told me. When I was done, Luke asked me what I was going to do. I am not sure Luke. I don't know what the right thing to do is. After a few minutes, Luke and Stacy excused themselves. They had plans they told me and had to leave. Quick hugs all around and then they were gone.

I sat there lost in my own thoughts until the phone rang. It was Sam. He wanted to see how my visit with Molly went and how she was doing. I started to answer his questions but just felt overwhelmed by it all. Sensing this, he asked me if I would like to have dinner. *Dinner?* At this point, I couldn't even remember the last meal I had. I thought about the offer and decided to go. I would drive over. On my ride there, I wondered what was going on with me. My daughter was in rehab, and my son seemed to be off in his own world, and I was having dinner with a very attractive man whom I hadn't seen since high school. Surely, I thought, I must be losing my mind. I was under a tremendous amount of stress, and he was quickly becoming a beacon of light. *I will analyze all this later*, I thought.

When I pulled up, Sam was waiting at the door. What a welcome sight he was. I walked in and sat down on the couch. I can't explain it, but in a very weird sense, it was almost like coming home. I felt safe and much less alone. He didn't press me for answers to his questions. He just waited, waited until I was ready to talk to him. His wait was not long. I told him of my visit with Molly and how terribly sad she was. I told him about my conversation with Ann. All the while, he just sat there and listened. When I was done, he asked me if I had any thoughts on what I was going to do. I still had no idea. This was all so new to me. I told him I thought that bringing her home was the right thing to do, but after my conversation with Ann, it didn't seem to be. I just was so out of my element with all of this. He told me that I didn't need to make a hasty decision, that I should think about what was best for Molly, give it a few days. I felt a sense of relief at not having one more person telling me that I need to decide right away.

We got up and went into the kitchen for dinner, and I was touched to see the trouble he went to, to make me feel comfortable—there on the table was a vase full of roses. He told me to have a seat, and then he proceeded to pull out a platter of food. "You cooked?" I asked.

"No," he replied, "but I did heat it up, so doesn't that count?"

We sat and had the most pleasant meal that I could remember. Light conversation and lots of laughter. It was so very enjoyable. I can't remember how long we lingered over that meal. I just know that it was getting late and I had to leave. I realized that I really didn't want to; I wanted to stay right there safe and warm. But I did have to go. As we said our goodbyes, Sam asked me if I wanted to have lunch the next day. Oh yes, I did, but first I had to see what Luke was doing. If Luke was going to be home, I needed to be there with him. Sam understood. We left it as I would call him the next day. Off I went, happier than when I first got there.

On the drive home, I got to thinking again. *What am I doing? My life could not be more upside down at this point. Why am I getting involved in a hopeless situation? I truly must be mad.* By the time I got home, I had convinced myself that the situation with Sam was just a pleasant distraction. I would just call him and thank him for a few lovely evenings, but I really needed to keep my full attention on Molly and Luke. I was sad at the realization of this but felt like it was the right thing to do. Strengthened by my new resolve, I walked into my house and straight to the phone. I called Sam and tried to explain to him that I really needed to give my full attention to my kids, and while I really enjoyed the time we had spent together, it just didn't seem right.

As always, he listened to what I had to say, and when I was done, he calmly said, "I will be here if you need me." We said our goodbyes and hung up.

Chapter 5

Even though I was sad, I felt it was the right thing to do. While I was still sitting there, the phone rang; it was Luke. He was calling me to tell me that he was going to stay at Stacy's house. Her parents were "cool" with it. It was late, and they didn't want him driving home. "Well," I said, "as long as they are okay with that, then it's fine with me."

After we hung up, I walked upstairs into Molly's room; I sat down on her bed and looked around. Everything seemed the same—normal. I remembered countless times sitting there, talking to her as she was getting ready to go out. I thought to myself, *Did I miss something? Were there signs that I didn't see? How could this have happened?* As I sat there, the answer became crystal clear. Molly would go on to the next facility, wherever Ann though she should go. I was going to do whatever they suggested. I was going to give Molly every opportunity to succeed no matter what. I was determined to be that 1 percent.

The rest of the weekend passed by in a blur. I was exhausted but somewhat relieved that I had come to a decision. I saw Luke and Stacy late on Sunday afternoon. They came by to have an early dinner with me. They told me that they had plans to meet up with some of their friends. I was sad to see them go, but they were young and full of life and adventure. Luke told me not to wait up, that he would most likely be home late. "Not too late," I said. "After all, you have school the next day."

As he kissed me goodbye, he whispered, "Don't worry, I got this." And off they went. As I watched him drive away, I thought how much I loved him and how much I wanted to freeze this moment in time. I went back into the kitchen to straighten things up, lost in my own thoughts. My mind wandered to Sam. What was he doing tonight? Had I made the right decision? So many questions floated through my mind. I realized that my best bet was to go to bed. I didn't think I would get much sleep, but as soon as my head hit the pillow, I was out. All of a sudden, I woke with a start. It was still dark outside. I looked at the clock; it was 3:00 a.m. I wondered what had woken me. Everything seemed quiet in the house. I got up to check on things. I walked down the hall to Luke's room. His door was partially open—there was just enough moonlight to see his sleeping body. Part of me was relieved to see him there. Although I wasn't sure why I was relieved, he was exactly where he should be. I walked back into my room to try to go back to sleep. The rest of the night, I tossed and turned, plagued by my doubts about my decision to extend Molly's treatment. I prayed I was making the right decision.

Monday morning came early. I woke with a headache, sure it was from stress. As soon as I got to my office, I called Ann and told her that I decided to follow her advice and have Molly continue treatment. Ann was very happy that I had come to that decision. She encouraged me to find peace in it. She spoke about Molly's increased chance of recovery. She also told me to prepare myself, that it was a good bet that Molly would be very angry with me when I told her. "Tell her," I said. "Isn't that your job to do?"

"No," Ann said, "you have to tell her, but we here at the facility will fully support you."

"Great," I said, "one more reason for Molly to be angry with me. How soon should I tell her?"

"Well," Ann said, "there is the Wednesday support group meeting. If you are coming to it, you can talk to her then. Or you can wait until Saturday visiting day. Either way, you need to have that conversation before her program ends in a week."

"One more week?" I asked. "How can that be? Has it been almost thirty days already?"

"Yes," she said, "it has been."

I told her I would decide which day I would do and call her back. She told me that in the meantime, they would look into long-term facilities that Molly could go to—long term. *How long?* I wondered.

After hanging up with Ann, I immediately called Sam. Not even realizing what I was doing but just naturally reaching out to him. When he answered, my words just came rushing out. I tried to explain how my conversation with Ann went and the next decision I was faced with. He listened calmly, and when I was done, he said, "Why don't you come over after work? We can sit down and talk this through."

"Okay," I said. "I can be there around six o'clock."

After we hung up, I called Luke. I just intended to leave him a message, but to my surprise, he answered, "What's up?"

Instead of telling him what I called him about, I asked him why he had answered my call.

"I'm in between classes and had my phone out to call you."

"Why?" I asked. "To tell you that I am going to Stacy's house right from school. Today is her dad's birthday, and they are having a special dinner for him."

"All right," I said, "please wish him a happy birthday for me."

We exchanged "I love you" and hung up. I tried to knuckle down and get some work done, but my mind kept wandering. I felt confident that I had made the right decision to extend Molly's treatment, but I was hesitant about telling her. After all, I didn't want to appear to be the bad guy again. Before I knew it, the day was over. While I walked to my car, I kept wondering why I called Sam. My only answer was because I needed a friend, someone who knew what was going on and had no judgement. Since he was the only one beside Luke and Stacy that knew the story, he was the natural choice.

When I pulled up, he was waiting at the door for me. As soon as he saw me, he opened his arms, and I naturally walked into them. He just stood there hugging me as I started to cry. I hadn't realized how much I missed having someone just hug me and let me cry. I had been holding it together the best I could for weeks. Standing there in

Sam's embrace was just what I needed. When I was all cried out, he led me into the house. We took our now familiar seats on the couch facing each other and talked. I once again told him my decision to keep Molly in treatment. I also told him how Ann said that it was up to me to tell Molly. We spoke about my hesitation in doing so. I explained how awful it was when I had to take her to this facility and how I was scared to do it again.

Sam just listened, and when I was done, he said, "You are doing all of this out of love, and one day, she will see that."

I hoped he was right. We talked some more, and I decided that I was going to talk to Molly on Wednesday. It seemed like the best time to do it. She would have four days to process it before she had to leave and go somewhere else. *But where?* I wondered. I prayed that it was at least someplace decent.

We talked for several more hours. Just talked. It felt good to share this with someone. Before long, I realized the time. It was getting late, and I needed to go home. Sam walked me to the door. As I was walking out, I turned to say "Thank you for being there" when he gently kissed me. It was no more than a soft brush of his lips. But it spoke volumes to both of us. We stood there looking at each other for a minute or two, and then I left.

Driving home, I hardly knew what to think or feel. I knew I felt grateful to have someone so caring in my life, but I also felt afraid. Afraid for what was happening. When I got home, Luke was in the kitchen. He had brought me home a piece of the birthday cake. I sat down and looked at him; he looked tired. I asked him how things were going. He told me that things were fine. He hesitated, then as if he had more to say, I waited, sensing he wanted to talk. After a few seconds of silence, he got up saying he had some homework and needed to do it; the moment had passed. I was reluctant to let him go. I saw so little of him these days. I decided to share with him my conversation with Ann and my decision.

After looking at me for a minute or two, he shook his head and said, "Good luck with that," and left the room. I was both stunned and saddened by his response; I was stunned at how cold he sounded and saddened because of his lack of feelings for his sister.

Chapter 6

The next day, I called Ann. I told her that I would be at the meeting on Wednesday, that I would tell Molly then so she would have some time to process everything. She agreed that it was a good idea. She also told me that they had found a place for her and that they would tell us both about it on Wednesday. The rest of the night as well as the next day passed uneventfully. I left work a little early on Wednesday to make my way to the facility. On my way there, I called Sam I wanted a little pep talk to get me through the next hour or so. We spoke for about ten minutes. He told me that what I was doing I was doing with love, that I needed to be strong and that I should call him when I left. Once again, I pulled into the familiar parking lot and made my way into the meeting room. Beth was again the meeting leader. Since mostly everyone was familiar to each other, Beth went around the room just asking each of us how we were doing and if anyone needed to talk. Much to my surprise, I raised my hand. I explained to everyone what I was going through with Molly. I spoke of my concern over her reaction to my decision. I spoke of my concern over her feelings toward me once I talked with her. Everyone listened to what I had to say, and when I was done, Beth asked the group for their thoughts. Everyone was in agreement that I was making the right decision. Some felt more strongly about it than others, but they all agreed it was the best course of action.

After the meeting was over, a woman came up to me. Her name was Lucille. She went on to tell me that her son Paul was a client at the facility. He had only been there a week, but this was his second stint in rehab. He completed a thirty-day program once, but when he was done, he went home. He stayed clean for two months before relapsing. She was sorry that she didn't take the advice given to her to send her son to a long-term facility. She hugged me then and wished me luck and told me once again that I was doing the right thing. I thanked her and made my way to Ann's office. I walked in and took a seat. She then told me about the program she found for Molly. It was a state-run facility that focused on recovery. It ran six months to a year. She of course was suggesting a year. Since it was state-run, it was funded by the state. There would be no out of pocket cost other than a small weekly allowance that I could give to Molly. I asked her if the facility was safe. Was it clean? Was it good?

"Yes," she answered to all my questions. She went on to tell me that the program focused on the person's history, on what brought them to drug use and what they needed in order to stay clean and sober. Once we got there, I would be given much more information, but for right now, what Ann told me would have to be enough. At that point she asked me if I was ready to talk to Molly.

Was I ready? I thought, *Who could be ready to tell their child that they couldn't come home?* Filled with dread, I took a deep breath and said yes.

Ann left to go find Molly. In those few minutes of waiting for her, I thought to myself once again, *How did we get here? How could everything have gone so horribly wrong?* I felt the sting of tears and quickly wiped them away. I had to be strong—if not for myself then for Molly.

Molly came walking in with Ann flashing her bright, lovely smile at me. I wondered to myself how much longer would she be smiling for. She came over to me and gave me a hug. I held on longer than normal; she felt so good. After a minute, she took a seat. "What's up, Mom?"

I looked at her for a minute and then spoke the sentence that would forever change our lives. "I have decided that you need to stay in treatment, that on Monday you will be going to a facility that has a longer program."

She just looked at me. I was ready for the crying, for the yelling, for the begging, for anything but what happened next. She looked at me with absolute hatred. She stood up, looked me square in the eye, and said, "No, no, I am not." She then started to leave the room. As she got to the door, she turned to me and said, "Don't bother coming back on Saturday. I won't see you." And then she was gone.

I hadn't realized I was holding my breath until she was out of the room. Once out, I immediately broke down. Giant sobs came out of me. "What have I done?" I kept saying. Ann waited until I somewhat calmed down before speaking. She said that Molly's reaction was normal, that she would come around but that I would need to stand firm in my decision, no wavering. I listened to what she said, trying to wrap my mind around everything. We continued to talk for a few more minutes, and when I was calm, she walked me out. I asked her if I really should stay away on Saturday.

"Yes," she said, "give us time to work with Molly and help her process this. We will be in touch." Then it was over.

As I walked to my car, I was both relieved and sad. Relieved that the conversation was over but sad at the outcome.

My drive home was long this time, and I was exhausted. Pulling into my driveway, I saw lights on in my house. *Good*, I thought, *Luke is home*. A welcome sight after a grueling day. I walked in, and there he was cooking. Stacy sat at the table, and the radio was on. I stood there for a few minutes, just basking in the normalcy of the moment. After a while, they noticed me. Stacy asked me how things went.

"Not so good," I answered.

Luke asked me if I was hungry.

I really wasn't; I actually felt sick, but I said, "Yes, yes, I am." I wanted to spend time with them. We sat and ate and talked. It felt so nice to have this time together. When dinner was done, Luke asked me if he could talk to me alone.

"Sure," I said.

Once out of the room, he asked if he could have some money.

"Sure," I said. "How much?"

He asked for fifty dollars. He told me he was taking Stacy out on the weekend and was a little short. I gave it to him. He hugged me and said that he was going to take Stacy home, stay for a while, and then head home. "Don't wait up."

Wednesday slipped into Thursday, then into Friday. I hadn't heard from Molly or anyone from the facility. I decided to call after work to make sure that everything was okay. I spoke to Ann; she assured me that everything was fine. Molly was still very angry with me. She did not want me to visit her on Saturday. The staff was working with her to help her understand my decision and to come to terms with it. She suggested that if I didn't hear from Molly by Sunday morning to call her. I thanked her and hung up. I next called Sam. I hadn't spoken to him since Wednesday. It seemed like forever. We spoke for a few minutes, and he invited me over. "Eight o'clock," he said.

I thought about it for a minute and then agreed. It was beginning to be a steady kind of thing—after a terribly stressful week we would get together. Easy it seemed.

So once again, I drove to his house. There he was waiting at the door as usual. I was very happy to see him. We walked in and sat on the couch, our usual spots. He waited until I was ready to talk. "So," he asked, "how did it go with Molly?"

I tried to explain how terrible it was. I told him that once I told her my decision to extend her treatment, to send her to a place with a longer program so that she could learn more, get more therapy, she got angry, very angry. I told him how she told me that she was not going to go anywhere else. That I could not force her to go. I told him that she also told me not to bother coming to Saturday family day. She would not see me. When I was done talking, he opened his arms to me and gave me a reassuring hug. He told me that he thought that I was doing the right thing for Molly. That if her counselor believes she needed more help, then she probably did. He asked me how Luke was taking all of this. I explained to him that Luke seemed a little distant when I talked about Molly. He didn't really want to talk about it. I guessed it was because the whole situation made him uncomfortable.

We continued to sit on the couch by the fire talking. Sam told me that he wanted to be there for me. He wanted to help in any way he could. I was so amazed that anyone would want to knowingly get involved in this kind of situation, but he did. I was so grateful to have someone to lean on and to help me navigate these uncharted waters. After a while, I glanced at my watch and realized that it was well after midnight. I could not believe how fast the evening had gone. I got up to say good night, and as I did, Sam hugged me and brushed his lips across my forehead and whispered, "Remember I am here for you." He walked me to the door and asked me to call him when I got home. I said that I would and left.

On the drive home, I called my friend Leslie. She answered on the first ring. "Are you okay?" she asked.

"Yes, I'm fine," I answered.

"Good," she said, "but do you know it's after midnight?"

"Oh my goodness," I said, "I am so sorry. I didn't even think about the time."

"It's okay," she said. "I was up anyway. What's up?"

Well, at this point, I hadn't told her about anything. No Molly and no Sam. I still wasn't ready to talk to her about Molly but I desperately needed to talk to her about Sam. I started slowly. About our meeting again after so many years, about our spending time together, and about our kiss. She listened, and after I was done, she asked me how I felt about all of it. I told her that I was happy about reconnecting with him. I also told her that I thought it could lead somewhere. He made me very happy, and that's what I needed in my life. She was happy for me, she said, but she also advised me to take things slow. She didn't want to see me get hurt. After a few more minutes of talking, we said our goodbyes. I promised her I would call her during the week.

Once I got home, I called Sam to let him know I was home. He was happy to hear that. He asked me what I was doing the next day, since I wasn't going to be visiting Molly. I told him that I had no plans. He asked me if he could come by. He had an idea, and he wanted to share it with me. I told him that as long as Luke was not going to be home or need me, I was in. I would call him in the morning. Once off the phone, I went into Luke's room to check on him; he was sound asleep. I stood there for a few minutes just looking at him. *Peaceful* was the word that came to mind. I closed his door, satisfied. I went to the kitchen for a glass of water and saw the note from Luke. He and some of his friends were going to the beach early. He would be gone most of the day; he just wanted to let me know. I walked into my room and eased into bed. I was exhausted. I set my alarm for 8:00 a.m. I wanted to catch him before he left.

Before I knew it, my alarm went off. Surprisingly, I got up with ease. As I walked out of my room, I heard voices downstairs. It was Luke and Stacy in the kitchen. I was happy to see them both. They apologized for waking me. "No, don't worry. You didn't wake me. I set my alarm because I wanted to see you before you left."

They appeared to be rushing a bit. Luke explained that a group of their friends were meeting up to spend the day at the beach. They were going to do a bonfire and just hang out. "Great," I said.

He asked me what time I was leaving to see Molly.

"I'm not," I answered. "She won't see me today."

Luke volunteered to stay home with me so that I wouldn't be alone. "No," I said, "you go have a good time. I have plans myself."

"Really?" he asked.

"Yes," I assured him. "You go have fun and don't worry about me." I stood in the doorway watching them pull away, wondering once again what had happened to our lives. In that moment, it felt surreal. I tried to think about what I wanted to do next, but I suddenly found myself exhausted. I decided to lie down for a few minutes and try to sort things out. I thought about Sam. Then I thought about what Leslie said. Until I spoke to her, I hadn't realized just how fast things were moving between us. But even though things were moving fast, it felt right—very right. I decided to throw caution to the wind and spend the day with him. After all, I was intrigued as to what he had planned.

Chapter 7

I called him to tell him that I was in, to ask him if I needed to wear anything special and also what time would this adventure begin. He expressed his happiness that I was going to see him. He said casual, jeans would be fine, and he would pick me up at one o'clock.

"Okay," I said, "I will see you then." After we hung up, I showered and thought about calling Molly. No, I decided I would give it until tomorrow as Ann advised.

Promptly at one o'clock, Sam knocked on my door. As I opened it, I couldn't help but smile. I was very happy to see him and to see what he had in store for us. I hadn't felt this happy and excited in a long time.

We got into his car, and off we went. I still had no idea where we were going. As we got on the parkway, he smiled and said, "I hope you will enjoy this day." To say that I was intrigued would be an understatement.

We drove for about an hour before getting off at a very familiar exit. "Where? What?" I asked him. He just smiled and kept driving. Before I knew it, we were pulling into the parking lot of our old high school. He parked, and we got out. He took my hand and together we toured the whole outside of the building. We peeked in through the various doors and windows and talked about all those years ago and about what high school meant to each of us. How we had our dreams and whole life before us. Next stop was the park—the park where we had both spent many a weekend day at. How we used to ride our bicycles there to meet up with our friends. How life was simple, not complicated like it was now. We held hands again as we strolled around the lake. In that moment, I felt peace. A peace so complete and warm, a peace I hadn't felt in a long, long time. I looked up at Sam, and all I could say was "Thank you. Thank you for giving me something that I so desperately needed."

He just looked down at me and smiled. Our next stop would affect me more than the other two could ever possibly affect me. A short five-minute ride and we were pulling onto my childhood block. He parked right in front of my house and looked at me. I just sat there, looking at the house I grew up in, the house where I had lived with my parents for twenty years. As I sat there, I was flooded with memories—memories that choked me up and a profound loneliness at the loss of my parents at such a young age. After what seemed like an eternity, Sam got out of the car and said, "Let's go."

"Go?" I said. "Go where?"

"Why, up to the door of course. Let's knock and tell the owner this used to be your house. Maybe they will let you walk through it."

"What? No, I don't think that's a good idea."

"Come on," he said. "The worst thing that can happen is that they say no."

"Okay, I'm game, let's go."

So up to the door we went. After knocking twice, the door opened, and much to my surprise, the person who opened the door was the same person we had sold the house to ten years before. I could not believe it; she remembered me and welcomed us in and told us we were free to look around. The outside of the house was almost exactly the same, but the inside was very different. Everything had been upgraded and changed, but to me it still felt somehow the same. It had the same coming "home" feel. After a short time, we thanked her and left.

Getting back into the car, I felt exhausted but a good kind of exhaustion. Sam looked over at me and asked if I was ready for our last stop. "I don't know," I asked him. "Am I?"

He said for this one, I had to close my eyes and I could not peek.

"All right," I said. "Here goes."

Off we went. After driving about five more minutes, Sam said, "Okay, we are here. You can open your eyes." I opened them with a little trepidation. What could this be? Once opened, I saw that we were in the parking lot of one of the oldest, most popular restaurants of our day. I could not believe it. It was a place that I had hoped Sam would have taken me back in the day. We went in, and except for a few minor changes, it looked almost exactly the same. We had a lovely time. We laughed over some memories, became introspective over others, but most of all, we enjoyed our time together. When we were done with dinner, it was time to head back. We were both more or less quiet on our ride back, both lost in our own thoughts. Sam pulled up to my house and walked me to my door. Luke wasn't home yet, so I asked him in. I wasn't ready to explain him to Luke, so I knew it would be a short visit, but I wanted him to come in if only for a few minutes.

We both sat down, and I thanked him again. I told him that it was just what I needed. That it gave me peace, that it made me remember who I was all those years ago. That I was a stronger person than I gave myself credit for. That my roots were planted firmly and that I could do this—that I had to do this.

I looked at him then, really looked at him, and asked him, "How did you know, Sam? How did you know what I needed when I didn't even know what I needed?"

He looked at me for what seemed like an eternity and simply said, "I knew because I love you, Brenda. I know you may think I'm crazy, but I do." My eyes filled with tears. I loved him too, I realized, but was terrified at the thought. How could I possibly love someone who had just reentered my life after such a long absence? But we had known each other for many years before. Was this all possible? I was probably going through the worst time in my life but, at the same time, what was shaping up to be the best time as well. I didn't know much at that point, but what I did know was that I loved Sam and I told him. Despite my initial fears, I loved him. We sat there together for a little while longer, basking in the glow of our newfound love. After about an hour, Sam decided it was time for him to go. I walked him to his car and thanked him again for the wonderful day. He pulled me into his arms, held me tight, and kissed me goodbye.

I watched him leave and slowly walked back into my house. My mind was racing with thoughts, oh so many thoughts. I worried about Luke and about Molly; I worried about what I was doing. What was I doing? Was I going crazy? Maybe, but for right now, I was going to enjoy it for whatever it was. I made myself a cup of tea and sat in the living room, thinking and waiting for Luke. I don't really know how long I was sitting there, but before I knew it, Luke was walking in. I startled him when I said hi to him. The room had grown dark, and he said he was surprised to see me sitting there. I reached over and put on the light—he seemed jumpy. I asked him how his day went, and he said fine. He asked me if I had a good day. Yes, as a matter of fact, I did. I was having a little trouble keeping the grin off my face. Luke leaned over gave me a quick hug and said good night. I continued sitting there for some time, thinking that something felt off, something about Luke that I couldn't put my finger on.

The next day dawned bright and sunny. I was up early, but Luke was up even earlier and gone already. I again had a nagging not-quite-right feeling. I would talk to him when he got home tonight, I thought. I walked into the kitchen to make myself a cup of tea, all the while thinking how my life was at such odds. On the one hand, I was unbelievably happy. I was venturing into uncharted waters with a man that I trusted 100 percent. On the other hand, I was so sad, sad for the *little girl lost.* Sad for myself and for the failing within me.

I don't know how long I sat there lost in my own thoughts, but I do know that the ringing of the phone pulled me out of my trouble thoughts. I answered and was surprised to hear Molly's voice. After all, it was a Sunday, not her usual day to call me. I was so happy to hear her voice. She, on the other hand, did not seem happy to be talking to me. "How are you?" I asked.

"I am doing just fine. I am just calling you to let you know that I have agreed to go to the next facility."

Hearing her say those words made my heart sing. I was so thankful. "That's wonderful," I told her.

After a minute or two of silence, she said simply, "You really didn't leave me much choice, did you? It was either your way or I would be homeless."

"Molly, please don't think of it that way. Try to think about it as an opportunity."

"An opportunity for what?" she asked.

"To learn more about your problems."

"My only problem, Mom, is that you are forcing me to do something that is totally unnecessary. Maybe you are the one who needs help. You should look into that."

I didn't want to fight with her, so I changed the subject to what time I would be coming for her tomorrow. She told me that she wasn't sure and that Ann would be calling later in the day. She said she had to go and hung up before I had a chance to even say goodbye. Again, I sat there lost in my thoughts. Molly sounded so distant and cold. It broke my heart.

A short time later, Ann called me. "I know you just spoke to Molly," she said. "I just wanted to go over her discharge plan and answer any questions you may have."

"Okay," I said.

Ann proceeded to tell me that I would need to be there on Monday by 10:00 a.m., that I could bring a few more things for Molly like some books to read, a notebook, and pens for her to start journaling in. She could also have a ten-dollar phone card so she could use the pay phone to call me.

"Okay," I said.

She also told me to prepare to be there for several hours as the intake would take a while.

"All right," I said, feeling slightly overwhelmed by this point.

"Do you have any questions?" she asked.

I thought a minute. "Well," I said, "how did you get her to agree to go?"

"Well," she said, "it really was a team effort. Each person on her treatment team spoke with her. We gave her all the information necessary to make the wise decision, but in the end, what really sealed the deal was her fear of being homeless. She really believed that you were not going to let her come home."

I sat there a minute, wondering if I really would have been able to stand behind that. I was very glad that it had not come down to that. I couldn't think of anything else I needed to ask at that point. I thanked her, and we hung up. I got up, went to my room, and started to cry. Was it sadness or relief? I wasn't too sure at that point. After I caught my breath, I took a shower. When I got out, I heard voices. I dressed and went downstairs to the kitchen; it was Luke and Stacy. Luke was putting plates on the table. "What's up?" I asked him.

Stacy told me that they had ordered pizza so we could have lunch together. "Great," I said. Just what I needed—to spend some time with my son. I realized that in the month that Molly had been gone, I hadn't spent too much time with Luke. I chalked it up to my being gone every Saturday and his increasingly busy eleventh grade life. So I was grateful to be spending this Sunday afternoon with him. The pizza came, and we sat down and ate. During lunch, he asked me how Molly was doing. I told him that she was leaving the facility that she was in and I was bringing her to another one.

"Wow, she must be thrilled," he said.

"Well, she's not happy with me at the moment. I am picking her up tomorrow morning and bringing her to another facility closer to the house. It's a state-run facility that offers her a longer program."

As I was talking, I noticed Stacy looking at Luke under her lashes. She was also very quiet, which was unusual for her. "Stacy," I asked, "are you okay?"

"Yes," she answered, "just tired."

"Okay," I said, but I was again hit with a slight feeling of unease. When we were done with lunch, Luke said that they were taking off. They were going to a movie with friends and would see me later.

"All right," I said. "Have fun and be careful."

After I cleaned up the dishes, I decided to call Leslie. I hadn't talked to her very much lately. We had only had that one brief conversation. I made myself a cup of tea and called her. It was about time I shared with her how my life had changed this past month. She answered on the first ring almost as if she was waiting for my call. "Brenda," she said, "it has been ages. How are you? How's life?"

It took me a minute or two to gather my thoughts—where and how to start? I started with Sam since I had already told her a little bit about him. I told her how he took me to our old neighborhood, how we were spending as much time as possible together and how we had said I love you. She listened to everything I had to say, mostly without comments.

When I was done, she told me how happy she was for me. She was glad that I had found someone so special to me. But she said, "I wouldn't be me if I didn't just say be careful. I don't want you to get hurt."

"I'm going to be okay," I promised her.

She then went on to ask me how Molly and Luke were handling my new romantic situation.

I hesitated for a minute, weighing my words. "Well, Luke doesn't know anything yet. I have been going to Sam's house, so I haven't had to talk to him yet." I took a deep breath and continued. "Molly doesn't know either, Leslie, but the reason why is much more complicated she is in a thirty-day drug rehab facility. There it was out. I told someone other than Luke and Sam. Now I waited, waited for the judgment that I was sure would be coming. After a few seconds, I heard Leslie say, "Oh, Brenda, what can I do?"

"What do you need?" I was stunned I was so sure that she was going to pass judgment on me. But in that short span of time, I began to realize that I was the only person passing judgment. She asked me what I was doing now and I told her nothing really. Why? She told me that she was going to come over, that she would rather talk about this in person. We hung up with her promising to be over in an hour.

I paced nervously around the kitchen while I waited for her to arrive. How much should I share? Didn't I have an obligations to protect my daughter's privacy? Wasn't it my job to do better for her? As I waited and paced, I slowly came to the realization that I wanted to tell Leslie the whole ugly truth. I needed to share my burden with someone who knew my sweet Molly for whom she used to be, for whom I hoped with my whole heart would be again. The ringing of the doorbell brought me out of my reverie. I opened the door to Leslie. In that instant, I knew I had made the right decision to let her into my confidence.

We sat down and I took a very deep breath before beginning. I told her that Molly was addicted to pain pills. I wasn't really sure how or when it started. I told her how on Monday morning, I was moving her to a longer program. How her counselor told me that she had a greater chance of success if she completed a six-month to one-year program. How terrified I was by all of it. And most importantly, how I felt responsibility and shame. Leslie sat there just listening. I couldn't read her, didn't know if she was blaming me or just pitying me. When I was finally finished talking, she got up walked over to me and hugged me. Then she sat back down and started talking to me. She started by telling me that this was not my fault, that if I watched the news or read a newspaper, I would see that this was becoming an epidemic out here in the suburbs. I wasn't alone and should not feel that way. She encouraged me to be more open with my other friends to let the people who cared about us in. She continued on by saying that this was a stressful time for me and having a support system would be important to me as I continued on this journey. I told her that at the facility Molly was currently in we were also encouraged to get a sponsor, to go to meetings, to work on ourselves. Families tend to get lost in their loved one's addictions. Leslie agreed that this was something I should probably do. After a few more minutes of conversation, Leslie got up to leave. As she was going, Luke walked in. At first, he seemed startled to see her, but a minute later, he was his charming self. "How are you, Leslie? We haven't seen you in a while."

"All good here, Luke," she replied. "I was just talking to your mom about Molly. I can imagine it's been rough on you as well."

His answer shocked me. "Not really," he replied. With that, he walked away.

Leslie and I took a minute to digest what he just said. I shook my head and said, "He has been acting a little strange lately."

I walked her to the door. As she was leaving, she gently said, "Brenda, please think about what we talked about today. It's important." I thanked her for coming by and promised her that I would. After closing the door, I went to find Luke. He was in his room, listening to music with his headphones on. He didn't see me at first, so I waited a minute, just looking at him. What was going on? I wondered.

He finally saw me and took off his headphones. "What's up, Mom?" he asked me.

"What was that all about Luke? What did you mean when you told Leslie you weren't surprised by what was going on with Molly?"

He took his time answering me. "I'm not shocked by anything Molly has done. I am only surprised by how long it took you to figure out."

I stood there for what felt like an eternity, just looking at him. I was shocked at what he just said. When I finally was able to speak, I asked him why. "Why, if you knew what was going on, didn't you say anything to me?"

"I didn't know exactly what was going on, but I knew something was wrong."

"Well, you could have told me that at least—told me something, anything so maybe I wouldn't have been totally blindsided."

He just looked at me, shaking his head. "Luke," I asked, "is everything okay with you? I know that I may seem preoccupied lately, but I am here for you. I hope that you know that."

"Yeah, I do, Mom. I know you are here for me, but really, everything is just fine." I stood in his doorway for a minute, watching him put on his headphones again. I took that as my cue to leave. I walked out and to my room, feeling somewhat troubled. So much to think about at that moment, so much that I felt overwhelmed.

I decided to call Sam—talking to him had a calming effect on me and right now I needed to feel calm. The phone rang several times before he finally answered; he sounded a little out of breath as if I had interrupted him. "Hi," I said, "it's me."

"Hey, me," he replied. "How are you doing?"

"I'm okay, I guess—I had a nice visit with Leslie this afternoon. I finally told her everything that was going on. It was a relief to get it all off my chest."

"Well, how did she react?" he asked. "She was very supportive and understanding. She agrees that I should probably start going to support groups. I think I should but really don't even know how to start. Molly is leaving the facility tomorrow, so I won't be able to go to that group anymore, so now what? Where to start now?"

Sam suggested doing an Internet search of drug and alcohol support groups. I told him that I would look into it. We spoke for a few more minutes and then said our goodbyes. Something about that phone call did not leave me feeling calm. If anything, it had the opposite effect. I sat there thinking about it all. Molly, Luke, Stacy, and now even Sam. So much to think about so much to worry about. I decided to take a walk to try to clear my head. After walking for what seemed to be about an hour, I felt better. Maybe I just needed fresh air or maybe just a break from myself. Either way, I felt better. When I got home, I decided to just go to bed to make it an early night. After all, Monday, I realized, was probably going to be a difficult day.

Chapter 8

Eight o'clock on Monday morning came early. I went into Molly's room to collect the additional things I needed to bring for her. Luke was already long gone. I left him a note letting him know that I would be gone most of the day, that I would try to be back by dinner. I just wasn't sure how long I would be at this new facility.

One more time, I made the drive to the facility. Funny how on my first trip out there I was filled with such hope. This time, I was filled with dread—I was dreading this trip because I knew Molly was still very angry and reluctant to go anywhere but home. I pulled into the familiar parking lot and walked into the building. There she sat, my sweet Molly, surrounded by her meager belongings. To say I was a little surprised to see her sitting there was an understatement. As I walked up to her, I said, "Why are you out here and not in your room?"

Her answer shocked me. "Since I am leaving today, they want to get my room ready for someone else, so I had to wait for you here."

For me, as Molly's mother, this was an emotional experience, this whole rehab program. But I found out for the facility, it was just another day. Business as usual. I asked her if there was anything I had to do before we left, and she said no. She had done all of the paperwork and had all the information she needed to go to the next program. "Okay," I said, "then let's go."

As we were walking to the door, I heard my name being called. I turned and saw Ann walking toward me. "I was really hoping I would get a chance to see you before you left with Molly," she said.

"Well, I am glad I got to see you as well," I said. "I want to thank you for everything you did for Molly and for me. You gave me a better understanding of what this disease is and does."

Ann looked at me and said, "Brenda, please remember this is not your fault. And please stay strong—you need to be for yourself and for Molly. This is a long road and you will need support along the way." I thanked her again, and we walked out.

Into the car and off to the next facility we went. For the first ten minutes of our ride, there was awkward silence. I was lost in my thoughts, and so was Molly. After a bit, I broke the silence with a total mom question: "Are you hungry?"

Molly simply shook her head. More silence. I had so many questions I wanted to ask her. I wanted to know why, why did this happen to us? What had I done wrong? But I thought better of it. I decided that this ride should be as pleasant as possible. "So, Molly," I said, "I'm glad that the weather hasn't been really bad lately." It had always been a running joke with my kids that I hated to drive in the rain, in the snow and in the dark. I thought that perhaps my bringing up the weather would break the silence.

Molly didn't say anything right away but as I glance over at her I saw a hint of a smile cross her face, followed by a giggle and then a sentence that took me by surprise: "So all it took was for me to get hooked on drugs to get you to drive?" She looked over at me with her beautiful laughing eyes and said, "Too soon?"

I couldn't help but laugh and say, "Yeah, maybe." That exchange broke the ice. We spent the rest of the ride just chatting like we had always done on the countless rides we had taken together, and for just a little while, I forgot the world around us. All too soon, I was pulling into facility number two.

As I drove up the road leading to the main building, I thought, *This place looks scary*. It was a tall, old-looking brick building at least five stories high. I pulled into the closest spot I could find and got out. Molly did the same and grabbed her bags. Together we both went into the building. The inside was really not much better than the outside. It had that institution feel to it. Together we walked to the reception desk, the woman asked our names, and Molly introduced herself. She was then checked in and asked to take a seat. We both sat there and waited, trying to process what was going on. After about ten minutes, we heard Molly's name being called. We both got up and followed the counselor down a long hallway. We entered an office, and we both sat down. The counselor introduced himself. He told us that his name was Barry and he would be doing Molly's intake and that later in the day, she would meet her regular counselor. Barry proceeded to go over the rules for living there. He told Molly the things that absolutely would not be tolerated. He told me what I could and could not do. The things that I could bring on visiting day and what she could not have. After that, he asked Molly for her bags. Barry looked at us and explained that he needed to go through everything just to make sure that there was nothing that she couldn't have. I told him that she had just come from another facility and could not possibly have anything. He looked at me sadly and said, "I'm sorry, I still have to check. You would be surprised by what some people try to bring in."

I looked at him confused at first, and then realization hit me. "You think I supplied her with things she shouldn't have? You are kidding me."

He shook his head and simply said, "Nothing surprises me anymore." I was both shocked and angry. But realized that there was nothing that I could do.

Molly was just sitting there calmly the whole time. "Mom," she finally said, "it's fine. Just let him do his job please. Don't make a scene."

Molly gave Barry everything she came with as well as the bag I had brought from home. He proceeded to go through everything; again, I was given a pile to take home with me. When he was done, he gave Molly back her bags and told her to say goodbye to me. "Wait," I said, "I was told by the last facility that I would be with her for several hours."

"No," Barry explained, "intake with Molly will take several hours. Your part is done."

My part? My part was only that of a taxi driver. This could not be happening again, but it was. I was escorted out after a brief hug from Molly. "I'll call you," she said. And then she was gone. Once again, I was standing in a lobby with an armload of things to take home again…again.

Once in my car, I called Sam. As soon as he answered, my words came rushing out. I told him everything that happened from the time I picked her up until right that very second. When I was done, he simply said, "Brenda, can you please come over tonight? We need to talk."

Now what? I thought. "Sure," I said, feeling anything but sure.

As I drove home, I wondered what Sam could want to talk to me about. I didn't feel ready for anything more right now. I felt raw and broken already. I didn't think I could take one more thing. I pulled into my driveway, exhausted. As I was opening the front door, I heard the phone ringing. I dropped everything and ran to pick it up. I was very glad I did when I heard Molly's voice. "Hi, Mom," she said.

"Oh, Molly, I am so glad to hear from you. We didn't get a chance to really say goodbye."

"I know," she said. "It's all business here. After you left, I talked to Barry for a while. He asked me a ton of questions about my addiction, my drug of choice, the program I was working, and the facility I just finished at. When we were done, he brought me into another office and introduced me to my counselor. Her name is Amanda, and she is about thirty years old and has been in recovery for ten years, and I just love her. She's great. We talked for a while, and she told me that I would be meeting with her alone three times a week and she would also be running one of my groups as well."

Well, to say that I was happy to hear Molly so excited would be an understatement. I was thrilled it further validated that I made the right decision. She told me that she had to go but would be able to call me once a week. We decided to stick with Wednesday evenings since it was right in the middle of the week. I told her that I loved her, and she said the same. We hung up, and I felt a sense of peace wash over me. In that moment, I knew without a shadow of a doubt that I did the right thing.

Before long, Luke came home from school. When he saw me sitting at the kitchen table, he walked over. "Hey, Mom," he said, "what are you doing home?"

"Hi, Luke. Today was the day I moved your sister from one facility to the other."

"Oh," he said, "I forgot—well, how did it go?"

"Surprisingly well," I said. "The car ride there started out a little awkward but after a few minutes it got better. But the place I brought her to kind of looked like a movie set from a horror film. It had a long driveway up to a brick building that almost looked rundown. I could easily picture it being an old psychiatric hospital. The inside was not much better—I had to leave her there after about fifteen minutes. But she called me a little while ago and seemed upbeat. She will be calling again Wednesday night. It would be nice if you were home to talk to her."

"Maybe," he replied. Well, for Luke, *maybe* was the best we could hope for. We talked for a few minutes more, and then he went to his room. Again, I got a nagging feeling that something was off.

For the rest of the morning, I did odd chores and paid bills and worried about Sam and what he could possibly want to talk to me about. I thought things were going well, but maybe, just maybe, this was becoming all too much for him. It was possible. It was too much for me, and Molly was my daughter. She was nothing to him. I made myself a cup of tea, still thinking. Then I heard the doorbell ring. *Oh no, now what?* I thought to myself. When I opened the door, there standing in front of me was Susan—my dearest friend. Before I had a chance to say anything, she said, "Brenda, it's been far too long since we saw each other or even talked. I have given you space even though you didn't ask for it. I somehow sensed you needed it, but I am here now, and we are going to lunch."

This was the last thing that I wanted to do right now, but she gave me no choice. I went back in to leave Luke a note as he was gone again, and his phone appeared to be off. As we pulled out of my driveway, I wondered what exactly I was prepared to tell her. We pulled up to one of our favorite lunch spots. A place that we shared many a lunch together. After we sat at our usual table and ordered, she simply asked, "What is wrong?"

"Wrong?" I asked. "What makes you think that there is anything wrong?"

"Oh, I don't know—maybe it's because you all but disappeared, or maybe it's because the boys haven't seen Molly in over a month, or maybe it's because we are just that close that I just know."

As I was listening to her, my mind was swirling as to what to tell her. Every fiber of my being was screaming, *Nothing is wrong! Everything is fine! Molly has just been really busy.* But a little voice was nagging at me reminding me that I needed people in my life for support. People who loved me and who would be there for me.

I took a deep breath and looked at my friend, remembering all the other lunches we had in this very restaurant. Lunches where we sat and talked about less serious subjects—where we planned Molly's sweet sixteen party, where we talked about how great it was that our kids found each other. Susan had twin boys, Robert and Jeffrey. They had all met when they went to middle school and had been inseparable since. Molly and Robert were especially close; they had dated through most of high school. Now here I sat, wondering what to say.

Susan just sat there, looking at me, waiting. I didn't feel as if she were rushing me or pressuring me. In that instant, I knew I could talk to her. As I started to speak, I felt my eyes fill up. Once again, I told Molly's story. I told her everything from my finding out about her addiction to my running into Sam. I told her about it all. Every last detail. It was almost like purging my soul. When I was done, I looked up at her. Our eyes met for an instant, and then she started to cry. She reached across the table took my hands in hers and said, "I don't know what to say other then I am here for all of you, whatever you need, whenever you need it. I'm just so sorry that I didn't know sooner. You should not have been juggling all of this on your own."

I looked at her and asked her the question that was burning in my mind. "Susan, do you think that I missed something with Molly? Do you think I somehow failed her?"

Susan took a minute to answer, and when she did, she answered no. "I don't think that it's anyone's fault. Hopefully you guys will figure this out together." She asked me what the plan was moving forward, and I told her that Molly was now in a longer program. I wasn't sure yet how long she was going to be there; I just knew it was going to be longer than the first program. I asked her not to say anything about this to anyone. I told her I was not ready to share this; I didn't know how Molly felt about our small town hearing about all of this.

Susan totally understood and agreed. She promised to keep it to herself until I told her otherwise. "How has Luke been with all of this?"

"I'm not too sure," I told her. "He hasn't seen or even talked to her since she left. At times he seems fine, but at other times, he seems really off. When I ask him about it, he says it's just the stress of being a junior. I am not going to push him right now, but if things stay this way, I will have to."

"Okay," she said, "so tell me more about Sam."

"Well, there really isn't much to say. We reconnected the week that Molly first went to the first facility. He's stuck around through all of this so far. We have exchanged I love yous, which by the way feels so good. I'm supposed to meet him at his house later tonight. He has to talk to me. I am not sure what about, but I am worried. When we spoke last, he sounded off. I am a little nervous about this conversation."

"Well," she said, "don't worry until you know there is something to worry about." We talked for a little while longer and then we left. I was happy that I told her what was going on. When we said our goodbyes, she reminded me again that she would always be there for me, that no matter the time of the day or night, she was there. I thanked her and said I was happy to hear that.

Chapter 9

By the time I got home I realized that I wouldn't have much time before I needed to head to Sam's house. I was literally exhausted by now and thought about calling him and telling him I couldn't make it. But I realized that I would much rather get it over with. I went to find Luke to talk to him. He was in his room on his phone. When he saw me, he said goodbye and looked at me saying, "What's up?"

I asked him if he was going to be home for the rest of the day/evening. "I am going out for a bit and want to make sure you are going to be okay."

"I'm fine, Mom," he replied. "I am leaving myself. Stacy and I are getting a quick bite to eat."

"Okay," I said, "but please don't stay out too late. It's a school night."

"Yeah, Mom, I know. I am well aware that today is Monday."

"Okay, Luke, I'm just being a mother."

"I know," he said. "I know."

After I left his room, I went to mine to get ready to go. I was hardly prepared for this evening, but I knew that it was something I had to do.

After a quick shower, I went to find Luke to say goodbye. I caught him as he was just leaving. "I'm going out now. I won't be late. Please be careful, and give Stacy my love."

"Okay, Mom, I'll be fine. Have fun," he said as he walked to his car.

Fun, I thought. *I can't remember the last time I had fun.* I drove to Sam's house, dreading the conversation to come. I knew in my heart that we had run our course. But I was thankful for our time together when I needed a shoulder.

As I pulled up, Sam was waiting for me at the door. We walked in together and took our "spots" on the couch. I took a deep breath and waited. Sam looked at me and said, "Brenda, please let me say what I have to say. Hear me out before you say anything."

I looked at him and said, "Okay, go ahead."

He cleared his throat once than a second time before he started. "Brenda," he said, "these past few weeks have been incredible. I have watched you go through a parent's worst nightmare and realized that I want to be with you, help you, and comfort you through this journey. I want to be there for Molly and for Luke. It's hard for me to just sit back and watch you juggle all of this alone."

I sat there just staring at him when he was done. I didn't know what to say. This was not what I thought he was going to say. He reached over and took my hand and pulled me to my feet. "Come with me. I want to show you something."

I followed him up the stairs. He showed me two bedrooms. "One," he said, "is for Molly, and the other for Luke." I was speechless. What could I possibly say to this warm, wonderful, selfless man? Part of me wanted to jump at this opportunity, but part of me knew it was just too soon. I tried to explain that all to Sam. I told him that Molly was in a program for the long haul. That she had so much going on that I could not possibly tell her about him, and Luke... well, Luke was a whole other story. Luke wasn't quite himself these days. I felt like something with him was off, and I wasn't sure what it was but I knew that I needed to find out. Sam listened patiently, only saying, "I will wait then."

I couldn't believe what I was hearing. He would wait? We went back downstairs to talk some more. He asked me about Molly's facility and how I felt about it. I told him again that I wasn't too sure about it. I didn't have enough information yet. But we were willing to give it a try. I told him I thought that I would know more when I saw her on Saturday. We talked a little longer, and then I told him I had to go. I didn't want to be gone too long, and I was exhausted. It was a very long and emotional day. As he was walking me to the door, I asked him, "Remember the other day when I called you and you sounded distracted and a little out of breath? What were you doing?"

He looked at me and simply said, "Moving furniture."

I couldn't help myself; I grinned from ear to ear. "Thank you" was the only thing I could say.

On the drive home, I was flooded with emotion. I was both happy and sad. Happy that I had Sam in my life but sad at the set of circumstances that we were in. When I got home, I went to find Luke. He was in his room on the phone. I waited until he looked up. "Can you please get off the phone? We need to talk."

"Sure, Mom, hang on." He finished his conversation quickly and hung up.

I took a seat and a deep breath.

"What's up?" he asked.

"Well, to start, I'm worried about you. You haven't been acting like yourself lately. Is something wrong?"

He just looked at me for a minute before answering, and when he did, his words cut me like a knife. "How would you know how I am acting? You are either with Molly or out somewhere. To notice if a person is acting differently, you need to be around to actually see it."

I felt tears sting my eyes. I couldn't believe what I was hearing. All I could muster at that point was "I'm sorry. I'm sorry if I am failing you."

"It's fine mom. Are we done'? I have homework to do. Yes, I said—I turned to leave—as I got to his door, I looked back at him. I love you Luke so very much. It wasn't till years later that I would learn this was called deflection. I walked back to my room with a heavy heart. I was just devastated by my son's words. Could I really be failing both of them. Before I had a chance to really give it much thought, the phone rang. It was Sam. "I'm just checking to make sure you are all right."

"Yes," I said. "I am okay, just really tired. I'm going to bed in a minute." I couldn't bring myself to share with him my conversation with Luke. It was too fresh, too painful. We said our goodbyes and hung up. I could not believe how tired I was. I got into bed, wondering if I was going to get any sleep.

I woke with a start to the sound of the phone ringing. For a minute, I felt disoriented, not sure where I was. I shook my head clear and grabbed the phone. "Hello, hello," I said.

"Hi," a voice answered back, "is this Brenda?"

"Yes," I answered.

"Well, this is Amanda, and I am Molly's counselor here. I wanted to chat for a few minutes if you have the time." She went on to tell me that she met with Molly the previous day. They had a very long conversation, she got to know her better, and together, they set goals. They talked about working her steps, and Molly reported to her that she was up to step 2. That she had worked with her counselor from her previous facility on step 1. Molly told her that she hoped to complete all twelve steps before leaving there.

I advised her not to put a timeline on step completion. "Some steps take longer to complete than others. Work at a steady pace."

"Brenda," she then said, "Molly has some concerns about you."

"Me?" I said. "Why would she be worried about me?"

"She's worries that you aren't getting the help you need, that you are isolating yourself. It's a common practice of family members when their loved ones become addicted to various substances."

"Well," I said, "please tell Molly not to worry about me. Let her know that I have shared this with two of my closest friends, that I am not carrying this alone."

"Molly will be happy to hear that. As I said, she's been worried. She is also worried about Luke, worried that she hasn't seen or even spoken to him in a month."

It saddened me to hear that. I was sad by that myself. Molly and Luke had always been close—they were their own little island in the rocky waters of my previous relationship. But as I listened, I started to realize that in the last six months or so, they hadn't been that involved with each other. Could it have been because Luke knew about Molly and her addiction, or was it something else? I wondered. Amanda and I spoke for a few more minutes, and just as we were getting ready to hang up, she asked me if I was going to be at family day on Saturday.

"Of course," I answered.

"Good," she said, "it's always a plus when the family is support-ive. Perhaps you can bring Luke."

"I'll try," I replied. "I'll try."

I could not believe how tired I was at just ten o'clock in the morning. I got up, showered, and got dressed. I was already late for work.

I drove to my office, all the while wondering what I was going to say to Gail. Gail had been my co-worker or partner so to speak for the past three years. She was the one who had trained me. To say we were friends was a stretch. We were friendly at the office, but that's as far as it went. So again, I wondered just what I was going to say to her. As I walked in, I decided to keep it simple and to just say that I overslept.

Tuesday ran into Wednesday, and then it was time for Molly's call. I was so happy to hear her voice. "How are you doing, Mol? Are you adjusting?"

"I'm fine, Mom. Everything is okay here."

I exhaled, not realizing that I was holding my breath. I was thankful to hear she was okay. She proceeded to tell me a little bit about this facility. She was in a room with three other women. Two were her age, and one was much older. The older woman took on the role of house mother. She sort of looked after the three of them. The girls her age were Tiffany and Carla. The older one was named Barbara. Molly told me that she had different groups every day, and she met with Amanda on Mondays, Wednesday, and Fridays in the morning. Some sessions with her lasted an hour; some longer depending on what they were covering. She told me that the program was better than she thought it would be. She also told me that the women had one wing of the facility and the men the other. They ate separately and only really got together when they had certain groups.

"Why would you have co-ed groups, Molly? Isn't it uncomfortable to discuss all of your issues in that setting?"

"No, Mom, it's good for us to learn to share and trust one another."

"Oh, okay, I guess." I said it a little hesitantly. I went on to ask her how she was eating, sleeping, the regular questions any mom would ask.

"Well, the food here is okay, kind of like bad camp food. I sleep just fine. If you have trouble sleeping, they offer you sleep meds."

"Sleep meds? I am not sure how I feel about that." I thought I would call Amanda and see about that. She went on to talk a little more about her roommates, and then we had to say goodbye. It's amazing how fast fifteen minutes goes by.

I sat at my desk after we hung up, thinking about our conversation, not really sure how I felt. I was happy, of course, to hear from Molly and glad she was settling in but troubled that she would be offered sleep medication—what was that really all about? I decided to call Amanda and ask. As I was getting ready to call, the phone rang.

It was Susan. "Just calling to check up on you and to see how things are going."

"Oh, Susan," I said, "things are going as good as can be expected. I heard from Molly a few minutes ago, and she seems to be settling in. She told me about her counselor, whom she likes, and she told me about her roommates. So I guess that's saying something. I am, however, concerned that she told me that she was offered sleep medication if she had trouble sleeping."

"I agree," Susan said, "that is concerning. What are you going to do?"

"I am going to call her counselor to get some information about it."

"Good idea," she said. We spoke for a few more minutes, and then right before we hung up, she reminded me that she was here for me that no matter what time of day it was and to call her if I needed her. I thanked her and we said our goodbyes. I had forgotten how good it was to talk to her. She was one of my closest friends, and I had completely shut her out. When I needed people the most, my foolish pride, guilt, and shame got in the way.

I got up to go talk to Luke about coming with me Saturday. He was of course in his room but not on the phone this time. This time, he was sitting there with Stacy. "Hey, you two, what's going on?"

Luke looked at me and said, "Nothing, Mom, we are just talking."

Stacy then turned to me to say hi, and I could see in her eyes that something more than just talking was going on. "Are you okay, Stacy?"

"Yes, I'm fine, just a little stressed with school. I was talking to Luke about it."

"All right," I said although I wasn't completely convinced. "Well, I just want to ask you, Luke, about coming with me on Saturday to visit your sister. You haven't seen her in over a month, and I think it would be good for her if you came with me to see her."

He sat there, staring at me, not saying anything, Stacy was staring at him, almost as if she was trying to send him a message. "I don't know, Mom. Let me think about it, and I will let you know."

I stood there looking at him, not really sure what to say. "Okay, Luke, I'm not really sure what there is to think about. It's your sister we are talking about, not some random stranger. But if you need to think about it, go right ahead, but I will need to know by Friday morning."

"Will do, Mom." I stood there a minute longer and then turned and left his room.

Halfway down the hall, I remembered that I had something else to tell him. As soon as I was nearing his door, I heard Stacy crying and saying, "Now what, Luke, what are you going to say to your mom? Are you going to go on Saturday?" I had the same nagging feeling.

As I was about to knock, I heard the phone ring. I turned to go answer it just as Luke and Stacy came out of his room. They were both startled to see me. Once again, I asked if everything was okay.

"Yes, Mom," Luke said with a tone of pure frustration. "I'm taking Stacy home. Is there something you need?"

"No, Luke, but I wish you would talk to me instead of shutting me out."

"I would," he said, "if I had something to say to you." I stood there watching them walk down the hall, once again wondering what was going on, what was happening.

I don't know how long I stood there lost in thought, but the ringing of the phone pulled me out of my thoughts. I hurried to answer it. It was Amanda; she was returning my call from earlier in the day. "Thanks for calling me back," I said. "I have a question for you. When I spoke to Molly earlier, she mentioned that she was offered sleep medication. I am a little concerned about that."

"Amanda explained that often clients have trouble sleeping in early recovery so they are offered sleep medication but that they are monitored and only offered them for a short amount of time. I'm not sure how I feel about that," I told her.

"Well, don't worry," she assured me. "Molly was not interested in taking anything."

I was relieved to hear that. Amanda then asked me if Luke would be coming with me on Saturday. "I'm not sure," I told her. We spoke briefly about it. "Luke isn't sure if he wants to come, but he will let me know by Friday."

"Well," Amanda said, "it seems very important to Molly to have him there."

"I will do my best," I told her.

"Good," she said. "On another note, Molly is doing well, I know it's early in her program, but she is working hard and participating in every group."

I was relieved to hear that. I thanked her for calling me back and told her I would see her on Saturday.

I continued to sit there, thinking and trying to digest everything that had happened in the last hour or so. I heard the front door open and Luke yell, "Mom, I'm home. I'm tired—I am going to do some homework, and then I'm going to bed."

I got up and went to his room. "Okay," I said. "I love you. Sleep well."

"Will do, Mom."

Again, I had a nagging feeling—that was twice in one day. I decided that I needed help with this, I went to my room and decided to call Leslie. She answered on the first ring. "Wow," she said, "I was just about to call you."

"Well, I beat you to it. How are you, Brenda? How is everything?"

"I'm doing all right. I heard from Molly today. She seems to have settled in. She's working hard."

"Great, I am so glad to hear that. I'm relieved myself. I still hadn't been sure I made the right decision, but now I was."

"Good," Leslie said. "I am glad too. So what else is going on over there? How is Sam?"

"Actually, everything with Sam is great. He asked me to move in with him. He even got the two extra bedrooms in his house ready for Molly and Luke. He wants in for the long haul, as he says."

"Wow," she said, "that is kind of fast, don't you think? What did you say?"

"I said just about the same thing. I also said that the kids were not ready for this. Leslie, he told me that he would wait. Crazy, right?"

"No, not really. It's very sweet."

"It is, isn't it?" I said. "Leslie, I wanted to talk to you about Luke. He hasn't been himself lately. He has been distant and dismissive. He won't commit to coming with me on Saturday to see Molly even though I told him that her counselor thinks it's important for him to be there. When I try talking to him about any of this, he just keeps telling me everything is ok."

"Well," she said, "this has to be very hard on him as well. So many changes in such a short period of time. He went from having his sister at home to now having her in a drug rehab. Imagine you being his age and having to deal with all of this."

"I am at my wits' end," I told her. "I don't know what to do. I just know that I am worried about him."

"Well," she said, "have you ever thought that he may be worried about you too? I mean, after all, he thinks this has all fallen on just you. He has no idea that you have someone in your life who is helping you shoulder this responsibility. Maybe, just maybe, it would be a good idea to tell him a little bit about Sam. If you slowly tell him, then down the road, it won't be such a shock."

"I'm not sure if this is the right time to start with all of that, but I will give it some thought." We talked a little more and then hung up. I was exhausted and needed to go to bed. Morning would come sooner than I wanted it to.

I woke the next day surprisingly well-rested. I went into the kitchen for a cup of tea and to catch Luke before school. He was already walking out the door. "Morning," I said. "Leaving early today?"

"Yeah," he said, "I promised Stacy a ride to school."

"Okay, will you be home for dinner tonight?"

"Yep," he said.

"Good. I'm cooking and really want us to have dinner together."

"Sure, Mom, that sounds good. See you later."

"Have a good day, Luke. I love you."

"Love you too," he said. As I was getting ready for work, I thought about my conversation with Leslie. Maybe she was right. Maybe I should begin to talk to Luke about Sam. I just wasn't sure. I decide to call Sam later in the day to see how he felt about it.

Midway through the day, I had a few spare minutes to call Sam. He answered just as I was about to leave him a message. "Hi, hope I am not disturbing anything."

"No," he said, "I'm free now. What's up?"

"I just wanted to touch base with you about Luke."

"What about him?"

"Well, as you know from everything I have told you, he has been acting off. I spoke to Leslie yesterday, and she thinks it may be because he is worried about me. About me having to handle all of the things that are going on right now by myself. She thinks that maybe if I started to tell him a little about you, it may ease his mind. So I would like to know how you feel about that."

"I feel fine about it," he said. "I think that it's a good idea. I think that if we are serious about this, which I am, then the sooner they know about us, the better. We don't want Luke to think that we have been keeping a secret from him that can affect his life, and if and when you decide to move in, it will most certainly affect his life. So I say that you should talk to him."

"Well, as long as you agree, then I will start talking to him at dinner tonight. Sounds like a plan," he said. "I hate to rush you off the phone, but I have another call, Brenda. Please call me tonight when you get a chance. I want to know how it goes with Luke."

"Will do," I replied.

Chapter 10

The rest of the day went on uneventfully. I was busy at work, which was a good thing. It didn't leave me much time to worry about my dinner with Luke. I stopped at the supermarket on my way home to pick up some supplies for dinner; I wanted to make him one of his favorite meals. When I got home, I was a little surprised to find that he was not home yet. I hoped he did not forget about our dinner. As I was getting everything out, in he walked. I was so happy to see him. He asked me if he could give me a hand. I gladly accepted. He got to chopping and mixing and, most importantly, joking around the way he used to. Well, before I was ready to end our banter, the meal was done. We sat down to eat. I asked him how his day was, and he asked me about mine. It was a very pleasant meal. When we were almost finished, I took a deep breath and asked him if I could talk to him about something important. Something that I had been wanting to talk to him about for some time.

"Sure, Mom, what is it?"

"Well," I said, "about the same time that Molly went into her first rehab, I ran into an old friend of mine. Someone that I had gone to school with, someone who I hadn't seen in a long time. We got to talking and got together a couple of times. He was a friend when I desperately needed one."

"Oh," Luke said, "is it serious?"

"Well," I said, "not yet, but I think that it could be." He didn't say much more other than asking if Molly knew.

"No," I told him, "not yet. I don't think that this is something to bring up to her at this time."

He sat there for a few minutes longer and then said, "I want to meet him."

"You do?"

"Yes," he said, "I do."

"Okay, I think that I can arrange that. Whenever you feel ready, just let me know."

"All right, Mom, I will." We continued to sit there for a few minutes longer each lost in our own thoughts. I got up to start to clear off the table, and he asked me if I needed any help.

"No, I'm good, but thanks anyway."

"Okay then. I am going to my room to do some homework, and Mom, thanks for dinner. I enjoyed spending time with you."

"I enjoyed our time as well. I will be in to say good night later."

When I was done clearing off the table and loading the dishwasher, I went into my room to call Sam.

"How did it go?" he asked.

"Surprisingly well. We prepared dinner together and then sat and had a really good conversation. I told him about you. I didn't get into the seriousness of our relationship—I thought that it may be too much all at once."

"What did he say?"

"Well, he didn't really say anything other than he wanted to meet you."

"All right, when?"

"Well, he didn't say when. I just told him that when he was ready, I could arrange it. It went better than I expected. Although I don't know what I expected him to say or do. But I guess that based on his behavior of late, I was prepared for the worst."

"Well," Sam said, "I am glad that things went well. I can't imagine you having one more thing on your plate right now."

"Agreed."

"Well," Sam asked, "are you busy tomorrow night? Or do you want to come over?"

"I am not sure yet. I wanted to see what Luke had planned before I made a decision."

"Well, just let me know. We can have dinner."

"I will, Sam. I will call you tomorrow."

"Great, Brenda, looking forward to it. Have a peaceful night— and remember I love you."

I still took great delight in hearing him tell me that. I hung up with a smile on my face. I sat there thinking about my dinner with Luke and how it went. What was I really afraid of? After all, he was my son and most of the time had a very clear head and kind heart. I realized that I was borrowing trouble these days quite a lot.

I went to Luke's room to see what he had planned for the next evening. He was on the phone with Stacy. He gave me the one-minute signal and got off the phone. "What's up, Mom?"

"I wanted to ask you if you had plans for tomorrow after school."

"Well, I actually do. Stacy and I are supposed to be getting together with her friends for a movie night at one of their houses."

"Sounds like a nice evening."

"It should be. Why, what do you have going on?"

"Nothing too much. I may go visit my friend. I just don't want to leave you here alone."

"Oh, Mom, come on, like I haven't been home alone like a million times before."

"I know. It's just that things are so different these days. It just makes me feel bad to know you are here by yourself."

"Well, don't worry about me. Have a good time with whatever you decide to do."

"Thanks, Luke."

"Well, good night. I love you, Mom."

"I love you too, Luke. See you in the morning." I went to bed peacefully, more at peace then I had been in quite some time.

The next morning, as I was getting up, I heard a knock on my door. It was Luke. He came to tell me that he thought about going with me to see Molly and that he just wasn't up to it this time, but he promised me that he would go with me next Saturday. He just needed more time to get used to the idea. Well, I was disappointed, but I told him that I understood. I would try to explain it to Molly the next day. He left saying goodbye and that he would see me later that night; he assured me that he would not be out too late. "Well, have a good day at school and have fun tonight. Please be careful."

"I will." And out the door he went.

As soon as I was dressed and ready for work, I called Sam. "Yes, Sam, I am free tonight. I would love to come over after work." This time, I told him, I would bring dinner with me.

"Are you sure, Brenda? I don't mind 'cooking' again."

"No, Sam, it's fine. I will stop on my way over and grab something. Do you have any preferences?"

"No, anything you pick up would be great."

"All right, I will surprise you then."

"Great. Looking forward to it. See you later. Oh, and Sam, I just wanted to let you know that I love you. I know that I didn't say it last night when we spoke, but I want you to know that I do. It was such a new and foreign feeling for me that it takes some getting used to."

"Have a great day, Brenda. See you later."

Off I went to work in a much better mood than I had been in such a long time. When I got there, Gail was waiting for me. "What's up?" I asked her when I walked in.

"Nothing much—we have a meeting this afternoon at five o'clock."

Oh no, I thought. Five o'clock. I had dinner plans. Now what? I would have to call Sam and tell him that dinner tonight wouldn't work out for me. I was so disappointed. He understood and told me not to worry about dinner, to just come over when I was done with work, and we would just relax, have a glass of wine and catch up. Again, it had been days since we saw each other. I told him that I wouldn't get there until almost eight o'clock as I still had to go home and feed my dogs.

"That's fine," he said. "Whenever you get here, you get here."

The day dragged on and on. It seemed never ending. Right on the dot of 5:00 p.m., we both walked over to the main building for our meeting. I prayed that it would go fast; the last thing that

I wanted was for it to go on and on. Luckily, I wasn't the only one who felt that way, and it went quickly. After all, it was a Friday night, and we had all just worked a whole week and wanted to get home. I said goodbye to Gail, wishing her a good weekend, and off I went. Homeward bound to feed my dogs, change my clothes, have a quick snack, and drive to Sam's house. I was so looking forward to spending some time with him. It was long overdue.

When I got home, I called out to Luke to see if he was home. I was met with silence. I remembered then that he told me he was going out with Stacy for the night. Well, I was disappointed that I didn't get a chance to see him before he left. I quickly let the dogs out and fed them. Grabbed a quick bite and changed my clothes before leaving the house to head to Sam's. The drive there was quite familiar these days, and I made quick time of it. As always, Sam was waiting for me in the doorway. As I walked up to him, he opened up his arms for a reassuring hug. It felt so nice to have someone to "come home to." We walked into his house arm in arm and took our usual places on the couch to settle in for a catch-up session.

He wanted to know in more detail how my conversation with Luke went. I told him that I didn't go into many details, only that we were old friends who happened to run into each other the week that Molly went into her first rehab. "Luke then asked me if it was serious, and I just told him that it wasn't yet but that I thought it could be. I didn't want to tell him too much too soon, and I thought that this was a good beginning."

Sam looked at me for a minute before he spoke. "I guess that is a good way to start. I'm not crazy about him not knowing that we are serious, but I guess you know him better, and if you think that this is a good start, then I am okay with it."

I smiled at him and said, "Thank you."

Sam looked at me and asked, "What are you thanking me for?"

"For just being you and for being so understanding about my life, crazy as it is."

"Well, Brenda, as I said before, I am here for you in any way that I can be. So tell me, what is on the agenda for this weekend? Is Luke going with you to visit Molly tomorrow?"

"No, he isn't. We spoke briefly about it, and he claims that he is not up to it. He needs more time to get used to the idea. I am hoping that he will come with me the following Saturday. Molly's counselor has told me that it's very important to Molly to see her brother. I told her that I would really try to bring him."

As we were sitting there, I heard my cell phone ring. I got up to go get it; it was Luke. As soon as I heard his voice, I started to worry. I knew that he was out with Stacy, and it was very unusual for him to be calling me. "Is everything all right? Are you okay?"

"Yeah, Mom, I am fine. I was just wondering if you were home. I wanted to talk to you for a minute, and I didn't want to drive all the way home if you weren't there."

"No, honey, I am not home right now, but I can leave and meet you at home in a half an hour."

"No, Mom, it's fine. Just tell me where you are, and I will come to you."

I hesitated for a minute before carefully answering him. "I am at my friend's house. Do you want to drive here?"

"Sure, I can do that. Just give me the address."

I gave it to him and said, "I will see you soon," and hung up the phone. I looked at Sam and shook my head. "I am not sure what that is all about. It's odd that Luke wanted to come here and not just meet me at home."

"Well," Sam said, "maybe his curiosity has gotten the best of him, and he wants to meet me and to make sure that you are okay."

"I guess," I said, "but I am a little nervous about this whole thing."

"Relax," Sam said, "it will be fine."

I waited and paced a little, not sure what this was all about. I silently prayed that things would not be too difficult and that this would not be too much for Luke to handle. He certainly did not need another thing on his already full plate. After about a half an hour, I saw headlights coming up the driveway. He was here. I took a deep breath and walked to open up the door. There stood Luke and Stacy. They both looked fine; they didn't seem like anything was wrong, which I still thought was the reason why Luke called me.

Sam stood behind me, beckoning them in. "Please," he said, "come in and have a seat." He reached his hand out to shake Luke's hand. Automatically, Luke reached for his hand and gave it a shake. I silently thanked his private school training for his automatic response. First hurdle over with. Luke and Stacy walked in and took a seat on the sofa. Sam and I sat on the opposite side of the room across from them.

Once all settled, I asked Luke what was up. Did he need to talk to me in private?

"No, Mom, I'm fine right here."

"Okay, I said, I saw Stacy reach for his hand. Up until that moment she hadn't said more than a very quiet hello. She cleared her throat and started speaking. She was speaking for the both of them. Luke and I talked about what you told him the other day, about Sam. We both just thought that it would be a good idea for us to meet him. Luke then jumped in and said that they just wanted to make sure that I was okay and that Sam was a good guy. I was so touched by what I was hearing. My son appeared to be taking on the "man of the house" role. As I looked at him, I started to realize that in fact he was the man of the house at this time. I felt overwhelmed by emotion at the thoughtfulness of this son of mine.

We sat there for a long time talking. Sam asked both of them some very insightful questions. He wanted to know about school and college plans and life plans. I listened to both of them, answering his questions with ease. After a while, Sam asked if anyone was hungry. "Yes," replied both Luke and Stacy at the same time. Stacy said that she was starved.

"Okay," Sam said, "let's go to my favorite restaurant. It's not very far from here. We can take one car, or if you prefer, Luke, you can follow us."

Luke and Stacy decided that they would just follow. As we were getting up to leave, I grabbed Luke in a hug.

"What was that for?"

"It was for nothing other than my love for you. See you at the restaurant."

Chapter 11

As we pulled into the parking lot, Sam looked at me and said, "Luke seems very nice, very respectful. I think we will be fine." We waited for Luke and Stacy to park, and then we all walked into the restaurant. Everyone there seemed to know Sam, and we were immediately shown to a table even though it was a fairly busy Friday night. Once seated, choices were made, and dinner was ordered. We proceeded to have a very lovely conversation. Sam was engaging with both Luke and Stacy and asked a lot of the questions that had been on my mind. He was interested in what Luke thought of school. Was being a junior different then he thought it would be? How were they faring in school? He was interested in all that they both had to say.

For most of the evening, we did not speak of Molly. Toward the end of dinner, Sam ventured to ask about Molly. He wanted to know how Luke was dealing with all of this. Luke honestly said that he didn't know how he felt. He felt sorry that Molly was going through all of this. He felt sorry for me as well. He hadn't been sure how I was managing, but now he knew. Sam had help with this. It made him feel relief that I wasn't doing this on my own. As I was listening to what he had to say, I was reminded that Leslie had said something similar to me—she thought that Luke may have been feeling that way. Worried about me but not really knowing how to voice his concerns. I was so grateful that Sam was there asking these questions. I felt that Luke was being more honest with him than he would have ever been with me.

Then Sam asked the one question that I silently hoped would not be asked: "When are you going to see your sister?"

I held my breath, waiting for Luke to answer. It took a minute or two for him to finally give the answer that I was hoping for. "I have decided to go tomorrow. I think that it's time that I see her and talk to her. Mom, what do you think?"

"Oh, Luke, I think that is a great idea. I know that Molly will be so happy to see you. It's been over a month since you saw her."

"Well, just as long as you are sure that it will be okay, I would like to go."

"I am sure that it will be just fine. She has been asking about you every time I talk to her."

"Okay, then count me in. What time will we be leaving?"

"Well, it's an all-day thing. We have to be there at nine o'clock, so I think that we should leave by eight-fifteen, okay?"

"Yep, fine, I will be ready."

"Well," Luke said, "thank you, Sam, for dinner, and it was great to meet you."

"Thank you," Sam said. Stacy replied, "I had a nice time too."

Luke got up and said that he needed to get Stacy home and that he would see me at home. Sam also stood up and shook Luke's hand again. He also said that it was great to meet them. He hoped now that everyone met, that he would be seeing more of them. He wished Luke luck for tomorrow and told him that he was sure that it would be a good day. Luke bent down and kissed me on the cheek, told me that he loved me, and out the door they went.

Sam sat back down and looked at me with a big smile on his face. "I think that it went well," he said. "How about you?"

I just looked at him smiling. "Yes," I said, "I think that it went better than I ever thought it would go. I was so worried about how you would meet, worried about how Luke would be, worried that the two of you would not get along."

"Well," Sam said, "I think that things went fine. Luke is a very nice young man. He seems to have a good head on his shoulders, and

Stacy is very nice as well. A little on the shy side but very nice. They seem like a very nice young couple."

"Yes," I said, "they are a nice young couple." At that moment, I was filled with a mother's pride. "I am so happy, Sam, that Luke is going with me tomorrow. I don't know what changed from yesterday when he told me that he didn't feel ready to see Molly."

"Well, Sam said maybe he had more time to think about it, or maybe he and Stacy talked about it. Either way, he has agreed to go. Let's start with that. Don't worry so much about everything. Take it for what it's worth and see where it goes."

"Agreed." We sat in the restaurant for a bit more time, just basking in the success of our first dinner together. After a while, we decided to leave. I wanted to make it an early night because I had to get up early the next day for my first visiting day with Molly in her new facility. I was quite on my way back to Sam's house. I had so much to think about. So much to digest. I was so happy that the first meeting went so well. We got to Sam's house, and instead of going in, I walked over to my car to get in and go home. Sam looked a little disappointed that I was leaving, but he understood that I had to. He gave me a hug and wished me luck. I stood in his embrace just a while longer, thanking the stars above for bringing this wonderful man into my life again.

My drive home was a blur. All I kept thinking about was our dinner together. Could this be the start of a more fulfilling relationship all around? I hoped so but was not going to dwell too much on that as I had been disappointed in the past and did not want to set myself up for something like that again.

Once I got home, I called out to Luke. "Luke, are you home?"

"Yeah, Mom, in here."

I followed his voice and found him in the kitchen eating ice cream right out of the container. Ordinarily, I would have told him to get a bowl, but I was more interested in finding out how he felt things went at dinner. I proceeded to put the kettle on for some tea, waiting to see if Luke would bring dinner up or if I would have to. My wait wasn't very long. So Luke said, "Sam is a very nice guy. He seems genuine. I like him, Mom, I really do. Stacy thinks he is nice as well. She told me to tell you again thank you for letting her be included in dinner tonight."

I breathed, not realizing that I was holding my breath. "I am really happy that you both liked him. Sam liked you as well. He thinks that you have a good head on your shoulders and that Stacy is sweet. To tell you the truth, Luke, I was a little nervous about how things would go once you met each other. I couldn't be more pleased about the evening. What I am happier about is that you are going to go with me tomorrow to see your sister. I think that it's really great that you are going. I know that it was a hard decision for you to make but one I am glad you made."

"Well, Mom, I really want to see her and to talk to her. Do you think that she and I will get some time to talk, just the two of us?"

"I am not sure, Luke. I don't know anything about this program. This will be my first time there as well. All I can say is we'll see."

"Okay, I guess that will have to be good enough for now."

"All right, Mom, I am going to get some sleep. I love you and I will see you in the morning."

I decided to call Susan to let her know about my evening. I wanted to share with her my good fortune, tell her how our unplanned dinner went. I also wanted to let her know about Luke agreeing to go with me to visit Molly. I walked into my room to call her when I realized the time. Too late to make the call. I sighed. It will have to wait until tomorrow. I got into bed with mixed emotions. On the one hand, I was happy about our dinner and how well things went with Luke and Sam. But on the other hand, I was nervous about how our visit with Molly would go. As I was laying there, I realized that perhaps I wasn't' ready for what lay ahead of us.

Much too soon, my alarm went off, signaling that whatever the day had in store for me was about to begin. After a quick shower, I went to find Luke; he was on the phone in his room. I paused waiting for him to see me standing in his doorway. Once he did, he said goodbye, hung up, and turned his attention to me. "Hey, Mom, what time are we leaving?"

"I thought we should go by eight o'clock. We have to check in at nine o'clock. It should only take us about thirty minutes to get there, but I want to make sure I have plenty of time to get situated. I don't want to rush or, worse yet, be late."

"Okay, Mom, I will be ready. Can I bring Molly anything?"

"I'm not sure, Luke. I have no idea what visiting day at this facility is like, so let's not bring anything this time. Would you like me to fix you breakfast?"

"No, Mom, I'm fine. I'm just going to shower and call Stacy back. I'll be down by eight o'clock."

"Okay," I said. I went to the kitchen to fix myself a cup of tea. Glancing at my watch, I realized that I didn't really have enough time to call Susan, but I did have enough time to call Sam.

He answered on the first ring, almost as if he was waiting for my call. "Brenda, I am so happy that you called. I wanted to talk to you but wasn't sure of your schedule for today, so I waited, hoping you had a minute to call me."

Just hearing his voice took some of my nervous edge off. "I'm glad I got you, Sam. I am just so nervous and anxious about this visit, but talking to you always helps."

"Brenda, don't borrow trouble. Let Molly's counselor lead the visit. Try to relax and enjoy all being together. Thank you, Sam. You always have a way of making things less complicated. I'll call you when I get home."

"All right, Brenda, we will talk later." We said goodbye and hung up, and I gathered my things together and finished getting ready. Luke came down, and into the car we went. I was more than a little apprehensive about the visit for many reasons.

Chapter 12

The ride was quick at that time in the morning. After all, it was a Saturday, not your typical work day. As we pulled into the parking lot, Luke said, "You left her here? It looks like an abandoned hotel."

"Thanks, Luke," I said, "that comment certainly makes me feel good about my decision."

With that, I parked and we got out. Into the building we went; the lobby was surprisingly crowded already. I guessed everyone had the same idea that I did. We signed in one at a time, and then were ushered into a very large room. Luke and I took seats and waited, watching an endless parade of people coming in. "Mom, is it always like this?"

"Well, Luke, in the last place Molly was in, we all sat in a room much like this, listening to a speaker before we got to see our loved ones. It looks like it works the same way here."

At exactly 9:00 a.m., a middle-aged man walked in. He waited until everyone settled down. He cleared his throat and began. "Hi, everyone, my name is Paul. Some of you have heard me speak here before, I usually come in to speak when there is a large group of new families here. To begin, quite a few years back, my wife and I sat in those very seats that you all are sitting in today. Like you all are today, we were hopeful as well. We hoped that our daughter Claire would get the help that she so desperately needed. That this was just a short detour on her road to the life my wife and I saw for her. The only problem was that Claire saw a different life for herself. A life very, very different from the one we thought she deserved. Claire completed this program. My wife and I attended every family day. We did everything we were told to do while she was here. What we failed to do was listen to Claire. Oh, we heard her words—they were the words that she thought we wanted her to say. She was fine. She was sorry. She was trying. But my wife and I never really heard Claire's voice.

"When she was done here, she came home. We picked up life where we left off, almost as if the past several months didn't exist. While she was here, we told everyone that Claire was traveling, 'finding herself' before she went to college. No one questioned us. It seemed like a plausible explanation. Once home, Claire followed the party line. The script we had written. She saw her friends, went out shopping with her mother for the usual college things, did what every kid does in the month before school begins. What she didn't do was go to meetings, find a sponsor, or work on herself. But we didn't think it was necessary. She was "cured." Well, let me tell you all something, and if you only take one thing away from what I say today, it should be this: it is necessary, very necessary. To us, Claire seemed just fine, back to her old self.

"The night before we took her up to college, her mom cooked her all her favorite foods. After all she wouldn't be back until Thanksgiving. Four months of college food. We invited the grandparents and some close family friends. After all, it was a celebration. For us, it was being able to put all of the ugliness behind us for good. For Claire, it was the beginning of her life.

"Bright and early the next day, we packed the car and headed off. The drive took us five hours. It was a lovely ride. Claire seemed excited. We were happy too. We had great conversations. Claire told us what her plans were. She was excited to meet her roommates. She wondered out loud how much of her past to share. My wife and I thought it best to keep the drug part to herself; after all, it wasn't that big a deal. It was a youthful mistake. Claire agreed, although she did so a little hesitantly.

"Once at school, we unloaded and helped set her up. Before long, her two new roommates and their families arrived. Vanessa and Regina. Everyone introduced themselves, sharing a little back history. The girls seemed like a good fit. Much earlier than we were ready too, we had to leave. The girls had freshman orientation, so we all had to go. Once in the parking lot, we parents exchanged information. We all agreed that it was good to be able to reach one another. Back in the car we went. The car ride back was a good one. My wife and I were happy Claire was back on track; life was finally normal again.

"The days turned into weeks. We spoke to Claire every few days. She sounded good, tired from her class load but good. She assured us she was eating and sleeping. She was excited to come home for Thanksgiving. We agreed that she could take the college bus home as most of the kids were doing. She told us the day and time she would be arriving at the station. It was all set.

"Two days before she was due home, we received a call that would forever change our lives. It was Vanessa, her roommate. At first, I couldn't understand her. She was crying, I begged her to please breathe and to calm down. I needed to be able to make out what she was saying. Finally, I heard her. 'Claire was rushed to the hospital by ambulance. You need to come now.'

"'Oh my god, what happened?' Vanessa had no answers for me.

"My wife and I raced to the car for what felt like the longest ride of our lives. We prayed the whole way there. 'Please God, please let her be okay.' Once at the hospital, we were told that Claire was brought in unresponsive. They had no medical history, but they told us that they did find an empty pill bottle on her bedside table. We were so shaken that I thought we may pass out. How could this be happening again? She was doing so well. The doctor came into the room, shaking his head. My wife immediately began to weep. I started yelling, 'No, please no!' The truth was that at this point, Claire was brain dead and there was nothing that anyone could do to help her. They brought us in to see her. She looked so peaceful as if she was just sleeping. My wife and I sat with her for a while.

"No parent should ever have to go through this. I realized that we never really made her work this very necessary program and that you are never 'cured' as we thought. I have told this story over one hundred times. It never gets easier, and the story always has the same ending. Our lives will never be the same again. But if I can save just one family from this anguish and heartbreak, I will feel like more of a success then failure. So please take away from this a few things. It's most important to follow the program that is laid out for you. Your addicts are never cured. Listen to your loved ones, not just their words but their souls, and don't hide in the shame of addiction. Share your story with everyone who will listen. You never know who is struggling with the same thing. Thank you all for your time." With that, he walked out.

When he left, there was hardly a sound in the room. I did hear some soft sobbing but nothing more. I myself was speechless. I looked over at Luke; his eyes were closed. I wondered what he was thinking.

As we all sat there with our own thoughts, Barry walked in. He introduced himself and proceeded to speak to us. "I am sure for some of you, that was hard to hear. Sometimes reality is, but unfortunately, this is every one of your realities now. Take away from Paul's story something positive. Take the painful knowledge that he learned— maybe it will save you all some pain. In a few minutes, the clients will join us. Try to keep this visit pleasant. They have all heard Paul's story on day one. Later on today, individual counselors will also join you. I am here if anyone has any questions." He left the room, once again leaving all of us with our own silent anguish.

Once again, I looked at Luke. This time, his eyes were open. "Are you okay?" I whispered.

"No, Mom, I'm not. I need some air. Can I go out for a minute or two?"

"Yes, I guess, as long as you are quick."

He got up and practically ran out of the room. I know for me hearing that story was difficult. I could only imagine for him how it was. After about ten minutes, I saw Molly. I could not get to her fast enough. I grabbed her in my arms and hugged her as if to never let her go. "Okay, Mom, okay…are you all right?"

"Yes, Molly. I'm fine, just so happy to see you."

Once I let her go, she looked around. Her eyes clouded over with sadness. "No Luke? He didn't come?"

Before I had a chance to answer her, I saw him come charging in. He grabbed Molly from behind and spun her around. When she was facing him, she threw her arms around him. "I am so glad you finally came, Luke. I haven't seen you in forever. I have missed you so much."

"I missed you too, Mol. When is Mom springing you?"

"I'm not sure yet. Amanda thinks I need to be here for a while. I, of course, do not agree."

"Okay, you two, let's find a seat so we can talk. As usual, they both rolled their eyes at me. This time, it was okay. I missed it—it had been a while since they were together and able to do it. Once we were situated, I asked, "Molly, how are you really doing?"

"I'm doing good, Mom, really I am. I am going to all of my groups and participating. I see Amanda three times a week one on one, and I see her in a women's group as well. We are covering a lot of ground, and I am working my steps with her."

"Wow, Molly," Luke said, "it sounds like you have things going in the right direction."

"I'm really trying. The faster I get this, the faster I get to leave here." "But you shouldn't rush through the program." I said.

As I was talking to her, I thought about Paul's story. "Please, Molly, stay as long as Amanda thinks is necessary. It's so important."

"I will, Mom. I'm doing everything that I'm supposed to do."

"Hey, Mom," Luke said, "relax. She's got this."

"Thanks, Luke. I know she's 'got this.' I'm just concerned."

"Yeah, I know you are, and I get why."

Molly looked at both of us with a questioning look, but before she had a chance to ask anything, Amanda walked over. I was internally relieved. I was not interested in explaining any of my exchange with Luke to her. After all, I wanted to keep this visit light. Amanda sat down with us and introduced herself to Luke. "I am glad you were able to join us today. I know Molly has been missing you. She talked quite a lot about you."

"Well, I have missed her too. When will she be getting out?"

"Well, Luke," Amanda said, "it's not exactly jail. She doesn't 'get out.' This is purely a voluntary program. Molly stays until she feels ready to leave. We, of course, lay out a program we think that she will benefit from, and give her suggestions, but it is really up to her. After all, it's her life, her failures or successes. Brenda, I wonder if you have a few minutes to talk?"

"Sure," I said, though I really preferred to stay and spend time with my kids. Off I went with Amanda to her office. As I was leaving the room, I looked back over my shoulder; it did my heart good to see Molly and Luke deep in conversation. I wondered for a minute what they were talking about.

Once in Amanda's office, I took a seat across from her and waited. My wait was short lived. "I'm very glad that Luke decided to come with you. I always stress to my clients' family members that addiction is a family disease. In order for Molly to succeed, the whole family needs to participate. Molly told me that she was sure that you would do whatever was necessary to help her, but she wasn't too sure about her brother. I'm very glad that he decided to come and see her today. I'm hoping he will make it a regular occurrence."

"I hope so too, Amanda. It's hard for me to read him these days. There is so much going on in all of our lives. Brenda, the next thing I'm going to talk to you about is a much more sensitive topic." *Oh boy*, I thought. I held my breath waiting.

"Well, as you know, I meet with Molly alone several times a week and at least once in a group setting. Two days ago, in group, it came up that people turn to drugs for many reasons. The easiest excuse is curiosity. In my professional opinion, this is almost never the case. In most cases, women turn to drugs to numb feelings. To numb pain. In Molly's case, it seems she was trying to numb herself."

"But why?" I asked. "What was she trying to numb?"

"Well, Brenda, I'm not sure, not yet. We are working on this together. What I am sure of is that she is not ready to share this with me—or anyone else for that matter. I'm telling you this so you will be prepared."

"Prepared?"

"Yes, once she talks about it—and she will need to—there won't be any turning back. It's important to remember you are a family there to support one another. It may be helpful for you to get a counselor for yourself. Perhaps there are things you need to talk about as well."

I sat there, trying to digest all that Amanda was saying to me.

"I know it's a lot to take in. Take some time to think. We can talk again next week." I stood up, more confused than ever before.

"Oh, and Brenda, please wait for Molly to approach you about this."

"Okay, Amanda, I will." With that, I left her office. I started walking back to the main room, I had to stop a minute to catch my breath. I wasn't really sure how to process any of this. I did, however, know how to put a smile on my face for Molly and Luke's benefit.

I found them right where I left them, but this time, there was someone with them. A little bit of a girl. She was sitting next to Molly, engrossed in their conversation. When Molly saw me, she jumped up and introduced me to her friend. "Mom, this is Nancy. She just got here yesterday, so no one can visit her yet. I thought it would be okay if she hung out with us for a bit."

"Sure, it's fine with me."

At this point, Luke voiced his hunger. "Hey, Mom, it's after twelve o'clock. Do they feed us here or what?"

"I'm not sure. Molly?"

Just as we were trying to figure it out, Barry came in again. "Hey all, I am sure most of you are wondering about lunch right about now. Well, normally we serve lunch, but on visiting day we give families the option of getting takeout from any of the local places. There is plenty of time if that's what you want to do. There is a pile of menus to look at."

"Well, Luke, there is our answer. Why don't we decide what everyone is hungry for? Nancy, would you like to join us?" (I was getting much better at sharing my time with Molly.)

"Sure, thank you, I would like that. Okay, everyone, what are you in the mood for?"

Molly suggested sandwiches from the nearby deli.

"Thoughts?" I asked.

"I'm good with that," said Luke.

"So am I," said Nancy.

"Okay then, sandwiches it is."

Luke volunteered to make the deli run. I was happy to let him go. I gave him the car keys, and off he went.

"So, Nancy, tell me a little bit about yourself."

"Okay, but there isn't much to tell. This is my first rehab. My parents really don't know how to handle any of this. They were disappointed that they couldn't come today. But there are happy to know that they will be able to come next week. I actually went to school with Molly."

"Yep, Mom," Molly said. "Nancy was a grade behind me. We weren't really friends in high school. We just had different circles of friends. But we saw each other in the halls from time to time."

"Oh, got it." I wondered what drug brought Nancy here. My wait was short-lived.

"I'm here because I got hooked on heroin."

Wow, I thought, *that's heavy stuff.* I wasn't sure what my response was supposed to be. I was saved from having to say anything by the return of Luke. "I'm back!" he yelled as he crossed the room. We got up to move to a table.

Once situated, Luke asked, "So, Nancy, what are you in for?" Leave it to Luke to pose that question.

"Heroin," Nancy said.

"Wow, that's tough, how are you doing?"

"Well," she said, "the first few days at the detox facility sucked, but now that I'm here, it's been better."

"Good, good to hear that," Luke said.

Desperate to change the subject, I asked about the girls' roommates. "Well," Molly said, I don't have any right now. The three people in my room left. Carla and Barbara went on to sober houses."

"Sober houses?" I asked.

"Yeah, Mom, apparently that's the last step before you get to go home. I have been told that it's like a transition between a rehab and home."

Oh, something more to worry about, I thought.

"Tiff checked herself out. She was done with this place. I'm worried about her, Mom. She wasn't doing any work."

"I don't have any roommates either," said Nancy. "Molly and I asked Amanda if we could room together. She is supposed to let us know tonight."

Luke had been quiet through this whole conversation. He just seemed to be taking everything in. We chatted for the rest of the visit, just lighthearted conversation. It was a very pleasant day. If we weren't in this building, it would have felt just like a typical Saturday. But the stark setting quickly brought me back to reality.

Right at 4:00 p.m., Barry came in again. "Okay, all, it's time to say your goodbyes. I hope you all had good visits. For those of you who are new to our program, we do this every Saturday."

I got up to give Molly a hug goodbye. "I love you, Molly girl. I will talk to you on Wednesday, and will see you again next Saturday."

"Bye, Mol," said Luke. "Talk soon?"

"Sure, Luke, sure." We said our goodbyes to Nancy, and off we went.

Chapter 13

Once in the car, I turned to Luke and asked, "Well? How are you? How did it go for you?"

"Well, Mom, to tell you the truth, it was a lot. I was totally not prepared for any of it. Paul's story was terrible. It makes me worry about Molly."

"I know, honey. I guess I should have prepared you better. I'm still trying to adjust to this myself."

"I know, Mom. I don't think I can come every Saturday—it's too much for me."

"I understand, Luke, it is a lot. I would like you to come at least once a month though."

"Once a month? How long do you plan on making her stay?"

"Well, Luke, as Amanda pointed out, I'm not making her stay. She can leave whenever she wants to. But the longer she stays, the better her chances are."

"Well, Mom, I'll think about it. Let me ask you, when do you plan on telling her about Sam?"

"I'm not sure yet. I am planning on talking to Sam first then to Amanda. I don't want to do or say anything that she isn't ready for."

"Okay, Mom, but keep in mind that I knew something was going on with you before you told me anything. I wouldn't be so sure that Molly doesn't feel something."

"Duly noted, Luke."

The rest of the car ride was silent, both of us lost in our own thoughts.

Before long, I found myself pulling into our driveway. Immediately, Luke jumped out and asked if he could head over to Stacy's. She had invited him to dinner, and he felt like he needed the break. "Sure," I said, "after all, today was a heavy day, and I was sure he needed the break."

He came around and gave me a quick hug. "I love you, Mom, and I'm sorry you are going through this."

"Thank you, Luke, for coming. I love you too. Be careful driving and don't be late tonight."

"I won't," he said, "I promise."

I walked into the kitchen to make a cup of tea and breath. I hadn't realized how exhausted I was until I sat down. It was an emotional day for all of us. First there was Paul's story, and then my conversation with Amanda. A lot to take in. I sat there for a little bit, just going over the day again. I was so engrossed in my thoughts that I almost missed the ringing of my phone. I jumped up to answer. It was Sam. "Hi, Brenda, are you okay? I hadn't heard from you and I was worried. I thought visiting ended at four o'clock."

"Oh, Sam. I'm sorry. I was going to call you. I just got lost in my thoughts."

"Well, as long as you are okay. Yes, I'm okay, just drained. Why are you worried?"

"Because, Brenda, it is seven o'clock, and as I said I didn't hear from you."

"Seven o'clock...how can that be? I can't believe that I have been sitting in the same spot for two hours. Oh, Sam, I'm okay really. It was just a very emotionally draining day."

"Well, I was wondering if you are up to some company? I thought if you were up to it, I would come over."

"That would be great, Sam. See you soon."

After we hung up, I got up and went into the bathroom to wash my face. The face staring back at me in the mirror looked harried, lost, and vacant. It was at that moment that I realized I had no idea what was really happening. I knew that my daughter was in rehab, but I had no idea what had driven her to this very dark place. Amanda talked to me about trauma, but what? What could have happened that I didn't know about? It wasn't until years later that I was to find out just what had happened. I quickly splashed water on my face and got ready to face Sam. My wait wasn't too long; I saw his headlights pulling into my driveway. As soon as I saw him, I started to cry. I didn't realize how hard I was holding myself together until I saw him. He just stood there holding me in his arms while I cried. When I was done, when there was absolutely nothing left in me, he led me to the sofa and waited. He waited patiently until I was ready.

I started off by telling him about Paul's story. I then told him about meeting Molly's friend, Nancy. I told him about my meeting with Amanda, and then finally, I told him how Luke handled it all. After I was done, Sam just looked at me, shaking his head. "Oh, Brenda, I wish I could go with you, be there for you, help you navigate this."

"Sam, I wish for that as well, but it's too soon. Molly is too fragile. She has so much on her plate right now. But I promise as soon as the time is right, I will talk to her."

"Okay, Brenda, whatever you think is right. Just know that I am here for you." We just sat there for a while, each lost in our own thoughts.

I was the first one to break the silence. "Sam, you must be hungry. Let me fix you something to eat."

"No, Brenda, let me fix you something."

"You, Sam?"

"Sure, I make a mean scrambled eggs and toast bread."

"Breakfast for dinner, count me in."

Off to the kitchen we went. Halfway through the meal prep, my doorbell rang. We looked at each other. "I'm not expecting anyone, and Luke has keys."

I opened the door, and there stood Susan. "Hi, Sue, what's up? Are you okay?" I asked.

"I'm fine," she said. "I was just checking on you. I was afraid if I called you, you may not have answered, or if you did, you may not have told me anything other than you are okay. I wanted to come over and talk to you, see you."

"Oh, Susan, thank you for caring so much. Come in, I would love you to meet Sam."

"Brenda, I don't want to interrupt anything."

"Don't be silly—you could never interrupt. Come in please." We walked into the kitchen. "Sam. I would like you to meet my best friend, Susan. Susan, this is Sam."

"Hello, Susan. Brenda has told so much about you."

"Well, Sam, I wish I could say the same thing, but my friend has been a little reluctant to share too much with me."

"Well," I said, "that's not entirely true. I really was waiting to tell Luke about Sam before I told too many people."

"Well," Susan said, "from the look of things, I'm going to guess that you have told Luke?"

"Yes, I have. I was going to call you to tell you all about it, but it was too late when I got home. As a matter of fact, Luke and Sam met last night."

"Really, how did it go?"

"It went very well," said Sam. "I think his curiosity got the better of him and he wanted to meet me. We had a lovely dinner, the four of us, last night."

"The four?" Susan asked.

"Yes," I said, "Stacy joined us as well."

"I like him very much," said Sam. "They both seem like very nice young people. It went so well that Luke agreed to go with me today to see Molly."

"How is she? How was your visit?"

"She is doing well," I answered. "She seems to like the facility or at least doesn't hate it. She told me she participates in her groups. She even met someone whom she went to high school with. She's a year younger, but it's a familiar face at least. I met with her counselor who told me that she is doing all she needs to do there. I was happy to hear that. Luke seemed a bit overwhelmed by it all. I am hoping he will continue to come with me. Having the whole family involved will be really beneficial for Molly's recovery. I'm just not too sure how much of this Luke will be interested in doing. I'm taking a wait-and-see attitude at this time."

"Sounds like a good idea to me," said Susan.

"Susan," Sam said, "please join us. I'm making a simple, light dinner. I want to make sure that Brenda eats."

"Oh, thanks for the invite, but I ate already. But I would like to stay and chat for a while." We moved over to the table and continued on with our conversation. Susan was asking Sam all kinds of questions. They were getting to know each other, these two very important people in my life. At one point, I sat back, watched, and listened. I was happy to see them getting along. Susan was one of my dearest friends, and Sam—well, Sam was turning out to be very important to me in his own way. I was happy to see it all. Although I was just feeling a little guilty about feeling happy about anything.

As the evening was winding down, Luke walked in. At first, he looked a little startled to see both Susan and Sam in our kitchen. Without a word, he looked at me and gave me his trademark one-eyebrow raise. I just looked back at him with a faint smile barely touching my lips. It was a kind of silent acknowledgment just between us.

"Hi all," said Luke, "what's going on?"

"Hi, Luke," replied Susan, "not too much here. I came by to check on your mom to see how she was doing, and Sam seemed to have the same idea. She told us that you went with her today to see Molly. How was it for you?"

"It was okay. She looks okay, but the place she's in looks like a dump. Did Mom tell you about the really sad story we heard today?"

"Yes," Sam said, "she told us about it. It's a terrible thing to have to have gone through."

"Yes," Susan mumbled, "I don't know if I could ever survive that."

"Molly is way stronger than that," said Luke. "She's going to get through this."

"Well, I'm beat. Today was a really long day. Good night, Luke," we all said in unison. After he walked out, Susan and Sam both got up to leave.

"Good night," Susan said.

"Susan. I'll call you tomorrow."

"Maybe we can get together if you aren't busy."

"Okay, sounds great. Thanks for checking on me."

Next, it was Sam's turn to leave. I walked him to the door. He took me into his arms and whispered, "I hate you having to go through this alone. Remember I am here for you. Anything you need. Please remember that."

"Thank you, Sam. That means a lot to me. And thank you for coming over. I love you."

I gently closed the door behind him. I was exhausted. It was a long, emotional day.

I walked to Luke's room to talk to him for a minute. His door was closed. I peeked in to find him sound asleep. I guessed that today was a lot for him as well. Well, I guess it was off to bed for me too. I was wondering if I would get any sleep at all. I was plagued with questions. Again I wondered what brought us here. Amanda mentioned Molly wanting to numb herself, but from what? What kind of pain could she have suffered? I had more questions than answers and no time frame for when I would get those answers. I lay there in bed, tossing and turning for most of the night.

At first light, I got up. I decided to start my day; lying there plagued by my worry was serving no purpose. I took a quick shower to wash off the remnants of a restless night and to try to take myself out of my sleep-deprived stupor. I made myself a cup of tea and sat in my kitchen. I was startled when I heard Luke's voice. "Mom? Mom, are you all right?"

"Yes, Luke, why do you ask?"

"Because I have been calling you for five minutes and you didn't answer."

"Oh, I'm sorry. I must have been lost in my own thoughts."

"Okay, as long as you are all right, Mom."

"I'm fine, honey. Promise."

"Okay, then I'm leaving in a little while. Stacy and I are hanging out with some of our friends for most of the day—unless you want me to stay home. I don't want to leave you home by yourself."

"I'll be fine, Luke. I'm either going to spend some time with Susan or Sam. I want you to go. Have fun and give my love to Stacy."

"I will, Mom. I love you. Try not to worry so much."

"I'm trying, Luke, I am trying."

After a while, I heard Luke yell, "Bye, Mom, I won't be late!"

Chapter 14

I decided I needed to get moving or I would just end up sitting there in my kitchen. As I was deciding what to do and whom to call, my doorbell rang. *Now what?* I thought. I went to my door and pulled it open, dreading to see who may be there. But to my very happy surprise, it was Leslie. "Brenda, I know I should've called, but I was worried you may have told me not to come, so I took a chance and just showed up."

"Come in, Leslie. I'm happy you are here. Can I get you anything?"

"No, Bren, I'm good. Let's just sit—you can fill me in on what's been going on."

"Well, so much has happened since I saw you last. Molly has moved from her thirty-day program to a long-term facility somewhere that wants the residents to stay for at least six months. Luke came with me yesterday to visit her. Luke and Sam met, and Sam met Susan. It's been a busy few weeks."

"Wow," said Leslie, "I'll say. So tell me everything. First tell me how Molly is adjusting. How did you get her to agree to go?"

"It wasn't so much me as it was her counselor Ann. She with the help of her staff helped Molly understand that it was in her best interest to go. She didn't really want to go but I guess agreed because she believed that I would not let her come home."

"How is she adjusting?"

"Okay, I guess. She hasn't been there that long. She has a friend there, someone whom she knew from school. Maybe that helps. I'm hopeful."

"Okay, so now tell me about Luke meeting Sam."

"Well, as it so happened, it was just this past Friday. I was at Sam's house. Luke called saying he wanted to meet me there. I was a little apprehensive, but Sam said let him come. So he and Stacy came there. It was a good thing. Sam ended up taking everyone to one of his favorite places for dinner. They enjoyed each other's company and seemed to genuinely like each other. I was not sure what changed for Luke, but he decided to come with me to visit Molly. It was a good visit. I am hoping that Luke will come with me more often. As far as Susan and Sam's meeting was concerned, that was purely by chance. Sam was over last night, and Susan stopped by. Again, they seemed to get along just fine. So right now, in this very moment, everything is fine. I don't want to say that too much."

"Well, I am glad for you, Brenda. It's been a rough ride thus far." We talked for a while longer before Leslie got up to leave.

"Thank you for coming over to check on me."

"You are welcome, my friend."

After she left, I felt much better. I was beginning to see how sharing this with the people in my life was helpful. I felt less alone, less isolated. *Maybe my next step should be finding a counselor for myself. I'll give it some thought,* I promised myself. *Now I will just enjoy a second cup of tea and think about the small successes of the last few days.* In the span of three days, Sam had met my son and one of my best friends. Luke had gone with me to see Molly, and Molly seemed to be settling in and adjusting to her new facility. It's all I could hope for at this time. After a while of just sitting there, I decided I needed something to do, so I called Susan. I got her answering machine. I left a short message.

I then called Sam. He answered right away. I smiled when I heard his voice. "How are you today, Brenda? I am doing okay today. I thought maybe if you weren't busy, you may want to get together."

"I would love to, Brenda. How about I come and get you in an hour?"

"Sure, I'll be ready." I quickly got dressed and grabbed my gloves and hat. It was a cold, crisp winter day, so I would need the hat and gloves for sure.

Sam, as always, was right on time. I couldn't help but smile when I saw him. He had a way about him that always made me smile even at my lowest point. "So, Brenda, where would you like to go?"

"I don't really care. I thought I would leave it up to you since you always come up with great ideas."

"Well," said Sam, "I was hoping that you would say that. I know just the place."

Off we went; we took the scenic route to the east end of Long Island. Once we parked, Sam grabbed my hand, and we walked together down to the water. I was to find out that this was Sam's place to find peace. We walked together in quiet reflection, each lost in our own thoughts, the crashing of the waves the only sound that could be heard. As we walked further and further up the beach, I thought to myself, *Now I understand why Sam comes here.* It was so peaceful. I could think clearly; the noise and confusion in my head was calm and quiet at last. After a while, Sam asked me if I wanted to leave if I was too cold. I said that I hadn't realized how cold it really was. "Yes, sure," I said, "I'm ready to leave."

Off we went, back to the car to head home. "Brenda would you like to stop for a quick bite, an early dinner?"

"Sure, Sam, that sounds good." This time, it was I who suggested a place to go.

After a quiet dinner and relaxed conversation, we headed back to my house. It was still early, so I asked Sam in. "Sure, I would love to," he answered.

Once inside, I called out to Luke. "Are you home, Luke?"

"Hey, Mom, I'm here. I told you I wouldn't be late." He came out of his room as he was talking to me. "Oh hey, Sam, I didn't know you were here."

"Hi, Luke. I'm just staying a minute. Wanted to make sure your mom was in and okay."

I didn't see it as much as I felt them looking at each other over my head, almost in silent agreement that I needed taking care of. On some level, it warmed my heart that these two very special men in my life cared so much.

"So, Luke," Sam said, "how was your day? Do anything special?"

"No, not too special. I hung out with Stacy and some of our friends."

"Sounds about right. Just what I was doing at your age."

"Well, you two," said Sam, "I'm going to head out. Early day tomorrow."

"Night, Sam," said Luke.

I walked Sam to the door. "Thank you again for a beautiful day, Sam. It was just what I needed."

"Anytime, Brenda. I'm here for you always." With that, he was gone. I quietly closed the door and walked back in.

Luke was waiting for me in the kitchen. "Mom, can I ask you something?"

"Sure, honey."

"Is it serious with Sam?"

I thought for a minute before answering him. "I think it could be, Luke. But I don't want to rush anything. So much is going on. I don't want to get hurt or hurt anyone either. I worry about Molly, about you."

"Me? Why are you worried about me? I'm fine," he said.

"I worry, Luke, because so much is changing. What once was is no longer. I don't know what our new normal will look like."

"Mom, I just want you to be happy, and if being with Sam makes you happy, then I say be happy. Molly and I will be fine with this, I promise."

"Thank you, Luke. I love you."

"I love you too, Mom. I'm going to bed. See you in the morning."

I sat there in my kitchen, thinking about my conversation with Luke. Glad that we had the kind of relationship we had. I too decided to call it a night; after all, tomorrow started a new work week. As I lay in bed, I wondered if sleep would elude me again. Much to my surprise, it did not. Before I knew it, my alarm went off. Surprisingly, I felt well-rested. I went to the kitchen looking for Luke. I caught him as he was leaving. "Have a good day, Mom. See you tonight."

"Bye, Luke. I love you."

"Love you too, Mom." As he was leaving, he looked back at me to tell me that Stacy would be coming over later for dinner, and then he was gone.

Well, I thought, *at least he gave me some kind of a heads up.* I was glad for that. I guess I would stop on my way home to pick up something to cook. After a quick shower, it was off to work for me. On the short drive there, I thought about Molly and about the things she was working through. I said a silent prayer for strength for her and for myself. I pulled into my normal spot at my office, and as I was walking in, I ran into Gail. "Hi, Gail," I said, "how was your weekend?"

"Good, quiet, just the way I like it. How was yours?"

"Same," I replied. In we went to start our work week together.

Monday blended into Tuesday and then into Wednesday. The only difference was that on Wednesdays, I got my much-anticipated call from Molly. Right on time, the phone rang. "Hi, Mom," she said.

For some reason, just hearing her say that brought tears to my eyes. Quickly wiping them away, I answered back. "Hi, Molly. It's so good to hear your voice."

"I miss you so much, Molly."

"Miss me, Mom? You just saw me four days ago."

"I know, but it's just so different. I am used to seeing you every day, being able to talk to you whenever I want to."

"Oh, Mom. This is not going to be like this forever. You know that."

"Yes, I know, Molly, I know. So tell me, how are you doing?"

"I'm doing good, Mom. Don't worry so much. Nancy and I are now rooming together, which is a good thing. They moved us into a smaller room, which is even better. Smaller room means that they can't move anyone else in with us."

"Well, that's good, I guess. How are your groups? How are your sessions with Amanda? My groups are going good. I'm working though some things with Amanda."

"Oh good," I said, "anything I can help you with?"

"No, Mom, not yet."

"Okay, well, I'm here if you need me."

"Thanks, Mom. Mom, how is Luke doing? Is he coming on Saturday?"

"Luke's doing good. You know him, he doesn't say much. And no, honey, he's not coming this Saturday. But he did promise to come and visit again soon."

"Oh," Molly sighed. I could hear all her disappointment in that one sigh. To be honest, I was disappointed myself. I had hoped that he would come again on Saturday, but maybe it was just too much for him. I didn't share any of my thoughts with Molly. Instead, I asked her more about her days there. She told that it was much the same most days. They got up, had an hour to get ready for the day, then they went to breakfast. They went there first before the men. After breakfast, they had their individual appointments with their counselors, then it was on to women's group, lunch co-ed group, and then women's group again. At that point in the day, they got to go back to their rooms to journal or talk or rest before dinner. Dinner was at 6:00 p.m. After dinner, they all met in the big room for an in-house recovery-based meeting.

"Wow," I said, "they really keep you busy."

"They do, Mom. Our days are really filled." I was starting to realize that our time was going by and we would have to hang up soon, so I asked her if there was anything she needed or wanted me to bring her on Saturday. "No, Mom, I'm good. I have everything I need. I'm glad you are coming though."

"Of course I'm coming. I will always come to see you, Molly—it's what I do." We talked for a few more minutes before we both heard the familiar clicking of the phone, indicating that our time was up.

"I love you, Mom."

"I love you, Molly. I will see you on Saturday."

"See you, Mom." And then she was gone. I sat there for a few minutes, replaying my conversation with Molly. I missed her so much. Missed our time together, but I knew she was in the right place.

I finally got up to go find Luke, to see if he was going to be home for dinner. As usual, he was in his room on the phone. I stood there, waiting for him to see me. I took the opportunity to look at him, really look at him. It was then I realized that he looked thin. As soon as he realized that I was standing there, he ended his conversation. "What's up, Mom?"

"Not too much. I just got off the phone with your sister."

"Oh, how is she? She's doing good. She's rooming with Nancy now, which is making her happy. She has established a good routine at her facility. I told her you wouldn't be going to see her on Saturday. She seemed disappointed."

"Well, Mom," he said, "I told you I wasn't going to go with you every time you went."

"I know you did, Luke, but I was hoping that you would have changed your mind."

"Well, I'm sorry, Mom. I didn't. I'll go see her again, just not this weekend."

"Okay, Luke, that's fine." It was something more than I had hoped for. "Well, Luke," I said, "moving on, any thoughts for dinner?"

"No, not really. I will eat whatever you make."

"Okay then, dinner is in a half an hour."

"Okay, Mom."

On my way to the kitchen, I thought about our conversation. I thought, *Well, it's something at least.* Luke and I had a nice dinner. We stayed away from topics that were difficult to discuss; instead, we talked about work, school, and Stacy. Then Luke asked me about Sam. He hadn't seen him since Sunday. So he was wondering what was going on.

"Nothing is going on, Luke. We don't see each other every day. We each have our own lives and responsibilities. We mostly see each other on the weekends."

"All right, Mom, just checking. I wanted to make sure. So, Mom, when are you going to talk to Molly about Sam?"

"I'm not sure yet, Luke. I don't want to overwhelm her with too many things all at once."

"I get it, Mom, but don't you think it would be better to talk to her now, when she's got people to talk to?"

I thought about what he said. Maybe he was right; maybe this would be the best time. I wasn't sure, though. I thought that I would talk to Amanda on Saturday. After dinner, Luke excused himself to finish his homework. I decided to call Sam. I wanted to hear what he had to say about telling Molly. Although in the past he expressed his thoughts, he thought that it would be a good idea to meet Molly to show her that I had support, that I wasn't going through this alone. I called him but didn't get an answer. Maybe it was just as well; I was feeling a little down. I realized that I had moments like this. One minute I would feel good, and then out of nowhere, reality would crash over me and just engulf me again. Maybe I did need a counselor. I decided to call it a night. I was suddenly exhausted. I went to say good night to Luke.

Chapter 15

The next day was a repeat of the day before minus my call with Molly. On Friday, I was busy with back-to-back meetings. I didn't have much time for anything else. When I finally had a break, I checked my messages; there were two. One from Luke telling me he would be out tonight, plans with Stacy. The second one was from Sam. He was asking me if I wanted to get together for dinner. First, I would call Luke to check in to see what his plans were. Then I would call Sam. Luke answered right away. "What's up, Mom? Just got a chance to call you back. I got your message about your having plans tonight."

"Yeah, Mom. I'm taking Stacy out to dinner. Do you want to come with us?"

"Oh no, Luke. You go and have fun."

"I don't want to leave you alone, Mom."

"I'll be fine. Sam also called. I haven't called him back yet, but I will. He wanted to have dinner, but I wanted to check with you first."

"Go, Mom. I think it would be a good idea."

"I will, Luke, I will. Since you are taking Stacy out to dinner, let me give you some money."

"Oh, Mom, you don't have to do that."

"I know, Luke. I want to."

"Well, if you are sure, Mom…"

"I'm sure, Luke. I want to. I'll see you at home."

My next call was to Sam. "Hi there," I said when he answered the phone.

"Hi, Brenda, how are you?"

"I'm good. Sorry it took me so long to get back to you, crazy day here at the office."

"It's fine, Brenda. I just wanted to see if you are free tonight."

"Yes, as a matter of fact, I'm free. Luke is taking Stacy out, so yes, I'm free."

"Okay, do you want to come over?" he asked. "Or would you like to go out? I would love to come over," I replied.

"How about at seven o'clock?" Sam suggested. "Sounds perfect."

After we hung up, I went back to my desk. Gail was already back. "Good call, Brenda?"

"What makes you say that?"

"Oh, nothing, but the big grin on your face."

"Care to share?"

"Maybe," I answered, "just not yet."

Gail just nodded and turned away. After several more hours of work, it was time to leave. We said our usual goodbyes and have a good weekend, followed by "See you Monday," and into our cars we went.

Once I got home, I fed the dogs and let them out and then jumped into a quick shower. Once done, I sat down and waited for Luke. My wait was short-lived. He came in almost rushing past me. "Luke," I said, "slow down. What's the rush?"

"Oh, hi, Mom, I didn't know you would still be home."

"Of course I'm home. I wanted to see you before I left."

"Sorry, Mom, I'm just in a rush."

"It's okay, Luke. Do what you have to do. I'll wait." As I waited, I thumbed through the mail. Nothing too interesting. Before long, Luke was down and ready to walk out the door. "Hey, slow down. I have some money for you."

"Mom, it's really okay. I am fine."

"No, please just take it. I want to make sure you have enough."

"Thanks, Mom." He kissed me goodbye, and out the door he went. I wasn't long behind him.

I made the short drive to Sam's, and as what was becoming our evening ritual, he was waiting for me at the door. Again, I realized what a welcome sight he was. Once inside, he asked me if I would rather stay in for dinner or go out for dinner. "Stay in, please."

"Perfect," he said, "let me just order something. Go into the living room. I took the liberty of pouring you some wine."

"Why, thank you. It's much needed after my long week." I took a seat by the fire and slowly sipped my wine, waiting for Sam to appear. My wait was short lived. He took his seat next to me on the couch and asked me to fill him in on my week. There wasn't much to tell him other than my conversation with Molly and then Luke. Sam agreed that I probably should talk to Molly. That was so when she finally heard about it, she wouldn't feel like I kept such a big secret from her.

I thought about it again. "Perhaps," I said, "but I think I'm going to get some feedback from Amanda first." As soon as I said that, I felt my eyes fill up with tears.

"Brenda, what's wrong? If you don't want to tell her, don't. The last thing I want is you to be upset. I want our relationship to bring you happiness, not sadness."

"Oh, Sam, it's not that—it's just that I always thought I had the kind of relationship with Molly that we could talk about anything, and now I know it's not true. She couldn't talk to me about what was happening to her, and I have to ask someone else what I can and cannot say to my own daughter. That's what makes me sad."

"I'm sure it does, Brenda, but remember, it won't always be this way."

"I hope you're right." We sat there, looking into the fire, just content to be for a few minutes.

Before long, dinner arrived. We set it up and enjoyed a quiet meal together. At about 9:30 p.m., my phone rang. It was Luke. He wanted to know if he and Stacy could come over. I looked at Sam with a questioning eye.

"Of course," he said, "tell them to come."

I relayed the message and hung up. "Sam," I said, "thank you."

"Why are you thanking me? They are always welcome here." We sat waiting for them to arrive. I wondered if there was a reason for the visit.

I didn't have to wait long for an answer. They both walked up to the door, smiles on their faces. "Come in quickly," I said. "It's freezing out there."

"It sure is," replied Stacy. In they came.

As Luke passed me, I whispered, "Is everything all right?"

"Yeah, Mom, we just wanted to hang out with you guys."

"You do?" I said. "Yes, Mom, we do."

Wow, I thought, *how nice*. Once we were all settled, Sam asked Luke and Stacy if they were hungry.

"No," Stacy answered, "we just had dinner."

Luke spoke next; he wanted to know if Sam wanted to shoot some pool on the cool pool table he saw in Sam's game room. "Sure," Sam said.

"Okay, let's go then."

"Hey, Stacy, why don't you hang here with my mom while we play?"

"Sure, Luke." I didn't miss the look that passed between them.

As they left the room, I looked at Stacy and said, "So what's up? What's going on?"

"I'm not really sure. On the way over here, Luke told me to keep you company when he left with Sam, so here I am."

"Well, do you know why Luke wanted to be alone with Sam?"

Stacy just shrugged her shoulders. "No, I don't. He just wanted time with Sam."

Okay, I thought. *There isn't much I could do at this point other than wait*. Stacy and I talked about school and the upcoming junior prom. She wanted to go; Luke did not. He kept telling her that he would take her to his senior prom. He just didn't want to go to his junior prom. I promised her that I would try to talk to him.

Before too long, Sam and Luke came back. They were both laughing. Sam went on to tell me that Luke was a bit of a pool hustler. He beat him two games out of three. "Really?" I asked. "I didn't even know you played pool, Luke."

"Mom, my friend Brian has a pool table. We play often."

"Oh well, good to know," I said. We all sat and talked and enjoyed each other's company. The one person missing was Molly. I could feel her absence. It was a profound ache in my heart. As I was sitting there lost in my own thoughts, Luke got up. He told us that it was getting late and he had to get Stacy home on time. Sam and I got up to walk them to the door.

"Drive safely, Luke. I'll see you at home. I'm leaving shortly myself."

"Thanks, Sam," said Luke and Stacy. "It was nice to hang with you."

"See you again soon," said Sam.

Once back inside, I asked Sam what was up with Luke. His answer surprised me. "Well, Brenda, it seems as if you are raising a good man. He wanted to make sure that my intentions were good ones. Seems as though he is worried that you will get hurt and he wanted my promise that I wouldn't hurt you intentionally. I promised him I wouldn't. I told him how I felt about you and I told him that my intentions were to have you all move in here. He seemed surprised by your hesitation to do so. I explained to him that you didn't say no—you just said not yet."

"How did he react?"

"Well, he's hard to read, but he didn't seem overly upset by the prospect."

I sat there, trying to digest what Sam was telling me. Luke was able to read more into what he saw than what I felt able to share with him. Sam and I just sat there, once again each lost in our own thoughts. Just sitting there with Sam's arm around me made me feel safe. I wondered if Luke was seeking that same security. I owed him a conversation when I got home. I hadn't realized how late it was until I happened to glance at my watch. I jumped up telling Sam I had to go. I had an early day tomorrow and was getting tired. He walked me to the door, pulling me into his arms, whispering, "I love you, Brenda. Drive safe, and please call me when you get home."

"I will, Sam, and I love you too. Thank you again for talking with Luke."

"I'm always there for all of you."

On my drive home, I thought about my night. I always felt better when I was with Sam. I felt safe, cared for, and not so alone. I thought again about Luke and how he may also be missing those feelings. I really needed to talk to him. I pulled into my driveway and noticed that there wasn't a single light on in my house. I went in and didn't hear a sound. I walked to Luke's room and saw him sleeping peacefully. I walked back to the kitchen, flipped on the light, and saw the note he had left me. He was tired. He wanted to go to sleep as soon as he got home. He reminded me that he had to get up early because he was going with Stacy and her family to Connecticut for the weekend. He said that he would be back on Sunday. To be honest, I had forgotten that it was this weekend. I scribbled a note telling him to wake me up before he left no matter what time it was. I then went to my bedroom to call Sam and let him know I was home safe and sound.

"Good, Brenda, glad you are in. What did Luke say?"

"I didn't actually get a chance to talk to him. He was asleep when I got home. I forgot that he was going to Connecticut with Stacy and her family for the weekend."

"Well, there will be plenty of time to talk to him when he gets back."

"You're right, Sam. Well, thank you for another wonderful evening."

"Good night, Brenda. Please call me when you get home from seeing Molly." I set my alarm for early the next morning. I wanted to make sure that I saw Luke before he left.

I was up bright and early the next day and already in the kitchen when Luke came down. "Morning, Luke. Morning, Mom. I didn't expect you to be up this early. I tried to be quiet so as not to wake you. I really wanted to see you before you left. I wanted to make sure you had everything you needed," I said. "I'm only going overnight. Don't worry so much," Luke replied.

"I'm trying," I told him. "When will you be back, Luke?"

"Some time in the early evening on Sunday."

"All right, can you please call me when you get there? I won't be able to answer but at least I will get your message when I leave Molly."

"Sure, Mom, if that makes you feel better."

"It does, Luke, it does."

I walked him to the door and gave him a hug, holding him tighter and longer than I normally do. "Okay, Mom, okay. I'm only going overnight," he said again.

"I know—it's just that I will miss you."

"All right, but I have to go now. I don't want to be late. Say hello to Mol for me."

"I love you, Luke."

"I love you too, Mom," he said and then he was gone. I walked back into the kitchen to have a cup of tea and think about the day ahead. I decided to talk to Amanda about Sam, see what her thoughts were. I wasn't sure what I was going to do, but it would be good to get her input. Before long, it was time for me to leave for my visit with Molly. I traveled the now familiar route, parked in a spot and proceeded into the lobby. I signed in took a seat and waited. Again, I watched as more and more people came in. Some of the faces looked familiar; I had seen them last week. Once again, at exactly 9:00 a.m., a new speaker walked in.

This time, it was a young woman. She introduced herself, "Hello, my name is Martha, and I am going to tell you my story. It started when I was fifteen. I am the oldest of three. I have a younger sister and a younger brother. Our dad died of cancer when my brother was two. It was then just myself, my siblings, and my mom. My mom was a nurse who worked many hours to keep our family afloat. I first noticed little changes in her six months after my dad died. Sometimes I would find her sleeping, sitting up on the couch. I thought that it was because she was so tired from working her long hours. After all, I was fifteen—what did I really know? But then things got worse, my mom would disappear for hours at a time coming home really late, looking terrible. Then one day, I came home from school early to find her passed out on the couch with a needle lying on the floor next to her. I was so scared at fifteen I didn't know what to think.

I just knew that I needed help so I called 911. It seemed like I was waiting forever for an ambulance to get there. The paramedics asked me all kinds of questions, most of them I couldn't answer. I watched as they lifted my mother onto the stretcher and took her into the ambulance. They were taking her to the hospital, they told me. I stood in the doorway watching as the ambulance drove away. Our next-door neighbor came over to check on me and to see what had happened. At fifteen, I didn't know that this subject was taboo. My neighbor just hugged me and asked me if I had called anyone. No, I told her I didn't. I guess I was in shock. She suggested that I call my grandparents. After she left, I walked over to the phone and called my grandma. I told her what I saw and what was happening. I told her everything I knew, which at this point was very little. She told me that she would be over right away. She was there with my grandpa very quickly. My grandma wanted to know what hospital they took my mom to so she could go there. My grandpa would stay with us, she said. It wasn't until the next day that I was to find out what was going on. It seemed that my mother was a heroin addict. It hadn't started that way. At first, she was addicted to pills. She took them to help her stay awake, then she took some to help her sleep. It was a cycle of ups and downs. When that didn't seem to work anymore, she moved on to bigger and better stuff. Until she arrived at heroin. I hardly understood what was being told to me other than my mother was going to be sent to a rehab and my grandparents were moving in to take care of us. I remember being scared and confused, but at my age, I didn't really understand what was being told to me. My sister and brother were told that Mom was sick and need to get well, so she was going away for a while.

"This established a pattern over the next five years. Mom would go away for a while, get clean, and come home. Sometimes her being home would last months, other times it was only weeks. Each time she came home, she looked less and less like herself. My grandma cried a lot. My grandpa, once the funniest person I knew stopped smiling and even stopped talking much. The toll this took on my family is something I can't put into words even now. As I said, this cycle lasted five years before it was over. I am standing here to tell you all this, my story, so that your family never has to suffer as we have. My mother died a year ago on my sister's eighteenth birthday. My grandpa, my mom's dad, was the one who found her in her room with drug paraphernalia spread around her. He was the one who had to tell my grandma and all of us. I will never forget the look in their eyes as they had to say goodbye to their daughter. I will never forget hearing my grandma crying in my grandpa's arms, saying no parent should ever have to bury their child. I will never forget having to try to console my siblings while I was choking back my own tears. I choose to remember my mother as she was the person she used to be before all of this. I choose to only talk of the good times and share the good memories with my siblings and I chose to forgo college for right now to stay home with my family. We have already lost too much. Six months after my mom died, my grandpa left us. My grandma says that he died of a broken heart. Thank you for letting me share this with you all." And then she was gone.

The room was eerily silent after she walked out. My heart was pounding. I thought, *Please God, please let us be okay. Please let us survive this. I can't bear the thought of being a statistic.* After a minute or two, Barry came in. He told us that hearing other people's experiences would be very important to us. It illustrated how serious this disease is. He asked us if we had questions. No one said a word. "Okay then, your loved ones will be joining you in a minute." There was a collective sigh of relief as we all waited for our loved ones to join us.

As always, Molly was one of the last people to walk in to the room. It really didn't surprise me as she always took longer than anyone I knew to get ready. As soon as she saw me, she ran over to me. "Hi, Mom," she said as she hugged me.

"Hi, Molly," I answered back, holding on to her a little tighter and a little longer than was necessary. Funny thing is, she didn't seem to mind it. Once we were ready to let go of each other, we walked over to the nearest couch and took a seat. I looked at her as if to drink her in. I was happy to see her more so after hearing Martha's story.

Just looking at her, I found myself silently praying, *Please oh please let us be the 1 percent.* I also found myself wondering if she had heard the same stories that we heard. I secretly hoped not. "Well, Molly," I said, "how are you?"

"I'm doing good, Mom! Not too many things are different from our conversation on Wednesday. Still working the same program. She told me she was happy to be rooming with Nancy. They had a lot of things in common. They knew some of the same people."

"I see," I said, wondering if this was going to be a problem.

All of a sudden, Molly jumped up. "What," I said, "are you okay?"

"Yes, Mom, it's just that I saw Nancy and her parents, and I wanted you to meet them."

"Okay, Molly, but don't startle me like that again please."

"Sorry, Mom, I didn't mean to startle you, I was just excited to see her. We talked about you guys meeting today. We thought it would be a good idea."

"I'm fine with that, honey." We walked over to where Nancy and her family were sitting. As we stood there, I noticed how fragile her mom looked. I could remember feeling the way she looked.

Nancy proceeded to introduce her parents to me. "Mom, Dad," she said, "this is Molly's mom, Brenda, and Brenda, these are my parents, Max and Julie. It's so nice to meet you both. Nancy has spoken about you both last week. It's nice to meet you as well, Brenda, and thank you for including Nancy in your family time last Saturday. We were disappointed that we couldn't see her, but you know rules are rules."

"Oh, you are welcome," I replied, "it was my pleasure. I enjoyed getting to know Nancy. Max invited us to join them for their visit with Nancy."

As much as I wanted time alone with Molly, I heard the quiet desperation in his voice. I turned to Molly with a questioning look. Sure, she answered, we would love to chat for a while. We both took seats and proceeded to exchange stories. Molly was very honest in what she shared. She told them about her previous thirty days. She told them that she was sure that this was it, that she understood this "situation" and would never go down this path again. They listened to everything she said, and when she was done, Julie said, "That's so good to hear. I am glad you feel so strongly about it."

Julie then turned to Nancy and said, "I am so glad you are sharing a room with Molly." All the while, I just sat there and listened. Maybe I was jaded already, or maybe I just heard too many stories that did not have a happy ending. Either way, for the third time that day, I found myself silently praying for strength, for peace, and for guidance for my daughter. As we were sitting there chatting, I was glancing about the room looking for Amanda. I thought that this would be the ideal time to try to talk to her.

While Molly was busy with Nancy and her parents, I finally spotted her. "Can you guys excuse me for a few minutes?" I asked. "I want to have a word with Amanda."

"Sure," they said.

As I got up to leave, Molly leaned over and whispered, "Everything okay, Mom?"

"Yes, honey, I just wanted to ask Amanda something, nothing to worry about."

"Okay, Mom, if you are sure."

"Yes, Molly, I am sure."

Chapter 16

I got up and walked across the open floor to where Amanda was sitting. As soon as she saw me, she got up and said, "Brenda, I was going to come over to speak with you. Do you have a few minutes now?" she asked me. "Yes, I do. As a matter of fact, I wanted to speak to you as well. Okay, good, let's go to my office where we will have more privacy." I agreed and followed her to her office.

Once situated, I started taking several deep breaths to calm my nerves. I was ridiculously nervous and had no idea why. "Amanda," I said, "I wanted to speak to you about a personal matter. One I know I should be speaking to Molly about, but I want to make sure that the time is right. I don't want to do or say anything that may be detrimental to her recovery. I then went on to share with her my chance meeting with Sam, all the way up to present day. I told her about him wanting us to move in with him, of his meeting Luke, and most importantly about him wanting to meet Molly. She listened to me, never interrupting my long story."

When I was done, she asked me what my thoughts were. "Well," I said. "Molly and I had always been close, or so I thought we had the kind of relationship where we talked about most things. But honestly, Amanda, I don't know anymore. I didn't know about the drugs or what drove her to them. So I don't know what the right thing is anymore."

"Well, Brenda, what is the relationship with Sam like?"

I thought for a minute. "Well, Amanda, it's an important relationship, one that I can see a future in. One that I would like to share with my family. Luke seems to like him, and he told me that when Molly finds out she will be mad that I kept it from her. He also said that he felt like she already knows something is going on just like he did before I told him anything. Amanda, I'm just not sure what the right thing to do is."

"Well, Brenda, Molly is still Molly."

"I know, it's just that I don't know how to talk to her anymore. Just the same way you always have said, Amanda. I thought about what she said. I guess I'll give it some thought."

"Well, if you decide to talk to her, I think you will be pleasantly surprised by her."

"I hope so, I really hope so."

"Well," said Amanda, "I wanted to talk to you as well. I have been working with Molly a lot on her personal trauma. I even broached the subject of maybe including you in on one of her sessions. She is not ready to even think about that. Brenda, you need to prepare yourself for the possibility that Molly may never share this with you. You will need to make some kind of peace with that."

"What? How can I make peace with something I know nothing about? With something that made turning to drugs the only answer."

"Well, she said, sometimes we never get the answers that we are searching for. I just looked at her, hoping she was wrong about this. We then moved on to discuss another situation that had Amanda concerned. Molly and Nancy, it seemed, had forged a powerful bond. At first, Amanda was glad for it, but recently, she had some concerns. They were quickly becoming co-dependent on each other."

"Co-dependent?" I said.

"Yes, what that means is that they rely too much on each other in a way that may cause a problem. Relationships like this worry me," she said. "I always say in these types of situations, if one falls, they both will fall. I have been meeting with both of them together and alone to try to explain how this isn't always a good thing, but I'm sure I don't have to tell you, your daughter has a bit of a stubborn streak."

"No, Amanda, you don't have to tell me, that I know."

After a few more minutes together, I got up to rejoin the others. "Thank you for your time. I will give everything you said some thought. You're welcome, oh, and Brenda, have you given finding your own counselor any more thought?"

"No, not yet," I answered, "but I will."

Once I left her office, I stopped before going back to Molly. I wanted a minute to think about what Amanda had told me about talking to Molly about Sam. I wanted to tell her, I didn't want her to be worried about me and I also didn't want to keep it a secret any longer. We had always been a family who didn't keep secrets from one another, and here I was keeping a secret from Molly and realizing that she was keeping her own secret from me. I had the power to talk about mine and hopefully the courage to accept the fact that I may never learn her secret. With a new resolve, I walked back into the main room to rejoin Molly, Nancy, and her family. "Sorry it took me so long," I said.

"No problem," said Julie, "it gave us some time to really get to know Molly better and to learn more about this program.'

"Well, if you will excuse us now, we will leave you to your visit," I said.

Molly and I walked away to find our own place to sit. Once situated, Molly asked me if I was okay, if everything was okay. "Yes," I answered, "I just wanted to speak to Amanda about a few things."

"Care to share, Mom?" It was right at that moment that I decided to be honest with her, to let her know what was going on at home. I reached over and took her hand in mine and started to tell her about Sam. I started slowly. I told her about running into him at the store. I shared with her how I was at his house the night she called to tell me about her friend Julie. That up until that point I hadn't told Sam about this part of your life. I told her how Sam was becoming an important person in my life. How he had met Luke and Stacy, as well as Susan. All the while I was looking at her face, watching for any indication of how she was feeling about this. When I was done, when I had told her everything, I waited.

Molly sat there just looking at me. I could not read a thing on her face. After a few more seconds of silence, she started to talk.

"Well, Mom," she finally said, "I'm glad you finally told me. I knew that something was different with you. I knew that it had to be something important. I just want to know why it took you so long to tell me. You know, Mom, Luke and I have spoken on the phone a few times, and every time, I asked him what was going on with you he said to ask you. So I'm glad you finally told me."

"Wait, Molly, what do you mean every time you asked Luke? I didn't know you talked to him."

"Well, Mom," she said, "I do. What's the big deal? He is my brother after all. Yes, I know that it's just that I thought you were only allowed one call a week. No, Mom, I never said that I said that I'm only allowed one call with you a week. I'm allowed one call with him a week as well."

My mind briefly went back to all the different times I saw him on the phone. How many of those times could he have been talking to her?

"Mom, that's not important. What is important is this. Is this serious?" she asked me with an intensity that I had never seen before in her. I measured my words. "Well, I think it could be. Sam makes me happy, I told her, but me being happy while you are going through this makes me feel guilty."

"Mom, this is a situation that I put myself in. It's something I need to work on, something I need to fix. Punishing yourself will not help anyone or anything. I want you to be happy, you deserve to be. But I am a little mad at you for waiting this long to tell me. I am part of this family and deserved to know the truth. Mom, I am clean and sober, and I can't do secrets and lies and hope to stay that way."

I just sat there looking at my daughter; she had changed so much in her time away from home. I was proud of how mature she had become. "I'm sorry, Molly, you are right. I should have shared it sooner."

"It's all right, Mom, but more importantly, when can I meet him? After all, it seems like everyone else has had the pleasure of meeting him."

"You want to meet him, Molly?"

"Yeah, I do, Mom. I think that it's important that we meet each other."

"Well, let me talk to him. I know that he wants to meet you as well."

"Okay, Mom, just please don't wait too long."

"No, Molly, I won't."

We both sat there for a few minutes, silent, thinking about our conversation. A few minutes later, Barry came in and announced our lunch break. "Okay, Molly, I said you pick it, what do you feel like eating?"

"Burgers, Mom, definitely burgers."

"Okay then, I'll be back shortly with burgers and fries." On my ride to pick up lunch, I listened to my messages. The only one was from Luke. He arrived safely, he said, he would see me tomorrow night. He wanted me to say hi to Molly from him and to tell her that he would try to come next weekend to see her. I was happy to hear that he would at least try to see her again. I thought more about the fact that the two of them talked every week. I was happy about that but curious as to why neither one had ever told me before. I picked up our lunch and headed back. Molly had found us a table by a bank of windows. It was a sunny day, so sitting there was very pleasant. We ate our lunch as Molly filled me in on some of the other things that were going on. She told me that she finally found a sponsor. Her name was Mary, and she met her at one of the in-house recovery-based meetings. She had been in recovery for over eleven years. She was older than Molly by at least ten years, but they got along just fine. They had a connection, and as she put it, the connection was key to a good relationship. She also explained to me that it was now with her sponsor that she would work her steps. She would be able to reach out to Mary if she felt herself struggling at all. They are encouraged to work with their sponsors as much as possible. It was a relationship that would last past her stay in rehab. I was happy to hear she was making so much progress. The rest of the afternoon flew by. We had lovely light conversations. She told me funny stories, and we laughed together, and for just a minute or two, it felt like it always had between us.

Before long, Barry came back in to announce that the day was almost over. I could not believe how fast the day went, and I said as much to Molly.

"I know, Mom. I look forward to seeing you, and then it feels like the day speeds by."

"I miss you, Mom, and I miss being home."

"I know, honey. I miss you terribly too." We stood up, and I hugged her. I didn't want to leave her. It was much harder to leave her this time. I'm not sure why I just knew it was. She walked me as far as she could go and stood waving to me. I thought I saw her crying. I wanted to go back to her, but she was gone. I slowly walked to my car for the drive home. Once home, I realized just how alone I was. Except for the sounds of our dogs, the house was silent. The silence was all-consuming. It filled me with sadness. I took a minute to just sit there, gathering my thoughts before the tears came. I sat there, crying, not really sure why. All I really knew was the profound emptiness that filled my being. When I was spent, I got up to wash my face. It was then that I heard the ringing of my doorbell. As I walked to the door, I realized how dark my house was. It didn't seem that dark when I came home. I flipped on some lights as I walked to the front door. I glanced out the door before I opened it, and there on my stoop stood Sam.

"Sam," I said as I opened the door, "is everything okay? You're asking me if everything is okay with me? I'm here because I was worried about you. Worried about me? Why? He came in and looked at me before he spoke again. I was worried because you never called me when you got home, and I have been calling you for over an hour, and you haven't answered any of my calls. Do you realize that it's after eight o'clock?"

I stood there listening to him. I could hardly believe that it was so late. "I'm sorry, Sam, I didn't mean to worry you. I guess I was so wrapped up in the day and my thoughts that I completely lost track of the time."

"Well, Brenda, just as long as you are okay."

"I am, Sam, thank you for caring about me so much."

"Always," he said. He continued to stand there for a minute longer before saying, "How about coming back with me to my house for the rest of the weekend since Luke is gone? I would feel better if you weren't alone."

I thought about it for a few seconds. I liked the idea of not being alone, but I wasn't sure that I was ready to take that next step. As if reading my thoughts, Sam said, "No pressure, Brenda, we will do whatever makes you feel comfortable."

Hearing that was enough for me to make the decision to go. "Let me just grab a few things and pack up the dogs." I stopped a minute and asked, "I can bring them, can't I?"

"Of course you can. I wouldn't expect you to leave them here." It took me less than ten minutes to gather everything I would need and get into his car. Off we went to Sam's house. On the way there, he asked me if I wanted to stop and pick up something for dinner.

"To tell you the truth, I'm not really that hungry. How about breakfast for dinner again?"

"Sounds good to me," he replied.

Once at his house, I set up the dogs' beds, showed them where their food and water was, and let them out. While I was doing that, Sam went about getting everything ready for dinner. I offered to help him, but he told me to sit down and relax. I gladly took him up on his suggestion. I hadn't realized just how exhausted I was. Once dinner was ready, we sat down, and Sam asked me if I wanted to talk. I realized that more than anything that's exactly what I wanted to do. I started at the beginning of my day with the meeting of Nancy's parents up to my conversation with Molly about him. When I was done, he said, "So she wants to meet me? Is that a good thing?"

"I guess," I replied. "She seemed happy that there is a you in my life. Her only comment was that she had wished I had told her sooner. She didn't like being kept in the dark."

I did, however, explain to her why I didn't tell her right away. I also found out that she speaks to her brother every week. I didn't know about that; neither one had told me before. It only came up when she told me that she had asked him if something was going on with me. "Does it bother you that they speak?" he asked me.

"No," I said, "I don't think it does."

"Well then," Sam said, "it sounds like it was a good visit."

"I guess it would seem that way, yet both Molly and I cried today, separately and not in front of each other. As I was leaving, I saw her face, and I saw tears rolling down her cheeks, and I cried as you know or didn't know when I got home."

"I'm not sure exactly why I was crying other than the fact that I was alone and somewhat feeling lost. Brenda, that's why you should move in here. You won't ever have that feeling of loneliness."

"I know, Sam, maybe we can revisit that after you meet her."

"Okay, I can wait until then, which now leads me to ask you when, when can I meet Molly?" I thought about it for a few minutes. Part of me was ready for them to meet now, but there was a part of me that was just not quite ready yet. I wasn't sure why I felt like that. I wondered on some level if their meeting would mean that things between us would then have to move on to the next step. Although Sam never pressured me about anything. He was patient, always assuring me that things would move at my speed.

I decided, in that instant, what the right thing to do was. "Sam, if you want you can come with me next Saturday. I will just talk it over with Molly, and if she agrees, we can do it then."

Sam looked at me and smiled, "I'd like that, Brenda."

We talked for a little while longer. Sam wanted to hear what today's speaker had to say. I repeated Martha's story to him. He just sat there listening, and when I was done, he just put his arm around me pulling me closer. He whispered in my ear, "I don't know how you do it each week, hearing one tragic story after another."

"I don't know how either," I said. "I worry that Molly hears these same stories and has to deal with them also. Although I think we look at them through a different perspective." We continued to sit there looking at the fire and sipping our wine.

After a while, I turned to Sam and said, "I hope you don't mind, but I am exhausted. I would really like to go to bed."

"Sure," he replied, "let's go." We walked up the stairs together hand in hand, and for the first time in a long time, I felt at peace. We walked towards the master suite together; at the door, he stopped to look at me for a minute, gauging my reaction. I hesitated for a minute before I nodded slightly, and together, we walked in the room.

Chapter 17

It was later than normal when I woke the next morning. I felt totally rested. I couldn't remember the last time I felt so calm and relaxed. I looked over at Sam, he was still sleeping. I took a minute to study his face. I was filled with love for this man. This man that came into my life at perhaps the worst possible time, who was willing to step into the fire with me, who not only was opening his heart to all of us but his home as well. He had quickly become my hero. In that moment, I knew that he was destined to be in my life forever.

As I was staring at him, he opened his eyes and looked at me. "Brenda," he said, "I love you. I love our time together and I don't want you to ever leave. Will you marry me?"

I lay there, staring at him not quite sure if I was really awake. Maybe I was dreaming. I had to be dreaming. *How could this be real? How could any of this be happening?* I just stared at him.

He reached over and stroked my cheek. "Don't say no. Just think about it."

"Sam, I am truly speechless. I couldn't say anything even if I wanted to. I promise, though, that I will give it serious thought." We continued to lie there for some time, both wrapped up in our own thoughts.

I was the first to break the silence. "Coffee?" I asked. "How about I take you to breakfast was his answer."

"Sounds good to me." I suddenly realized I was ravenous. Sam suggested I use the master bath to get ready; he would use the guest bath that way we could get done and get out.

"Perfect," I said. "I'll meet you downstairs." Thirty minutes later, I was in the kitchen feeding the dogs and letting then out.

Sam walked in, asking me if I minded that he picked a restaurant. "No, of course not," I answered. "I'll go wherever you want."

"Good," he said. "I have the perfect place in mind. It's a small cafe right on the water. It's a perfect day for it, cold but sunny."

"I'm ready," I said, "whenever you are." Into the car we went for a short ride; we drove down a lovely little street that ended right at the water, and there, sitting right at the edge of the dock, was a little cafe. It had only four table, but the owner seemed to know Sam. Sam introduced me to him; his name was Gus. It seemed that Sam came to this cafe quite a lot. Gus told me that Sam generally came in with a good book and took the table closest to the window with the best view of the water.

I looked at Sam, who just shrugged and smiled and said, "I'm just a water kinda guy."

We took his usual table, ordered coffee, and relaxed. "So, Brenda, what time is Luke due home?"

"He called me earlier and told me that he should be home by five o'clock."

"How is he doing? Is he having fun?"

He said he was; he told me that he took Stacy to the seaport yesterday and today they were doing a little shopping before they headed home. Well, then, it looks like we have the whole day in front of us. "Is there anything special you want to do?"

"No, Sam, not really. I would like to just relax today if that's okay with you. We can stop on the way back to your house and get some groceries, and I can make an early dinner for you if that's okay with you."

"I would love that," he said. After a leisurely breakfast, we said goodbye to Gus.

Once back in the car, we headed to the local grocery store. The store where it all began. "What do you feel like eating?" I asked him.

"Whatever you feel like making. How about I make some spaghetti and meatballs? I know that Italian food is your favorite. That would be great," he replied. We loaded up on groceries and headed back to Sam's house.

Once back, I got to making the sauce. Sam put on some music and came into the kitchen to keep me company. It seemed so natural to me, a Sunday afternoon together doing what most families do. These thoughts were running through my mind when I heard my phone ring. "Sam, do you mind just grabbing that for me while I dry my hands?"

"Sure, no problem," he replied.

"Hello," he said. "Brenda's phone. Can you please hang on? She will be right there."

I saw the expression change on his face, and then I heard him say, "Yes, this is Sam. Oh hello, Molly, so nice to hear you too. I couldn't dry my hands fast enough." I reached for the phone, but Sam stopped me. I had to sit there and listen to a one-sided conversation. "I am very glad I answered your mom's phone too. Yes, she is doing okay. Yes, I'm trying. I will talk to her about that, and as long as she is okay with it, I would be happy to come with her. Yes, I want to meet you as well. Okay, Molly, it was very nice talking to you. Here is your mom."

I took the phone, just then realizing that my heart was racing. "Hi, honey, how are you?"

"I'm good, Mom," she said. "I got to call you today because we are having a special meeting on Wednesday night. I wanted to ask you if you could come."

"Of course, Molly, I will be there."

"Oh, Mom, I asked Sam to come. I really want to meet him, and I don't want to wait until Saturday. So please, Mom, please bring him."

"Let me talk to him, honey. I can't make any promise. But I will definitely be there."

"Okay, Mom, I have to go."

"I love you, Mom. I love you too, Molly."

"Bye, Mom," she said. "See you Wednesday, oh and Mom, it starts at six o'clock. Okay, hon, see you then." There was a click, and then she was gone.

I turned to look at Sam. He was leaning against the counter, smiling at me. "It's up to you, Brenda. I would love to go with you to meet Molly, but if you are uncomfortable with it, then I understand completely. Can I think about it and let you know I asked?"

"Sure, that's fine. I'll wait to hear from you." I finished cooking and we sat down to enjoy our dinner. But in the back of my mind, all I was thinking about was Wednesday's visit. Once dinner was done, I decided to head home. I wanted to be there when Luke came home.

Sam walked me to the door, gently kissing me on the forehead. He whispered in my ear, "Remember, Brenda, I love you, and everything will work out."

I just looked up at him and said, "I know, Sam. I know." On my drive home, my mind was racing. I wanted Molly and Sam to meet, I did, but I wasn't sure if I was ready for that yet. I was worried about how their meeting would affect her. Was she ready for this? What if she didn't like him? I decided that I would talk to Luke tonight. Since he had spoken to Molly, maybe he had some thoughts for me.

I was having a cup of tea when I heard Luke come in. "Mom? Are you home?"

"Yes, Luke, I'm here in the kitchen."

He came in like gangbusters. I was really happy to see him. "Luke, I missed you so much."

"Mom," he asked, "are you okay? I mean I'm glad you missed me, but I was literally gone one day."

"I know, honey. It's just that things are so different these days. Did you have fun? Yes, Mom, we did. What did you do while I was gone?"

"I saw Sam. It was a quiet weekend. Luke, can I talk to you for a minute?"

"Sure, Mom, what's up?"

I told him about Molly calling and talking to Sam and of her wanting me to bring him on Wednesday. It seemed like they are having a special meeting. She didn't want to wait until Saturday to meet him. So I wanted to get your thoughts."

Luke thought about it for a minute and then said, "I think you should bring him."

If Mol wants to meet him and Sam wants to go, "I say, go for it."

"Just do it, Mom. Why wait?"

I couldn't argue with him. There really was no reason to wait. Sam was an important person in my life, and Molly was my daughter. There really was no reason why they shouldn't meet. Is there anything else you want to talk about, Mom?

"No, Luke. Thanks, I appreciate your input."

"No problem, Mom."

"Night, Luke."

"Night, Mom."

After Luke left the room, I decided to call Sam. I wanted to let him know what I decided and to make sure he still wanted to come with me on Wednesday. "Hi there," he said when he answered.

"Hi, Sam. I wanted to tell you that I spoke to Luke when he got home and he agreed with everyone. He thinks that you should meet Molly sooner rather than later. So if you still want to come, I would very much like it."

"Of course, Brenda, I still want to go with you, what time should I come to pick you up?"

"I think we will be okay if we leave here by five-thirty."

"Okay then, five-thirty it is. Don't worry, Brenda. Everything will be okay."

"Thanks, Sam. I will see you then." After we hung up, I sat down and felt a calm wash over me. It felt good to have a plan. No more wondering. I called it a night and went to bed. I had a restful night and woke up refreshed. Luke had already left for school by the time I made it to the kitchen.

Time to start another work week for me. Monday and Tuesday passed by, relatively uneventful. But by midday Wednesday, I was nervous again. Gail asked me several times if I was okay.

"Yes, Gail, I'm...I'm sorry if I seem a little distracted."

"It's okay, Brenda, as long as you are okay."

"Yes, I'm good. Thank you, Gail, for asking, though."

Before I was ready it was time to leave work, on my drive home, I kept worrying about tonight's meeting. When I got home, I went right to Luke's room. I wanted to see him and talk to him. He was lying down on his bed. I dropped down and sat on the edge. "Hey, are you okay?" I asked him.

"Yeah, Mom, I am just a little tired is all."

"Are you sure?' I was worried Luke almost never stopped.

"Yeah, I'm okay." He quickly changed the subject by asking me if I was okay. Was I worried about tonight's meeting? he asked.

"Of course I am, Luke," I answered. "I am hoping that it all goes well."

"Mom, please stop worrying. It will be fine. It's Molly. The one thing about her that has never changed is her heart. She has a good heart, always has, and I am sure, Mom, she always will."

"I know, Luke. You are right, but I still worry. I don't want this to be too much for her."

"Mom, what time are you leaving?" I glanced at my watch and told him that Sam should be by at any minute. "Well then, Mom, you better get going. Tell Molly I said hi and that I will talk to her soon."

"Okay, Luke, as long as you are sure you are okay."

"Yes, Mom, please stop worrying."

"I'm trying to, Luke. I am trying to. I will see you when I get home and let you know how everything went. I love you, Luke."

"Love you too, Mom."

I quickly changed my clothes, washed my face, and fed the dogs just in time. Sam was, as always, prompt. "Bye, Luke!" I yelled again.

"Bye, Mom, and Mom, don't worry." As I got in, Sam's car a feeling of dread washed over me. Sam must have seen my face because he reached over and squeezed my hand. "It's going to be fine, Brenda. Please try not to worry."

"I hope so, Sam, I hope so." We drove to the facility in silence. I wondered what Sam was thinking about. Once we pulled in, I told Sam again how this part of the program worked. "A speaker comes in, talks a little bit, and then our loved ones join us." I wasn't sure if that was going to happen tonight, but I wanted to make sure he was prepared.

We walked in and, as usual, signed in. I saw Barry, so I took the time to introduce Sam to him. "Nice to meet you, Sam. Glad you both could be here tonight. Brenda, I just want to let you know that tonight's meeting will be a little different from our Saturday gatherings. At six o'clock, Molly will be joining you. This is what we call an in-house recovery-based meeting."

He went on to explain that every night, they have these meetings. "Some nights it's broken up into two groups—one is the men's meeting and one is the women's meeting. Sometimes they do a co-ed meeting, and once a month they do a meeting with family members."

"Okay." I turned to Sam and said, "Well, I guess you are going to meet her any minute now."

"Brenda, it will be fine. Please try to relax."

"I'm trying, Sam. I really am." We walked into the meeting room and took seats. The room was quickly filling up. I was somewhat surprised to see so many people. As I was looking around the room, I saw Molly. She was walking in; she hadn't seen me yet, so I walked toward her. Before I got to her, she saw me. "Hi, Mom. I'm so glad you were able to come."

"Me too, honey. Me too." She was looking around, I guess trying to see if I was by myself.

"Yes, Molly. I brought Sam with me." I saw a smile touch her lips.

"Okay then, I am ready to meet him." Hand in hand, we walked over to where I had left him sitting.

"Hi, Molly," said Sam as he stood up. "I am very happy to finally meet you. Your mom has told me so much about you that I feel as if I know you already."

She looked at him as he was talking as if to study him. "Hi, Sam. I wish I could say that my mom has told me about you, but we both know that wouldn't be true. I am glad she finally brought you, though."

With that, Barry came into the room. "Okay, everyone, as is our usual practice, we have a speaker, so I will ask you all to find some seats. Once the speaker is done talking, we will have our regular meeting, and then you will have time with your families."

Everyone took their seats quickly; I was sitting between Molly and Sam. I leaned over to Sam and whispered, "Here goes."

A young man walked into the room. He looked around slowly, then he spoke in a loud, clear voice. "My name is Benjamin. I am twenty-five.

"One month ago, I got the phone call that every one of you in this room dreads. The call was to inform me that my baby brother's life was taken by an overdose of heroin laced with fentanyl. He was twenty-two. He had a baby, a baby. He was trying to turn his life around. He was a good man, a kind man who was dealt a bad hand in life, but he was trying, really trying. My niece will never know her father. Will never know anything about him other than the fact that he is gone. Our parents will never be the same. Life will never be the same. There will forever be a void in our hearts." He then turned and left the room.

Again, as in the past, there wasn't a sound in the room. Silence—heavy, sad silence—filled the room. Barry came back in then and told us that was all Benjamin had in him. He told us that he would be conducting tonight's meeting in ten minutes. I turned to look at Molly; she had silent tears running down her face. I hugged her to me; I had no words. She leaned into me and continued to softly cry. *How hard must this be for her?* I wondered. Sam reached over and took my hand. He looked at me with a pained expression. I found it hard to read anything else on his face. The three of us sat together in silence. I heard low whispering all around us, but I couldn't find my voice. I couldn't think of anything to say. After the ten minutes were up, Barry told us to move our chairs into a circle. Once we were all situated, he proceeded to ask if anyone would like to share.

A young man stood and introduced himself. "Hi," he said, "my name is Evan, and I am an alcoholic."

"Hi, Evan," said everyone. "I am sharing today because Benjamin's story touched me. I also have a baby, and I can't even imagine not being in her life. I am trying to beat this. I am trying to find a way to make this a small chapter in my life, not my whole story. I am scared and I know that I can't fail. That's why I keep coming to these meetings. My name is Evan. Thank you everyone for listening."

To my surprise Molly was the next person to stand. "Hi, my name is Molly, and I am an addict." My heart skipped a beat. I had never heard her say those words out loud and with as much conviction as she did. "I am sharing today because Benjamin's story hit me as well. Not because I have a baby but because someday I may want one, and I know that I need to be well, to have this all behind me so that I never have to put my child through this."

Next was Courtney. She spoke about being sad after hearing about Benjamin's story. "It's horrible. I feel bad for his brother's baby. It's just so tragic." Many people in the room were nodding and murmuring their agreement. Another young man joined the conversation he was in agreement that while it was terrible, he thought that Benjamin's brother should have tried harder to get help. The room was split; some people saw it one way and others saw it from his point of view. But everyone agreed that it was terrible. Molly was extremely quite through this whole discussion. I wondered what it was that she was thinking. Once everyone who wanted to share was done, Barry asked everyone to link hands. He started to recite the Serenity Prayer. Everyone who knew it joined in. Once they were done, Barry told us that we could spend thirty minutes with our families. Then he walked out.

Once he was gone, I turned to Molly and asked, "Are you okay? I mean that was a rough meeting."

She looked at me and said, "No, not really, Mom. We have meetings that are really bad. Meetings that have speakers that rip your heart out."

I couldn't help myself. I had to know. "Why, Molly, what is the point in that? Why would they bring in speakers that tell such horrible stories?"

"Because, Mom, they want us to know the realities of our disease."

Throughout the whole meeting, Sam was terribly quiet. I turned to him and asked, "Are you okay, Sam?"

"Yes, Brenda, I am okay. How about we find a quiet place to sit down and talk?"

"Sounds good to me." Molly took my hand and led us over to a little alcove. Once seated, she looked at Sam. "Well, Sam," she said, "thank you for coming tonight. I'm glad that Mom decided to listen to me. I wanted to meet you once she told me that there was a you. I was the last one to hear about you, and that makes me sad."

"Oh, Molly," I said, "I'm sorry I would never do anything purposely to make you feel sad."

"It's okay, Mom. I'm just glad you both came tonight. Well, Sam, now that I have finally met you, I want to ask you a question."

"Sure," he replied. "What are your intentions with my mom?"

"Molly," I gasped, looking at my daughter, absolutely speechless.

"It's fine, Brenda. I will happily answer the question. My intentions are honorable, Molly. I love your mother. As a matter of fact, I asked her to marry me. She promised me she would think about it."

"Mom? Did you think about it?"

"Hang on, you two, let's slow down a bit. Sam, we just talked about this last weekend, and Molly, you just met him."

"I know I just met him, Mom, but let's look at the facts. You ran into him at the beginning of this nightmare. He has been by your side through it all, and he is here right now, meeting me here in this rehab. I am sure that he has better things to do with his time. Oh, and Mom, he's kind of cute." The last line was spoken in the typical Molly fashion with the twinkle in her eyes and the smile that crinkled up at the sides. The smile that I hadn't seen in a very long time.

Sam just sat there, looking from Molly to me with a giant grin on his face. "Okay, you two can we talk about something else please."

"Sure, Mom, whatever you say."

"Good," I answered. "Molly, how are you doing in your groups?"

"I am doing okay, Mom."

"In yesterday's group, Amanda told us about sober living. What's that?" Sam asked.

"Sober living is the phase after this one. It's living in a house with other addicts in recovery. You have a mentor living in the house with you—they are the ones that hold you accountable for the things you do. You learn to transition from a facility to a house to living on your own. From the way Amanda explained it, it's something that I am looking forward to."

I glanced nervously at Sam. "It sounds good, Molly, but don't rush things. From everything I have heard, you need to work the program step by step."

"I know that, Mom. It's just something for me to look forward to."

The rest of our visit was filled with good-natured conversation. Molly wanted to know what we had been doing, how Luke was doing, and how her dogs were doing. I assured her that everyone, and everything was going well. Before long, Barry came back into the room to inform us all that we needed to say our goodbyes and leave. I couldn't believe how fast time tended to go whenever I was with Molly. She walked with us to the door, at which point I grabbed her into my arms and hugged her. I missed her already, and I hadn't even left her. It was getting so much harder for me to leave her.

She whispered in my ear, "Thank you, Mom, for coming and for bringing Sam to meet me. Being here makes me feel like I am missing so much, I feel lost without you all, and it's hard when I know that things are happening in my family that I don't really know about."

"Oh, Molly, I'm sorry. I won't keep you out of things anymore. It's just hard to know what to talk to you about. I know you have so much going on here. I don't want to overload you with other things."

"Don't protect me, Mom. I am fine. I am growing and changing, and I need to be included in our family."

"Promise me, Mom. Promise me that you won't keep me in the dark anymore."

"I promise, Molly, I promise."

To my surprise, she went over to Sam and hugged him as well. "Thanks, Sam, for coming tonight, and thank you for taking care of my mom. She doesn't do such a good job of that herself."

"You are welcome, Molly. I am hoping to come again, but I leave that up to you and your mom." She stood in the doorway watching us leave. This time, there was a smile on her face.

Chapter 18

Once in the car, I exhaled the breath that I hadn't realized I was holding. I looked at Sam and asked, "Well, how do you think it went?"

"I think it went well. I never thought that there would be a problem. Brenda, you are raising two great people. Molly just ran off the tracks a bit. It's not forever, it's just a bump in her road."

I looked at him, hoping that he was right. We drove the rest of the way back to my house, engaged in light conversation. Sam pulled into my driveway and noticed that quite a lot of lights were on in the house. I wondered what was going on. As soon as I opened the door, I realized that Luke had some friends over. "Hi, Mom. Hi, Sam. How did the visit go?"

"Good, Luke, we can talk about it at another time when you are less busy."

"It's fine now, Mom. Everyone is getting ready to leave anyway."

"Okay then, I will wait for you in the kitchen."

Sam and I went into the kitchen; to tell you the truth, I was exhausted from the day. Before long, Luke joined us. "So, guys, how did the visit go? How was Molly? How did the meeting go?"

Sam was the one to answer. "The visit was good, Luke. Your sister seems to be in a good place. As far as the meeting is concerned... well, that was a more difficult situation. I know for me, it was difficult to hear the story we heard tonight. But after the speaker was done, everyone who wanted to share or ask questions got a chance to do so. That part of the meeting for me was really important."

"I agree with Sam, although it seems to me that it gets harder for me to hear the speakers tell their stories."

"Yeah," said Luke. "I had a hard time listening to the story when I went there. I'm glad, Sam, that you were finally able to meet Molly now she can stop asking me what is going on. And speaking of that, Sam, did you ask?"

"Yes, Luke, I did. Still waiting for an answer, though."

I sat there looking from one to the other. "Okay, guys, what gives? I'm sitting right here, you know."

"You didn't give him an answer yet?" asked Luke.

It took me a minute to realize what they were talking about. "Okay, you two, enough," I said. "I would think about it, and I will. I don't want to be rushed."

"Okay, Mom, I get it, but please don't make your decision based on me and Molly."

"I won't, Luke, I won't."

Sam got up at that point and said that he had to head out. I walked him to the door, promising him I would give his proposal serious thought.

Once he was gone, I went to find Luke. He was in his room. "Luke," I said, "can you please explain to me what that was all about?"

"Nothing really, Mom. Sam asked me to stop by his house, which I did, he told me how he felt about you and that he wanted to ask you to marry him. He wanted my okay to do so. So I told him that I was okay with it and that I was sure that as soon as Molly met him, she would be in agreement. Mom, it was important to him that we were okay with him and with him being a bigger part of all our lives. Mom, he loves you, and I'm guessing that you love him too. He is willing to take on a family that isn't his. Why are you not jumping at this?"

"It's complicated, Luke. But I am going to give this serious thought. Thanks for telling me about your visit with Sam. Good night, sweetie. I'll see you in the morning."

"Night, Mom." I walked to my room, lost in thought. Luke was right. I did love Sam, and I knew that he loved me too. He was accepting of the current situation that our family was in. So I wasn't sure what was holding me back. I did know that I didn't want to make another mistake. Could not, would not put my kids thru another ugly divorce. I decided to talk to my two best friends. I called Leslie and Susan and asked them if we could meet for dinner the next night. To my relief, they were both free and would be glad to get together. We set the time for six o'clock, enough time for everyone to get to the restaurant from work. I felt much better once I made the plans. I decided to call it a night. It had been a long and emotionally filled day.

I was up bright and early the next day, I wanted to catch Luke before he left for school. I found him in the kitchen. "Morning, Mom. I was hoping to see you before I left for school. I wanted to let you know that Stacy asked me if I could have dinner at her house tonight, and I said yes. I didn't think you would mind. That's fine. As a matter of fact, I'm meeting Leslie and Susan for dinner myself so it works out good."

"Okay, Mom. Have a good day. Don't stress so much. Everything will be fine." I reached over and hugged him and asked him when he got so grown up.

He shrugged and said, "I guess it was when you weren't looking," and off he went with a half-smile on his face.

After a pretty uneventful day at work, I headed home to let the dogs out, change my clothes, and check the mail. I had a little time before I had to meet them. As I walked into my house, I noticed once again how quiet it was. I realized how much I disliked the quiet. I would much rather the noise and confusion of a full house of young people. The quiet I was experiencing these days was deafening. I quickly fed the dogs and let them out. I checked the mail—nothing important. I changed my clothes and put on some lights so the house wouldn't be dark when I got back home. All of a sudden, I couldn't wait to leave. I drove to the restaurant we had decided on. It was pretty close to where we all lived. I, of course, was the first one there. Thankfully, my wait wasn't too long.

Susan walked in with Leslie right behind her. "I'm so glad you called us, Brenda. I didn't want to bother you. I was hoping that you would reach out," said Leslie.

"Me too," echoed Susan. "Well, I'm glad you both were free. I want to talk to you both about something pretty important."

"Is everything okay?" asked Susan.

"Yes, everything is fine. I just wanted your opinions on something." I took a long, deep breath and began. "Sam asked me to marry him." There, it was out. Now I waited for the reactions.

"Wow," said Leslie. "I haven't met him yet, but from what you've said about him, I guess I am not totally surprised." She turned to look at Susan.

Susan didn't say anything for a minute, then she spoke. "Brenda, Luke called me. He was on his way home from his visit with Sam. He wanted to talk to someone, and he knew it couldn't be you. She went on to tell me that Luke shared with her that Sam had intended to ask me to marry him. That he wanted to ask Luke for his blessing so to speak."

I just sat there in stunned silence for a few minutes. I was trying to digest what Susan was telling me. I was somewhat curious as to why Leslie wasn't surprised to hear about the proposal. "Did everyone know about it but me?" I turned to Leslie. "So you knew too?"

"Yes, Brenda. Susan called me. I hadn't met Sam, but Sue had, and she wanted my thoughts. Okay then, what are your thoughts?"

Susan spoke first. "I like him. I liked that he took into consideration Molly and Luke's feelings. I like that he stuck by you, is sticking by you. I think it's a good sign that Luke likes him. I don't see why you wouldn't say yes."

Leslie spoke next. "I know that I warned you about moving too fast, but after hearing what Susan and Luke told me about Sam, I agree."

"How did Molly like him?"

"She liked him. We had a really good visit with her, and in typical Molly fashion, her first question to him was what his intentions were. So of course, he told her. You guys have given me a lot to think about. I don't want to rush into anything. I want to make sure this time."

"Well," Susan said, "if you are that worried, why don't you move in with him first and see how that goes?"

"I agree," said Leslie.

"I'll think about it and talk to Molly and Luke," I replied.

"So," asked Leslie, "how is Molly doing?"

I sighed, weighing my words. "She seems to be doing well. She is participating in her groups, she sees her counselor several times a week, and yesterday at the meeting, she shared. It was the first time that I heard her say she was an addict. It shook me a little to hear her say it out loud, but I suppose it's an important part of her healing." The rest of our dinner was spent catching up on other things in each of our lives. Once done, we walked out together. I embraced them both, thanking them for being there for me. They both told me that they would always be in my corner.

I walked slowly to my car, thinking about our conversation and thinking about Luke calling Susan to talk to her about Sam's proposal. In spite of my feelings of being alone, I really wasn't. I had friends who had become my family. I realized at that moment, I was indeed fortunate.

On my drive home, I decided to talk to Luke to get his opinion on Sam, the proposal, and the possibility of a move. When I got home, I found Luke rummaging thru the refrigerator. "Hi, Mom," he said when he saw me.

"Hi, hon, what are you doing? I thought you were having dinner at Stacy's house."

"I did, Mom, but the food wasn't really very good. So I'm starving."

"Sit down," I said. "I will fix you a sandwich, and we can talk."

"Sure, Mom, that sounds great. What's up?"

I thought for a minute as I was getting everything out. "I want to ask you about Sam and how you honestly feel about him and things moving forward." I could see in his eyes that he was giving my question serious thought.

He finally answered, "Well, Mom, since you are asking me, I'll tell you. I like him a lot. He treats me like an adult. He didn't have to say anything to me about how he feels about you. When he talked to me that day, it was like it mattered to him what I had to say. I'm sure that talking to you was important to him."

"I agree, Mom. It's the feeling I got. Mom, just so you know, Molly and I talked about this. She likes him too. We both think you would be crazy not to say yes."

"Well, Luke," I said, "I was going to talk to Molly on Saturday and get her feelings, but since you already did, then what I was thinking of doing was maybe moving in with Sam first. You know to get a feeling of how things would be. Of course it would be me and you at the beginning but then Molly when she gets out of her program."

"I think that's a great idea, Mom. How does Sam feel about this?"

"I don't know yet. I haven't talked to him yet. We are supposed to have dinner tomorrow night. I thought I would talk to him then. Would you and Stacy like to join us?"

"Sounds good, Mom. I'll just check with Stacy, but I don't think we have any other plans. Thanks, Mom, for the sandwich. I have some homework, so I'm going to say good night. Good night, Luke, and thank you."

"For what, Mom?"

"For just being you." After he left, I decided to call Sam. I wanted to tell him about my dinner with the girls as well as my conversation with Luke.

I was happy to hear his voice when he answered the phone. "Hi, Brenda," he said. "How are you doing?"

"I'm good, Sam, I was just calling to say hi and see how you are doing."

"I'm good, Brenda. How about you?"

"I'm good. I had dinner with the girls tonight. I hope you don't mind that I shared with them everything that was going on with us."

"I'm fine with that, Brenda. I also had a long talk with Luke and I came up with an idea that I would like to talk to you about tomorrow over dinner. Is that all right with you?"

"Sure, Brenda. I'm fine with that. How about you come over around six o'clock then?"

"Sounds good to me, and oh, I invited Luke and Stacy. I hope you don't mind."

"The more the merrier," he replied.

Chapter 19

I woke up the next day with a pounding headache. *Maybe a hot shower and a cup of tea would help clear it up*, was my first thought. After doing both, I realized that was not the case. I decided to stay home from work; after a quick call to my office, I returned to bed. As I lay there thinking, I realized that today was the first day in a very long time that I was just lying in bed. I had nothing to do in the immediate. I was exhausted, both physically and mentally. There was so much going on in my world. The next thought I had was, *What time is it?* I had fallen asleep. A much-needed sleep. I looked over at the clock and saw that it was 2:00 p.m. I could not believe that I had slept the whole morning and most of the afternoon. I knew I was exhausted, but I guess I hadn't realized just how exhausted. As I lay there thinking about my exhaustion, I realized that my headache was gone. All I was left with was a feeling of grogginess. I decided to jump in the shower to wash it off.

As I was getting out, I heard the phone ringing, I rushed over to answer and caught it just as Luke was getting ready to hang up. "Hi, Luke, I'm here."

"Hi, Mom. I was just calling to let you know that I am going to meet you at Sam's. Stacy can't come."

"Why, Luke? She has to go to her grandmother's for dinner. She wanted me to go with her, but I told her that I was going with you to Sam's house for dinner. She was disappointed but understood."

"Sounds great, Luke," I said. "Are you coming home first or just meeting me there?"

"I'll just meet you there, Mom. That way I can hang with Stacy for a little."

"Sounds like a plan. We set the time and hung up."

On my drive over to Sam's house, I thought about what I was going to say and how I hoped he would receive it. The more I thought about it, the more I liked the idea of us living together. I only hoped that Sam would like the idea as well. I was surprised to see Luke's car in the driveway when I pulled up. As I got out of my car, I saw Sam standing in the open doorway of the front door, his usual place when I came to his house. "Hi, Brenda. As you can see, Luke beat you here."

"Yes, Sam, I see that."

I shook my head because Luke was never early for anything. I took this as a good sign. "Come on in, Brenda. Can I get you something to drink?"

"No, Sam, I'm okay for now. I had a terrible headache all day today. It's gone, and I don't want to take any chances."

"Understood," was his reply.

"I took the liberty of ordering Thai food. I hope that it's okay with you. Luke told me that he has never had Thai and was very willing to give it a try."

"I love Thai food, Sam. Thank you for ordering dinner." We all sat in the living room, catching up on our week. To me, it felt so natural, as if it were something that the three of us had been doing forever. I decided that this was as good a time as any to tell Sam about my dinner and about the idea that I had.

I cleared my throat and began. "So, Sam, as I told you last night, I had dinner with Leslie and Susan. You gave me quite a lot to think about, and I wanted to talk to my friends about it. I also had a long conversation with Luke, whom I have come to find out had a long conversation with Molly."

"I love you, Sam. I really do. I love the fact that you want to have a relationship with Molly and Luke. But I don't think that I can marry you right now. I don't think the timing is right for me. But

I also don't see myself without you, so I was wondering and hoping that you would be in agreement with my idea. I thought that maybe we could move in with you to see how things went before making a lifelong commitment." I looked up at him but I was unable to read his face. I sat there waiting and hoping against hope that he would be okay with this sort of compromise. My wait, thankfully, was short lived.

"Of course, Brenda. Move in, all of you move in. I would love that, and maybe just maybe you will see that we are great together." I exhaled the breath I was holding. I looked at Luke; he had a giant grin on his face.

"Well then, if you both don't mind, I would like to go upstairs to decide which bedroom is mine."

Sam just laughed and said, "Go right ahead. After all, this is our house now."

I sat there, basking in the feeling that we had made the right decision. "So, Sam, I am going to talk to Molly tomorrow when I go to visit her. I think that she will be happy about this."

"Sounds good, Brenda. When do you guys want to make the move?"

"Well, I think that it will take me a few weeks to pack everything up. I am thinking about renting my house for the time being, so I want to pack up everything, I want to store my furniture and the things that I am not bringing with me. After I talk to Molly, I will have a better idea as to what she wants me to pack for her to move over here."

"Okay, sounds like a good, solid plan. Are you happy, Brenda?"

"Yes, Sam, I am. I am very happy about the decision that we made."

"Good. All I really want is for you to be happy."

I leaned over and kissed him. "Sam, you are a wonderful man. Thank you." The rest of our evening was filled with laughter and good times. Luke told us that he decided to take the bigger room. He thought that he could sell the idea to Molly by saying that he was giving her the room with the walk-in closet. He thought that she would rather have that room than the bigger room.

"Hmm," I said, "I don't know about that, Luke."

"Mom," he said, "that's the spin I will put on it. Maybe she won't realize that my room is bigger."

"That's a thought," I said, "but probably not realistic."

"Well, Mom, if that doesn't work, then I will just tell her that I was here first."

The next day, I went to visit Molly. I went by myself because I wanted to have time to talk to her alone. I wanted to know how she was doing, really doing, and how she thought Wednesday night's meeting went. I went thru the usual process and sat in my regular seat and waited for the speaker to come in. I honestly dreaded this part of my visit with Molly.

As was the usual routine of things, Barry came in first. He explained how this meeting would go for the people who were new. Then he introduced today's speaker; her name was Helen. A woman walked in and stood in front of us. She thanked us for coming today and explained how important it was for our addicts to have the support of their families. Then she told her story. It seems that Helen was an addict. She started using drugs when she was fifteen. She told us that she was forty-five years old on her last birthday. She had been in and out of rehabs for twenty-plus years. In between her stints in rehabs, she had some clean time but nothing that lasted longer than a couple of months. In those clean periods she managed to get married, have two babies, hold down numerous jobs, and even bought a house with her husband. But of course, the addiction always had a hold on her and she lost everything. The first thing to go was her marriage. Her husband just couldn't understand what was going on and didn't want to be educated. She was in her first stint in rehab after their last child was born. He came to see her and told her that he wanted a divorce. He just couldn't, wouldn't put himself or their kids through this.

"I begged him to stay. I made promises that I knew I couldn't keep, but I made them anyway. He just looked at me and told me that he loved me, but he loved our kids more and that they would be better off without me. As you can imagine, that devastated me more than I ever thought could have been possible. When I got out of that rehab, I started what would be the worst downward spiral of my life. I had no home, nowhere to go, and nothing at that point to lose. I lived on the street doing whatever was necessary to survive and to get my next fix. Days blurred into weeks, into years. And then one day, while I was sitting in my usual spot, a woman came up to me and said, 'You look lost. Can I help?' Of course my usual response was, 'No, I am fine.' I laugh now as I say those words. I was the farthest from fine that a person could be. She gave me her name and a phone number and told me that if I ever changed my mind to give her a call. I tucked her number away, thinking that I would never use it. Days later, I came across it again and decided to give her a call—what did I have to lose at that point? We met at a coffee shop, and she told me about a program that she worked for. She told me that there was help for me if I wanted it. I did want it. I didn't want to live the rest of my life like I had been living. I had finally reached my rock bottom. And everyone here needs to know that every addict has a rock bottom, and until they hit that, they are not likely ready for real change. I was about to begin a program that worked for me. I now have five years of clean time. I have my own apartment, job, and the beginnings of a relationship with my kids. It has been a long and hard road, but it's a road that every addict can travel if they do the work and put in the time. I know that I am just one pill away from a relapse. I live with that fear every day, but by working the program every day and doing the things that I need to do, I know that I will never walk down that road again. I'm Helen, and I am here to tell you that there are success stories out there. Thank you all for listening." Then she was gone.

I sat there for a few minutes, thinking about Helen's story. I had hope, real hope for the first time in a long time. I must have been deep in thought because it took me a few minutes to hear Molly calling me. "Oh, honey, hi. I'm sorry. I was just thinking about the story the last speaker told us."

"Oh yeah," she said. "Helen spoke today, right?"

"Yes, she did, and I have to say that it was a welcome change from all of the sad stories I am use to hearing every time I come here."

"I know, Mom, but those stories are our realities. We are told about them as are you so that we all know what can happen if we don't work our programs."

"I guess, Molly, but it is a welcome change to hear that some good can happen."

"I guess, Mom."

"So, Molly," I said, eager to change the subject, "how are you?"

"I'm good, Mom. Not too much has happened since I saw you two days ago."

"It just seems like so much longer than two days ago," I said.

"So, Mom, how are you? How are things going on the home front?"

"Things are good. I had dinner the other night with the girls. They both send their love and can't wait to see you."

"That's nice, Mom. Please tell them that I say hi and am just as eager to see them."

"Will do. I wanted to talk to you, Molly, about our visit Wednesday night. I want to know how you think it went?"

"Don't you mean how I liked Sam, Mom?"

"Well, that's part of it. I don't want to do anything that you wouldn't be happy about. I came up with a plan that I wanted to get your thoughts about, and if you are in any way uncomfortable with it, then I need you to tell me."

"Okay, shoot."

"I thought that it would be a good idea for us to just move in with Sam at first to see how things work. His house is big enough for you and Luke to have your own rooms with plenty of room to move around without getting into each other's way. I want you to feel comfortable with this plan."

"Well, Mom, I don't see why that wouldn't work. I liked Sam. I think that it's a good sign that he chose to get involved with you while this is going on."

"I agree, Molly, but it's really important to me that both you and Luke are comfortable with this situation."

"Trust me, Mom we both are."

I sighed with relief. Maybe, just maybe, this would all work out.

The rest of our visit was lovely. We shared the other things that were going on in our lives. Molly seemed to be working the program and getting things out of it that were important to her. As we were sitting there, Nancy walked over to say hi. "Hi, Nancy," I said, "are your parents here?"

"Yes, they just went to talk to my counselor, so is it okay if I just hang here for a little bit?"

"Of course," I said. "So tell me, Nancy, how are you doing?"

"I'm doing good, Brenda. I am so grateful that I get to room with Molly. I am less lonely."

"Well, I am glad to hear that," I said. "I like that we room together too," said Molly.

As we sat there, a young man approached us; Molly seemed to light up when she saw him. "Mom," she said, "I would like you to meet my friend Vinny."

"Oh hello," I said, "nice to meet you."

"Hello, Mrs. Brooks."

"Vinny, please call me Brenda."

"I would much rather. Okay, nice to meet you, Brenda."

"Would you like to join us?" I asked.

"Sure, but only for a minute or two. I have a session to attend." He sat down and joined the conversation that Molly and Nancy were having, I just sat back and observed. Molly seemed to be looking at Vinny quite a bit from under her eyelashes. I wondered what that was all about and decided to ask her about it later when we were alone again.

"Don't you agree, Mom?" said Molly.

"I'm sorry, honey. I must have been thinking about something. Can you repeat your question please?"

"I just said that the people we meet here can become important people in your life."

I thought about that for a minute. Was she telling me something without telling me? "Well, I think that the people you meet here hold a different kind of relationship with you than your school friends do."

"Mom, that's not what I mean, but sure, fine, I guess you are right about that."

After a few more minutes, Vinny excused himself, saying that he had a session and needed to leave.

"Well," I said, "it was very nice to meet you."

"Same here," he said, and off he went. I sat there, trying to figure this out. We sat together for a bit longer, and then I saw Nancy's parents walking over. She got up and said a hasty goodbye and walked over to them. I was alone again with Molly.

"So, Molly, is everything okay with Nancy? She seemed a bit distracted and upset."

"Yeah, I think so. I know that Amanda wanted to talk to her parents about her stay here. I don't think that she will be able to stay as long as I can. I hate the thought of being here without her."

"Well," I said, "you should stay as long as Amanda thinks is necessary. As much as I like Nancy, I don't think that you should rush anything."

"I know, Mom, I know."

"So, Molly, who is Vinny?"

She rolled her eyes at me and said, "He's a friend, Mom. I just told you that."

"I know what you told me, Molly, but it's not exactly what I see."

"Mom, must you always do this? Please stop, you are making more out of this than necessary."

"If you say so, Molly, if you say so."

"Mom, why is it so important to you to make a big deal out of everything?"

"It's not, honey. I am just concerned."

"Well, don't be. There is nothing for you to worry about."

"Okay," I said. The rest of our visit was pleasant; we both stayed away from topics that would cause friction. Before I knew it, it was time to say goodbye. To me, the day seemed to fly by. As Molly was walking me to the door, she asked me when I thought that we would be moving in with Sam.

"I was hoping to move in by the beginning of March," I replied. "I have to pack the house up. I am going to be putting our furniture into storage and just taking what we will be using."

"Okay, Mom, but I want to take everything that is in my room, furniture, and all."

"I know, Molly. I was sure that's what you would want."

"Thanks, Mom. I love you and will talk to you on Wednesday night."

"I love you too, Molly."

Chapter 20

The next few weeks were a blur for me. I spent the weekdays at work and the evenings packing. I walked around the house putting stickers on the things that were going into storage, going with us and going into the garbage. The weekends were spent seeing Molly and going to Sam's with Luke. He was eagerly setting up his room; he seemed genuinely happy to be moving. Everything seemed to be moving at warp speed to me. Before I knew it, it was moving day. I have to admit that I was a little apprehensive. One chapter of my life was closing, and I was hoping that things would work out for all of us. Sam arrived right on time with the movers right behind him. He instructed them to put the items marked for storage in first as we were going to his house to unload everything that was staying, and then we would head to the storage unit that I rented to store everything else. Luke was already at Sam's house, unpacking everything that he could stuff into his car. As I walked down the stair outside of my house, I felt a pang of sadness; after all, this was my home. The house I brought my babies home to the house I made into our home. Sam, sensing my sadness, put his arm around me and told me that this was not just the end but a new beginning. A clean slate to start over. I looked up at him and thanked him and told him that I would meet him at his house. I needed a few minutes. He understood what I was saying without me having to actually say anything out loud.

"Of course, Brenda, take your time. I'll see you at home."

Home, I thought. *His house will now be our home.* I sat in my car, looking at my house. I had such a bittersweet feeling. But I knew in my heart of hearts that I was making the right decision for everyone. With one last glance, I hit the road heading for Sam's house, our home now and a new beginning.

When I pulled up, I was greeted with a scene right out of a movie. There was mass confusion. Luke and Stacy were trying to unload boxes from the truck to find his missing things. Sam was directing the movers to put the boxes in the rooms that they were marked for, and I could hear the dogs barking in the house. Part of me was glad for all the distractions, and part of me just wanted to find a quiet place to hide. Realizing that that was not an option, I rolled up my sleeves and jumped right in. I decided that the best place for me was in the house making sure that all of the boxes ended up in the right rooms. With so many hands helping out, we were done in no time. Sam found me in the kitchen, sitting at the table surrounded by boxes. "Brenda, are you okay?"

"Yes, Sam, just a little overwhelmed at this point."

"Take your time, Brenda. Everything does not have to be done right now."

I looked at him and smiled. "Yes, Sam, it kind of does."

"Okay then," he replied, "how about I just go with the movers to the storage unit and direct that unload?"

"That would be great, Sam. Thank you."

"No thanks necessary, I will see you in a bit." And then he was gone.

Luke and Stacy came down to see if I needed help. "Sure, but don't you need to do your own unpacking?"

"Mom, we are all done. My room is set up just the way I want it to be. The only thing left is my TV, and Sam told me that he would help me hang it up tomorrow."

"Oh, well, that is great guys."

Brenda said, "Stacy, I hope you don't mind, but I unpacked Molly's clothes and put them away. I didn't know when she would be here, and I didn't want any of her clothes to get ruined."

"Thank you, Stacy. I really appreciate that. If you guys are serious and want to help unpack, maybe you can go into the den and deal with those boxes. I want to try to get the kitchen set up before Sam gets back."

"Will do," they replied. We all set about getting our various jobs done. I guess I was lost in thought as I unpacked boxes because I didn't hear Sam come in. I was a little started when I heard him calling my name.

"I am in the kitchen, Sam."

"How is it going, Brenda?" he asked.

"It's good, Sam. I am almost done with the kitchen boxes. Luke has his room all set up, and Stacy was kind enough to unpack Molly's clothes. They are both in the den trying to unpack those boxes. I hadn't realized how much stuff I had until we got to unpacking. Maybe I took too much. After all, your home is already so beautiful."

"Brenda, I want you to use as much space as you want to. I want you to make this your home as well. Be as comfortable as possible. Please relax."

"Thank you, Sam. I really appreciate that and thank you for making us feel so welcomed."

Sam just looked at me and said, "I'm really glad that you are finally here."

"Me too, Sam. Me too."

Before long, both Luke and Stacy joined us in the kitchen, announcing that they were starving. "Is there anything to eat here?" Luke asked.

"How about I just order pizza for tonight?" suggested Sam.

"Sounds great," was the consensus to that suggestion. After eating way too much pizza, I decided to call it a night. Luke, Stacy, and Sam decided to hang out a little longer. After saying my good nights, I went up to my new room. Everything seemed so strange to me that night, and it would take me several weeks to feel like myself again.

We all developed a routine. Luke had to get up for school much earlier than he did when we lived in our old house. We had decided to keep him in the same high school to finish and graduate next year with his friends. So he left the house first most mornings. Sam left next as he had over an hour's drive to his job. I was the last person to leave as I was actually closer to my job after the move. Monday through Friday, it was business as usual. On Saturdays, I would visit Molly. Sometimes I went by myself, and other times, either Sam or Luke would come with me. I was almost getting used to the stories that I heard, although they didn't get any easier to hear. Interestingly enough, almost ever visit I had with Molly would involve either Vinny coming over to say hi to us or there was some mention of him in our conversation. Each time I asked Molly about him, she would just roll her eyes and tell me to stop making such a big deal about her friend. I had a nagging feeling that something more was going on.

Chapter 21

Early one Friday morning in the middle of April, I got a phone call from Amanda asking me if I could bring Sam and Luke with me to see Molly the next day. "Sure," I said. "Is everything all right?"

"Yes, everything is fine. It just would be helpful if you all came tomorrow."

"We will be there," I promised. When Luke came home from school, I was waiting for him in the kitchen. When he saw me, he asked me what was wrong. "Nothing," I answered. "It's just that I got a call from Amanda today and she asked me if you and Sam could join us tomorrow for Molly's visit."

"I guess so, Mom, if that's what you want me to do."

"Yes, Luke. If Amanda is asking, then I am sure it's important."

"Okay, Mom. I'll be ready in the morning. Is it okay if I go to Stacy's house now? I will probably stay for dinner but will be home early."

"I guess so, Luke, but please remember to get home on time." It had become a habit of his to miss his curfew at least once a week. I wasn't sure why, but I let him know on more than one occasion that it was unacceptable and that if he did not correct this habit, he would lose the privilege of driving the car.

"I told you I would be on time, Mom. See you later," and out the door he went.

I was sitting in the living room when Sam came home. "Hi, Brenda, how was your day?"

"It was fine, Sam. How about yours?"

"All good, happy to put the week behind me, though."

"Sam, Amanda called me earlier today and asked me if we could all be there tomorrow to see Molly. She assured me that everything was fine but said that it was important for all of us to come. I already spoke to Luke, and he surprisingly did not give me a hard time about it. You know that I will do whatever I can to be there for you and Molly, so count me in for tomorrow."

"Thank you, Sam. I really appreciate it."

"No thanks necessary, Brenda. We are a family now. This is what families do for each other." Once again, I was exhausted after my week at work. I was beginning to realize that this was more mental exhaustion than anything else. I was eager to call it an early night.

The next morning, we were all ready on time. This in and of itself was no small feat. Into the car we went for the drive to the facility. It was such a familiar route these days. We went through our usual routine and found our seats. As always, Barry came in to the room first to introduce himself and to talk a little about the program for the families that were new. I considered us seasoned veterans by this time. After all, Molly had been in this rehab for almost three full months. He then introduced an older woman. Her name was Rebecca, and she had a story to tell us. A story that I will never in my life forget. Rebecca was the grandmother of three beautiful children. She showed us all their pictures. Her only daughter had married her high school sweetheart, and though it broke her heart, they moved two states away so that her son-in-law could pursue a wonderful career opportunity. Her daughter was happy, loved, settled. She spoke to her every day on the phone, and she got to speak to her grandchildren as well. She waited for the mail every day because her grandchildren were always sending her their drawings. She missed her daughter but was happy in the knowledge that she was happy and living her life. Rebecca went on to say that it had been much too long since she saw her daughter and grandchildren and was so happy when her daughter called to let her know that her husband had some time off and that they were planning on driving out for two weeks.

"I went out and bought new bedding for all the bedrooms in my house. I wanted everything to be fresh and new. I started cooking days before they were due to arrive. I wanted everything ready, everything perfect. We spoke the night before they were getting on the road. The grandchildren told me that they were so excited to visit. Their mom, they told me, bought them all sorts of things to do on the trip to keep them for being bored. They told me how excited they were to be spending a night in a hotel because the trip was too much to do all at once. I told them that I had surprises waiting for them and that I loved them so much and couldn't wait to see them. I spoke to my daughter once more before we hung up. The next morning, as I was eagerly waiting for them to arrive, I heard a knock on my door. I looked at my watch thinking that they made really good time. maybe they left earlier than they expected to. I ran to the door, expecting to see my daughter. Instead, I saw two police officers. They asked if they could come in. At this point my brain could not register anything. They led me to a chair and told me their story. My son-in-law's car had been hit head on by a drunk driver. The driver walked away without a scratch, but my daughter's entire family died on that stretch of highway. I just sat there looking at them. Nothing registered with me. How could this possibly be happening? I think that I was in shock. Maybe it was a bad dream. Unfortunately, all of it was true. In the span of one horrific decision that someone else had made, I lost my whole family. My daughter and son-in-law and my three grandchildren, whom I will never get the chance to see ever again. I am here standing before you to tell you, to beg you, please think before you do anything to damage yourselves or anyone else. You are all someones's child or parent. Thank you all for listening."

I just sat there once again numb from the pain of Rebecca's story. I could not believe the courage that she had to come here and to tell us her story. I looked over at Sam and Luke, both of them sitting in stony silence. The looked on their faces were unreadable. Barry once again joined us and told us that our loved ones would be joining us shortly, then he walked over to us and said that Amanda and Molly were waiting for us in Amanda's office. We could follow him now to see them. *Oh boy*, I thought this must be serious. We all followed him; once there, he left us outside the door and wished us luck. What did that mean? I wonder. I gently knocked on the door as I opened it.

"Come in, guys," said Amanda. Molly jumped up when she saw us and threw her arms around Luke. I was next followed by Sam. I noticed that she was in a really good mood. I was encouraged by that.

"Have a seat, everyone," said Amanda. "So I guess you are all wondering why I asked you to come in today."

"The thought had crossed my mind," I answered.

"I asked you here because Molly has indicated that she thinks that she is ready to leave, to move to the next step." I just sat there staring at Amanda.

"Leave," I repeated.

"Yes, Mom, I am ready. I have learned here that I can follow my own schedule and I am ready to leave. Not go home but go to a sober house."

I sat there feeling like someone punched me in the stomach. I was not even sure how to react to this news. "I thought that you would be here for at least six months."

"Yeah, Mom, I am sure that is what you thought, but it's not what I thought." I sat there in stunned silence, wondering if this was something that she could actually do.

Amanda spoke next. "I know that this comes as a shock to you all. But as Molly said, this is her decision. We here believe that she would benefit from a bit more time here, but she doesn't agree with that, and as you know, we can't force her to stay. The only thing that I am encouraged about it that she has agreed to go to a sober living facility. She will need to get a job, go to meetings, and continue seeing a counselor. The unfortunate thing is that I won't be able to keep seeing her. But I can help her find someone that she is comfortable with. Why don't I leave you all alone to talk a little more about this?" With that, she got up and left her office.

Once Amanda left, I turned to Molly and said, "Molly, do you really think that this is in your best interest?"

"Yes, Mom, I do. I don't think that I can get any more out of being here." She turned to look at her brother, waiting for his reaction.

Luke took his time answering her unspoken questions. "I think it's a great idea, Molly. Nothing like starting your new life sooner rather than later."

Sam spoke next. "Well, Molly, you are the only one who can know if you are ready for this next step. I support whatever your counselors think is right for you."

I just sat there in stunned silence. I was not ready for everyone to side with Molly. I was hoping that they or at least Sam could see that this was not a good idea.

"Thank you both for understanding what is important to me. Mom," she said, looking at me, 'I promise you I am okay to do this. I will have all the support and help that I need. If I didn't think that this was the right thing for me, I wouldn't do it." After another round of debate, we decided that Molly would leave next Saturday. She would move into a sober house further out east. It was an all women's house, and the "housemother" would drive her to get a job and to get to and from her meetings etc.

I was quiet on the drive home. I had a lot on my mind. I wasn't sure that we were making the right decision, but it was quickly brought to my attention that the decision was not mine to make. I could either fight it or support it. Every fiber of my being wanted to fight it, but I knew that all I would do if that was the route I decided to take would be to alienate Molly. As I sat there, I felt Sam's hand on mine. When I turned to look at him, he simply smiled at me and said, "Please don't worry. I think it will be okay."

I shook my head slightly and whispered, "I hope so." The remainder of the ride home was a quiet one, each of us lost in our own thoughts.

When we got home, Luke asked if he could go see Stacy.

"Sure," I said, 'but don't you want to come in and talk about this first?"

"No, Mom, not really. I don't think that anything anyone says at this point will make any kind of difference. You already agreed to let her go to this sober house. So what would be the point of talking about it now?"

"I guess you are right, Luke. I just thought that it would be a good idea for us to talk about it."

"Well, I don't have anything more to say, so if you don't mind, I would like to go to Stacy's house."

"Okay, Luke, will you be home for dinner?"

"No, I don't think so, Mom. I just need some time away from all of this."

"Well, be careful and don't be late."

"I won't, Mom. See you, Sam."

We walked into the house and sat down; I really didn't know what to say at this point. The decision was made, and there was nothing more to do but accept it. Sam and I made a plan to go pick up Molly together and bring her to the sober house she was going to live in. I tried to keep my mind off of the impending move for the rest of the night. It was very difficult for me. I was scared that she was leaving too early. I was scared that she hadn't learned everything she needed to learn, and I was scared that she would be mostly on her own for the first time in a long time. I wasn't ready for this, but more importantly, I didn't think that she was ready either.

The rest of the week flew by, and before I knew it, it was Saturday morning, time to head off to pick up Molly. Sam and I got in the car and headed to the rehab for the last time. When we got there, Amanda was waiting for us, as was Barry. "Is everything all right?" I asked.

"Yes, we just like to meet one last time with the family before you head out. Have a seat," said Barry. Sam and I both sat down and waited to hear what they had to say.

Barry spoke first. "Brenda, I have some concerns."

Oh great, I thought.

"My biggest concern is that Nancy is leaving today as well. They are headed for the same sober house. Nancy and Molly have formed a bond, a very tight bond. Now this can be a good thing because in the right circumstance, they will hold each other up. But I am fearful that if one of them falls, the other one will as well. They have what I call a co-dependent relationship, and that is worrisome to me."

I looked at Amanda, gauging her reaction to this. Amanda spoke next. "I have to agree with Barry on this one. While I do believe Molly is much stronger than Nancy is, I agree that if one of them falls, they both will. I have spoken to Molly about this on several occasions. She doesn't seem to think that this is a problem. Nancy, on the other hand, only wants to get out of here, so she is less receptive to what I had to say. We have found them two separate counselors who are aware of our fears and concerns who have assured us that they will be working with them on this issue. All I can say is that you have my number, and if you have at any time concerns, don't hesitate to call me." She went on to tell me that Molly had a list of things that she would need to buy to bring with her to the house. The basic supplies would be provided for her, but any personal items that she wanted in her room would need to be provided for her by us. With that, they both stood up and walked us back out to the lobby.

Sam and I sat down and waited. Our wait was short lived. Molly came rushing in with several bags full of her possessions. "I'm ready," she announced. "Let's hit the road."

"Hang on, Molly," I said. "I just want to make sure that you have everything you need."

"I'm ready, Mom. I signed all of the paperwork and made sure that my room was cleaned out. Nancy and her family left a little while ago. I promised her that we would meet them for lunch before we hit the store to buy the things I need."

"You did, I see. Well, how did you know that we would be okay with this plan?"

"Because I know you, Mom. Is it okay with you, Sam?"

"Sure, Molly. If your mom agrees, then I have no problem with your plan."

"See, Mom, it's all okay."

I rolled my eyes for a change and said, "Fine, let's go then."

Molly went over to Amanda and Barry and thanked them both for everything they did to help her. Barry leaned over and whispered to her loud enough for all of us to hear, "Be careful, Molly. You are new at this, and I don't want to see you back here again."

"Oh, don't worry, Barry. You won't ever see me here again. Goodbye," Molly said.

Amanda said, "Remember everything you learned here, and remember if you are feeling lost, go to a meeting or meet with your sponsor or reach out to someone. Don't go down that road again."

"I won't, Amanda, I got this." With that, she walked out the door. We followed behind her, not quite sure how to feel.

Once we were settled in the car, Sam asked her where we were headed. Molly gave us the name of a local diner; it was on the way out to the sober house. It didn't take us very long to reach our destination. Molly jumped out and told us that she had seen Nancy's parents' car in the parking lot. "That means that they are here already, Mom? Can you please hurry up? I don't want to keep them waiting too long."

"I'm coming, Molly. Just relax please." We walked in behind her and over to the table that Nancy's parents had secured.

"Hi, everyone," said Molly.

"Have a seat. We just got our menus, so there is no rush," said Nancy. We joined them and looked over the menu. Once our choices were made, we started to discuss this next part of the girls' journey. It seemed as if Nancy's parents were much less worried about things than we were. They were treating this almost like they would if they were dropping their daughter off at college. There were so many things that I wanted to say to them. I wanted to ask them if they were worried about Nancy relapsing. I wanted to know how they felt about the girls living in a sober house together, and most of all, I wanted to ask them if they thought that this move was too soon. Of course I kept everything to myself. I choked back the words, the fears, and the silent tears. I prayed that this lunch would be over soon so that we could get back in the car. I wasn't sure how long I could keep the smile plastered on my face. Thankfully for me, Molly and Sam did most of the talking as did Nancy and her parents. The meal was over soon enough, and we agreed to meet at the store so that we could let the girls shop together. I found out that they would be sharing a room again and they didn't want to buy any of the same things. Off to the store we went. The girls went up and down pretty much every aisle, looking for just the right things for their room. I followed along, feeling like I was losing my mind. Everyone seemed happy and upbeat; all I felt was dread. I couldn't believe that this was happening. I felt sure that we were not ready for this. Thankfully, the shopping trip did not last too long; the girls needed to be at the house by a certain time, and we were getting very close to that time. Back to the cars we went with, in my opinion, too many bags of unnecessary things.

Once we got to the house, the girls checked in and were assigned their room. We helped them unload their things and were told that we were not allowed to go into the house. The front porch was as far as we were allowed to go. We said our goodbyes; Molly hugged me extra hard and thanked me for letting her do this. I told her I loved her and that she should call me later tonight once she was settled in. "I will, Mom, I promise." She turned to Sam next and thanked him for buying her everything she wanted. He had insisted in the store that she get whatever it was she wanted. He would take care of it.

"You are welcome, Molly. I hope that your first night here is a good one." She smiled at both of us grabbed as much as she could carry and went into the house.

Once we got back in the car, I did what I was afraid that I would do at any given moment of that day I cried. I was so scared of the unknown. Was Molly ready for this? Did she have enough tools to handle what would be coming her way? I had no way of knowing, and that thought terrified me. Sam just leaned over and held my hand and let me cry. When I was done, he looked at me and again told me that it would be all right. Molly had a good head on her shoulders and was surrounded by good people. He pleaded with me to take it easy and not worry unnecessarily. "I will try, Sam. That's all I can do."

The drive home was a very quiet one. I don't think Sam knew what else to say, and I certainly did not feel up to talking. When we got home, I told him that I needed to lie down; I had a terrible headache again and wanted to try to get some sleep. "Whatever you need, Brenda, I'm here for you."

"Thank you, Sam, for going with me and for being so supportive of Molly."

"No thanks necessary," he replied.

Chapter 22

I could not believe how fast time was moving. April crashed into May and then into June. Molly had been in her sober house now for three months, and as far as I knew, there had been no problems. She had a job, she had a sponsor, and she went to meetings. There was a saying, "90 in 90," which translated to ninety meeting in ninety days. She was happy and was blooming. I could not believe that we had been on this journey with her for over six months already. To me, at times, it seemed an eternity, and at other times, it seemed to be only a blink. Things at home were on track as well. Luke was finished with his junior year at school. He took Stacy to the junior prom, and they seemed to be flourishing as well. Unfortunately, I was not seeing Luke as much as I would have liked to; he was constantly busy with his friends and with Stacy. Now that we lived further away from his friends, his drive time was longer. But all in all, things were going well. Sam and I were happy with our arrangement; there did not seem to be any rush to get married at this point.

Things once again changed in July. We got a call from Molly she was ready. "Ready for what?" I asked.

"Ready to come home, Mom. You didn't think that I would live here forever, did you?"

"Honestly, honey, I didn't give that much thought. I remembered what Amanda had told us that Molly should stay in a sober living situation for at least a year. It would take that long for her to

reestablish herself in her new sober life." Once again, in my opinion, Molly was rushing things.

"Well, Molly, I will talk to your brother and Sam and call you back. This is not just my decision to make."

"Sure, Mom," she replied, "but, Mom, I am not staying here much longer."

After we hung up, I went to find Sam. He was out in the backyard doing some yard work, getting ready for his annual Fourth of July party. "Hi, hon," he said, "what's up? You look awfully serious for this early in the morning."

"I just got off the phone with Molly. She called to tell me that she was ready to come home. I am not sure how I feel about that. Other than I feel like she is rushing things again."

"I understand how you feel, Brenda, but remember, this is exactly how you felt when she was leaving the rehab, and look how things worked out. I think that as her mother, you will always worry about her timing of everything."

I thought about what he said, and part of me agreed with him. This was all new territory to me. I knew how to navigate the waters of adolescents, but the waters of drug addiction were very new to me. "So, Sam, what are your thoughts? Do we bring her home?"

"Of course we do, Brenda. We are her family and this is her home. Can you imagine how she will feel if we tell her she can't come back home? It was always our plan that she would have a place here once she was done with this part of her program. After all, her clothes are hanging in her room, and her boxes are in the closet, just waiting for her to unpack them. So if you are asking me how I feel, I say bring her home. Have you talked to Luke yet?"

"No, I just hung up with her. I came to find you first. I am going to talk to him now."

"Well," Sam said, "the last I saw of him, he was in the gym working out. Maybe he is still there."

"Okay, that will be the first place I check then." One of the great things about living with Sam is that he had a full home gym in the basement of his house. Luke had begun using it, and he was loving it. I was welcomed into the gym with the ear-shattering noise of the music he was exercising to.

As soon as he saw me, he turned down the music, grabbed a towel, and asked, "What's up, Mom?"

I jumped right in. "I just got a call from Molly. It seems as if she is ready to come home. I already talked to Sam and I wanted to talk to you."

"Are you asking me if I agree with her coming home?"

"I guess I am," I replied.

"Well, then, I say yes. Why wouldn't you want her back home?"

"It's not that I don't want her back home, Luke. It's more that I worry if she is ready to come home. Where she is, she has a full support system. She sees a counselor three times a week and she goes to meetings every day. What can we offer her here?"

"Well, Mom, I think you need to make it clear to her that you expect certain things. If you let her know ahead of time, then it's her decision whether she wants to come home or not."

"I think that's a great idea, Luke, thanks. Enjoy the rest of your workout." I went back upstairs to call Molly back and let her know what I thought was the best course of action.

She answered quickly as if she was waiting for my call. "Oh, hi, Mom, what's up?"

"Well, I told you that I would call you back once I talked to Sam and Luke about your plans of coming home."

"Right, right," she said. "So what's the decision?"

"We would love you to come home. But there are going to be certain things that you are going to have to do."

"Like what, Mom? Well, you need to continue seeing your therapist. You are going to still have to make meetings and meet with your sponsor. Everything that I have learned from visiting you in rehab is that you need to continue working the program."

"Yes, Mom, I am aware of that. Anything else?"

"Well, you need to find a job."

"Got it, Mom. So when can you come and pick me up?"

"How about on Friday afternoon, then you will be home for our Fourth of July party."

"Sounds perfect. I will let the housemother know I will be leaving then."

"Thanks, Mom."

"You're welcome, honey." Once we hung up, I sat there thinking for a minute. Suddenly, I was sure that my call was not the one she was waiting for. She almost sounded disappointed when she heard my voice. I wondered what was going on. Now that the date for Molly's return was set, I decided to take a look at her room. I wanted to spruce things up a little before she got there, maybe add a few touches to make if feel more like home for her.

I decided to take the day off from work on Friday. I wanted to cook some of Molly's favorite foods so that she would feel comfortable coming home; after all, when she left in early January, she had left her childhood home. For the last several months, she had lived in three different places, and now when she was finally leaving, she was coming home to a totally different house. I wanted her to feel welcome. I was delighted when I heard Sam walk in. He decided to cut his day short so that he could come with me to pick Molly up. Once again, I realized just how lucky I was to have him in our lives. We headed out to Molly's house, taking a slow ride so that we would have time to talk. I wanted to let Sam know just how worried I was about her coming home. I didn't feel prepared, wasn't sure what to say or to do anymore. Sam assured me that I should just treat her exactly how I always treated her. She was still Molly. I thought about what he was saying and realized that he was right. I just had to relax. When we pulled up Molly was outside it appeared as if she was talking to a young man. As I got out of the car, I saw her briefly hug him. I wondered as I walked over who it was.

"Hi, Mom," said Molly. "You remember Vinny, don't you?"

"Vinny?" I said.

"Remember, Mom, from the rehab."

"Oh yes, sorry. I do remember. Hi, Vinny. How are you?"

"I'm fine. I was just actually leaving."

"See you, Molly. Nice to see you guys again." Then he was gone.

"So, Molly, why was he here? I thought this house was for women only."

"It is, Mom. He was just passing by and stopped to say hi. Why make such a big deal about it?"

"I'm not making a big deal about anything. It was only a question." It seemed as if she was annoyed at me already. "Hi Sam," she said. "Thanks for coming with Mom to pick me up. I have everything packed right inside the door. Claudette said that you could come in and grab whatever I can't carry myself."

"Sure, Molly, I'll just go in and grab it all. Why don't you just wait in the car with your mom?"

"Okay, Sam, thanks." Once Sam was out of earshot, I looked at Molly and said, "So what's going on with you already you seem very short with me and that is not exactly how I was thinking we should start this next chapter."

"Oh, Mom, are you seriously going to start this? I am fine. I don't know why everything has to be a big deal with you."

"I am not making everything a big deal, Molly. I expressed some curiosity about your friend Vinny being here, that's all."

"That's all it ever is with you, Mom."

"Okay, Molly. Let's just forget it. I wanted today to be about new beginnings. I am excited for you to see the house and to see your room."

"Me too, Mom." It took Sam less than ten minutes to load the car, and off we went. "So, Sam, Mom tells me that you guys are throwing a big Fourth of July party. Yes, we are. Is there anyone that you would like to invite?"

"Hmm, can I think about it and let you know?"

"Sure, we are fine with that right, Brenda? Right, I think that it would be good for you to invite some of your friends. On the ride home, Molly told us that Nancy had gone home about a month ago. Really, you never mentioned it before. I know, Mom, but I am mentioning it now. She hated being in the sober house. She didn't want to follow the rules, and she didn't like her counselor she was also in the habit of missing meetings. It really never worked with her being in sober living, so her mom picked her up. To tell you the truth, I can't believe that she lasted as long as she did."

"Do you still talk to her?" I asked.

"No, not really. She called the house a few times after she left but stopped. Which brings me to my next question. Do I finally get a cell phone? I have been without one for over six months now, and I think it is time for me to get one."

"Well, Molly, I don't disagree with you, but let me give it some thought please and I will let you know later tonight."

"Okay, Mom, sounds good."

As we turned onto our block, I turned around to see Molly's expression as we pulled up to the house. As Sam pulled into the driveway, he said, "Welcome home, Molly. I hope that you will be happy here."

Molly's face was priceless; she had the biggest grin and the widest eyes that I have ever seen. "Wow, guys, this is where we live? Yes, honey, this is home now. I can't believe it, it is absolutely gorgeous and tremendous. Well, go in and find your brother please so that he can come out here and help with your stuff."

"You got it, Mom." She ran up the steps and burst into the front door. I heard her yelling for Luke. I walked over to Sam and put my arms around him, thanking him once again for being such an amazing man.

"You make it easy, Brenda." Out of the house came Luke, Stacy, and Molly. All of them were talking at once. Luke was telling Molly that he would give her the tour once they moved her stuff into her room. Everyone joined in to help bring Molly's stuff into the house. Before they went upstairs, I asked for dinner ideas. I told them that I had cooked some things and could start dinner now or they could give me ideas for takeout.

Molly looked at all of us and said, "Pizza. I would love pizza."

Sam chuckled at that suggestion and replied, "Don't threaten me with a good time." What Molly didn't know yet was that one of Sam's favorite meals was pizza. He took the liberty of ordering and told us that he would go get it so we would have time to show Molly the house. First things first, though—she wanted to see her room. Up the stairs we all went, carrying as much stuff as we could. Stacy led and opened the door to Molly's new room with a flourish.

"I hope that you don't mind, Molly," said Stacy, "but I took the liberty of hanging up all of your clothes."

"Thanks, Stacy."

Luke made a big deal about her walk-in closet, hoping that it would leave enough of an impression to make seeing his room less painful for her. We put all her stuff down and went on to show her the rest of the house. When Luke brought her into his room, I held my breath. It was, after all, the bigger of both rooms, and Luke knew that the deal was if Molly wanted the bigger room, he would have to give it to her. When she looked around, all she said was, "At least I have a walk-in closet." The next stop was the home office, followed by our room. We took her downstairs to the main level and showed her the kitchen, dining room, living room, and den. She, of course, loved it all, but Luke saved what was, in his opinion, the best for last. He took her downstairs to the home gym.

"OMG," was all she could say.

"Yeah, Molly, pretty cool, right? Sam and I come down here mostly every night and work out. He has shown me some new things to do to get into better shape."

"I can't wait to start working out in here," was her answer to that statement.

"Hello, hello, where is everyone?" we heard from upstairs.

"Okay, guys, let's go upstairs. It sounds like Sam is back with dinner."

Chapter 23

We managed to get through all of July without a bump in the road. Molly was going to meeting; she had found a counselor that she liked and found a sponsor. I was happy about that. The only concern I had was her blossoming relationship with Vinny. Sam and I both had concerns about this. We had many discussions. I even called Amanda to get her input. All she would tell me was that generally speaking, new relationships were frowned upon in the first year of sobriety. It was important to concentrate on sobriety instead of relationships. I did have my concerns. I was deep in thought sitting at the kitchen table, so I didn't hear Molly calling me. I was startled by her hand on my shoulder.

"Mom," she said, "I called you several times."

"I'm sorry, honey. I didn't hear you. What's up?" I asked.

"I just wanted to tell you that I was going out. I have a job interview."

"Wow, that's terrific. Where is it and what will you be doing?"

"It's a waitress job at a local steakhouse."

"Waitressing? You have never done that before."

"Yes, Mom. I am aware of that, but how hard could it be?"

"Wish me luck."

"Good luck, honey," I continued sitting there long after she left. Once again, I was startled when I felt Sam tapping my shoulder.

"Sorry," he said, "I didn't mean to scare you. I was just going to tell you that Luke and I are leaving."

"Where are you guys going?"

"To pick up the car. Don't you remember me telling you?"

"Oh, Sam, I'm sorry I just have a lot of things on my mind right now."

"It's okay, Brenda, can I help?"

"No, not really. It's just some things that I need to work out for myself."

"Well, if you change your mind, I'm here for you."

"Thank you, Sam. I really appreciate that more than you can ever really know." The house was really quiet after they left. I realized that I had the house to myself it was the first time in a really long time that I was alone. I took the time to call Susan and let her know about Molly's job interview. Since I had dinner with Susan and Leslie, I found it so much easier to talk to them both. I had found my footing with my friends once again.

As I was talking to Susan, Molly came running in. "Mom, Mom, where are you?"

"Can I call you back, Sue?"

"Sure," was her reply.

"I'm in here Molly. Mom, I got the job. I am so excited about it. I told the manager that I didn't have any experience, and he told me that he would assign me with someone who had a ton of experience and that in no time, I would be fine on my own."

"Congratulations, Molly. That's terrific, when do you start?"

"Tomorrow night, my shift will be from five o'clock till closing which is around eleven o'clock."

"Great, maybe once you are comfortable there, Sam and I will come and have dinner. Would you, Mom?"

"Yep, we will." At that point she told me that she was meeting Vinny for lunch; they were going to celebrate her new job.

The next few weeks went rather smoothly; Luke was hanging out with Stacy and the rest of his friends mostly at Stacy's house, and Molly was working and seeing a lot of Vinny more then I was comfortable with. Sam and I went to the restaurant for dinner once a week. We enjoyed the food, and it was fun to see Molly at work. She seemed to be blossoming in her newfound responsibilities. Again, though, I had a nagging feeling. The owner liked her so much that he was training her to be a bartender. I wasn't sure that this was a good idea although her drug of choice had never been alcohol. She did drink socially with her friends, but she never abused it. We had a really good August, and September was shaping up to be just as good. Things were going so good that Sam and I finally decided to get married. We picked the last weekend in September. We both always liked Indian summer. We choose just a small group of our closest friends.

The morning of the wedding was sunny and bright. Sam wanted the wedding to be in the backyard; he wanted to be able to take advantage of the lovely weather. I was a little worried that if it rained, we would be in trouble. Sam, however, had faith that the weather would cooperate, and as luck would have it, he was right. We had a lovely ceremony. Molly was my maid of honor, and Sam asked Luke to be his best man. The day was perfect in every way possible. As I stood looking around, I was once again amazed at how far life had come. If someone told me less than a year ago that I would be marrying the love of my life and that my daughter would fall victim to drug abuse and be clean for almost ten months, I would not have believed them. Yet here we were. At that very moment, life was perfect.

We would continue riding the wave of bliss until the week before Thanksgiving. I woke to the knocking on my door. I looked at the clock and saw that it wasn't even 7:00 a.m. yet. I got up and went to the door to find Luke standing there looking distraught. "What's wrong, Luke, are you okay?" I asked.

"Yes, Mom, I am fine, but I have something to tell you."

I felt my stomach drop like a lead balloon. "What, Luke?" I asked. Silently praying that it was nothing terrible. "Molly isn't home. She went out last night after you went to sleep. She asked me to cover for her. She promised me that she would be home before you guys got up, but she's not home yet. I tried her phone and it goes right to voice mail. Mom, I'm sorry I woke you, but I didn't know what else to do. I don't know where she is."

"Luke you did the right thing by waking me. Covering for her, on the other hand, is something we will discuss later."

I went back into the bedroom to find Sam. He was just getting out of the shower. "What's up, hon?" he asked as soon as he saw me.

Without meaning to, I just started to cry. "Oh, Sam, it's something terrible. Luke just told me that Molly isn't home and hasn't been since last night. She asked him to cover for her and promised him she would be back before anyone was up."

"Okay, Brenda, let me get dressed and make a few calls. We will find her, I promise you."

I paced the floor, sick at the thoughts running through my head. After what seemed like an eternity, Sam came into the kitchen. "Okay, Brenda, I found her, but I am going to go get her. You stay here."

"No, Sam, I want to come with you."

"I'm sorry, Brenda, but I promised her I would come alone. Please just wait here. I will text you when she's with me I swear to you I got this."

I took a deep breath to steady myself and said okay to his suggestion. I resumed pacing until I heard my phone go off. It was from Sam, and it was one line. "I have Molly. She is okay. Talk soon." That was it, nothing more. I couldn't bring myself to go to work. I was sick, physically sick. I couldn't imagine what had happened. Not knowing what else to do, I just sat; I sat in the living room, waiting and waiting. I would like to have been able to say that my wait was short lived, but it wasn't. I sat in that very seat all morning and well into the afternoon.

Luke came home from school and asked me if I heard anything. "Yes," I told him, "Sam found her and picked her up hours ago. He sent me a text that she is okay, nothing more. So I am waiting, waiting for them to come home."

"Can I wait with you, Mom?" I could tell that Luke was much more worried than he let on.

"Sure, have a seat," I said. Thankfully, we didn't have much more of a wait. Sam and Molly walked in Molly looked terrible, and Sam did not look much better. Molly looked up at Sam, and he gently nodded. I looked from one to the other, not quite sure what was going on, then Molly went up the stairs. I heard her door shut. Then Sam asked Luke if he wouldn't mind going to his room.

"Sure, Sam. Call me if you need me."

Sam walked over to me and took my hands. "Brenda, I know that you are worried, and you have every right to be. But you have to trust me on this: Molly is going to come down soon to talk to you. It's really important that you hear this from her and that you try really hard to stay calm."

I couldn't imagine what was about to come; not in my wildest imagination was I prepared. Sam and I sat there together, waiting for Molly; it didn't take her too long to come down. I noticed that she had changed her clothes and washed her face. I also noticed that she had terribly dark rings under her eyes. Molly didn't sit. She stood in front of us with silent tears running down her face; just looking at her broke my heart. "Mom, I'm sorry, so very sorry that I worried you. I didn't mean for this to happen, not any of this."

"Okay, Molly, as long as you are okay, we can fix anything, you know that."

"Mom, some things are just not fixable by you. This is one of those things." I could see her struggling to find the words that she had to say to me. I could feel Sam's fingers getting a little tighter on my hands.

After seeing her take a few deep breaths, she blurted out the words that would once again forever change our lives. "Mom, I relapsed." There it was, out in the open. I just sat there, looking at her, not trusting myself to speak. After all, what could I say? I had no words.

"Mom, please say something, anything."

I took a deep breath than another and another. I still couldn't speak, so I stood up and pulled her into my arms and just held her. It was at that moment that I felt how thin she was. I hadn't noticed it before; maybe it was because of the choices of clothes she wore or maybe it was because she was always dashing off to work, spending little time at home. Whatever the reason was, I felt it now. "Mom, are you mad?"

"No, Molly. I'm not mad, just concerned as to what we do now. Where we go from here? Why don't you go to your room and let me think about this, talk to Sam and try to figure it all out?"

"Okay, Mom, and Mom, I love you."

"I love you too, Molly."

Once she left the room, I turned to Sam and asked him, "So how did you find her, and where did you find her?"

"I made some calls, Brenda, and tracked her phone. She was holed up in a very questionable motel."

"Was she alone, Sam?"

"No, Brenda, she was not." At that, I decided it would probably be better for me to stop asking questions. Sam and I continued to sit there, discussing the possible options open to her at this point.

"Maybe she should go to another rehab," I said.

"I think we have to wait to see what she decided she wants to do," said Sam.

"Really? You really think we should leave it up to her? I hardly think that she is equipped to make any kind of decision, much less this one."

"Brenda, as much as you don't want to see it, Molly is legally an adult and has to make her own decisions."

"Fine, Sam, we will leave it up to her."

At that, I got up and walked up the stairs to our room. I was beyond annoyed at him for not seeing things my way, it was a situation that we would find ourselves in more than once over the next several years.

Chapter 24

The next day was Thanksgiving, and we were hosting a very large gathering at our house. I wanted to cancel it, but Sam would not hear of it. He thought that it would be better to just celebrate the holiday and deal with things afterward. I, on the other hand, just wanted the decision to be made and to move on. As it turns out, Molly had her own plan of what she wanted to do. She found us in the kitchen and told us that she would be leaving to meet Vinny for a little while and would be back in plenty of time to help me in the kitchen. I stood there looking at her when she told me her plan. When she was done, all I could say was, "Are you kidding me? You are not leaving this house until we make a decision as to what the next step for you is, and then you are leaving to go to wherever it is you decide to go."

"Well, Mom, I decide to go to Vinny's."

"Very funny. You know exactly what I am talking about, Mom," she said with her usual annoyed tone, accompanied by her customary eye roll. "I will be back later to help you." With a flip of her head and a wave of her hand, she was gone. I just stood there, not quite sure what had just happened.

Luke came bounding down the stairs next, talking as he was walking into the kitchen. "Gotta run. I promised I would have breakfast with Stacy since I can't go with her to her grandma's house, and she can't come here." And he, like his sister, walked out the door. I

175

just stood there in the middle of the kitchen, shaking my head. That's exactly how Sam found me when he walked in. I took one look at him and asked him if he was leaving as well. He looked at me, not quite sure what to make of that question.

"I'm wondering, Sam, if you have some place to be? I mean Molly left then Luke left, so I was wondering if you were leaving too."

He walked over to me and took me in his arms. "No, Brenda. I am not leaving. I am here to help you get everything together. As a matter of fact, I bought us a present."

"You did?"

"Yep, hang on. I will get it." He came back into the kitchen with a gift-wrapped box. "It's a joint present," he announced, "but you open it."

"Okay, here goes." After unwrapping it, I opened the box to discover matching aprons. His and hers. I had to smile when I saw them; it was so like Sam to do something so whimsical. "Thank you, Sam."

"You are very welcome, Brenda. I wanted the first official holiday that we are hosting to be special."

"Well, it didn't start off that way, Sam, but I am sure with these aprons, we can get back on track."

"How about a little music to cook by?" he asked.

"Sure, sounds good to me." It didn't take long for us to get into a preparing and cooking groove. By the time the kids got home, everything was pretty much done. They both decided to shower and get dressed since it didn't seem as if we needed too much help from them. It made no sense to me, but there was a part of me that was happy to be sharing this holiday as a family. Sam was right in his thought to not cancel. Right on time, our friends and family started to arrive. We were to spend the next several hours surrounded by the love you can only get from your truly good friends and family. We sat around the table eating, laughing, and telling stories. I totally enjoyed myself although there was a little nagging feeling in the back of my mind wondering what Molly was going to do.

Somewhere around 8:00 p.m., everyone started to leave. "Thanks for having us guys," "The food was terrific," and "We had such a great time" were some of the comments we heard. When the last couple left, I shut the door, leaning against it exhausted. I looked at the table and the kitchen and sighed. I had my work cut out for me. But to my happy surprise, everyone pitched in and helped me. Before I knew it, we were done.

"Thanks, everyone, for all your help. I couldn't have done it by myself."

"Of course. Why wouldn't we help?" they asked.

I just shrugged. "For so many years prior to this one I had no one to help me. This was a wonderful change."

"Mom, Sam, can I talk to you both?" asked Molly.

"Sure, honey, what's up?"

"I have decided that I need to go into another rehab. I called my counselor and my sponsor as well as Amanda. You remember her, right, Mom?"

"Of course I do."

"Well, anyway, we all decided that I need to go back into a rehab. That as much as I think that I can handle this on my own, I know that I can't."

I sat there for a minute before I commented, "I think that is a really good idea, honey. Have you found one?"

"No, Mom. I was hoping that you could help me with that."

"Sure, I absolutely can. I can start making calls tomorrow morning. Maybe we can find a facility that can take you tomorrow."

"No, Mom. I won't go into a place until Saturday."

"Why, Molly? Why wait?"

"Because, Mom, you know that it has been our tradition to decorate the house for Christmas the day after Thanksgiving, and I don't want to miss out on that." It had been our family's tradition since the kids were old enough to help with the tree, and I could understand why Molly didn't want to miss it.

"Okay," I agreed, "but I am still going to make calls tomorrow."

"I know you are, Mom."

"Good night, you guys."

"Good night, honey," we answered.

Next, I heard Luke yell down the stairs, "Yeah, night, everyone."

The next day dawned gray and cold. It seemed as if the last few years, the day we decorated was always cold. It didn't seem to bother Luke or Molly; they bundled up along with Sam and went outside to do the decorating on the outside of the house. It had always been Luke's special job to orchestrate the outside decorations. He was very possessive of how the house should look. I stayed in to make calls for Molly. Once again, I discovered that the facilities would only give me general information but could not give me specific details; they would need to speak to Molly herself. I was, however, able to make a list, a rather small list of facilities that had open beds. Once my calls were done, I went outside to check on the progress of the house design. Each year, Luke had a new design idea. I enjoyed it very much. It was bittersweet this year, however, as I knew that Molly would most likely be in a rehab facility at Christmas.

"Hi, Mom," she called when she saw me. "I can't wait for you to see how it looks when we flip the switch tonight."

"I can't wait either. Are you guys almost done?"

"I think so," answered Molly, "but you never know what Luke has in mind. I will go ask him and let you know."

"Okay, I am going to go in and start pulling the boxes out so that we can get to working on the inside of the house when you guys come in."

"Sounds like a plan, Mom."

As I sat at the table opening the boxes of decorations that we had accumulated over the years, I thought to myself, *Here we are again*. I had truly believed that we would be the 1 percent, that we would never be in this situation again. I was to find out that the percentage was actually less if that could be believed.

I was still sitting there thinking when Sam walked in. "Brenda, are you okay? You seem so lost."

"Hi, Sam, I didn't hear you come in, but yes, I am okay. I was just sitting and thinking that we are on this road again. I never thought that we would have to be traveling it again. Yet here we are."

He put his hand on my shoulder and said, "I know, Brenda, but we will get through this. Molly will get through this. We are much wiser than we were the last time. We know what to expect and how to handle the different hurdles that come our way."

"I know, Sam. It's just that I never ever wanted her to go through this again."

Luke came charging in at that point, breaking up what was turning out to be a much more serious conversation than what I wanted it to be. "Hey, guys, are you ready to start on the inside yet?"

"Yes, honey, we are. Let's get going. We all walked into the living room to start unpacking and decorating the rooms." Molly walked in and announced that she found a place that could take her tomorrow. She seemed happy with her decision. She proceeded to ask if Vinny could join us for dinner; she wanted to spend some time with him before she left.

"I guess it's okay," I answered, not really sure if it was okay but agreeing nonetheless. We all got busy then, decorating the house. There was a bit of a heaviness with decorating that year. There was a part of me that just couldn't shake the sadness that I was feeling. It was just getting dark when we finished, and Luke called us all outside. There was the usual anticipation of Luke flipping the switch, but this year was made even more special with the celebration being at our new home. Dinner that night had a bittersweet quality to it. It was nice to have Molly and Luke home for dinner, and the addition of Stacy and Vinny made it seem as if we were having some sort of celebration. As I sat at the table that night looking around at all the faces that were there, I took a moment to think about how far we had come as a family but at the same time how much further we had left to go.

Chapter 25

I woke early the next day to the sound of rain on my windows. It was a rainy, gloomy day just like the mood I was in. I lay there for a few minutes, savoring what was left of the normalcy of my life. Before long, I felt Sam stir. He rolled over to look at me, surprised when he saw that I was up already. "How long have you been up?" he asked.

"Just a few minutes. I was just lying here listening to the rain and dreading what today would bring. I guess we should get up and get ready to start this day."

By the time we made it downstairs, Molly was already in the kitchen. "Morning, Mom. Morning, Sam," she said. "I wanted to get up and get ready early so that we could get on the road. The rehab facility is about two hours away, and I don't want to get there too late."

"I know, honey," I said. "We are ready to leave, so if you have everything you need, we can get on the road."

"Yes, I am ready. I already saw Luke, and my bags are by the front door."

"Okay," said Sam. "It sounds like we are all ready to go then. I will just go put the bags in the car, and we can be off." We all walked out and got into the car to head to Molly's new facility.

The ride there was one that I would not soon forget. Molly started to talk to us before we even got off the block. "Mom, Sam,

I just want to say I am sorry. I don't know what happened, and I don't know how I got back here again. I was going to meetings, I was talking to my sponsor and of course seeing my therapist. It's just that there were things that we talked about, things that I don't want to or can't face, not now and maybe not ever. The more we talked, the more I found myself wanting to forget, to run away and escape. In the beginning, I started missing my therapy appointments. Then I stopped calling my sponsor. And then it was the meetings I couldn't face going anymore. The only way that the thoughts, the pain, the anguish would stop was by picking up again. I know that you are disappointed in me, Mom. I am disappointed in myself. More than you can every understand. I found the escape I was so desperately seeking in the drugs that I took."

I just sat there listening to her speak; I didn't know what to say to her. My heart was breaking for her and for whatever it was that drove her to this. I remembered my conversation with Amanda in the beginning. I remember her telling me that Molly had things that she needed to work through and figure out; she warned me that I may never know what it was that drove Molly down this path. I sat there wondering if I should ask her. Maybe this was the time maybe she was ready to share with me whatever it was that plagued her so. I took a deep breath and started to speak. "Molly, I am so sorry that you are going through this. I wish you would have come to me, to us, when you started to struggle. Maybe there was something that we could have done to help you."

"Mom, I know that you think that you can help me with everything, but sometimes you need to realize that this is my burden and that I need to figure this out. I am sorry that I ever started using drugs again, and I am sorry that you have to do this again."

"Well, Molly, I am sorry too, sorry that you feel that you need to do this on your own."

Through this whole exchange, Sam didn't say a word. When we were finally done, all he said was "Molly, I hope you know that your mom and I love you and will support you in any way we can."

"I know, Sam," was her answer. Before long, we were pulling up to the new facility. Sam parked the car, and we all got out. I was thankful that it had finally stopped raining. We each grabbed a bag and trudged up to the door. We were immediately greeted by a young man. "Hello, can I help you?"

"Hello, I'm Molly, and I am supposed to be admitted today."

He looked at his clipboard to find her name. "Yes, I see it. Okay, so you need to leave your bags with me, say goodbye to your folks, and then I will bring you back to meet the staff."

I was prepared for this. This is how it seemed to work. Molly turned to us and hugged us both and whispered, "I will be okay. I will call you as soon as I can."

"I love you, Molly," I said. "Be careful, work the program, and please take care of yourself."

"I will, Mom, I will." With that, she was gone; it seemed to me that she was gone a lot lately.

The young man turned to us and introduced himself to us. His name was John, and he would be handling our orientation. "Okay, folks," he said, "please follow me into my office so we can get started." I reached down for Sam's hand, holding onto it as if it were my lifeline. We followed him to his office and took seats. He looked down at his clipboard again and said, "I see by the initial intake that we are Molly's third round of rehabs, is that correct?"

"Yes," I answered, "she was in a facility in January and February but followed their program for several months. She has been clean for almost a year now."

"I see," he said, 'so I am assuming that you know the drill here. The first thing that I have to do is go through her bags to make sure that there is nothing in them that is not on the approved list. Let's get started with that." Sam and I both sat there watching as he took everything out of her bags and put them on the table. Once he was done with that, he gently unfolded everything and checked pockets and the few books she brought with her.

"Is that necessary?" I asked.

"Yes, it is. You would be surprised what people try to bring in with them." I sat there watching him, and even though I had been through this before, it still bothered me to watch it. It felt like an intrusion to me. Once he was done, all he handed back to us was

Molly's cell phone. I remembered the last time leaving with armloads of her belongings. I was somewhat relieved that I wouldn't have to go through that again. He went back to his desk to sit down and go over this program. He began by telling us that in this program, the clients work intently on themselves, that's why they don't have weekly visiting.

I looked at Sam then back at him. "What do you mean? We can't come and see Molly every Saturday?"

"No, I am afraid not. We find that our program works better if there are no interruptions in treatment, but what we do have is what we call family weekend."

"Family weekends? What is that?"

"Well, that is a weekend devoted to you, her family. You come back on your designated weekend and spend the weekend with Molly and the group of people whom she will be working with. It will give her the chance to speak to you in an honest way to discuss the things that are troublesome to her. We have found this to be very effective."

"Okay," I said, "so when will that be?"

"I'm not sure yet. That decision is left up to her team of counselors. I am sure that you will have plenty of notice, so don't worry. Also, we encourage the whole family to be at this weekend, as well as any significant other. Okay, so moving on, Molly will go to the detox unit first. She will spend seven to ten days there. Once she is out of active withdrawal, she will begin working with a medical doctor, a psychiatrist, and of course, a primary therapist."

"A psychiatrist?" I asked.

"Yes, very often, we find that our patients have what is called a duel-diagnosis."

"What is that?" I asked.

"We find that some of our patients have an underlying psychiatric issue. The use of drugs or alcohol seems to exacerbate it, bring it out, and makes it more prominent. We find that in treating both at once, our patients have an increase chance of success."

"Oh, okay, then what?"

"Well, then, we work with her on what may have caused her to start using drugs in the first place and then what made her pick up again. It's a long process but one that needs to be done. Everything we do here is to give Molly the best chance of long-lasting sobriety."

"I never heard of the psychiatric piece. I am glad that it is something that you address here."

"Molly is, of course, allowed to call home once a week. She will discuss that with her counselor in the next day or two and a day, and a time will be set that will work for you both. Now one last thing—I will need you both to sign this paper. It is giving us consent to speak to you both. If Molly signs her part of it, then we will be good to go."

Once the paperwork was signed, we were free to leave. As it was the first time, I left with a sense of dread in my heart. Even though I had been through this before, it didn't make it any easier for me to go through it again.

Sam and I walked out hand in hand, not saying a word to each other. What was there to say anyway? We were walking this road again, a road that I was sure we wouldn't be down ever again. We got into the car for a silent two-hour ride back home. I couldn't find my voice; I was choked with sadness for my daughter for what she was going through, for what she went through to lead her here.

Once home, Sam and I sat in the driveway of our house just sitting there, looking at the decorations that we so painstakingly put up just yesterday. I looked at him and said, "Sam, was it only yesterday that we did all of this?"

He looked at me and said, "Yeah, Brenda, it was. To me it feels like an eternity." There was a sense of sadness and loss that was surrounding us; neither one of us could shake it. It would be many, many days before we felt like ourselves again.

I was at my desk on Tuesday when I got a call from Molly's new counselor. She introduced herself; her name was Renee, and she was Molly's main counselor. "I called you today, Mrs. Roberts, to give you an update on Molly's progress thus far."

"Please call me Brenda. I have a feeling we will be speaking quite a bit. How is Molly settling in?"

"She's doing fine. The first two days were a bit difficult for her, but it usually is with patients in detox. She is doing much better today. She made her first group this morning, which is a good sign.

She will probably only need a day or two more of detox before we move her into her room."

I breathed a sigh of relief. I was very glad to hear that. Renee went on to tell me what the treatment plan looked like for Molly. First, she would meet with the medical doctor. He would assess Molly's overall health to make sure everything was okay. She would then meet with the psychiatrist to see if she had any underlying psychiatric conditions that we didn't know about. Then she would be assigned another counselor.

"Oh," I said, "I thought that you were her counselor."

"Yes, I am, but she will be assigned another one. We each work with her in different ways. She will get the benefit of both of us. Her days will be pretty full. She will have various workshops and meetings. She will meet with myself and her other counselor at least twice a week. And of course she will have group therapy. We give our patients every opportunity for success here."

I was very glad to hear that.

"So, Brenda, do you have any questions you would like to ask me?"

"Well, when can I speak to Molly?"

"We usually wait about two weeks before we let our patients speak to any family members. After the wait, they are allowed to call one person off their approved list for twenty minutes."

"Can I ask you who is on the list?"

"No, unfortunately, I can't share that information with you, but I can tell you that you are on her list."

I was happy to hear that. "But let me understand this, since there is obviously more than just me on the list, I may not get a call from her every week?"

"Yes," she said, "that is correct. However, you can always call me to find out how she is doing."

"Well, I am slightly relieved to hear that, but I would like to talk to her every week."

"I know I find it most difficult for parents to get used to the idea of not being able to speak to their kids more often."

"Okay, I have another question: when can we visit her?"

"Well, that is a little more difficult. We generally plan a family weekend once every six weeks, and you just missed the last one. So we won't have another one for five more weeks."

"Wait, so let me get this straight: I won't get to see her for five weeks and there is no guarantee that I will get to talk to her every week?"

"Yes, that is correct, but please keep in mind what we do we do with the belief that we are giving them the most chance for long-lasting sobriety."

After we hung up, I just sat there staring off into space. I couldn't believe this; essentially, we would have almost no direct contact with Molly for perhaps five weeks. I was still sitting there in shock when Gail walked back in from lunch. "Brenda, Brenda, are you okay?"

"Yes, I am fine. I just got a phone call that left me a little confused, but I am okay."

"Do you want to talk about it?" she asked.

"No, I'm okay, I promise. I'm just going to take my lunch hour now that you are back. See you in an hour."

As soon as I got to my car, I called Sam; he wasn't at his desk. His secretary told me that he was at a meeting, but if it was important, I could call his cell phone. *Yes*, I thought. It was important but perhaps not important enough to bother him in his meeting. I tried Susan next; to my great relief, she answered right away. I was so relieved to hear her voice; my words came rushing out. I am sure that she had a hard time following what I was saying, but she listened wordlessly. When I was done, I waited for her reaction; I could tell that she was measuring her words carefully. Well, Brenda, maybe it's better this way. It seemed like she learned a lot at her last rehab, but it didn't last. Maybe this time, the way they are doing things will have a lasting effect. I heard what she had to say and thanked her for taking the time to listen to me and hung up. I sat there thinking for a while; her reaction wasn't what I had expected. I wanted her to be as outraged as I was. While I was sitting there, Sam called me back. I again repeated Molly's treatment plan this time. However, I was much calmer when telling Sam about it.

"Well," he said, "maybe this is a good thing. Maybe Molly will have less distractions and can work on herself more."

"Maybe," I replied. "I guess that remains to be seen." We hung up, and I sat there thinking about what Renee had told me, then what Susan had to say and of course Sam's input as well. Maybe I was being shortsighted; only time would answer that question. I had hopes that this time would be the time.

Chapter 26

I t had been a full two weeks since I last saw or spoke to Molly. Sam and I were sitting on the couch talking when my phone rang. It was Molly. I was overjoyed to hear her voice. "How are you doing, honey? Can I put you on speaker phone? Sam is sitting here with me."

"Sure, Mom, that's fine. Hi, Sam."

"Hi, Molly. How are you?"

"I am doing good. I have been working really hard here. I like this program so far. I am learning a lot."

"I am glad to hear that, Molly. I was hoping that we would hear from you."

"Well, Mom, I wanted to wait until my head was clear before I called you."

"Well, I am just glad to be able to hear your voice."

"I know, Mom, how are things there? How is Luke doing?"

"Everything here is good. You know your brother, he doesn't really say much. Can you tell me when we can come and see you?"

"I am not too sure, Mom. Renee told us in group yesterday that once they figure out the weekend, you will get an e-mail. So I guess you should be on the lookout for that."

"Okay, I will then, so tell me, do you have roommates?"

"No, not yet. Renee told me that I may not get anyone, so I'm good with that. I don't really like living with strangers anyway."

"Are you lonely by yourself?"

"No, I am only in my room really to sleep. They keep us really busy here."

"That's good," I replied. "I miss you, honey."

"I miss you too, Mom, but I am where I need to be right now."

"I know, I know." We talked for a little while longer, catching each other up on the day-to-day things that were going on in our lives. Before long, she had to hang up. She promised to call us again soon.

"Bye, Mom. Bye, Sam. Love you both."

"We love you too, Molly, and then she was gone.' We both sat there after she was gone looking at each other.

Sam spoke first. I thought she sounded good.

"I guess," I said. "I miss her, Sam. I miss just being able to pick up the phone and talk to her. I even miss the anticipation of her Wednesday night calls."

"I know, Brenda. I am sure that this is hard for you, but you have to agree she is in the right place to meet her needs."

"I guess you are right, Sam."

Luke walked in while we were still sitting there. "Hi, guys."

"Hi, Luke," I answered.

"Are you okay, Mom?"

"Yes, I am I just got a call from your sister, so I guess I am just a little sad. I miss her."

"I know, Mom, but you can't mope about it."

"I am not moping, Luke. I am just thinking about her and this situation."

"If you say so, Mom. Are you making dinner tonight?"

"Yes, I am. I'm making spaghetti and meatballs."

I saw Sam and Luke exchange a look. "What?" I asked.

"It's nothing, Mom. It's just that whenever you are upset by anything but especially by Molly, you make spaghetti and meatballs."

"Do I?"

"Yes, honey," said Sam, "you do. It was the first meal you ever cooked for me and you seem to fall back to it whenever you are upset. It's almost like your comfort food."

I had never realized that. "I can make something else if you both want."

"No, Mom, it's fine. I am going to do some homework, so just call me whenever it's time to eat."

"Will do," I told him. Sam walked with me into the kitchen, offering to help.

"No, I'm fine," I told him, "but I would really like the company if you aren't busy."

"Of course I have nothing to do, so I am all yours." I smiled at that, realizing once again just how lucky I was. I don't know how I could—or rather we could—have survived as much as we had without Sam.

On Friday, I received the e-mail that I was waiting for. They had set the date for family weekend; it was next weekend. By that time, Molly had been in the rehab for a full three weeks. It went on to say that they were doing it that weekend because Christmas would fall the following weekend. I read the e-mail in full to Sam that night when I got home. It gave us the name of the hotel that we could stay at; it was only a short distance from the facility. They asked us to arrive by noon on Friday. Once we got there, we would be provided with an itinerary of what would take place. The weekend would end by midday Sunday. Renee added a note asking us to bring Luke. I felt uncertain about that last part; I didn't know how Luke felt about going, but I could only imagine. I told Sam that we should ask him as soon as possible. He was in agreement, and we decided to asked him later that night. When I hadn't seen or heard from him by seven o'clock, I called him.

He answered his phone sounding annoyed. "What's up, Mom?"

"I'm just wondering where you are? I had expected you to be home by now or at the very least call me to let me know that you weren't going to be right home after school."

"Mom," he said with an edge in his voice, "I told you this morning that I would not be home for dinner, that Stacy and I had plans to see a movie, which is what I am trying to do right now."

"Oh, honey, I'm sorry. It must have slipped my mind."

"I'm sure it did, Mom. If you spent more time listening to what I have to say and less time on Molly, who isn't even home, then you might have remembered. I gotta go, Mom, talk to you later."

I just sat there after he hung up, feeling terrible. Was I only thinking about Molly? Did Luke feel slighted? I hoped he didn't, but I did realize that Molly occupied most of my thoughts. I decided that I needed to make more of an effort to be there for Luke.

Sam came into the kitchen and asked me if I found Luke. "Yes," I answered, and I relayed my conversation to him.

"Well," Sam said, "I guess Luke feels a little left out at times."

"It seems that way, Sam. I have to try harder. I don't want him to feel like he is getting lost in the shuffle."

"I have total faith in you, Brenda. You will figure this balancing act out."

"Thanks, Sam, I certainly hope so."

Saturday morning dawned snowy; we would have a white Christmas this year. I was in the kitchen making tea when Luke came in. "Morning, Mom. I wanted to apologize to you for how I talked to you yesterday. It's just that I was in the movies. I had told you in the morning that we would be going, and then you called me asking me where I was as if I didn't tell you. It's really frustrating at times."

"I am sorry, Luke. I know that I have been distracted lately, but I promise that it won't happen again."

"Mom, I wish that were true, but we both know that it is not."

"Well, I promise to try harder then."

"What did you want to talk to me about anyway?"

"I just wanted to tell you that I got an e-mail from Molly's facility telling us about family weekend."

"Oh, when is it?"

"It is next weekend. They told me that they usually like to wait a little longer, but since the following weekend is Christmas, they were doing it sooner."

"Well, Mom, I can't do next weekend. I have plans already, and I am not going to change them."

"But, Luke, her counselor asked me to specifically bring you. It will be much better for Molly if we are all there."

"Well, Mom, I can't go. That's that."

He was leaving the room as Sam was coming into it. "Hey, Luke, how's it going?"

"All good here. I am heading over to Stacy's. We are going Christmas shopping."

"Do you need any money, Luke?" asked Sam.

"No, I am good for now. Thank you, though."

"Well, be careful driving," I chimed in. "The weather looks bad."

"I will be fine, Mom. It's not supposed to snow all day. I will call you and let you know if we will be back for dinner."

"Fine, Luke."

Once he left, Sam asked me if I felt like going shopping. I thought about it for a minute but decided that I would rather start baking my holiday cookies. I was already late in baking them. Each year I was involved in a cookie exchange. I needed to bake a lot of cookies, and there was no time like the present to start. Sam offered to help, and this time, I gladly accepted. He put on Christmas music and donned an apron. "I am ready," he said. I had to smile at the sight of him, this big, strapping man wearing a lacy Christmas apron. As always, he found some way to make me smile. It didn't take too long before our house filled up with the smell of cookies. Of course, every time I took a tray out of the oven, Sam had to take a sample. Before long, our dining room table was filled with cookies, all different kinds. As was my tradition, I made ten different varieties of cookies. Looking around at the table, hearing the music and smelling the cookies, my heart was finally full of Christmas spirit. I had been missing it up to this point. This was the first year that Molly wouldn't be home for Christmas, but I was determined to make the holiday as festive as ever. I wanted Luke to feel special. I didn't want to make it about the absence of Molly; that's why we invited our usual crowd of people for Christmas dinner. Sam and I still had not come up with a reason that Molly would be missing; we didn't feel that it was our place to explain her absence for what it really was. We were working on what we would say.

Chapter 27

The week before heading to see Molly flew by, both Sam and I had taken Friday off so that we could get an early start. We didn't want to hit traffic or weather, so we decided to leave very early in the morning. We were both in the kitchen when Luke came down. "Hi, guys, are you leaving already?"

"Yes, Luke, we are. We wanted to get an early start. Are you sure that you don't want to come? It's not too late," I said.

"I'm sure, Mom."

"Well, Luke, I want you here alone every night. If you have any problems at all, call Susan or Leslie. They both know that you will be here this weekend alone."

"So what, Mom, you need them to check up on me?"

"No, honey, I just told them that you were here alone so that if you needed anything, they wouldn't be surprised."

"Mom, what could I possibly need? You will literally be gone two and a half days."

"I know, honey, but I worry."

"Yeah, I know you do."

"Luke, please don't give your mom a hard time," said Sam. "You know she worries about you and is nervous about this visit with Molly."

"I know, Sam. I am going to be fine, Mom, I promise, and if it will make you feel any better, you can call me anytime you want and as many times as you want."

"Thanks, Luke, but I don't think that will be necessary. Don't forget to let the dogs out and to feed them."

"Mom, come on, are you kidding me? I am not five years old. I got this."

"I know, I know." I walked over to him and pulled him into my arms. Leaving him was always so difficult for me. "I love you, Luke."

"I love you, Mom. You guys be careful driving and tell Molly that I am sorry I couldn't make it, but it was really short notice."

"I will." With that, he was out the door, heading to school.

"Do you think that he will be okay, Sam?"

"Yes, I am sure of it, and we will only be gone a few days. If it will make you feel better, I can call John next door and have him keep an eye on things."

"That would make me feel better, Sam, but please tell him not to let Luke know we have asked him."

"Will do. I will meet you in the car. I will walk over there now and ask him."

"Thank you, Sam." I walked out to the car, looking to make sure that we had everything we needed. I brought Molly's Christmas presents and a few tins of the cookies that we made. Sam was back in no time; he was able to catch John before he went to work and made the request. John was more than happy to keep an eye on things, he told Sam.

Once on the road, Sam took my hand and told me to try to relax. "I know that you are worried about everything, Brenda, but there really is nothing we can do at this point. Molly is where she needs to be getting the help that is necessary for her sobriety, and Luke...well, Luke is Luke, and he will be just fine."

"I know, Sam, it's just so hard for me to relax these days."

"How about right after the new year, you and I go on a getaway weekend? Nothing crazy, maybe just an overnight since I know that you don't like leaving Luke."

"That would be great, Sam, really great." We talked intermittently for the better part of the ride. I had so much on my mind, so much to think about that I was really quiet. I was so wrapped up in my own thoughts that I hadn't realized how quickly the ride went. The stopping of the car rousted me out of my reverie.

"Are we here?" I asked.

"No, but we are almost there. We have about another thirty minutes to go, and since we have plenty of time, I thought we could stop and grab a bite to eat."

"Sounds good, Sam. Thank you for thinking of it." Out we went into a very quaint-looking restaurant. The inside was just as cute as the outside was; we were immediately seated and offered menus. After a delightful meal, it was back in the car for the final leg of our trip. We spent the rest of the drive in pleasant conversation. Once we got into the small town that our hotel was in, we kept an eye out. There it sat at the end of the only road running through town. It was a lovely little hotel, very small, and from the outside it looked very old, but it had a charm that you don't find in the more modern hotels. We parked, grabbed our bags, and proceeded to check in.

Once in our room, I checked my e-mail again to see if the weekend itinerary had been sent to me. The only e-mail I received was from Renee; she was asking us to come to the facility at 1:00 p.m. to meet with her. I glanced at my watch and realized that we had an hour before we had to head there. I thought that I would take the time to call Luke, to let him know that we had arrived and to make sure that he was doing okay. Sam thought that I was being just a little over protective but didn't give me a hard time about making the call. I got Luke's voice mail. I again looked at my watch; maybe he was still at school, although I didn't think so. As a senior, he only had three morning classes. Maybe he was driving; I left him a message telling him we had arrived safely and that we were meeting with Molly's counselor in a little while, but I would call him back after that meeting.

"I love you, Luke," I said to his voice mail and then hung up.

"Okay, Sam, I am ready to go."

"Okay, Brenda. We will still be a little early, but if you want to go, we can."

"Yes" was my answer. Now that we were so close to seeing Molly, I was eager to get there. Back in the car we went for a very short drive to the facility that she was in.

Once we checked in at the desk, we let them know that we had a meeting with Renee. We were told that she was in a meeting and would be done shortly. As we were sitting there waiting, John came out; once he saw us, he walked over to see how we were doing.

"I guess we are okay, John," I answered. "The more important question is, how is Molly doing?"

"She is doing really well. I am sure that all the questions that you have can be answered better by Renee."

"Hello there. I hear my name," she said as she walked over to us. We stood up as soon as we saw her, eager to hear what she had to say. "Hi, Mr. and Mrs. Roberts. How are you both, and how was your drive here?"

"Renee, it is so good to finally meet you and to put a face to the voice. Everything is good with us, but please call us Sam and Brenda. We aren't really that formal."

"Great," she said, "can you please follow me to my office?" Once we were in her office, I was surprised to see so many more people waiting for us. "Have a seat and let me introduce Molly's team."

I looked at Sam, silently communicating, *Team?*

"This is Dr. Burke. He is Molly's medical doctor he was the one who worked with her in detox. He sees her once a week to monitor her vital signs and to make sure that she is medically sound. Next is Dr. Lewis—he is the psychiatrist who works with her weekly as well, and last but not least is Vivian. She is my co-counselor. She sees Molly also weekly—we both do actually but at different times. Once a week, we her team meet to assess her progress and any problems that may have come up. Each of us are here to help her in any way we can, and now we are here to answer your questions. We will also be working with you on this family weekend, to help her approach issues that she may want to discuss with you both."

I took a deep breath; it was a lot to digest. I looked over at Sam; he seemed to have been concentrating on what Renee was saying. He spoke first. "I'll start then. How is she doing? Her mother and I have been somewhat worried since we only spoke to her once since she has been here."

Vivian took the lead. "Molly is doing well. She is working with me every week on some issues that have been troubling her. We speak one on one and in group. There are some things I know that she would like to discuss with you both, but she is hesitant—that's why she was waiting for family weekend. I imagine that's why she has only called you once."

Renee joined in at that point. "I have to agree with Vivian. She is working hard. She is always very vocal at her group sessions. She, it seems, is trying to find her footing again. She is a lovely young woman trying to find herself."

Dr. Burke was next. He told us that her detox was harder than she thought it would be. She told him that compared to the first time, this time was worse. "I explained to her that the deeper you fall into addiction, the harder it is to come off the drugs she had been using."

"Can I ask you what drugs she was using?"

"I'm sorry, but that is confidential. If Molly wants to share it with you, then she will. Other than that, she is pretty healthy. We put her on a health plan—she goes to the gym once a week and eats very healthy meals."

I sat there, thinking if I had any questions for him but realized that I didn't.

Next, Dr. Lewis spoke. He was Molly's psychiatrist. He saw her weekly as well; it was his job to see if she had any underlying psychiatric illnesses. As of today, he had not seen anything too much out of the ordinary. However, he advised us that there was still so much stigma surrounding mental illness that he found that the patients here were sometimes less than honest with him about symptoms that they might be experiencing. He found that the longer they worked with their counselors, the better it was for him to diagnosis them.

When everyone was done speaking and all our questions were answered, everyone but Renee excused themselves. Once we were alone with her, she said, "I know that this is a lot all at once. We wanted to introduce you to her whole team so that when you meet everyone again during this weekend, everyone is familiar to you both so that you will be more comfortable with everyone."

"We understand," said Sam.

"Okay, then let me tell you how this weekend will work. We are done for today as far as you seeing any of us is concerned. However, you can take Molly out to dinner tonight if you would like. The hotel that you are staying at has a very nice restaurant, and we recommend that you take her there. We also ask that you keep tonight's dinner light—don't ask too much about her stay here. We will be covering that tomorrow. Talk to her about what you have been doing, how her dogs are, and the latest news around your town. You can tell her why her brother did not come to see her."

"What if she starts to talk about being here?" I asked.

"She won't," Renee assured me. "We have had a conversation with her about that as well. We find that those conversations are best had with her support team. Molly is waiting to see you, so if you don't have any more questions, I can go get her. Just be aware that she must be back here by seven o'clock tonight."

I looked at my watch, not realizing how long we were sitting with her team. It was already 5:00 p.m.; we had been talking for almost three hours. "I don't have any more questions. Do you, Sam?"

"No," he answered.

"Okay, then I will go get Molly. You both are free to wait here for her or in the lobby."

"I think we will go to the lobby," I answered.

"Okay then, I will see you there in just a few minutes." We walked back to the lobby, and to be honest, I was nervous. There were so many things I wanted to ask her that I was told not to. I wasn't used to having to monitor my conversation with my daughter.

I told this to Sam. He put his arm around me, kissing the top of my head, and said, "I know, honey, but you have to try. Keep in mind that this is what is best for Molly."

"I know, Sam," was my reply.

We had just reached the lobby when I heard a squeal followed by a "Mom, Mom, I am so glad you came." I turned around just in time to grab Molly in my arms as she launched herself at me.

"Oh, Molly, I am so glad to be here and more importantly to have you in my arms again." I stood there, holding her for as long as she let me. Of course she was the first to let go. I just wanted to stand there forever, just holding onto her. She then went over to Sam and hugged him as well; I could see in his eyes that he was just as happy to see her as I was.

"I am so glad you guys were able to come." I saw her looking over Sam's shoulder; I guessed that she was looking for her brother.

"Oh, Molly," I said, "Luke wanted to come, but we got the e-mail telling us about family weekend only a week ago. He had a midterm today that he couldn't miss. He told us to tell you that he was sorry that he couldn't be here."

"I know, Mom. He told me that yesterday when we spoke on the phone. I was just hoping that he would come anyway."

Hmm, I thought to myself, *so she has spoken to her brother.* I wondered who else she had spoken to since she has been here. I knew from Renee that the list of people she was able to speak to was carefully checked and monitored. I decided that asking her that would not be in anyone's best interest. So instead, I asked, "Are you hungry, honey?"

"Yes, Mom, I am starving. We eat lunch here at twelve o'clock, and to tell you the truth, the food is okay, not great, certainly not what I am used to eating at home."

Sam jumped in and said, "So let's go. Renee told us that the restaurant in our hotel is very good, so how about we head over there? Time is moving and we want to spend as much time with you as we can tonight."

"Okay," I said.

Molly said, "I'm ready, you guys just need to sign me out."

"Okay, where do I do that?" I asked.

"Right here, Mom, at the front desk." I walked over, signed the sign-out sheet, and off we went. We were back at the hotel in less than ten minutes; the restaurant wasn't too crowded. To my relief, we found a table easily. The waitress came over to give us the menus; she recognized Molly and asked how she was doing.

"I am fine, Jeanette. These are my parents, Brenda and Sam."

"Very nice to meet you both," she said. "Can I get you guys anything to drink?" We gave her our drink orders as well as our dinner orders. After she left, I asked Molly how she knew Jeanette.

"She comes to our meetings."

"She does?" I said.

"Yes, Mom, she has been in recovery for almost ten years. She used to live out of state, but she came here to this rehab facility about ten years ago. She got clean here and decided to stay. She told me that she thinks that's why she has stayed clean."

"Oh," I said. Now I had more to think about.

"So, Molly," said Sam, "how have you been?"

"I'm okay, Sam. They keep us pretty busy here, not much downtime."

"Is that good?" he asked.

"Yes, I think so. It doesn't give us much time to think about other things." Jeanette brought over our food. She explained that she knew that Molly was on a time table and wanted to give us as much time as possible with her, so she rushed our food out. I thanked her for her kindness. As soon as she left, Molly dug in. I took great pleasure in watching her enjoy her food. I barely ate any of mine; I was too busy catching her up on what was going on at home. I remembered to keep everything light and positive. I had even taken pictures of the dogs so that she could see them. We sat there, enjoying each other's company and talking. Sam even had a few funny stories to share as well. There was a lot of laughing that night; it felt good. We got Molly back just in time and promised to see her the next day. The "official" start time was 9:00 a.m. I told her that we would be sure not to be late. As she jumped out of the car, she thanked us again for coming and told us that she loved us.

"We love you too so much, honey. Sleep well, and we will see you tomorrow."

Off she went; she seemed to be in good spirits. Once we got back to the hotel, Sam asked, "You seemed very quiet after Molly told us about Jeanette. Are you worried that she may decide to stay here after she finishes this program?"

"The thought did cross my mind, Sam. I hope that she doesn't, but I know that the choice will be hers to make."

Chapter 28

I woke the next day feeling exhausted. I had one of the worst night's sleeps in a long time. "Morning, hon," I heard from across the room.

"Morning, Sam." I looked up to find him fully dressed with what appeared to be two cups of steaming coffee.

"How did you know, Sam?" I asked.

"Because, Brenda, you were tossing and turning all night, I was very hard not to notice how restless you were."

"I'm sorry, Sam. I didn't mean to wake you up."

"It's fine, Brenda. I don't sleep well in strange beds anyway." He handed me my coffee and sat down on the edge of the bed. "What's going on?" he asked. "Why so restless?"

"I don't know, Sam. I am worried about today, about what could possibly be going on that Molly can't just talk to us herself. Why do you think that she needs so much support?"

"I'm not sure that it's support she needs as much as maybe guidance on how to approach us with whatever it is she needs to say."

"But, Sam, she has always been able to talk to me, or at least that's what I thought."

"Let's not borrow trouble, Brenda. Let's wait to see what happens today first. Remember we will be together, and Molly has a whole team to help her through this."

"I know, Sam, just the thought of this makes my head ache."

"Well, why don't you get into a nice, warm shower and try to relax just a little? I will call Luke to check in, and then I will call John to touch base."

"Thanks, Sam. I would appreciate that." I sat there for a few seconds more and then headed into the bathroom. For a small hotel, the bathroom was quite big, and the shower was wonderful. After showering and getting dressed, I felt much better.

As I was coming out of the bathroom, I heard Sam on the phone. It sounded like he was talking to Luke, so I walked over to him and motioned for him to let me say hi. He put up one finger to indicate that I should wait. "Yes, yes, Luke, I totally understand. No, I think you made the right decision. I am sure that your mom would agree. No, she's in the shower. Yes, I will tell her. No, I am sure that she won't be mad. Okay, say hi to her parents for us too. Okay, I will have her call you later today." With that, he hung up.

I looked up at Sam with questioning eyes, waiting for what he had to say. "Okay, so here is what is going on. First off, Luke is fine. There was never a problem. Apparently, the snow that we left in yesterday got really bad as the day went on. He was concerned about making the drive from Stacy's house home. He asked her parents if he could stay. They of course told him yes. They agreed that it was not the best driving conditions for him. Next, he called John to ask him if he could go to our house to feed the dogs and let them out, as well as to leave some lights on for them, which of course John did. Luke was just worried that you would be mad at him for not going home. I assured him that he handled the situation in the right way. He didn't put himself in a bad position, and he didn't leave the dogs high and dry. Luke wanted me to be the one to tell you the story. He knew that you would be worried, and he didn't want the added worry to take away from our visit with Molly."

"I'm okay, Sam. I am not as fragile as everyone makes me out to be. I know that, Brenda, but you do have a lot on your mind most of the time. Luke handled the situation in a very mature manner, and I am proud of him for that."

"I am too, Sam. I am too." Sam offered to take me to get a quick bite before we left, but I didn't think that I could eat a thing. We sat in the room for a little while. Sam promised me that no matter what happened or what was said, he would be there; he was in my corner. He asked me to please try to keep an open mind and to try to listen to everything that was said before I reacted.

"Of course I will, Sam. I just want what is best for Molly."

"I know you do."

"So do I."

We headed over to the rehab facility to start our day, I had no idea what to expect; all I knew was that I had a pit in my stomach that refused to budge. At the front desk, we were asked to sign in. I looked around and saw other people in the lobby; this was the first time that we saw anyone else there. John came out and asked everyone to follow him, he brought us all into an auditorium like room. Once everyone was seated, he introduced himself. "Hi, my name is John. I have worked here for five years. Before that, I was in active addiction. This program saved my life. I was a heroin addict living on the streets for six years. I never knew where my next fix would come from or what I would have to do to get it. All I did know at that time was doing my next hit of heroin. I am guessing that you are all wondering how I wound up here. Well, my story goes like this. I got into drugs when I was fourteen years old. I started with smoking pot. I was a pretty good kid up until then, always went to school, and had a ton of friends. Then my folks got a divorce—no, that wasn't the reason I got involved with drugs. I got involved because I wanted to be cool. I started, as I said, with smoking pot. That of course opened the door to a whole new group of friends. That group introduced me to snorting pills then to shooting heroin. The first hit of heroin I ever took was the greatest feeling in the world. It made me feel powerful, euphoric, invincible. I spent the next five years chasing that first high. Let me tell you all something—you never, ever again feel that high quite the same way. I was living with my mother back then. When she could no longer handle me, she sent me to live with my dad. It took him just under two years to throw me out. My parents loved me, still do. They never mistreated me. They never did anything to me except make excuses for my bad behavior. Once my dad threw me out, I wondered the streets for a while, stealing whatever I could to get my next fix. After a while, I wandered to this town. I was on the street here for just over a year before I got arrested. I was thrown into jail, where I stayed for ten days before I had my day in court. I spent ten days in the worst throes of withdrawal that I can ever put into words. In those ten days, I wished for death. Death would have been easier than what I was going thru. But as luck would have it, it didn't kill me. When I stood before the judge, he offered me two choices. One was five years in jail. The other was coming here and getting clean and then checking in with drug court every week for five years. I am standing here before you because as you can see this was my choice, and I don't regret it, not for one moment. At the beginning, I was shaky in my recovery. There were moments that I thought that it would be easier to go back out on the streets, but then reality would hit me. What kind of life would I be going back to? And how long would it be before I overdosed and died? I couldn't do that to my parents. I couldn't have them bury me. So I pushed on. And now here I stand before all of you. I am here and alive to tell my story, to give you all hope that with hard work, dedication, and the burning desire to be more than their addiction, they can one day be standing before a group of people like yourselves to tell their story. Thank you all for listening. In a few minutes, your loved ones' main counselor will come in and bring you to their offices."

After he was gone, I looked over at Sam and said, "Wow, that was pretty powerful, don't you think? I had no idea that John was in recovery."

Sam replied that yes, in fact, John's story touched him as well.

I was still reeling from his story when Renee came for us. "Hi, guys, are you ready?" she asked.

"I don't know, Renee. Are we?"

"You both will be fine. Just try to relax. Molly and the rest of the team are in my office already. We are meeting them there." Off we went, following her to her office.

As soon as I walked in, Molly jumped up to give me a hug. I heard her whisper, "It's okay, Mom," in my ear. "Hi, Sam," she said next and walked over to him to give him a hug as well.

"Okay," Renee said, "I just want to let you know how this day is going to go. First off, this room is a safe zone, and what I mean by that is that Molly, as well as you Brenda and Sam, are free to say whatever it is that you need or want to say. There will be no judgment in here. We don't use labels, and we try to only use kind words. Everyone is free to ask questions. However, everyone is free to decide that they do not feel comfortable answering certain questions, and that's okay. What we share in this room I ask that it stay in this room once the day is done, and when you go out with Molly, you don't discuss anything that is said here any further. We have found that it serves no purpose. So does everyone understand everything I said?"

I looked at Sam, and we both nodded.

"Okay, then who wants to start?"

"I will," said Molly. I could see that she took a few deep breaths before beginning. "Mom, Sam, I want to apologize to you for using drugs in your house. I didn't intentionally break the rules—it just happened. I feel deep guilt and shame over doing it."

Vivian jumped in at that point to remind Molly that she should not feel guilt or shame over the effects of her disease; what she could feel was sorrow over breaking the rules. That guilt and shame served no purpose.

Molly started again. "I feel sorrow over breaking your rules. I am sorry that I did it. I also feel sorrow over not coming to either of you when I started to feel my life spin out of control." She stopped speaking and looked at both of us. I guess to either gauge our reaction or to see if one of us was going to say anything.

Sam spoke next. "I appreciate you telling us how you felt, Molly, and I agree, feeling guilty or shameful doesn't help the situation. I just wish that you had come to me or your mom. I hope that you know that you can always come to me. I promise you here and now that I will never judge you."

At that last sentence, I saw Molly's eyes fill with tears. She walked over to Sam and hugged him. I heard her whisper, "Thank you. Mom? Is there anything you want to say to me?"

I sat there measuring my words. I wanted so much to say the right thing. I didn't want to make her feel bad. "I agree with Sam, honey. I also wish that you would have come to me."

"Mom, I know how you are, though. I don't want to disappoint you anymore than I have already."

"What do you mean 'how I am'?"

"I don't know, Mom, it's just that you want us to be the stereotypical 'perfect kids,' and I know that I have already ruined that image once. I didn't want to do it again."

I sat there for a minute, trying to absorb what she just said. "Molly, I don't want perfect kids. I never have. I just want you to be happy, healthy, and secure in your life."

"I know that's what you think, Mom, but sometimes it's really hard to live up to your standards."

I just sat there. I had no words. I couldn't believe that was what she thought of me. Renee gently reminded me that right now Molly was being honest with me. By that, by letting me know how she felt, we could make changes, positive changes that would benefit our relationship. I sat there looking at Molly, and all I could think to say was, "I'm sorry, I never meant to make you feel like that."

"I know that, Mom. I know that you want the best for us, but sometimes it comes across a little controlling."

Dr. Lewis took this opportunity to jump in to tell us that he has been working with Molly extensively, and to the best of his knowledge, he did not think that she had any underlying psychiatric disorders. He thought that with the proper self-care and work, she would be her old self in no time. I was still thinking about what Molly had said to me, so Dr. Lewis's words really didn't sink in at that point.

"Mom, are you mad at me?"

"No, Molly, I am not. I guess I am thankful that you told me how you honestly feel."

"Mom, I don't feel like that all the time, just some of the time."

Vivian spoke again. "Molly, is there anything else you would like to address with your mom?"

Oh no, I thought to myself, *there is more?* I didn't know how much more of this I could take.

Molly looked at me again and said, "I was mad at you for a little while when I was in the other rehab because I am part of this family, yet I was the very last person to hear about Sam. You even told your friends about him before me."

This I felt comfortable addressing. "Yes, Molly, I know, but as I told you then, I didn't know how to approach you with things that were that big and important. There was a part of me that felt guilty that my life was moving along in a positive direction and you were in a rehab facility. I felt guilty for being happy when you clearly were not. And I didn't know if it would do more damage to you and I certainly did not want to do anything to put the work you were doing on yourself in jeopardy."

Once again, Vivian interjected, "We try not to use the word *guilt*. It really serves no purpose, and you were not doing anything wrong. Brenda, you were living your life, and Molly was living hers. Both of your lives were moving in different directions at that time."

"Molly, I am sorry that I did not tell you sooner. You are a very important person to me. You are my daughter, and I never intentionally did anything to diminish that."

"Thank you for acknowledging that, Mom. I appreciate it."

The rest of the day went along the same way. Molly brought up different things that she felt, and we had a chance to let her know how we felt. We had a short break in the middle of the day for a quick lunch, but for the most part, we just kept moving along. We touched on different subjects, but I felt like the most important things were said right in the beginning. Dr. Lewis and Dr. Burke excused themselves midday as they had other groups to get too. So for most of the day, it was just Renee and Vivian. I liked them both; they were two very different types of counselors. Renee had a warmer way about her, while Vivian was more no nonsense. What I was waiting for, however, never was brought up; we never spoke about what drove Molly to drugs in the first place. When I asked the question, she looked from Renee to Vivian and said in a very clear, no-nonsense way that it was something that she was just not ready to discuss with me. I wanted to push the topic, but I knew better. I realized that it was as Amanda once said; it was something that Molly would have to tell me when she was ready. But to try to accept that she may never be ready to share it with me. By the end of the day, I felt drained. It was a very emotionally charged day for all of us. I felt like we covered a lot of ground that day. I hadn't realized just how late it was when we finally stopped. It was 5:00 p.m. already. Renee told us that we could once again take Molly for dinner. She reminded us that we had to be back by 7:00 p.m. but that this time, we were invited to join their meeting. There would be a speaker, and she always suggested that families join in. We agreed that once we came back with Molly, we would join the meeting. I was a little apprehensive about it but thought better to keep my worries to myself.

Off we went, back to the restaurant in the hotel. Seated once again, we had Jeanette as our waitress. "Hi, guys, how is everyone today?"

"Fine, Jeanette," answered Molly for all of us. We placed our orders and sat there together in silence for a few minutes. I know I was trying to figure out what to say. I knew by what we were told earlier today that talking about anything that we discussed was off limits, and frankly, I wouldn't know where to start anyway. Sam broke the silence by telling Molly that it had snowed really badly the previous day. He also mentioned that we had brought her Christmas gifts with us and would bring them to her tomorrow before we left. She told us that she had gifts for us and Luke as well.

"Oh," I commented.

"Yes, Mom, I take an arts class, and I was able to make a few things for you guys. It's just a little something, no big deal really. I just wanted to have something for you guys to open on Christmas morning."

At that, I started to tear up; this was going to be the first Christmas without her.

"Mom, it's going to be fine, I promise. I can call you on Christmas Eve and Christmas Day. Don't be sad, Mom, it's okay. They do something special that day. We all come to this restaurant for Christmas dinner. It's different from what we are used to, but it's okay."

"I know, honey, I will still miss you."

"I'll miss you too, Mom."

Jeanette brought us our dinner and told us that she was leaving. She, it turns out, was the speaker at tonight's meeting. "I'll see you guys later?" she asked.

"Yes, we will be there," Sam answered.

We ate dinner, filling Molly in about our jobs, about the weather at home, and the usual gossip that we both so enjoyed. She asked about Susan and Leslie, and she asked if we were having our annual Christmas dinner. "Yes," I answered, "I didn't want to but Sam insisted."

"I am glad that you are doing it, Mom. Your life should not stop because of me. What are you going to tell everyone about my not being there?"

"We haven't figured that out yet."

"Well, Mom," she said, "you can always tell everyone the truth."

"You wouldn't mind that, Molly?" I asked.

"I don't really know, Mom. Let me think about it, talk to Renee. I suggested it because I felt sure that you wouldn't want to, but let me give it thought."

"Okay, Molly, let me know. I am fine with not saying anything about you being in rehab." We finished eating and headed back to the facility.

We found seats and waited for Jeanette to come in. Our wait was short lived; exactly at 7:15 p.m., Jeanette took the stage. "Hello, everyone. My name is Jeanette, and I am an addict. I have been clean and sober for almost ten years now. I am originally from Florida. My drug of choice was alcohol. I started drinking when I was sixteen. It started very innocently. It was on occasional Friday nights at my friend's house. Her mom worked nights. Her dad had died when she was a baby. So she pretty much had the house to herself on Friday nights. She was always allowed to have friends over. Of course, her mother never knew about the alcohol. She would get her older brother's friends to buy us beer. It really started slowly at first. A few beers, that was it. But as I got older, it started to get to be a problem. My friends didn't seem to want to keep drinking, but I did. So I found new friends, friends who liked to drink as much as I did. A few beers turned into vodka. I choose vodka because it had no smell. I found myself craving alcohol all the time—one drink turned into two then into three. I quickly found myself going through a bottle every two days. By the time I was twenty, I started to have blackouts. I was a drunk. By this point, my parents were aware of what was going on. They told me that if I didn't get help, I would not be welcome in their house anymore. I couldn't believe what they were saying to me. In my eyes, I just was enjoying myself. I remember the last night I was at home. My mother found me on the floor in a pool of my own vomit. I don't remember anything from that night. I remember waking up in the hospital several days later. My mother was sitting in a chair next to the bed. As soon as she saw my eyes open, she started to cry. I had no idea at that point where I was or why she was crying. I was to find out that the doctors did not think that I would make it. Later that day, my dad came to the hospital. He and my mom told me that I couldn't come back home. They had found a rehab facility that was willing to take me right from the hospital. The only catch was it was in New York. I didn't know a single person here. I told them both that I was not going. If they didn't want me to come home, that was fine with me. I would be fine on my own. I called my boyfriend at the time to come get me. He arrived right after my parents left. I will never forget the look on my mom's face. I believe that she thought she was seeing me alive for the last time. It took me another four years and three more hospitalizations before I finally hit rock bottom. I vaguely remember calling my mom and asking her to help me. She picked me up that night and took me right to the airport. I was fortunate enough to be able to get on the last flight out of Florida heading to New York. I remember feeling terrified, I didn't know what to expect, but more importantly, I was afraid to feel again. To experience real feelings. I was very fortunate to have found this place, to finally admit that I had a problem and be willing to do the work necessary to get clean and sober. Through the continued support of my counselor, my sponsor, and these meetings, I have almost ten years of sobriety. It took me a while to rebuild my relationship with my parents. To earn their trust again and to earn their respect. The journey was long and hard, but it was worth it. I am engaged to a wonderful man. We have a house in town, and I have a job I love, and whenever I can, I give back. I give back to a community that has helped me realize just how beautiful life can be if you are willing to live it the right way. Thank you all for your time. I wish peace upon all of you."

I was so touched by her story. I remember thinking that she was such a happy and positive person when we first met her in the restaurant; she had a wonderful outlook on life now. I would never have guessed just how dark things had been for her. I was so happy that she found peace. Molly turned to me and said, 'Isn't she great, Mom? She has done so much work and has been such a great example."

"I hadn't realized that you heard her story before."

"She was one of the first speakers I heard when I first got here. She seems like such a positive person," I said.

"She is, Mom. She has been through so much stuff. As a matter of fact, I am glad that you got to hear her speak. She has agreed to be my sponsor."

"That's wonderful, Molly."

"Yeah, Mom. It seems that we also have a lot in common. What did you think Sam?" Molly asked.

"I liked her too, Molly, and I am glad that you found a sponsor that you have a connection with. From what I understand, that is important."

We talked some more before John came in. He asked if anyone had any questions; people were looking at each other, wondering if anyone had anything to say. Since no one spoke up, John opened the floor for our families to share if we wanted to. Molly was the first one who spoke. "Hi, I am Molly, and I am an addict. I just wanted to share that I am very fortunate that my parents could be here this weekend. Thank you both for coming."

"You're welcome," I said. A young man in the back followed her lead, then another, and another. When we were done, everyone had spoken. It was a warm ending to the meeting.

Molly walked us to the door. "Don't forget, guys, you have to be back here tomorrow at nine o'clock. We only have until twelve o'clock, then the weekend is over. So please don't be late."

"We won't, Molly," Sam promised.

"Good night, honey," I said, "I love you," then I took her into my arms and hugged her tightly. I didn't want to let her go.

"Good night, Molly," said Sam. "I hope you sleep well."

She smiled at him and said, "I am sure I will."

The next morning, I felt much better than I had the morning before. Sam and I went down to the restaurant for coffee. I was happy when I saw Jeanette. "Morning Brenda, Sam."

"Morning, Jeanette," I said. "I just want to tell you how much hearing your story meant to us. It gave us hope to hold on to. Molly also told us that you are her sponsor, I am really happy about that."

"I am too. Molly is a really good person. She has a good head on her shoulders. She just needs some direction. She knows what I went through, and we have some similarities. That's why we connected. It's important to find a sponsor that you click with."

"I'm sure it is," I said. "Thank you for being there for her."

"You're welcome. She knows that she can call me day or night. Whenever she needs me."

"I know. That means so much to her," I said.

"Can I get you guys anything other than coffee?" she asked.

"No, I think we will be good with the coffee," Sam answered. "We need to be back to see Molly in just twenty minutes, so we only have time for a quick cup."

"Okay, hopefully I will see you before you guys leave. If I remember correctly, you end today at twelve o'clock. Depending on who her counselor is, you may get to take her out to lunch before you leave to go home."

"Well then, I hope to see you later."

After she left, we had a few minutes to ourselves. "Well, hopefully we will be able to take her to lunch today. It would be nice if we got to spend a little more time with her." We didn't know when we would be able to see her again after this. It was something that I was planning on asking Renee. I glanced down at my watch and realized that we had to head over. Again, I didn't want us to be late. We quickly paid for our coffees and hit the road. We had taken the time to check out already.

We got to the rehab right on time. This morning's visit was much more relaxing and much less emotional. Renee and Vivian met with the three of us; they went over what Molly's days looked like and, more importantly, what her continued treatment plan would look like. I took that opportunity to ask them when we could be able to see Molly again.

Vivian was the one to answer, "The day you come to pick her up."

I was a little startled by her answer.

"We only do one family weekend per admission. So this was your weekend. Of course you can speak to her when she calls you, but as far as coming back to see her is concerned, this was it."

To say I was a little surprised and disappointed would be an understatement. I wasn't happy about that, any of that. Especially since Molly didn't call us weekly.

"Mom," she said gently, "I will be fine. It will be fine."

I looked at Sam, not too sure that I believed any of that. There was, at that point, a lull in the conversation, so I took the opportunity to give Molly her Christmas gifts. I asked her to wait to open them until Christmas Day.

"Of course," she said. "I will wait to open them until I call you."

"Okay, honey, that sounds great."

Renee was the next to speak. "We are going to leave you guys alone now so you can enjoy the rest of your time together."

I looked at Renee. "Oh, I thought we would be able to take Molly for lunch?"

Molly looked at us and said, "I am really sorry, guys. It's just that the speaker who comes in at one o'clock is someone who I want to hear."

"Okay, Molly, then we can just enjoy our time with you here."

The remaining hour went by so quickly; before I knew it, it was time to go. Molly once again walked us to the door. "I love you both. I am so grateful that you were able to come. I think it went good."

"I love you, Mol," I said as I hugged her. "I hope you know that nothing could have stopped us from coming to see you."

She hugged Sam next, and I heard her whisper to him, "Please take care of her. I know that she is struggling."

"I will, Molly. You just work on you, and don't worry about anything." Then she was gone…again.

The drive home was to me a sad one. I thought back to our conversations with her on Saturday. I was astonished that Molly thought that I had such high expectations for her and Luke. I mentioned that to Sam, and he just took my hand and said, "Maybe you need to look into yourself a bit."

"What? You can't be serious?"

"Well, Brenda, you want the very best for your kids, every parent does, but I think that sometimes you set unattainable goals for them."

"So let me understand this, you think that I am responsible for Molly being a drug addict?"

"No, Brenda. That is not what I said. What I said was that maybe you just need to relax your expectations for them." The rest of the ride home was done in silence. I was beyond angry at Sam for insinuating that Molly's drug use was related to anything that I had done.

Chapter 29

Once home, I went to find Luke; he was of course in his room, and he seemed a little startled to see me. "Hey, Mom. I didn't even know you were coming home this early. Is everything okay?"

"Yes, everything is fine. I have a question, though, do you think that I push you too much? Put unreasonable expectations on you?"

He looked at me, gauging what his answer should be. "Luke, I want the truth please."

"Well, Mom," he said, measuring his words, "you don't exactly make things easy for us. I guess my answer to you would have to be that you expect us to be cookie cutter kids. You know, have the right friends, do the right things, be good in school. To try not to make any mistakes. But it's okay—Molly and I are used to it."

I stood there for a minute just looking at him, then I left his room. I heard Luke yell after me, "I'm sorry if I hurt your feelings, Mom, but you asked me." I went across the hall to our room and shut the door, I wanted to think about what he had said, what Molly had said, and most of all, what Sam had said. What was wrong with wanting them to be the best that they could be? To set high standards? Isn't that what a parent is supposed to want for their kids? To have more opportunities than we had, to do better than we had done? I wasn't sure anymore. In the back of my head, I worried that I pushed Molly too hard and she cracked.

I was deep in thought when I heard a knock on the door. It was Sam. "Can I come in, Brenda?" he asked.

"Sure," I answered.

"Brenda, I am sorry. I didn't mean to hurt you. I just meant that if you just accept Molly for who she is right now, things would be easier on you both. I think that you are a good mother, and all you want is the best for both Molly and Luke, and there is nothing wrong with that."

I sat there listening to what he had to say, and before I knew it, I was sobbing in his arms. I voiced to him my fear that I had caused this. "Brenda, you know better than anyone that you can't cause someone to become a drug addict. You have been to enough meetings to know that. I don't know what caused Molly to go down that path. From what Amanda and then Renee told us, we may never know what it was. Molly may never feel comfortable sharing that with us, and it's something unfortunately for you that you will have to come to terms with."

I sat there in his arms for a little longer before I pulled away and sighed, "I guess you are right. Maybe in time I will get to where I need to be."

I was busy that night and the rest of the week leading up to Christmas. I still had to wrap gifts, do some last-minute shopping, and of course come up with an excuse to explain why Molly was not home for Christmas. On Christmas Eve day, as Sam and I did our last-minute wrapping, Sam came up with the idea. Molly had been stricken with the flu. She was in bed with a fever, and since my mother-in-law was coming and was eighty-seven, we thought it best if she just stayed in her room. Besides the fact that she was so sick, she wouldn't have been able to come down anyway. It seemed like the easiest solution. I had to remember to tell Luke. I wanted to make sure that he didn't say something else. We decided to order dinner in that night. It was just going to be me and Sam. Luke was spending Christmas Eve with Stacy's family. It had been the plan for the last couple of years. They were at her house, and then on Christmas Day, Stacy was at our house.

Sam and I were sitting in the living room with only the lights from the tree on when Luke came home. "Hi, guys, I came home early in case you needed any help."

"Thanks Luke," said Sam, 'but I think that your mom and I have it covered. Everything is pretty much done."

"Oh, Luke, I just wanted to tell you that we are going to tell everyone who comes tomorrow that Molly has the flu and that is the reason she isn't coming down."

"Okay, Mom, whatever you say. I will tell Stacy that when she gets here in the morning. Good night, guys, oh and Mom, is Molly calling tomorrow? I want to talk to her."

"She is supposed to. I am hoping she calls in the morning."

"Okay, I'll see you in the morning."

Sam and I continued to sit there, enjoying the fire and each other's company. After a while, he asked me if I would like to open a present. He had a gleam in his eye that made it irresistible for me to refuse his offer. He went under the tree and brought out a small long box. "I hope you like it, Brenda. I saw it and I couldn't resist." I took the box from him and gently took the paper off. It was a beautiful black velvet box. My heart, for some reason, fluttered. Carefully I opened it up, and there sitting in the box was a beautiful heart-shaped necklace. I just stared at it; it was absolutely beautiful.

"Turn it over," he said.

I did and read the inscription on the back. "Now you will always have my heart. I love you."

"Oh, Sam," I said with tears in my eyes.

"I love you too. This is the most precious gift that I have ever had. I will wear it always."

"I am glad you like it, Brenda." We sat there for a little while longer before heading to bed. Tomorrow would dawn bright and early for me.

I woke before the alarm to an empty bed. I quickly showered and dressed and headed downstairs. Before I even made it all the way down, I heard two very loud, slightly off-key singers in my kitchen. It was Sam and Luke singing Christmas songs very loudly. As I walked in, I couldn't help but laugh. Never had I seen such a sight before.

Sam was trying to make pancakes and Luke was trying to make something—what it was I wasn't sure, but he was trying. "Morning, Mom," said Luke when he saw me.

"Morning, honey. Morning, Sam."

Sam came over to give me a kiss. "Merry Christmas, sweetie. Have a seat. Your breakfast will be ready in a minute."

I dutifully sat and waited. Sam and Luke brought over pancakes, bacon, and juice before joining me. Sam raised his glass and said, "To a great Christmas. It may be different this year, but it will be great nonetheless." We three enjoyed a delicious breakfast, and just as we were finishing, the phone rang. Luke jumped up, saying that he would get it. My heart sang when I realized that it was Molly that he was talking to. He walked in the kitchen with the phone and put it on speaker. We were all able to talk to her at once.

"Merry Christmas," she said. She sounded in remarkably good spirits.

"Merry Christmas, honey."

"Did you get a chance to open your gifts yet?"

"Yes, Mom, I just did. I love everything. Thank you, guys, for everything. I am sorry that I am not home, but I promise to be there next year."

"I know, honey. We miss you, but know that you are in the best place you can be for now."

"Mom, did you decide how you are going to explain why I am not there? Yes, we decided to say that you have the flu. I know it sounds kind of lame, but it's the best we could come up with given the circumstances."

"No, Mom, I guess it's believable, but at least if it's not, no one will be rude enough to question you."

"What are you plans for today, Molly?" asked Sam.

"Well, we can if we want to go to church, then we are all going to have lunch at the restaurant that was in your hotel. Then we can make one more call each."

"Sounds nice," I said. "Are you going to church?"

"Yes, Mom, I am, and before you ask, my second call today is going to be to Vinny. I want to be able to wish him a Merry Christmas too."

"Okay, honey, whatever makes you happy. Thank you for the gifts you made for us. We love the picture frame, and you are right—our wedding picture will look beautiful in it."

"You're welcome, guys. I love you, Mom, and you too, Sam. Have a great day today, take pictures, and mail me some. Can I talk to Luke now? My time is almost up, and I want to talk to him for a minute."

"I'm here, Mol. I am going to take you off speaker and go to my room. Is that okay with you guys?"

"Sure, Luke, if that's what you want."

Once Luke left the kitchen, Sam and I finished up and straightened up the kitchen. I wondered what Molly could be talking to Luke about that she didn't want us to hear. As if reading my thoughts, Sam said, "Stop worrying, honey, I am sure it's nothing. She probably wanted to make sure that you are okay."

"You're probably right." I pushed my worry to the back of my mind; I had so much left to do to get ready. Sam offered to help. "Thanks, Sam, if you could go around the house and put on all the Christmas lights, and then please bring the two leaves of the table up. I'm going to set the table next." We worked steadily for the next few hours.

Before I knew it, our family and friends started to arrive. We were fortunate that one of our good friends lived close to my mother-in-law and offered to bring her. It made things so much easier for Sam; he no longer had to make the two-hour round trip drive to go get her. As soon as she came in, Luke went up to her and wished her a Merry Christmas; she had a very soft spot for him. After she was done hugging him, she asked, "Where is your sister?"

Luke turned to look at me. Sam jumped in, saying, "Mom, she has the flu. We thought it was just a bad cold, but by yesterday afternoon, she developed a fever and just can't get out of bed."

This was the first time that I was happy that she was in a wheelchair because the way she looked at both of us, I felt sure that she didn't believe us, and if she could, I felt certain that she would march right up the stairs to see for herself. I quickly changed the subject by asking her if I could get her anything to eat or drink. "No, I am fine. Please just push me over to the tree. I would like to sit there."

Luke did the honors; he sat there chatting with her until it was time to go pick up Stacy. By that time, mostly everyone was there, and she had plenty of other people to talk to. I kept myself busy in the kitchen, getting everything ready. It was a bittersweet day for me. I always loved hosting the holidays, but this one was a little difficult for me. I enjoyed our family and friends, but a little part of me was missing that year.

Chapter 30

We had welcomed in the new year very quietly that year. Sam and I reflected on how much had gone on in the last twelve months. Now the holidays were over, and it was business as usual. We spoke to Molly just about every two weeks. I had figured out that every other week, she was calling Vinny. From everything that I could figure out, they were still a thing. I wasn't sure how I felt about it but knew better not to ask to many questions. I received a call from Vivian on a Friday morning in early March; Molly was ready to leave. I sat there for a minute before speaking. "What do you mean she is ready to leave?" I asked.

"Well, Brenda, she has been with us for three months, and she feels that she is ready to go home."

"Is she ready?" I asked.

"Only Molly can really answer that question. It's not up to us to keep her here. She is free to leave whenever she wants to go. You have always known that."

"Yes, I did know that, but I thought we would have gotten some kind of heads up, that she was talking about leaving…something."

"Well, as we have always told you, she is an adult. Her discharge plan only needs to be discussed with her. It is up to her as to whether or not she says anything to you in advance. But it is up to you whether or not she can come back to your home. It's a decision that you as a family would make. I take it from this conversation that Molly has not discussed any of this with you."

"No, Vivian, she has not. When is she planning on leaving there?"

I could tell that she was hesitating for a minute. "Brenda, I will share that with you, but the rest of the answers you are looking for will have to come from her. She is scheduled to leave tomorrow."

"Tomorrow? I have to make plans to get there. I really need a little more notice."

"Brenda, I am going to have Molly call you now. Let me go find her. Can you take another call?"

"Of course I can. Please have her call me. I am at my office, but I will stop what I am doing to speak to her."

Gail poked her head into my office. "Are you ok?" she asked.

"Yes, Gail, I am fine, just a little confused at the moment. Molly is going to call me in a few minutes. Can you cover for me while I take her call outside?"

"Of course I will, take your time."

I tried to concentrate on the work I had on hand, waiting for her to call me. I waited for over an hour before she called. "Hi, Molly," I said as I got up to go outside.

"Hi, Mom. Vivian told me that you wanted to talk to me."

"Yes, I do, Molly. She called to let me know that you were coming home tomorrow, is that true?"

"Yes, Mom, it is."

"Don't you think we should have talked about this, Molly?"

"Why? You always knew that I was coming home one day, didn't you? I am allowed to come home, aren't I?"

"Yes, of course you are, but don't you think that we should have had maybe a phone meeting with Renee and Vivian before you made this decision?"

"No, Mom, I don't. I feel as if I have made all the progress that I can being here. I am an adult and am free to make my own decisions."

"Well, I am not sure how I feel about all of that. What I do know, though, is you have really given me no notice to make arrangements to come up there to get you."

"Mom, I don't need you to come and get me. I have taken care of all of that. Vinny is coming up here tomorrow morning to get me and bring me home—that is, if I am still welcome there."

"Oh, Molly, of course you are still welcome back. This is your home."

"Okay, then I will see you sometime tomorrow. Bye, Mom." I hardly got the word goodbye out before she hung up the phone. I just sat there for a minute in shock. I couldn't believe that she was coming home just like that. We had no idea that she was going to be done so soon, or maybe it wasn't so soon. We really didn't have as much interaction with this facility as we did with the last one she was in. I decided to tell Sam and Luke about this when I got home. I finished the rest of my day in a haze of sorts. I had so much going on in my head. *Where do we go from here?* I wondered. Was there a plan for aftercare? I know that Amanda had made Molly's aftercare plan with all of us; she stressed how it was very important that Molly had aftercare. Maybe Vivian and Renee had worked out a plan for her. I had no idea about any of that, all I knew for sure was that she would be home tomorrow,

For some reason, I was the last one home that night. I walked in to find Sam, Luke, and Stacy looking at takeout menus. "Hi, Mom," said Luke. He was the first one to see me.

"Hi, honey," said Sam next. "Are you okay?"

"Yes, I guess so. I received a call from Vivian today. It seems as if Molly is being discharged tomorrow."

"Really?" said Sam. "What time do we have to leave to get her?"

"Oh, we don't. Apparently, Vinny is going to pick her up. I just got a courtesy call from Vivian to let me know that Molly was leaving. She did seem a little surprised that I was unaware of Molly's discharge. I guess she thought that Molly would have called to let us know she was leaving. It seems as if Molly feels like she has gone as far as she can go at this facility."

Sam just sat there and listened to me talk. When I was done, he asked if I was okay with it. "Sam, I don't think we have a choice about whether or not we are okay with this. The only choice that is ours to make is whether or not Molly can come back here."

Throughout our whole conversation, Luke and Stacy just sat there. When we were done, Luke said, "Mom, I don't think that Molly was willing to stay any longer, and that is why she probably didn't want to talk to you before now. She must have been afraid that you would try to talk her into staying longer."

"I guess, Luke. It's just that I am not sure what her plan is or even if she has one. In her last rehab, I was involved in her discharge. Amanda let us know what to expect Molly to be doing and, I guess, what not to do."

"Well, Mom, as you can clearly see, that didn't really work, did it?"

"No, Luke, I guess it didn't."

"Brenda, do we have any idea when she will be home?" asked Sam.

"No, not really. All Molly told me was she would see me tomorrow."

"Okay then," said Sam, "tomorrow it is. I know that you are probably really worried, Brenda, but there really isn't anything that we can do other then tell her that she can't come back here, and we both know that we would never say that. So let's try and look on the bright side: she is coming home."

"I guess you are right, Sam. It's just that I am worried. I wish that I had more information on her discharge plan."

"Brenda, I am sure that she will tell us what her plans are."

We tried to stay away from talking about Molly for the rest of the night. After a quick dinner, Luke excused himself and took Stacy home. I guess what should have been a nice evening suddenly took a different turn. I was sorry that Luke and Stacy once again got the brunt of my moodiness. Sam and I decided to make it any early night. I wanted to be as rested as possible and up early to wait for Molly. I had no idea what time she would be home. I must have been exhausted because when I rolled over in the morning to see what time it was, I was horrified to realize that it was almost 11:00 a.m. I bolted out of bed and went downstairs, looking for Sam. He was in the den reading the paper. "Sam, how could you let me sleep this late? You know that I wanted to get up early to get ready for Molly."

He carefully put the paper down and looked at me. "Brenda, first of all, you slept through your alarm. Secondly, when I tried to gently wake you, you just rolled over. So I decided that you must need the sleep, so I let you sleep. Molly is not home yet. She sent you a text message telling you that she would be home around three o'clock, so I saw no harm in letting you sleep until you woke up on your own. What is the big deal? Can't you just learn to relax and trust that I can make an intelligent decision on my own without your help?"

"Yes, Sam, I can, and I am sorry that I snapped at you. I am just so worried about all of this. What if this doesn't work this time either? Then what…then what do we do?"

"Well, Brenda, we won't know that. We will have to wait and see and trust that Molly has learned things from this rehab, and if nothing else, we can hope that if she relapses again, she will come to us for help."

"I guess, Sam. I just wish that all of this would be easier for her, and I guess for us as well. I am going to go back up and shower and dress. I want to run to the store to get a few of her favorite things."

"Of course you do," mumbled Sam under his breath. I paused for a minute when I heard what Sam said and then decided to just let it go. After a quick shower, I went to our favorite specialty store and stocked up on some of Molly's favorite things. I wanted to have things that I knew she would enjoy. I wanted her to feel welcome when she came home.

Luke came into the kitchen as I was unpacking the groceries. "Did you get me anything?" he asked. "Or is all just for the returning princess?"

"Luke, that is such an unkind thing to say, and to answer your question, of course I picked up a few things that I know you enjoy as well."

"Wow, what a surprise," I heard him mumble as he left the kitchen.

What is with all the mumbling today? I wondered why Sam and Luke felt like they needed to voice their distaste for this current situation. I decided to make a special dinner; after all, it would be our first dinner altogether in several months. I would make spaghetti and meatballs, that seemed to be what I made these days as our comfort food. Midway through the preparation, Sam came into the kitchen. "Just to let you know," he said, "I just saw Vinny's car pull up. I am assuming that they are back."

I was so excited to see her that I was waiting at the door for her. "Molly, I am so happy that you are home," I said as I rushed to hug her.

"Hi, Mom, yes, I am home, and it's really unnecessary to make such a big deal about it."

"Well, honey, it's a big deal to me."

"Hi, Vinny, thank you for bringing Molly home."

"You are welcome, Mrs. Roberts."

"Vinny, I told you to please call me Brenda. Molly, I made a special dinner for tonight. If you want to go up to your room to unpack and get ready, we will be eating shortly." I could see that Molly was a little hesitant, so I invited Vinny to join us as well.

"Thank you, Brenda, but I have other plans for tonight."

"Mom, I am sorry, but I told Vinny that I would go with him to his parents' house tonight." I could feel Sam's arm go around me as she spoke.

"Oh, I thought that we would have a special dinner tonight, honey, to celebrate your coming home."

"I wish I would have known, but I didn't, sorry. Vinny, just give me a minute to put all my stuff up in my room, then we can go."

Sam and I just stood there at the foot of the steps, watching her head to her room. I tried my best to hide the tears that threatened to run down my cheeks. As Molly was coming out of her room, I heard Luke. "Hey, Mol, I didn't know you were home yet. I am just heading out to get Stacy for dinner tonight. Isn't it just like Mom to cook a big meal to celebrate your return?"

"Yeah, it is, Luke, but I am not going to be here. I promised Vinny that I would have dinner with his parents tonight."

"You have got to be kidding me, Molly. You know Mom—she went to the store today to get you your favorite things, and she has been in the kitchen cooking for hours."

"I said I was sorry. I have other plans, Luke."

"Come on, Molly, you know Mom just as well as I. Don't you think that this is hurting her feelings? Can't you just give her a break?"

"Luke, I said I was sorry. I can't live my life worrying about everyone's feelings all the time. It's not how I want to live my life anymore."

"Oh, so you just want to live your life as a selfish bitch?"

I had heard enough at this point. "Please don't fight, you two. It's just fine. Molly, you go and do what you planned to do, and Luke, go get Stacy. We can have a great dinner, and maybe Molly and Vinny can come back for dessert." I looked at Molly at that point.

Maybe it was the desperation that she saw in my eyes or maybe it was just the right thing to do, but whatever it was, she said, "Sure, that sounds good. We will be back in time for dessert." She leaned over and kissed my cheek, and out the door she went.

Luke was right behind her. As he passed me, he put his arms around me and said, "I'm sorry, Mom, but you know, it's always the Molly Show. See you soon."

Once everyone was gone, I turned to Sam and broke down; I could no longer hide the tears. "What's happening, Sam?"

"I am not sure, Brenda. Maybe Molly is just trying to find her way again, or maybe it's something that she has explored in rehab—you know, being her own person. I am not sure what is going on, but maybe you and her should have a talk about it so that you don't get hurt again."

"Maybe, Sam. I'll think about it. I'm going to finish dinner, and then when Luke and Stacy get back, we can eat."

"Sounds good, honey. Can I help?"

"No, I think that I have everything pretty much covered."

Dinner that night had a somber feel to it; it was supposed to be celebratory, but with the absence of Molly, it fell short. As promised,

Molly came back with Vinny for dessert, but by that time, Luke had left to bring Stacy home, so it was just the four of us. Molly used that time to tell us her plans. She was going back to the restaurant that she worked at prior to going to rehab, but she also got another job across the street from the restaurant; it was working as a receptionist at a day spa.

"Wow, Molly," I said, "isn't that a little much?"

"No, Mom, it's fine. I will work at the spa during the day, and then when my shift there is over, I will just walk across the street to the restaurant. My hours will coordinate with each other. It will be fine. I want to keep myself busy."

I couldn't help myself from asking, "When will you find time to work your program?"

"Mom, I will have time to do everything that I need to do. It is my program to follow. I appreciate your concern, but this is something that I need to do for myself. I would really like it if you would trust me on this."

"I will try, Molly. That is the only thing that I can promise."

Chapter 31

As luck would have it, everything was going well. Molly had found her footing; she was successfully working both jobs and making meetings. She even found a sponsor that she liked. The only difference this time was that Sam and I had almost no involvement in her program. We learned not to ask too many questions and just waited for her to share things with us. We got back into the routine of going to the restaurant that she worked at on Friday nights. We would have dinner and then go into the lounge if Molly was tending bar. It was fun for us to see her at work. Things seemed to be going well. Molly had made arrangements with Sam to give him her paychecks and tips from bartending to save for her. We all thought that it was a good idea. Vinny was still in the picture; it seemed like the two of them were as thick as thieves. When she wasn't at work, she was at his house or he was at ours. Things with Luke were going well. He was a senior and had spent the better part of March and April filling out college applications. He was also pressured by Stacy into going to the senior prom. I thought that it was a great idea. I tried to tell him that the senior prom was a rite of passage and that if he didn't go, he would someday feel like he missed out on an important part of his senior year. He begrudgingly went and participated in the "after prom" activities; it was a whole weekend deal. I was happy to see that life, for all intent and purposes, was back to normal.

Luke graduated from high school on a sunny Friday in June. Sam had insisted on throwing him a graduation party. He thought that after the last few years, it was the right thing to do. Luke was thrilled with the idea of a party and handed me a guest list. What I thought would be a small gathering actually turned out to be a full-blown event. But nothing surprised me more than the graduation present that Sam had bought him. The morning of his party, Sam walked him down the stairs, and out the front door, there sitting in the driveway, was a new car. The look on Luke's face was priceless; it made my anxiety over the car more manageable. Luke was stunned. "Is it really for me?" he asked.

"Yes, Luke, it really is yours. Your mom and I thought that it would be a useful gift now that Molly took back her car. You won't need to work your schedule around hers anymore." He ran over to me and hugged me, thanking me and thanking Sam. He jumped in to try it out and then to tell us he was going to go get Stacy.

After he left, I just stood there looking at Sam. I had so many things I wanted to say, but I couldn't find the words. Never had anyone other than myself done anything this amazing for one of my kids. I was so grateful for everything that Sam had and was doing for us. "Thank you, Sam, although thank you hardly seems enough."

"Brenda, I love Luke as if he were my own. I hope you know that."

"I do, Sam, I do." Together we walked back into the house; we had so much to do to get ready for the party. I looked at the clock and realized that Molly hadn't made it downstairs yet.

I went upstairs to her room. I knocked on her door. After a minute, she said, "Come in." I opened the door to find Molly sitting in the middle of her room with a pile of books on her lap.

"What are you doing, honey?"

"Well, watching Luke going through his college applications got me thinking that I want to go back to school to finish my degree."

"You do? I didn't think that it was something that you even thought about anymore."

"Well, Mom, I only have one semester left to go to get my bachelor's degree. It seems like such a waste for me not to finish."

"I agree, Molly, but do you think that you have enough time? I mean you are already working at two jobs. You don't want to bite off more than you can chew."

"I know, Mom. That's why I am looking into it first. I want to make sure that I make the right decision. I already discussed this with Sam, he agrees that it would be a good idea."

"Oh, you talked to him?"

"Yeah, Mom. I wanted to see what he thought before I talked to you about it. Hey, I forgot to ask you, what did Luke think of his new car?"

"He loved it. Let me guess—you already knew about that."

"Yes, I did, Mom, but don't worry—other than me thinking about going back to school and Luke's car Sam is not keeping any other secrets."

I hope not, I thought.

"Do you need any help, Mom?"

"No, I think we are good. The caterers and waitstaff will be here shortly. I think that we are all set. What time did you tell Vinny to get here?"

"Three o'clock. That's okay, right?"

"Yes, that's just fine. I'm going down now to check on some things. Come down as soon as you are done."

"Will do, Mom." I went in search of Sam; I found him in the backyard orchestrating the setup of the outdoor tables and chairs. He smiled when he saw me. "How is Molly? Was she up and ready?"

"Funny you should ask," I answered. "Actually it looked like she had been up for quite a while. I found her looking through college catalogs. Apparently, she is thinking about going back to finish her last semester, although I am sure that it is not a surprise to you since she told me that she had already discussed it with you."

"Please don't be angry with me, honey. She talked to me about it only a week ago and asked me not to say anything to you. She wanted to give it thought before she talked to you, I promised her that I wouldn't say anything to you but that she would have to talk to you soon because you and I don't keep secrets from one another and I didn't want it to be ongoing."

"What do you think about her finishing college up?" I asked him.

"Well, I think that if she feels like it's something she can do, I say let her. Brenda, Molly is an adult. We have seen that with our own eyes. She is going to have to live her life on her own terms. As we have learned we can't make her do anything. I think or at least I hope that she has learned enough about her disease that she continues to make the right decisions."

"I hope so, Sam. It's just that I worry so much, I don't want her overextending herself. You heard the same stories that I have, so much can go wrong."

"Yes, but Brenda, so much can go right. I think that we have to trust her on this."

"Can we talk about this some more later? I want to get ready for Luke's party, and I don't want to worry about this anymore today."

"Sure, honey, whatever you say."

I went back upstairs to finish getting ready. I was feeling somewhat ill at ease, so I decided to take a minute to call Susan. She answered immediately. "Hi, Brenda, I was just about to call you. It's so weird that you called me."

"Hi, Susan, do you have a minute? I need to talk to you."

"Sure, what's up? Are you okay? Do you need me to bring something when we come?"

"No, no, it's nothing like that. It's just that two things happened already today that I am not sure how I feel about."

"Is Molly okay? She sounded a little panicked when she asked me."

"Yes, yes, of course she is. That's not it—it's just Sam bought Luke a new car as a graduation present. Of course he told him it was from both of us, but I had no idea about it before I saw it this morning."

"A new car," she said. "Wow, that's great."

"Is it, Susan? I mean don't you think that he should have talked to me about it first? I don't know, maybe, but what would you have said if he did?"

233

"I guess I would have been grateful to him for thinking of such a wonderful present."

"Okay then, what is upsetting you about this? His doing it without consulting you or his stepping in and taking some of the pressure and control off of your shoulders?"

I sat there thinking about what she said for a minute before answering her. "I guess it's the fact that he didn't consult with me before getting my son such an important gift."

"And there it is Brenda, 'your son.' I thought, as I am sure Sam did, that you are a family now, and being a family it's no longer your son and your daughter and his house—it's family, Brenda. I know that you came from such a dysfunctional situation before you reconnected with Sam, but you need to learn to trust him and let go of your crazy control over everything and everyone."

"Do you really think that I am that controlling?"

"Well, yes, in a way I do, but I get it, I get why you had to be for so long, but now you have a partner that cares about all of you. Let him do his job. Let him be there for all of you."

"I know, but I also found out that Molly talked to him about her going back to school. There was a time that she came to me with that sort of thing."

"Okay, but Brenda, aren't you glad that the burden of everything doesn't always fall on your shoulders? Doesn't it feel good that you have a partner who cares?'

"Yes, Susan, I am very glad for all of that—it's just so unfamiliar to me. I am not sure how to handle it."

"How about you just don't worry so much and let Sam drive the car for a change? Try not to worry so much."

"I will try, Susan."

"I'll let you go so I can get ready. Thanks for talking to me about this. See you later."

After we hung up, I thought about what Susan had said. I was so used to doing everything by myself for so many years I didn't have a choice. I wondered what it would feel like to let go, even just a little. To hand over some of my worry and some of the decisions that I felt I needed to make on my own. That thought at that moment was so foreign to me, but it was one that I was willing to explore. I also thought more about what Susan said about what she called my need to control everything. It worried me because that was to some extent what Sam had said to me a few weeks ago. As I was standing there thinking about everything, Sam walked in. "Brenda, are you okay?"

I turned to look at him and answered, "No, Sam, I am not okay, but I think that with a little help from you I will be."

"Whatever you need from me, I hope you know I will do. We are a team now, Brenda. You no longer need to shoulder the responsibilities of everything yourself. I hope that you know that."

"I do, Sam, and I thank you for that. I am going to get ready for Luke's party now. Can I meet you downstairs?"

"Sure," he replied. "But don't take too long. Luke is back with Stacy, and our guests should be arriving soon."

"I won't. It shouldn't take me too long at all." He kissed the top of my head and left. I stood there for a few minutes longer, just thinking about everything Susan said and everything that Sam said. I made a promise to myself that I would try to relax a bit and let Sam jump in wherever he felt his place was. Happy with my new resolve, I quickly got dressed and went downstairs.

Molly met me in the front hall and hugged me. I hugged her back and asked her what the hug was for. She replied, "It's for everything that you do for us and for being the person you are."

My eyes filled with unshed tears. *This is my Molly*, I thought. "I love you, Mom. Let's have some fun today." With that, she walked away. I didn't know what was wrong with me; it seemed as if these days I was much more emotional than ever. I found myself looking through the crowd of people to find Molly periodically throughout the day. It was wonderful to have her home and to have her back to her old self. Vinny seemed to hang on her every word, and they truly seemed to be happy. Luke's party was wonderful; everyone had a great time, and he had even more fun now that he had his new car to show off. I was happy and grateful that Sam had suggested that we give Luke a graduation party; it was just what we needed in our lives at that point. The rest of the month of June flew by; everyone seemed to be busy with their own lives.

Sam and I were sitting in our backyard, enjoying a typical Long Island Saturday in July. The weather was just perfect; we had not hit the oppressive heat yet so we were taking advantage of our yard. That is where Molly found us. "Hi, guys, do you have a minute? I would really like to talk to you both."

"Sure, honey, take a seat," I answered.

"What's going on, Molly?" asked Sam.

"I wanted to talk to you both about the decision that Vinny and I made last night." We both looked at each other, waiting for what was to come next. "We have decided to move in together. We found a really cute house to rent not too far from here, and we think that it would be a great idea."

I sat there digesting what she just told me, searching for the right words. Before I had a chance to say anything, Sam said, "Well, if you are serious about this, I think that your mother and I need to be able to speak to each other about this first and then talk to you and Vinny together."

"Okay, Sam, I'm fine with that. Vinny and I are supposed to grab a bite to eat later today before I go to work. Can we talk then?"

"Sure," he answered.

"All right. Then we will see you guys later. Love you, Mom, and please don't worry."

Once Molly was out of earshot, I turned to look at Sam. "Well?" I asked.

He looked at me as if weighing his words, trying to gauge I think what my reaction would be. "I think that we should let her do it. If she really thinks that they can make a go of things, then I say let her."

"Are you kidding me?" I said. "How can you possibly think that this is in any way a good idea? Don't you remember that Molly met Vinny in rehab? She can't possibly think that this is going to work out. We don't really know Vinny, and we don't know if he is working his program or pretty much anything else."

Sam just sat there looking at me. "Brenda, I think that if you try to stop her, she will do it anyway. I think that she will feel abandoned by you, and it will put a strain on your relationship with her. Let's face it—from what I know of Molly, she does exactly what she wants to do regardless of what you or, for that matter, anyone else thinks or says. If we support her moving out, then if she runs into any type of problems, the chances of her coming to us are better than if we try to stop her."

I thought about what he was saying, and I realized that there was a lot of truth in his words. I really didn't think that her moving out was a good idea—I did not in any way support it—but I knew that what Sam said was the truth. Molly would move no matter what we said to her, and I wanted her to succeed and I wanted to continue being a part of her life, so reluctantly, I agreed with Sam. "Brenda, if you don't think that you can sit down with both Molly and Vinny later today, I can do it and just say that you weren't feeling well."

"No, Sam. This has to come from me too. I will be fine. However, I think that we should tell them that we or, at the very least, you need to check out the place that they are thinking of moving into."

"Agreed," said Sam. Sam and I continued to sit outside for the better part of the day. It was a beautiful day, and I had so much on my mind that I didn't realize how fast the day was going.

Before I knew it, I heard Molly calling for me. "I am still out here, honey," I said.

"Hi, guys, have you been out here all day?"

"Yes, we have. The weather is just so nice we didn't want to waste the day by being inside."

Sam got up to shake Vinny's hand and asked them both to have a seat. I could tell by Vinny's mannerisms that he was nervous. So I got right to the point. "Molly tells us that you both think that it's a good idea to move in together. While Sam and I have some reservations, we have agreed to get on board with this idea." I could see by the huge smile on Molly's face that she was happy.

"However," Sam said, "the only condition that we have is that I can check out the house you want to move into."

At that, Vinny finally found his voice. "That's fine with me, but the house we would be renting belongs to friends of my parents, so I think you will be okay with it, but if you still want to see it, you can meet us there tomorrow. We are supposed to be moving some of our things in then."

I looked at Sam before I answered. "Yes, we can meet you there. Just give us the address and the time." Molly jumped up and first hugged me and then Sam and thanked us both for trusting her decision. It was clear to us that she was ecstatic about our answer, but what was also clear to me was that regardless of how we felt, she was moving. This troubled me quite a bit.

Bright and early the next morning, we headed over to the house that Molly intended to move too. Much to my surprise, the house was indeed adorable. It was wasn't very big—it was more of a cottage—but it was on a beautiful tree-lined street. When we pulled up, Molly came running out. "I am so glad that you are here. I have so much to do before we move in. I was hoping that you guys would help."

"Sure," Sam answered, "what do you have to do?"

"Well, Vinny brought a bed that he needs help setting up, and I want to clean the kitchen and the bathrooms. The landlord told me that everything is move-in ready, but you know me, Mom. If it's not up to your standards, I don't consider it clean."

I put my arm around her as we walked into the house "Sure, Molly. I am glad to help in any way I can."

We spent the better part of the day helping them get ready for the big move, which by the way was happening tomorrow. "Molly, Sam and I will be working all day. I wish you could wait for the weekend. We would be able to give you more help then."

"It's okay, Mom. Vinny has two friends meeting us at the house tomorrow, and Luke and Stacy said that they would help as well. I should be finished packing everything up tonight. We will be fine."

I smiled at that. For years, Molly's catchphrase was "I'll be fine." It was almost nice to hear her use it again. Molly spent the better part of Sunday evening packing up everything she owned. She made piles of boxes in the entryway of the house.

As Sam and I were heading up to bed, he looked over at all the boxes and commented, "How can one small person have so much stuff?"

She just smiled at him and said, "Well, if you guys would stop buying me stuff, I wouldn't have all of this."

"Okay," he said with a twinkle in his eyes, "we can stop."

"Don't you dare," said Molly. "I was just kidding."

"So was I," said Sam.

Molly was up when I came out of our room the next morning. "You are up early today."

"I know, Mom, but Vinny only has his dad's truck for a few hours this morning. We want to get everything moved over in one trip."

"Hey, what's all the noise?' asked Luke as he came out of his room. "Don't you guys know it's not even eight o'clock yet?"

"Morning, Luke. I thought that you would be up by now. Molly told us that you would be helping her with the move."

"Yeah, I said that, but no one told me that we would be doing this at the crack of dawn."

"Can you still help me, Luke?"

"Well, I'm up now, so sure, just let me jump in a quick shower so that I can clear the cobwebs."

"Well, good luck, honey. I have to leave for work. Just call me if you need anything. I can always stop over on my way home."

"Thanks, Mom. I am sure that we will be fine. I will call you when we are settled."

"Love you, Molly. Have fun. Tell Luke that I am making dinner tonight and if he is going to be home to just let me know."

"I will, Mom. Have a good day at work."

I made it to work a few minutes late. "Morning, Gail. Sorry I was late. Molly is moving out this morning, and I got caught up talking to her."

"You are fine, nothing going on now anyway."

"Molly is moving?"

"Yes, she and her boyfriend, Vinny, are moving into a house today."

"Really? I had no idea that it was so serious. They haven't been together for that long, right? Where did they meet again?"

"I am not sure how serious it is, Gail. You know Molly—she doesn't share her personal life with me anymore. They have been together for a little over a year, but I believe that in their world, that is an eternity." I tried to dodge the "Where did they meet?" question. I still wasn't sharing that part of Molly's life with just anyone, and even though Gail and I had become friends, I just wasn't ready to cross that line.

Sometime about noon, Molly called to check in. "Hi, Mom."

"Hi, Molly, how are things going?"

"Everything is going just fine. We have everything moved over here now. Now it's just unpacking the boxes and setting everything up. Luke wanted me to tell you that he is staying along with Stacy to help us unpack, so he won't be home for dinner."

"Okay, honey, just let him know that I still expect him to be home at a reasonable time."

"Will do, Mom."

As soon as we hung up, I called Sam. "Hi," I said when he answered.

"Hi, Brenda, what's going on?"

"Well, Molly just called. Everything is moved into their new house. Now all that is left is the unpacking. She wanted me to know that Luke won't be home for dinner—he volunteered to stay and help unpack."

"He volunteered?" asked Sam.

"Yes, apparently he did, although I think that it was Stacy who did the volunteering."

"That sounds more like it. Well, since no one will be home for dinner, how about I take you out?"

"That sounds terrific. I will meet you at the house, and we can decide where to go."

"Perfect," replied Sam. "See you later."

"See you later."

The rest of the day went by fairly quickly; before I knew it, it was time to leave. Gail and I walked out together. "Oh, Brenda, I meant to ask you, do you and Sam have plans for this Saturday? Tom and I are having a BBQ and would love it if you guys could come."

"I don't think that we have plans, but can I let you know tomorrow?"

"Absolutely, have a good night, Bren. See you tomorrow."

"Thanks, Gail. See you then."

On my drive home, I tried to figure out where I wanted to have dinner; I knew that Sam would ask me where I wanted to go. It was a constant struggle to pick a place to go to. I decided that I wanted to go to the little restaurant that just opened up on the beach; we hadn't been there yet, but it had wonderful reviews, and I knew how much Sam loved the beach. Besides, the weather was perfect. When I pulled up, Sam was already home. "Hi, honey," I said as I walked into the house. "I think I know where we should have dinner tonight."

"You do?" said Sam. "I picked a place too."

"Really?" I said. "We usually struggle to pick a place, and tonight we both came up with a restaurant."

"Well, Brenda, we can go wherever it is you want to go. What were you thinking?"

"I was thinking that we should try the new restaurant that just opened on the beach. It's a perfect night, and I know how much you love the beach."

He stood there and looked at me and said, "That's what I love so much about you—you know me so well. I was thinking the same thing."

Over a lovely dinner, I filled him in on the rest of what Molly had told me. She wanted us to finally meet Vinny's parents. I was a little hesitate about that. I felt like meeting them would elevate their relationship to the next level. "It may," said Sam, "but what other choice do we have? We can say no and look terrible, or we can just meet them and maybe get a better idea as to Vinny's character."

"I suppose you are right, Sam. I'll let Molly know that we would be happy to have dinner with them—oh, and speaking about dinner. Gail invited us over to her house on Saturday. It seems that she and Tom are having a BBQ and would like us to join."

"I'm fine with that," said Sam. "It's up to you."

"I say we go—we haven't really gone out with any of our friends in a while."

"Okay, then it's a date. I will let her know tomorrow."

After dinner, we took a walk on the beach; it was such a perfect evening. I hadn't realized how much I missed spending time with Sam like this. Luke was home when we got back. I found him in the kitchen with an enormous bowl of ice cream. "Are you hungry?" I asked. "No, I just was in the mood for ice cream. Molly ordered pizza for dinner tonight. It was kinda fun being there—everything is pretty much unpacked."

"Really, I thought it would take a few days."

"So did I, Mom, but Vinny's mom and dad came over to help."

"They did? Well, now I feel bad that we weren't there to lend a hand."

"Why, Mom, I am sure that if Molly needed your help, she would have let you know. It's Molly we are talking about, remember?"

"Yes, I know I just feel like I should have been there helping."

"Well, Mom, we were there, so it's fine. How do Vinny's parents seem? Molly wants us to meet them, but I am wondering if you got a feel for them."

"Well, let's see—I think that they are older than you guys. His mom seems a little out there."

"Out there?" I asked.

"You know what I mean, Mom, like a little ditzy. And she drinks a lot. She bought a bottle of wine with her. She does know that Molly and Vinny are in recovery, doesn't she, Mom?"

"I believe so, Luke, but who knows what other people feel comfortable doing?"

He shrugged. "Well, his dad seems more down to earth. I guess all in all, they are nice. Different from you guys but nice. I heard them asking Molly when they could meet you both."

"I know, Luke. Molly asked us the same thing earlier today. Are you going to meet them?"

"I suppose so Luke. Molly is living with him now, so it seems like the right thing to do. Enjoy your enormous bowl of ice cream. Are you in for the night?"

"Yep, Mom, I am tired, and Stacy is meeting some of her friends for a movie, so I am in."

"Well, then good night, honey. See you tomorrow."

"Night, Mom." On my way up, I thought about what Luke told me about Vinny's parents, I wondered if they knew that Molly was in recovery. I was hoping that Vinny would be honest with them the way that Molly was honest with us. Now I was troubled; I decided to call her to ask. When she answered, I made small talk, asking about the move and about the progress of the unpacking.

"Mom, believe it or not everything is unpacked and put away. Vinny's parents stopped by to lend a hand. Before you ask, they dropped in as a surprise—it wasn't a planned thing."

"It's fine, honey. I am sure that their intentions were to just be a help. I am glad that everything is unpacked. That's the important thing, right?"

"Yep, Mom, that's right. Did you talk to Sam or give it anymore thought about meeting Vinny's folks?"

"Yes, honey, actually I did, and Sam and I talked about it over dinner. We would very much like to meet them. What are you thinking? I can have everyone over here for dinner or we can go out somewhere."

"Thanks, Mom, but I was hoping to have you all here. I can cook dinner for everyone."

"Are you sure, honey? I don't mind if you all want to come here."

"No, Mom, I am sure. I would prefer if everyone came to my house for dinner."

"Okay, you just let us know when and what we can bring."

"Well, Mom, I was thinking that we can do it Sunday afternoon. It can be an early dinner the way you used to do when we were growing up, you know, like around three o'clock."

"Okay, we are good with that. What can I bring? How about some dessert?"

"That would really be great."

"Sounds like a plan, honey. We will be there with bells on."

"Thanks, Mom. I really appreciate everything you are doing. You know I would do anything for you."

"I know, Mom. I know."

"Oh, Molly, can I ask you one other question?"

"Sure, Mom, what is it?"

"Do Vinny's parents know that you are in recovery and that you two met in rehab?"

"I don't know, Mom. What does it matter?" The last few words were spoken to me with a little bit of an edge in her voice.

"Well, I just want to make sure that I don't say anything that I shouldn't say."

"Well, how about this, Mom? How about you just have a normal conversation like you would with anyone else? How about you just stay away from my personal life? How about you try that for a change? I have to run, Mom. Talk to you tomorrow." Then she was gone.

I sat there thinking about what had just happened; how could a perfectly normal conversation fall apart so fast? Everything was going so well, and then this. I was still sitting on the bed when Sam came up. He dropped down on the bed, groaning about how full he was; he couldn't move. "What happened?" I asked.

"Well, when I came in, I found Luke up to his elbows in ice cream. He offered me some. How could I say no? Which incidentally was exactly what I should have said. So I enjoyed a bowl of ice cream with him. Now I can't move." He rolled over and finally looked at me. "Hey, are you okay?"

"No, not really," I said. 'I just hung up with Molly. The beginning of the conversation was terrific, she filled me in on the move and how Vinny's parents just showed up to help. She then told me about all of us getting together to meet and have dinner, which by the way is next Sunday at Molly's house. Right before we hung up, I asked her if Vinny's parents knew that she was in recovery and that they met in rehab. Well, as you can imagine, that set her off. She hung up the phone on me after giving me a nasty attitude."

"Oh, Brenda, I am sorry for that. Maybe we need to stay away from sensitive subjects for the time being."

"Maybe," I said. "Maybe."

The next few days flew by. We had a busy weekend. Saturday was a BBQ at Gail's house, and Sunday was dinner with Molly. I had hardly spoken to Molly all week. I assumed that she was busy. At least I hoped so. I didn't see much of Luke that week either; he was seeing his friends before everyone went off to college. We had a lovely time at Gail's house and got home later then I would have liked to.

I was up early the next morning, I had a very restless night's sleep, and I guess my body just wanted me to get up and moving. I left Sam sleeping and went to make myself a cup of tea. I was troubled. I was trying to hide it from myself and everyone else. I believed in my heart that Molly was in way over her head. I remembered what we had heard in the meetings that we attended. It was strongly discouraged from getting involved with anyone in the first year of sobriety. The reason that they gave was that the person in recovery should be working on themselves and that's it; they should not be focusing on anyone else. We were also told that they should be really working on staying sober, to not overload themselves with too much. Here we were—Molly was in a relationship, had been for I can only guess, probably the whole time she was in her first facility. She was working two jobs, as well as looking into going back to school; my fear was that she could only keep this up for so long. I was worried, scared for her. But I tried to keep my fears to myself; as I found out from my conversation with her about Vinny's parents' knowledge, she could turn on me on a dime. It was a path I preferred to stay away from. I wanted to talk to Sam, but he always tried to make everything better. As much as I loved sharing with him, sometimes I just wanted to talk to him and have him just listen and not try to fix things. But that wasn't him—he was more of the "find and fix the problem" type of person. At that moment, I realized that what I had heard in that first meeting about getting my own sponsor was probably what I should have done. At this point, I didn't even know how to start to find one; we weren't going to any more meetings. I had no support in the recovery community. I felt as if I had I failed myself. I made a promise to myself that first thing tomorrow, I would call Amanda. Perhaps she could lead me in the right direction. For right now, I had to shake myself out of this mood and deal with the problem at hand, what to bring for dessert. I decided to go to my favorite store and pick up some pastries. I would bring a variety; after all, who didn't like pastries?

Just as I was about to leave, Luke walked into the kitchen. "Hi, Mom, you are up early."

"Morning, Luke. I couldn't sleep, so I decided to get a jump on my day. I was just on my way out to get some dessert to bring to Molly's. What are you doing up this early and on a Sunday?"

"I promised Stacy that I would take her to the beach before we went to Molly's."

"Oh, I hadn't realized that she invited you guys as well."

"Yeah, she did. I think she invited us for reinforcements—you know, in case something goes wrong."

"What is that supposed to mean, Luke? Mom, come on, you know how you can get. Molly was just worried that you may ask too many questions or put her on the spot."

I stood there for a minute, thinking about what Luke was saying. *Wow, I must be impossible, or at least my kids think I am.* "Mom, can you just relax and try to enjoy yourself at Molly's please?"

"Sure, Luke, I will be on my best behavior."

He leaned over to kiss me goodbye. "Love you, Mom. See you later."

"Have fun, Luke. Be careful, and yes, I will see you later." I finished my tea and hit the road. I picked up a variety of pastries along with a few loaves of the bread Molly liked. I was going to really try to make this a pleasant afternoon.

When I got home, Sam was in the kitchen. "Hi, honey. I was just about to call you. I was wondering where you were. I woke up and no one was home and there was no note."

"I'm sorry, Sam. I meant to leave you a note, but Luke came down and I got distracted."

"No problem, just making sure that you are okay. I'm fine, I just went to the store to pick up dessert for this afternoon."

"What did you get?" he asked as he was rifling through the bag.

"I picked up some pastries and some bread for us to bring. I am going to put it in the refrigerator. Do not touch any of it."

"Yes, I know. I won't. Don't worry," he mumbled as he walked away. I sat down at the table and decided not to tell Sam about my conversation with Luke or my decision to call Amanda. I wasn't sure how I felt about either, and until I did, I didn't want to share it with anyone.

Dinner at Molly and Vinny's house was very pleasant. His parents were very nice. I made sure to keep the conversation light and refrained from asking too many questions. I did not want to put Molly or Vinny for that matter in any kind of uncomfortable situation. I was surprised, however, to hear Vinny's mom ask a few questions of her own. I guess Vinny didn't have that conversation with his mom. All in all, it was a very pleasant afternoon. We all stayed until early evening, promising each other that we would get together again soon. Sam and I were the last to leave. Molly walked us out to our car and thanked me for not bringing up anything that may embarrass her.

"Of course, Molly, the last thing I would want to do is embarrass you."

"Thank you, Molly, for a really lovely afternoon," said Sam.

"You're welcome, guys. I am really glad you came."

"Us too," I replied.

On the ride home, Sam and I talked about the afternoon. We both agreed that the meal was delicious and that Molly and Vinny worked well together. We enjoyed his parents and decided that we would like to get together with them again. "Brenda, don't you think that Molly really had it together today?'

"Yes, she did, she didn't seem stressed in the least bit."

"I am really proud of how far she has come."

"I agree, Sam. I agree."

Chapter 32

I was up early the next day; I had had a much more restful night than the night before. I was ready to start my week. I got to work early and was at my desk before Gail even came in. "Morning," I said when she walked in.

"Morning, Brenda, you're here early today."

"Yes, I know. I came in a bit early because I need to make a phone call this morning and I didn't want to fall behind because of it."

"Brenda, it's fine. I can always cover for you if necessary. You know that I don't mind."

"I know, Gail, and I appreciate it, but I don't think that this call will be very long."

Mid-morning, I went out to my car to call Amanda. I was fortunate that she wasn't in any kind of group and was able to take my call. "Brenda, this is a surprise. To what do I owe this call?"

"Amanda, I was wondering if I could come over to see you some time this week?"

"Is everything okay?" she asked.

"Yes, I think so. I was just hoping to get some guidance from you."

"Can I get back to you, Brenda? I have to look at my schedule and see what my week looks like."

"Absolutely. I would appreciate that. If you get my voice mail, just leave me a message with the date and time, and I will make it happen."

"You got it, Brenda."

"Thank you, Amanda. I really appreciate it."

I pretty much waited the rest of the day to hear back from her. Amanda called me back at almost six o'clock that night. "Sorry for the late response, Brenda, but it's been a busy day. I checked my schedule, and I can meet with you tomorrow evening. We don't have a speaker coming in, so I will have about an hour free at seven o'clock. Will that be enough time?"

"Yes, it will be fine. Thanks again, Amanda. See you tomorrow."

When I hung up the phone, Sam asked me who I was talking to. I hesitated for a minute not quite sure what I wanted to say to him. After thinking about it for a minute, I decided to just tell him about my meeting with Amanda. "Do you want me to come with you?"

"No, Sam. I think it's important for me to just meet her myself."

"Is everything all right?"

"Yes, I just have some questions I wanted to ask her. I thought I would work an hour of overtime and go right there. You will be on your own for dinner. I hope that's okay with you."

"Sure, I will be fine. Maybe Luke will be home and we can just grab a bite to eat together. I am sure that he would like that," I replied.

I could not wait for the next day to end. I was anxious to speak to Amanda. I drove the familiar route to Amanda's facility and went through the familiar routine of checking in. As I was walking to the lobby, I heard someone call my name. I turned around, and there walking over to me was Barry. "Hi, Brenda, how are you?"

"I am doing fine, just really busy though. You know, Brenda, unfortunately it's a sad state of things out there. How is Molly doing? Is she here with you?"

"She's doing well, and no, she isn't here with me. As a matter of fact, she doesn't even know I came."

"How has she been doing with her program and her steps?"

"Well, I don't know if you knew this, but she relapsed right before the holidays and went to another facility about two hours from here. She went through their program, which I must say was quite a bit different from this one. She stayed there for a few months and now is home."

"I am sorry to hear about her relapse. But as you know, relapse is part of this disease, and if you aren't constantly working a program, you are more than likely to relapse."

"I remember. Unfortunately, I don't think Molly always remembers."

As we were talking Amanda joined us. "Hi, Brenda. Ready? We can go to my office."

"I'm ready. It was nice to see you again, Barry. Brenda, come find me before you leave. I think I may have something that Molly can benefit from."

"I will, Barry. Thanks again." Off I went walking down the hall that I had traveled many times before. Once we were in Amanda's office, I took a seat and started even before she was able to say a word.

"Oh, Amanda, I am so worried about Molly. She relapsed right before the holidays and went to another facility. She stayed there for a few months before she came home. The program she was in was very different from this one. They had only one weekend where we could go up to visit her. I didn't speak to her ever week because she was able to call more than just me and her brother. They let her give them a list of people she wanted to talk to, and then they either approved or denied it. She is in a relationship with Vinny. She met him here. They are living together, and she has two jobs. I don't know if she's working her program or going to meetings or even talking to her sponsor."

Amanda just sat there, listening to me without saying a word. When I was done, she started talking. "Okay, Brenda, let's talk about these concerns of yours one at a time. First off, I am sorry that Molly relapsed. I am glad that she went to another rehab, though, and as far as it being different from ours is concerned, that is not necessarily a bad thing. Each facility is different in how they approach addiction, but we all follow the same program. The way we get there may be different, but the goal is the same for all of us, continued sobriety. Now as far as her in a relationship with someone she met here, now that is a little concerning to me. We tell our clients that for the first year, they should focus on themselves and only themselves. The first year is the hardest by far. So you telling me that she is in a relationship is troubling enough, but then to add into it that it's with someone who is newly in recovery as well—well, that opens a whole new can of worms one that neither of them is prepared to handle. It doesn't matter that they are living together—that doesn't make it any better or any worse. They both have heard this more than once here, so in my opinion, they are being reckless. Moving on, Molly having two jobs says to me again that she is not putting her recovery first. If she were, then she would make time for meetings, sponsors and therapy, but with her life being as full as you are saying it is, I believe that she doesn't have time for the important things."

I sat there listening to everything that Amanda was telling me, and as I thought, my worst fears were coming true. "So, Amanda, what can I do?"

"Unfortunately, Brenda, there is nothing that you can do for Molly. What you can do is help yourself. You can find a sponsor for yourself, join a support group, and please find a therapist. Doing all of those things will help you keep your sanity. Believe me when I tell you that you cannot do anything to open Molly's eyes. She will have to see for herself what happens if she doesn't work her program."

I sat there not sure of what to say. I didn't know what I was hoping Amanda would say. But yes, maybe I did. I wanted her to tell me to bring Molly back and let them talk to her, maybe reinforce the important things to her, tell her the things that I clearly couldn't say to her.

As if reading my mind, Amanda said, "I wish I could tell you to bring her back here, but you know as well as I do that it's not some-thing you or I can do for her. She needs to do all of this for herself. Of course if she wanted to call me or come in and see me, I would never turn her away."

"I appreciate that, Amanda, thank you."

"Brenda, just in case you forgot, we have a meeting here every Wednesday night that you are welcome to attend. We have great speakers and, you may even be able to find someone you are comfortable talking to, maybe a sponsor."

"Thanks again, Amanda. I do remember about the meetings. Maybe I will come one of these days."

"Please try, Brenda. It will help you more than you can imagine."

Amanda asked me if I could find my way out. She was meeting with someone in a few minutes. "Of course I can," I told her. I thanked her again and left.

On my way out the door, I looked for Barry. I found him with no trouble at all. "Hey, Barry, I am done and wanted to say goodbye to you."

"Hang on, Brenda. I have something that I would like you to give to Molly if you don't mind."

"Of course not, Barry. I would be happy to give her anything that you have." He handed me a sealed envelope with just her name printed across the top.

"Thanks for taking this to her, Brenda. Please give her my best and tell her not to be a stranger. She can come back any night for the alumni meetings."

"I'll let her know." On my way home, I thought about what Amanda said to me. I agreed that I would probably benefit from finding a sponsor; talking to someone who had been thru this situation before would be a welcome relief. I was happy to have Susan and Leslie to talk to, but they could only understand so much. What I really needed was someone who had walked this path before me who was possibly walking it again.

When I got home, I went in search of Sam. He was sitting outside having a cigar and talking about life with Luke. I stood in the doorway watching the two of them; it made me so happy to see that Luke had a strong, positive male role model in his life. After a few minutes, Luke spotted me. "Hi, Mom, how long have you been stalking us?"

"I am hardly stalking you. I came home and was looking for you guys. Plain and simple."

"Sure, Mom. Well, now that you are home, I am going to hit the sack. I am exhausted."

"Night, Sam. Thanks for dinner and for the conversation."

"Night, Luke. Have a good night."

"I enjoyed spending the evening with you, so no thanks necessary."

As Luke passed me, he kissed my cheek and said, "You really picked a good one." That was the closest thing to any kind of approval anyone could hope to get from him.

"So, Brenda, how was your visit with Amanda? Did she help you with whatever it was that was troubling you?"

"Sort of, but not really."

"Hmm, what exactly does that mean, hon?"

"What I mean is that I told her everything that had been and is still going on. She basically told me that there was nothing that I could do about any of it, that it's all up to Molly. Her only suggestions were that I find a sponsor, a therapist, and a support group. She also reminded me that every Wednesday evening, there is a support group meeting at her facility and I am more than welcome to join it."

"I agree that there probably isn't anything we can do about any of this. Maybe you should try going to a support group meeting. Maybe you will meet like-minded people, and that will put your mind at ease."

"Maybe, Sam. I want to give it some more thought."

"Well, if you want to go, I would be happy to go with you unless you want to go alone."

"No, Sam, I would like it if you came with me."

"Well, let me know what you want to do tomorrow. I have no other plans." He said the last sentence with a wink.

"Thanks, Sam. I really appreciate all of your support. I am exhausted myself, so I am going to call it a night."

"Okay, Brenda. I will be up shortly."

I spent the better part of the next day debating with myself as to whether or not I would go to the meeting. I finally decided to go. What did I have to lose anyway? Maybe, just maybe, it would do me some good. I called Sam and told him that if he was still willing, I would take him up on his offer to go with me.

"Of course I would be happy to go. I will meet you at home and we can shoot right over."

"Thanks, Sam. I'll see you later."

The rest of my day passed in a blur of activity. I was grateful to be busy. I didn't want to overthink my decision. On my way home, I called Luke to let him know that Sam and I would not be home. "Okay, Mom, I'll just hang out at Stacy's for dinner, and see you when you get home."

"Perfect, Luke. Have fun, and please don't be late getting home."

"I won't, Mom." Sam and I were quiet on our ride to the facility. I suppose we were both wrapped up in our own thoughts. Once we parked, we made the familiar trek up and into the facility. It was no surprise to me that Barry was standing in his familiar spot, greeting everyone as they came in. When he saw us, he immediately walked over.

"I am so happy that you both decided to come tonight. I think that it is as important to family members as it is to the addicts to keep up with self-care. I find that family members very often feel as if the problems are only with the addicts. What I try to explain to everyone is that addiction is a family disease, and everyone plays an important part in the recovery process. I am happy that you are here tonight."

"Thanks, Barry. We are trying—this is all still so new to us."

"I know, Brenda, but the more you educate yourselves, the better things will get for you."

We excused ourselves and told him we would see him after the meeting.

"Okay," he said, but just one more thing. "Tonight may be hard for you both, more so than usual."

Once we found seats, I turned to Sam. "What do you think he means by that?"

"I am not sure. I guess we will just have to wait and see." He reached over and took my hand. "Don't worry before you know that there is anything to worry about, honey."

"I'll try," was my response.

As usual, the meeting started right on time. Barry started by introducing himself to everyone and thanking everyone for coming. He went on to explain a little bit about the program and how these meetings worked. He continued on saying that after the meeting, he would be available for anyone who had questions. He turned to look directly at me when he introduced tonight's speakers. "Everyone, this is Max and Julie, and they are here tonight to tell you their story."

As soon as I heard who it was, my stomach dropped. I looked over at Sam, trying to tell him without words that I needed to leave immediately. He just looked back at me and gently shook his head no.

"Hello, everyone. My name is Max, and this is my wife, Julie."

I could not believe how they looked; it seemed as if they had aged twenty years since the last time we saw them. "We are here to tell you about our daughter Nancy. I am going to tell you about her life. Nancy was a beautiful and happy child. She was friends with everyone. She didn't have a mean bone in her body, and she trusted everyone. In her world, no one was bad, no one lied or stole. Maybe that's what made it so easy for people to take advantage of her. She was an only child. We loved her so very much. Sometime, around the time she turned fourteen, we started to see a change in her. Her mom and I asked her multiple times if she was okay, if she needed to talk. Her answers were always the same: she was fine, school was a little more difficult for her, but she was fine. Gradually, over time, we noticed more and more often that she was increasingly moody and argumentative. Finally, we found the cause of the change. Drugs. It seemed that Nancy got mixed up in the wrong crowd of people. We tried to help her on our own, but we were not even close to being equipped to handle a problem like this. So we found this facility. She did great in here. She learned about her disease as did we. She worked a program that put structure back in her life. She reconnected with a friend in here, and she transitioned into a sober living facility. For all intents and purposes, things seemed to be moving in the right directions. What we failed to do for her was push her into sticking with her program. We believed that she was 'cured.' What we were not educated enough to know is that you are never cured. It is an ongoing problem that needs to be worked on every single day. We brought her back home and back into her life, the life that led her down the original path to drug abuse. By the time we realized Nancy had relapsed, it was too late. She was found in a rundown house in a very questionable neighborhood. The doctor told us that she had overdosed, and by the time someone called 911, it was too late. She was in a coma. My wife and I got to see her in the hospital and had to make the decision as to whether or not we should unplug her from the machine that was keeping her alive. Let that sink in. We, her parents who brought her into this world, were asked to make the worst decision a parent can make. Whether or not to unplug our daughter from life support, the machine that was breathing for her. You can't imagine the pain we felt standing there looking at her. The doctors let us sit there for a long time. I fooled myself into believing that she could hear my words to her. I apologized to her for letting her down, for not trying harder, for not understanding this disease better. I told her I loved her."

At this point, Julie spoke as Max could not go on. "I don't know where we went wrong, how this happened to her. I sat there holding my precious daughter's hand while they unplugged all of the machines. Max had to leave the room—he couldn't take it—but I stayed. I had to. I had to be there for her the way I always was. I kissed her forehead as she took her last breath. I believe that she knew I was there, in the end as I was in the beginning. We will never be the same. Our lives will forever be empty. We will always be broken. As difficult as it was for us to come here tonight, we felt it was important. We don't want anyone to ever feel this type of loss. So if you only take one thing away from this meeting tonight, please let it be that you have to do everything you can to make sure that your loved one follows a program, any program, don't let them get lost again. Thank you all for listening."

When they were done, I just looked at Sam. I couldn't even talk; my throat was choked with unshed tears. I was beyond sad; I was numb. How could this have happened to Nancy? She was so young, so vibrant, so alive. I took Sam's hand and got up. I needed to see Max and Julie. We left the room and found them talking to

Barry in a corner of the lobby. I stood there, unsure of what to say to them. Julie saw me and came right over, tears streaming down her face. "Oh, Brenda, I am so sorry that you had to hear about Nancy that way."

"Julie, how can you even apologize to me? I can't even put into words my sorrow at the news. I am sorry that we lost touch, Julie, so sorry. Oh, Brenda, we each got caught up in our own lives and in our hopes that this whole ugly situation was behind us, but it isn't. It never was. I just fooled myself into believing that she was okay, better, and that she had put all of this behind her. That will always be my biggest regret, my biggest sorrow."

At that point, I reached over and hugged her. We both just stood there and shed the tears that we both were holding back. Once we were cried out, Julie asked, "So how is Molly doing?"

"I think she's doing okay. She did relapse after she left sober living and went to a different facility. Now she is living with her boyfriend. She doesn't share much with me anymore. But whenever I see her, she seems good."

"Brenda, you need to push. I know what everyone here tells us not to. That we need to let them find their way, be their own person, work their own program. But we are their mothers. We know them better than anyone does. We need to be there. We need to question the work they are doing on their recovery, and we need to hover. More so now than when they were young. I think that if I had followed my instincts, maybe Nancy would still be alive."

"Julie, you can't blame yourself. We want to see exactly what it is that they show us. We want to believe." We stood together for a few more minutes talking, promising to keep in touch. Then they left.

After they left, Barry and Amanda walked over. Amanda spoke first. "Brenda, Nancy just passed away a few weeks ago. I am pretty sure that Molly doesn't know yet, and quite frankly, I am worried about how she will take the news."

I hadn't thought about that, but I was in agreement with Amanda. I didn't think that Molly was going to take this news well. I looked over at Sam; he was nodding. Barry spoke next. "Maybe you should encourage her to make next week's meeting. We can tell her then. That way, you are not the ones giving her this news."

Again, I looked over at Sam. He spoke. "I think that may be a good idea, but I want to have a chance to talk to Brenda first. We can call you in the morning."

"Sure," answered Amanda. "Tomorrow is fine." We thanked them both for their time, then we left.

We didn't say a word to each other on the walk to the car, but once in the car, my words came rushing out. "I can't believe that Nancy is gone. I don't know how her parents can go on. What, Sam, do we do about Molly? I thought that having her make a meeting here next week was the perfect plan, but I don't think so now. I think she is going to wonder why now, all of a sudden, I am pushing her to make a meeting here. The more I think about it, the more I think we should be the ones to tell her. Don't you agree, Sam?"

"Brenda, I will support whatever decision you think is the right one to make. I do agree that she will wonder why you are suggesting that she go to a meeting here all of a sudden. What if she doesn't want to go, what then?" he asked. It was decided we would tell her.

Sam suggested that I call her to see if she was home. Tonight would be as good a time as any. "I don't want her to find out from someone else" was Sam's biggest concern now.

She answered right away. "Hi, honey, it's Mom. Sam and I were wondering if you were home and if we could come by for a bit."

"Sure, Mom. I'm home. Of course you can come by. Are you guys okay?"

"Yes, honey, we are fine. We just wanted to see you for a few minutes."

"Well, then, come on over." After I hung up, I just looked at Sam. "Oh, Sam, I just don't know how I am going to tell her this. This is going to break her heart. You know how close she was to Nancy. Don't you remember when we went to pick Molly up from the sober house, she was disappointed that Nancy didn't stay as long as she did? I am sure that they kept in touch for a bit after they both went home."

"Well, Brenda, if you want, I can be the one to tell her."

"I don't know, Sam. Let's get a feeling for how things are when we get there."

The drive to Molly's house was a short one; we were pulling up into her driveway in no time. I tried to put a smile on my face before we got to the front door so that I wouldn't worry her. She was waiting at the door for us with a big smile on her face. "Hi, Mom. Hi, Sam. This is such a nice surprise. You should do this more often."

"Hi, sweetie," said Sam.

I couldn't speak, so I just hugged her. "What's wrong, Mom? And don't lie—I can tell by your face that something is wrong."

I took her hand and lead her to the couch. I cleared my throat once, then again, all of a sudden, I couldn't find my voice. I looked over at Sam, pleading with him to help me. He looked at Molly and in a gentle voice told her the story.

For what seemed like an eternity she said nothing, then she leaned into me and started to sob. She kept saying over and over again, "No, this can't be true." I held her the way I used to hold her when she was little. I had no words of comfort for her.

After a while, she got up and started to pace the floor. "Why wasn't I there for her? Mom, why didn't she call me, ask for help, something?"

"I don't know, honey. Maybe she didn't know how. Maybe she got caught up in something that pulled her down to a point where she didn't know how to get up. No one will ever really know what happened."

"Mom, how do you know about Nancy?"

"Well, Sam and I went to a meeting at your old rehab, and the speakers tonight were Max and Julie."

"Why did you guys go to a meeting?"

"Well, I spoke to Amanda yesterday. She asked me if I had followed up on her suggestions of finding a sponsor, a therapist, and meetings on my own. Of course you know the answer to those questions. I decided to go to a meeting, maybe connect with someone who could be my sponsor. As you can imagine, once we heard their story, any thought of doing anything else flew out of my mind. We spoke to them for a few minutes before we came here. We wanted to tell you ourselves."

"I am glad you did, Mom. I am not sure how else I would have found out if you didn't."

We sat together for quite some time before Molly asked us if we didn't mind leaving; she wanted some time to process everything that we told her and she wanted to call her sponsor. We hugged her goodbye, and as we were leaving, I heard Sam whisper, "Don't forget, Mol, if you need anything or to talk, you can always call me."

"I know, Sam, thank you."

The car ride home was silent. Again, each of us were wrapped up in our own thoughts. Once we got home, Sam asked me how I thought Molly was going to do once this sunk in. "I'm not sure, Sam. I know that she was close to Nancy. And I know that on some level she blames herself for not being there for Nancy. Although I am not sure what Molly could have done for her. I am going to wait until Saturday to mention to her that Barry suggested that she make a meeting there."

It hit me at that moment that I never gave her the envelope that Barry had asked me to give her. "Sam, how about we have dinner at Molly's restaurant tomorrow? I can give her the letter from Barry and we can see how she is doing."

"Sounds like a plan to me, Brenda."

Luke was coming out of his room when we went upstairs. "Hey, guys, how was the meeting?"

"It was very difficult," replied Sam. "We found out that Nancy overdosed and passed away a few weeks ago."

"Oh man, that is horrible. I can't imagine how bad Molly is going to handle this when she finds out."

"We just left your sister. We thought that it was best that she heard it from us."

"How did she take it, Mom?"

"She of course was very sad about it and had some feelings of guilt over not being there for her, but we told her that there was no way she could know that Nancy was struggling. Apparently, they lost touch a few months back. Amanda and Barry suggested that Molly try to make a meeting next week. I didn't mention it to her yet, but Sam and I talked about having dinner at her restaurant tomorrow. If we do, I think I will tell her then."

"This stinks, Mom. I think I am going to call her now to see how she is."

"I think that's a great idea. I'll say good night then. See you in the morning."

We never spoke about Nancy again. Molly never brought her up, and when I tried to, she just looked at me and walked away. She let me know without telling me that the subject of Nancy was off limits.

Chapter 33

The rest of the summer moved at a very rapid pace. Before we knew it, it was time to pack Luke up for college. He had decided on going to a college about two hours away. He would be living on campus; it was close enough to come home if he wanted to and for us to go see him. The night before he left, I made a special dinner, all of his favorites, and had Molly and Vinny over. It had a bittersweet feel to it. Stacy was devastated that he would be gone; she had one more year of high school to finish, and her plan was to go to the same college he was at. They were still inseparable, and this would prove to be very difficult for her. I had a difficult time adjusting in the weeks following his departure. For all intent and purposes, Sam and I were empty nesters. We had the house to ourselves. It was a new and slightly odd feeling for me, an adjustment that I was having difficulty with. Sam, on the other hand, was enjoying it. He thought that it was a much-needed break for him and me. It was, as he put it, "the honeymoon that we never had." There was no one to worry about but each other. Molly seemed to have settled into a routine; she and Vinny were doing well and we saw them once a week. Luke was settled into his dorm and was enjoying the classes he was taking. Things, he kept reminding me, were going well. Everything was right in my world. September rolled into October and then into November. Luke would be coming home for Thanksgiving, and I was so excited to see him.

The night before he was due home, I was out running around doing my usual last-minute things, when Sam called me. "Hi, honey, how long until you get home?" he asked.

"I'm not sure—probably about an hour. Why, what's up, do you need anything?"

"No, I'm good. Molly just called and asked if we could come over. I told her that I would let her know."

"I can come home now, Sam. I am pretty much done. The few other things I wanted to do can wait. See you soon."

On my drive home, I wondered for a minute why Molly called Sam and not me directly, but I really didn't worry about it too much. Molly and Sam had built a wonderful relationship; he was the dad she always wanted, and he took such joy in having a daughter.

Sam was waiting for me when I walked in. "Let me help you put everything away. I told Molly we would be there soon." After a few minutes of unloading, we were back in the car and headed to Molly's. In hindsight, I should have realized that something was wrong by the fact that Sam was quiet on our ride to Molly's house. As we were turning onto her block, I saw her; she was walking down the street. I thought to myself how odd this was as Sam told me that she was expecting us. Once Sam saw her, he pulled over and got out. Before I even had a chance to get out, he was walking back to the car.

"Brenda," he said, "why don't you drive to Molly's house? We will meet you there in just a bit. Molly wants to talk to me for a few minutes."

"Sam, what is going on?"

"I am not sure, Brenda, but just trust me on this. Please go to the house." I slid over to the driver's side of the car and drove on to Molly's house. I sat there for a few minutes. I had an odd feeling in the pit of my stomach. I finally got out of the car and headed to the front door. Vinny was waiting in the living room looking like death warmed over.

"Hi, Vinny, can you please tell me what is going on? I just saw Molly walking down the street. Sam is with her now."

Vinny just looked at me and shook his head and said, "I'm not sure myself. As soon as I walked in, Molly started to cry and walked out. I guess that's when you saw her."

We both just looked at each other and sat down on the couch, waiting. After what seemed like hours, Sam and Molly walked in. Molly was clinging to Sam's hand like it was her lifeline. He eased her down into a chair and came to sit next to me. My heart felt like it was beating out of my chest as I sat there waiting for what was to come. Sam spoke first. "Molly and I had a long talk about this, and she is worried and scared about what you both will say and do. I promised her that at the very least, you, Brenda, would be there for her." He then looked over at Molly and nodded.

Molly sat there for a minute before she started to talk; her voice was so low that I had to strain to hear what she was saying.

"Mom, I relapsed again." It was three simple words that once again changed our whole lives. I sat there for a minute totally speechless; I had no words. I didn't know what to say. I wanted to be sure that whatever I said would be supportive and not judgmental. My first instinct was to go over to her and hug her, but I wasn't sure if that was the right thing to do. I was the one that she usually came to with her problems; this time, she went to Sam. I was glad that she felt like she could go to him, but I wasn't sure what my role in this situation was.

As I was thinking about all of this, I heard Molly say, "Mom, please don't be mad at me. I am sorry that I did this again." Her words snapped me out of my self-centered daze.

"Molly I am not mad at you. I could never be mad at you for this. I am sorry that we weren't there for you when you were struggling so."

"I know, Mom. By the time I realized that I was struggling, it was too late—one thing led to another and here we are again."

Through our whole conversation, Vinny sat there in silence. He finally spoke up. "Molly, I am sorry that this has happened, but I don't think that I can go through this again. I want to be here for you, but I don't really think I can. I am going to stay at my parents' house tonight, and then tomorrow we can figure things out." With that, he got up and just left.

I was horrified. I could not believe that this man who supposedly loved my daughter could just get up and leave when she clearly needed him the most. Molly just sat there; she didn't seem in the least bit surprised by his behavior. "Molly," Sam said, "I think it would be better for you if you packed a bag and came home with us tonight. In the morning, we can figure out our best course of action."

"Mom, is that okay?"

"Of course it is, Molly. You never, ever had to ask if you can come home. It's your home too."

"Okay then, just give me a few minutes to pack some things to take."

Once she went upstairs, I turned to Sam and asked, "Did you know about this before we came here?"

"No, honey, I didn't. I just knew something was wrong. Molly called me earlier today and asked if we could come over. She wanted to talk to us, but apparently, she and Vinny had an argument before we got here, so that's why she was walking down the block. When I got out of the car, she asked me if she could talk to me alone, which as you know I said yes to."

"Sam, I am so glad that she feels comfortable talking to you. I don't know what any of us would do without you."

"Well, Brenda, you will never have to find out."

Molly came down a few minutes later with two bags. "I hope you don't mind but I really want to stay a few days, I just don't want to come back here."

"Of course, honey. You can stay as long as you want to," replied Sam. I myself wasn't so sure that would turn out to be the plan.

When we got home, Molly went right up to her room; she told us that she was tired and wanted to get some sleep. Sam and I went into the living room to talk. "What are we going to do, Sam? I think she needs to go back to a rehab facility, don't you?"

"I agree. I think we need to find one for her that isn't in New York."

"What?" I said. "You want to send her away?"

"Well, she has been to three facilities here, and they didn't produce long-term results. Maybe if we send her out of state, we will get a better outcome."

I sat there thinking about what he said. Maybe he was right, but I had no idea where to find one. "Brenda, how did you find the first facility you sent her to?"

"I looked online and found the only one that took our insurance."

"Well," he said, "maybe we should do some research and look for facilities that are out of state and takes our insurance."

"I guess we could do that."

We went up to our office to start our research; it didn't take long for us to find about a dozen websites that offered treatment. We were inundated with information. So much so that we were having trouble finding something that we thought would work for us. Finally, Sam found a website that sounded promising. There was an 800 number that promised to answer twenty-four hours and seven days a week. We decided to give this one a call. The phone was answered almost immediately by a very nice-sounding man. He introduced himself to us over the phone, telling us his name was Tim. He listened to everything we had to say. When we were done, he began asking us questions. Unfortunately, we were unable to answer most of them. He assured us that it was okay because eventually he would need to speak to Molly directly; he would need to find out what drugs she was taking and how much. He told us about the program his facility offered; he also told us that his facility was located in Florida.

"Florida," I said. I didn't know how I felt about sending her so far away. Tim went on to explain to us that he found that sometimes going out of state worked best, because there were no outside distractions. He told us that Molly would be able to concentrate on herself and no one else. He reiterated that addicts had the best chance of long-term recovery when taken out of their comfort zone. He told us about people, places, and things.

"If you put an addict back with the same people, they will find the same places and go back to the same things. Sending her out of state may be the best thing for her."

We thanked Tim for his time and told him that we would talk to her and get back to him the next day. He gave us his private cell number because he said he would be off the next day. But would be back again on Thursday. I thanked him and we hung up. I looked at Sam and asked, "Thoughts?"

"Well, what he said makes sense, but do we want to send her so far away?"

"I don't know, Sam. How about we sleep on it and talk to her in the morning?" he suggested.

"Sounds good to me."

We were up early the next day; I still had to get some things done before Luke came home. I couldn't believe that Thanksgiving was in a day. I felt so overwhelmed by everything. I was in the kitchen cooking when I heard Molly calling for me. "I am in here, honey."

When she walked in, I noticed for the first time how skinny she was. I couldn't believe that I missed seeing that. "How are you today, Mol?"

"I'm okay, just really sorry that I am putting you through this again."

"Molly, it's not me that you need to worry about. I am worried about you and what this is doing to your body."

"I'm okay, Mom, just so upset with myself."

Sam walked in at that moment so I decided that maybe this would be a good time to talk to Molly about the facility that we found in Florida. She sat there listening to everything we had to say. When we were done telling her all about it, she looked at both of us and said, "I think it's a good idea. I think that I will benefit from going away. How soon can I go?"

"I'm not sure, honey. We spoke to this person on the phone last night—he is an intake counselor and needs to speak to you himself. He gave us his number and told us to call him if we had any other questions or if you wanted to talk to him yourself."

"I think that I would like to talk to him, Mom. Can I have his number?"

"Sure, honey, let me get it." I went back up to our office to retrieve the paper that I had written his number on. As I walked back down, I saw Luke pulling into the driveway. I was waiting at the door when he came in. I was so happy to see him.

"Mom, were you waiting at the door for me all morning?" he asked with his typical twinkle in his eye.

"No, I was not," I laughed. "I was just lucky enough to see you as I was coming down."

"Where is everyone?" he asked.

"In the kitchen, where else would they be?"

As he walked in, he commented on the wonderful smell. "I have missed the smell of home cooking, Mom. I am glad to be home."

"Well, I am glad that you are home as well. Hi, guys," he said as he walked into the kitchen, "why is everyone so glum?"

"Hi, Luke," said Molly as she jumped up to give him a hug.

"Hi, Mols, how's it going?"

She hesitated for a minute before answering, "I relapsed, Luke. I just told Mom and Sam last night."

"Oh wow, that stinks. How are you handling it? And more importantly, what are you going to do about it?"

"Mom told me about a place I can go to in Florida. I think that it's my best option at this point. I was just going to call this intake counselor that Mom and Sam spoke to last night."

"Well, don't let me stop you. I'll hang out here with the folks while you do what you have to do."

It was much later before Molly came back down. "I had a really good conversation with Tim. He told me all about the program and what I could expect if I went there. I really want to go, Mom. I think that it's my best option right now.

"He told me that all you need to do is get me there. Someone from their facility will pick me up at the airport and bring me to the detox portion of the program first, and then I will go to the rehab side. He said that they can take me as soon as Friday or Saturday."

I sat there for a minute. My mind was racing. *Do we send her to Florida?* Some place where we couldn't see her. My heart was telling me that this was a terrible idea. She would be gone again for the holidays. But my head was saying that this was her best bet for long-term recovery. I looked at Sam; it was as if he was reading my heart and mind. He simply said, "We think you should go. If you believe that this will benefit you and help in your recovery, then we are all for it. I just ask that you stay until Saturday. This way, your mother and I can spend some time with you before you go."

Molly jumped up and hugged us both and said that she really wanted to stay until then; she turned to Luke and asked him if he would help her move out of the house she was sharing with Vinny. In her mind, they were over. If he couldn't support her now when she needed him the most, then they were done.

"Of course," Luke answered. "I can get a couple of my friends to help. We will have you out on Friday."

"Thank you everyone for supporting me. I am sorry that I have disappointed you all once again."

"Molly, honey," I said, "this is not about any of us. This is about you and getting you healthy again. We are your family and are prepared to do whatever we can to help you."

After that, she excused herself to go to her room; she wasn't feeling well and wanted to lie down. Once she was gone, Luke looked at us and said, "You know that she isn't feeling well because she is withdrawing from whatever it is she is on."

The thought hadn't crossed my mind. I just sat there thinking about this whole situation. Luke excused himself to go to his room to unpack. Once he was gone, I turned to Sam. "Now what?" I asked."

"We wait and see how the rest of the day goes." I guess that there wasn't much else we could do at this point. "Brenda, I'm going to look for flights going to Florida on Saturday."

"Thanks, Sam. I have to get back to preparing for tomorrow." I couldn't believe that Thanksgiving was tomorrow. I busied myself with preparing everything, I was trying not to think too much about what the coming weeks would bring.

Thanksgiving was a somber day in our house; we all put on a happy face so that no one would suspect that there was anything going on. I usually enjoyed Thanksgiving so much, but this year, all I could think about was Molly, I couldn't wait for the day to be over.

The next day dawned cold and rainy. It was our tradition to decorate the house for Christmas. This year, we decided not to do it.

Molly needed help moving out of her house, and to be honest, no one was in the mood to decorate. After we were done moving her, we spent the rest of the day together, just the four of us. Luke was strangely quiet and wanted to stay home with us. I even asked him why he wasn't seeing Stacy. His answer was, "I'm just not up to it today."

Bright and early the next day, we were driving Molly to the airport. She wanted to take the earliest flight possible; it was as if she couldn't leave fast enough. We stayed with her at the airport until the last possible second. When I hugged her goodbye, I didn't want to let her go. My heart was breaking for this gentle soul, my sweet baby girl. I waved to her until I couldn't see her anymore. Once she was gone, I fell into Sam's arms weeping as if my heart was breaking. He just stood there holding me until I had composed myself enough to walk to the car.

"Brenda," he said, "she will be okay. This is something I know. She is strong and resilient. She came to us to tell us that she relapsed—that is something in and of itself."

"I know, Sam. It's just that I feel like such a failure. How could this have happened again?"

"Brenda, only Molly knows what is going on. Remember what Amanda told you—she may not be ready to talk to you about the underlying issues that she is struggling with."

"I know, Sam. I just wish she would."

"I know you do."

When we got home, Luke was gone; he left a note telling us he was picking Stacy up and bringing her back to our house. They were both going to help us decorate the house. It made my heart happy that Luke was trying to make things as normal as possible despite the things that were going on. Midday, we received a call from Molly; she was settled at the detox facility. She was allowed one call to let us know that she was safe and settled. She would not be able to call us again until she was at the rehab itself. I felt a sense of unease at this.

Once we hung up, I called Tim. He explained that this was the policy but that I would be getting a call from Molly's counselor in the next hour or two; he also went on to tell me that if I had any questions or concerns going forward I could call him. This gave me a sense of peace; at least there was someone I could talk to if necessary.

True to his word, Tim had Molly's new counselor call us that afternoon. She introduced herself. Her name was Ruth, and she would be working with Molly once she got to the rehab. She gave us a rundown as to how things worked there. It was different than the other facilities Molly was in. Molly would be staying in Florida for at least six months. The first four would be at the rehab, and the following two would be in a sober facility. I told her that we were familiar with sober living as she had lived in one once before. She also told me that there was one family weekend before Molly moved into the sober house. She wasn't sure yet when it would be, but she wanted to let us know that there would be one. We spoke for a while; she sounded pleasant enough and told us that she would be calling us weekly to let us know Molly's progress. Molly herself would be able to also call us once a week. It was at that point that I asked her whom else she would be able to call. Ruth's answer was simple: no one but her parents. I was relieved to hear that. I didn't think that it was necessary for her to keep in touch with Vinny. As far as I was concerned, he was out of her life. I felt that a clean break was the best route to go. We spoke for a few minutes longer. Just before we hung up, Ruth said, "Remember, Molly is here because she feels that this is her best option, and please know that you are free to call either myself or Tim." I thanked her and we hung up. I went in search of Sam to let him know how my conversation went. He was happy and relieved to hear that things were going well. I, on the other hand, still had my concerns. But I vowed to myself that I would just ride it out.

Christmas came and went mostly low key. Luke came home for Christmas and was oddly quiet. I just chalked it up to Molly being gone again. As promised, I received a call from both Ruth and Molly once a week. Ruth's calls were much more informative, telling me how Molly was progressing. Molly's calls were almost like a check in as if she was just away at college. She really did not go into much detail as to what was going on and what her days looked like. At first, I tried to press her for more details, but when I realized that she really didn't want to discuss her days, I stopped asking. I just tried to enjoy her calls for what they were, Molly checking in. I did, however, speak to Tim nearly daily. We had an unspoken agreement; when I felt myself on the edge, I would call him, and he would talk me down. He was becoming my counselor, my sponsor, my friend. It is a friendship that to this day I still cherish. Tim had a back story as well. He was an addict who had twenty-plus years of sobriety. It took him almost losing his wife for the last time to realize that he needed to make changes, long-lasting changes. He considered himself one of the lucky ones.

When I asked him how he was lucky, his answer was simple. "I never killed anyone in the throes of my addiction, including myself. I was granted the gift of realization before it was too late." I totally cherished my conversations with Tim, and I credit him with getting me through this dark stage of our lives.

Chapter 34

Our life quickly set into a new normal. Sam and I went to work every day; we tried to maintain some kind or routine. I found myself constantly waiting for calls from Ruth, Molly, and Luke. My life revolved around waiting. I forgot how it felt to be happy and calm. Sam tried his best to keep things light. He was forever trying to find new things for us to do. I credit him for keeping me sane. I was sitting at my desk at work when I got the call. It was Ruth, and she was calling to tell me that Molly's family weekend was coming up. She gave me the dates and told me that it would be beneficial for us to come. I told her that I needed to talk to Sam and then let her know. It was the same day that Gail got the call that her dad passed away. We were both hit at once. Gail, of course, left immediately, promising me she would call me when she had more information. The rest of the day passed in a blur. I was thankful when it was finally time for me to leave. I was waiting in the living room for Sam to come home. As soon as he walked in, I told him about family weekend and about Gail's dad.

He sat down, asking me, "What now?"

"I am not sure, Sam. I guess I have to wait to hear from Gail. Once she gives me the details, we can make a decision as to whether or not we can go."

My heart was breaking; I couldn't bear the thought of missing this opportunity to see Molly. It wasn't until the next night that Gail finally called me. "Brenda, I am going to be missing the next two weeks of work. I am sorry to leave you with this burden."

"Oh, Gail, don't even worry about any of that. Work will be fine. Take all the time you need."

"Thank you, Brenda, I appreciate that." She gave me the information regarding the wake and funeral.

Once I hung up, I turned to Sam. "Well, we have our answer. I won't be able to go to see her, Sam. Gail will be gone for two weeks. We can't leave our office without coverage." Then I burst into tears. "How could I call me daughter and tell her that I couldn't come?"

Sam suggested that I call Tim and tell him what was going on. I checked the time before calling him; he answered fairly quickly. "Hi, Brenda, how are you doing?"

"I am terrible, Tim. Ruth called me yesterday to tell me about Molly's upcoming family weekend. Unfortunately, my co-worker experienced a death in her family, and I won't be able to make the weekend. I haven't told Molly yet, but I feel terrible about it."

"Brenda, you can't beat yourself up over what you have no control over. Molly is going to have to learn to accept disappointment and how to handle those feelings—what better place to do that than here?"

"I understand that, Tim, but that doesn't make me feel any less terrible."

"I'm sure it doesn't but you also need to learn how to not feel guilty about saying no to your kids. It's a habit I think you got into long ago and one that needs to be broken for all of you to build a healthy relationship moving forward." We talked for a while longer before I asked him to have Molly call me.

"I want to tell her about this sooner rather than later."

"Sure, I'll go find her right now and have her to call you. If you need to, you can call me when you are done talking to her." Not more than ten minutes later, I received the call I was dreading.

"Hi, Mom, what's up? Tim told me that you wanted me to call you."

"I did, honey. I didn't want to wait to tell you that Sam and I won't be able to come to visit you on family weekend. I am so sorry, but Gail's dad passed away, and I can't take the days off from work to get there."

"It's fine, Mom, how many more of these weekends can you come to anyway?"

"Molly, I would come to every one that there was if that's what it took to help you get through this."

"I know, Mom. I won't say that I am not disappointed, but I understand. Listen, Mom, I wish I could talk about this more, but Tim pulled me out of group. I really have to get back. Talk again later?"

"Sure, that's fine. I love you, Molly."

"Love you too, Mom." And then she was gone.

After I hung up, I sat there for a while thinking about our conversation. I was glad that she took it in stride. I was afraid that she would be angry at me, but clearly she wasn't. Sam found me still sitting there an hour later. "Brenda, are you okay?"

"Yes, Sam, I'm fine I spoke to Molly some time ago and told her that we would not be able to make the family weekend and she seemed okay with it."

"Good, honey. I knew she would understand. I don't think you give her enough credit."

We had traveled into the new year mostly unscathed. Midway through March, I received a call that I was hardly ready for. Molly was ready to move on to their sober living facilities. They were recommending that she go to an all-female house about ten minutes away from the facility she was currently in. This way she would be able to walk back and forth for her continued treatment. She would be transitioning from inpatient to outpatient. She would be required to get a job, make a meeting a day, and continue working her steps with her sponsor. I worried that once again it would be too much on her plate, but both Ruth and Tim assured me that she could handle it all if she stayed on program. I prayed that she would. Molly was excited about making the move; in typical Molly fashion, she made some new friends, and two of them were moving with her. Of course they were her "new best friends." It seems as if she found new best friends in every facility she went to. She gave me a list of approved things to send her so that she could make her room as comfortable as possible. She was excited about moving to her sober living facility, but she was even more excited about the prospect of coming home in two months.

Sam and I spent the next few days gathering everything that it was that she wanted. We sent out five care packages to her. Sam chuckled at the thought of Molly having to pack it all up and bring it home with her when she left Florida. The next two months flew by, and it was soon time to book Molly's return flight home. The night before she was due home, I had a really long talk with Tim. I was scared at the prospect of her coming home. Were there things that I needed to look for? Signs that I overlooked the last time? Things we should be doing and things we shouldn't be doing?

He assured me that Molly herself knew about her triggers and what she should avoid. She also knew how to work her program and what would happen to her if she didn't. I tried to be calm, but I just couldn't. I wanted things to be good for everyone, but I remembered what Tim had told me more than once: No one can control another person's happiness. That comes from each of us.

On the drive to the airport, I was somewhere between ecstatic and panicked. Sam, sensing my feelings, reached over and took my hand. As he kissed my fingers, he whispered, "Relax, it will be fine, but if it's not, we will get through it."

How I wished I had Sam's outlook on things. He dropped me off and went to park the car. I stood there in the warm June sun and silently prayed that things would be okay. That this time Molly would get it and that life would return to normal. I did have to chuckle to myself at the last line of my prayer. Normal, what was our normal these days? Sam and I walked over to the baggage area, waiting for Molly to come down. I saw her first before she even saw me. I took the time to look at her; it had been six long months since we saw her. She looked great—lean but not skinny, tan, not the pale Molly of months before. "Mom!" I heard her yell as I was still studying her.

"Molly, honey," I said as I opened my arms to catch this running, leaping, wonderful child of mine. Once I had her in my arms, I let go of the breath that I hadn't realized I was holding. It felt so good to have her in my arms again. Oh, how I missed her, missed the feel of her in my arms missed the way she hung on just the way she did when she was a little girl.

"Mom, Sam, I am so happy to see you both. I missed you guys."

"We missed you too, sweetie. Your mom has been running around all day getting everything ready, and of course cooking for you like you have not eaten in six months."

"Mom, I hope you made my favorite mac and cheese."

"Of course I did. It was the first thing I made."

"Let's get your bags, Mols, and let's get out of here," said Sam.

At that, Molly chuckled. "I have a few more things than just bags."

I saw Sam roll his eyes in that good-natured way of his. "How am I not surprised by that?" he said. The drive home was one filled with stories about what had been going on since we last saw her. She laughed at most things we told her. It wasn't until much later that day that she finally asked us about Vinny. Sam took over answering that question. "Well, Molly, right after you left, Vinny came by to talk to us. He wanted to try to explain why he didn't think he could support you this time. We listened to him, but honestly, neither one of us quite believed what he had to say. We haven't heard from him since. But what we do know for sure is that he moved back home right after you moved out."

Molly was quiet throughout the conversation. When Sam was finished, all she said was that she was glad that it was over.

It didn't take much time for Molly to get back into a routine. She had a sponsor whom she really liked; she was able to go back to her job at the restaurant but this time, it was just as a hostess. She made meetings every night, and when she wasn't working or at a meeting, she was at home. Things seemed, for all intents and purposes, to be moving in the right direction. Luke was back from school as well; he was working full time to save for an apartment for his sophomore year at school. He did not want to dorm again, and Sam told him that if he worked all summer, he would match whatever he made. So that was all the incentive that Luke needed. We were having a great summer, the kind of summer I had always hoped to have.

Mid July, Molly came home from work with a friend. She introduced us to him. His name was Adam, and they, it seemed, had gone to school together; he was a few years older but they had some friends in common. After that first day, Adam seemed to become a fixture in her life. Sam and I didn't exactly care for him. He seemed off somehow, but we couldn't put our fingers on it. It was Luke who finally came to us and told us what we, I guess, always knew but couldn't confirm. Adam had spent some time in jail. Luke went on to explain that he had been in jail for two years for selling drugs. Sam and I just stood there looking at each other, at a complete loss for words. "What do we do now? Do we confront her? Do we wait for her to come to us to tell us?" I had no idea what the right thing to do was. I suggested that we call Tim, maybe he would have an idea as to how to deal with this situation.

As always, he took my call. "Hi, Brenda, Sam, how are things going?"

We told him how things had been going and how things were now. When we were done, he asked us if we had any reason to believe that Molly relapsed. "I don't think so. She seems okay to me," said Sam.

"Brenda?"

"No, Tim, I think she is okay."

"Well, then we have some things that we can do. First off, you need to talk to her. Be honest. Remember, communication is key here. Tell her how you feel about the company she is keeping. Share with her your concerns. Ask her to explain to you why she thinks her involvement with this person is beneficial to her and her recovery, and remember, no matter what she says, hanging around with people like this is never a good idea."

"Tim," I asked, "do we forbid her from seeing him?"

"Well, guys, you can do that, but at the end of the day, we all know that Molly will do whatever it is she wants to do no matter what you say or what the consequences of her actions are."

"Great. I thought so. Basically, we are fighting a losing battle."

"Let's hope not," replied Tim. "I suggest that the sooner you have this conversation the better off you all will be, and remember, you can't keep Molly on the right track and you can't make her do anything she doesn't want to do. You can only control what you allow to happen in your house."

We both thanked Tim and hung up. We continued to sit there together, both lost in our own thoughts. Sam spoke first. "I think that we should talk to her tonight when she gets home."

"I agree, Sam, but first let's decide what we are okay with and what we are not okay with."

"Well, I'll start, Brenda. I am not okay with Molly bringing Adam to this house. I think that would only encourage her to keep seeing him."

"I agree, I also think that we should make it mandatory that she speak to her sponsor about Adam and that she should talk about him at her meetings. Maybe if she hears what her peers have to say, she will take that into consideration."

"I agree. So we have a plan?"

"Yes, Sam, we do." We continued our day waiting for Molly to return home. She walked in right on time and found us in the kitchen. Sam asked her to have a seat as we wanted to speak with her.

"Sure, guys, is everything okay?"

I started. "Molly, it has come to our attention that Adam may not be the best person for you to hang out with at this point."

I could tell by the way Molly's body changed in that instant that this conversation was not going to go well. "Well, Mom, I am sorry that you feel that way because Adam asked me to move in with him."

"He what?" I said much louder than I intended to.

"He asked me to move into his house with him. He lives at home but has a basement apartment and wants me to move in with him."

"You can't be serious, Molly."

"Oh, but, Mom, I am serious, very serious."

I knew that this conversation was inevitable. "I am sure, Sam, that you had your little spies out there checking him out."

Sam, who had been silent up to that point, jumped in. "As a matter of fact, Molly, I did. We love you and want to protect you. You are the most trusting person there is, and we didn't want you to get hurt."

"Yeah, I'm sure that's why," she mumbled under her breath. "Well, either way, I am going to move in with Adam, I would just appreciate it is you both would not be so uptight about everything all the time."

With that, she left the room; we both sat there speechless once again. How could this be happening again? I could not believe what I was hearing, Molly was moving out again, but this time she was moving in with a convicted drug dealer. Great, just great. What were her chances now of staying clean? I was so numb that I couldn't even cry. I just sat there in a daze. After a while, I heard the door slam. I jumped up only to see Molly lifting half a dozen bags full of what I can only assume were her clothes. Before I could even get out of the door, she was gone. Sam and I went up to her room to find it in shambles; it was as if she just pulled everything she owned out of her drawers and closets and dumped them into bags. I tried to call her cell phone, but it just went to voice mail. I was devastated. I had no idea what to do at this point. We didn't even know where he lived.

Hours later, Luke came home. "Hey, guys, is it true that Molly is living with Adam now? Do you think that it's a good idea?" he asked.

"No, Luke, of course we don't think it's a good idea, but we really didn't have a choice. We spoke to her when she got home and told her that we knew about Adam's background."

Before Luke could say anything, Sam jumped in to assure him that we didn't tell her he was our source of information. "Luke," I asked, "how did you know she moved out?"

"She called me, Mom. She was ranting about how you both are unfair and how you made your decisions about Adam without getting to know him."

"Well," said Sam, "I know all there is to know about him. As a matter of fact, I am going to make some calls right now to get the rest of his information." He got up and excused himself.

Luke and I were left sitting there. Luke spoke up. "Mom, I know that you are worried, but you know that there wasn't anything you could have done to stop her. She wants what she wants and doesn't care how it will affect anyone else."

I just sat there. I had no words left in me. After a few more minutes, Luke went to his room. He was meeting friends and wanted to get ready. Some time later, Sam came back in. "Brenda, I found out Adam's whole story. It appears that he was indeed arrested for selling drugs, but he is out on bail. He is waiting to be sentenced. If the judge has his way, he could be going upstate for several years."

"Oh, wonderful," I said. "Now what?"

"Now nothing, honey. There is absolutely nothing that we can do except be here for her."

I didn't hear from Molly again for several weeks. I tried calling her, but my calls always went to voice mail; she talked to Luke from time to time but she never talked to me or Sam. I was happy that she still talked to Luke because at least we knew that she was okay. Right before Luke was to leave to go back to school, Molly called me. She wanted to know if she could come by to get a few more things and to say goodbye to Luke. "Absolutely," I replied, "but please come alone. Adam is not welcome in our house."

"Of course, Mom, I am not stupid." And once again, she was gone. I had no idea what time she would be by, so I took the day off from work. Of course she showed up after 5:00 p.m. I watched her walk up the front path, noticing how thin she looked. She didn't have her usual jaunty walk; she was more subdued than usual.

"Hi, Mom," she said when she saw me at the door.

"Hi, honey, how are you?"

"I am fine, wonderful even."

"I am really glad to hear that. Are you hungry?" I asked her.

"No, I'm good. I just wanted to come by to say hi and grab some more stuff and to say goodbye to Luke."

"Well, he is upstairs doing his last-minute packing, and your room is exactly as you left it."

"Thanks, Mom. I will be done in a few." I proceeded to the kitchen to wait—for Sam, for Molly and for Luke. I was once again relegated to waiting.

Sam came in from work a few minutes later. "Hi, honey. From the look of things, I see that Molly is here."

"Yes, she is," I replied. "She just got here a few minutes ago. She's in her room now gathering some more stuff. Luke is in his room doing his last-minute packing as well. He is still insisting on leaving tonight."

"I wish he would wait until morning. Can you talk to him?"

"Sure, I can try, but as with everyone else in this family, when he makes his mind up, there is generally no swaying him."

"I would appreciate it though if you tried."

"Will do, let me just go up and change and see how everyone is doing up there. Be down in a jif."

I sat there thinking about how once again everything was changing; just when we were getting into a routine with Molly, she moved out. Now Luke was going back to school, and we would once again be just us. I wondered if other parents were feeling the same things as I was. Sam came down a few minutes later, followed by Luke and Molly. Molly was carrying two more bags. She stopped on the landing and reached out to hug Sam. I wondered what that was about. He stood there for a few minutes with her talking in tones too low for me to hear. I made a mental note to ask him about it when she left. She walked over to me next and hugged me. "I have to go, Mom. Sorry to just run in and leave, but maybe next week, we can have lunch or something. Can I call you?"

"Of course you can, sweetie, anytime you want to."

"Okay, baby brother, have a safe trip to school. I'll call you, but you know the phone works both ways—you can call me too."

"Yeah, I know, Mols, but you know me, I am not much of a phone person."

"Yeah, sure," she replied. "I am sure Stacy has a different idea about that." They gave each other a hug. It did my heart good to see them together; it happened so infrequently these days. Luke decided to walk Molly out to her car. I could see them talking at her car. Again, I wondered what was going on.

Luke walked in as his phone was ringing. "Hi, Stacy," I heard him say. "Yeah, I was planning on leaving tonight, but I can wait until tomorrow. What time are your parents planning on hitting the road? Okay, I can meet you at your house then. See you in the morning."

After he hung up, he explained that Stacy's parents didn't want to leave tonight; they wanted to leave in the morning, so he told them he would follow them up to school. As planned, Stacy was doing her freshman year at the same college Luke was at. "Luke, can I ask you what you and Molly were talking about?"

"You can ask me, but I don't think it's my place to tell you. Maybe you should ask Sam." He stood there for a minute before going to his room.

I went to the kitchen in search of Sam. He was rummaging through the refrigerator. "Hon, can I ask you something?"

"Sure, Bren, what's up?"

"What were you and Molly talking about on the landing?"

"I was planning on sharing it with you after she left. It seems as if Adam was finally sentenced. He will be serving three years upstate. He was transferred right from court to prison."

I just sat there staring at him. I could not believe what I was hearing. "When did this all happen?"

"Well, from what Molly told me, it happened two days ago."

"Two days ago and we are just finding out about it now."

"Yes, apparently, she didn't feel right sharing this with us."

"But she told you," I said.

"Yes, I know, but I think that the only reason why she told me was because she was worried that I may find out through work."

"Now what, Sam, what happens now?"

"Well, he serves his time in jail—that's what happens next."

"But what about Molly? What is her plan?"

"I believe that she plans to continue living in Adam's parents' house. He has a brother from what I understand who lives there as well. Apparently, his brother will be going up to see him and bringing Molly with him."

I just stood there staring at him. I was totally horrified by what I was hearing. "Are you okay with all of this, Sam?"

"Brenda, I don't really think we have a choice in this matter. It is what Molly intends to do whether we like it or not."

I walked away, shaking my head. I had no more words for this situation. All I knew for sure was that disaster was on the horizon.

Chapter 35

Unfortunately, my prediction was right. Molly got into the habit of going to see Adam almost every weekend. When his brother was unable to take her, she took the bus up to the prison to see him. I could not believe that this was happening. During this time, we saw very little of Molly. We kept inviting her over, and for one reason or another, she never came. It got so bad that Sam finally went over to Adam's house to see her himself. I was waiting anxiously for him when he got back. I saw him walking from his car to the house; the look on his face did not encourage me at all. When he walked in, he took my hand and led me back to the couch. "Brenda, what I am going to tell you is not good. I saw Molly. She looks terrible—she is skin and bones and very pale. Of course she insists that she is fine, 'just tired,' but Brenda, she has relapsed. This time, she has moved on to heroin."

At that last sentence, all I could do was cry. "Brenda, I offered her all kinds of help, but she is not interested in any of it. She claims she is happy with her life and does not want us to interfere in anyway."

"Oh, Sam," I wept, "now what? We know how this will end— we have been to so many meetings. It never ends well."

"I know, honey, I just don't know how we can help someone who clearly wants no help from us or anyone else. We just sat there together, both scared at what the outcome of this could be. Sam held me as I cried; for once in my life, I was hit with crippling panic. After what seemed like hours, I decided to call Tim. I needed his help now more than ever. I was taken by surprise when instead of hearing his cheery hello I got his voice mail. By that time, I was almost hysterical, so I am sure the message I left for him was almost impossible for him to understand. To my great relief, he called me back within the hour.

"Hi, Brenda, you okay? I could barely understand what it was you said."

As soon as I heard his voice, I started to cry again. Of course he couldn't understand a word I was saying, so Sam took the phone out of my hand and explained to Tim what was going on. Once he was done, he put Tim on speaker phone so I could hear what he had to say. He told us how risky Molly's behavior was; he told us that we needed to try to persuade her to go back into treatment. He said that heroin was the big time, that there was no going back now. Her new habit would lead her down a rabbit hole that she would not get out of on her own. I was sobbing through the whole conversation; Tim had put words to my worst fears. We asked him how we could get Molly the help she needed.

He spoke the words that I dreaded. "You both know that you can't do this for her. She needs to want to get help on her own. She will unfortunately need to hit her rock bottom before she can bounce up again."

"But, Tim, what if she doesn't get help before it's too late?"

"Brenda," he answered, "let's not think like that. Molly, I pray, will reach out to you both before it's too late.' We spoke for a little while longer and then hung up. I turned to Sam for answers. This time, he had none, he was just as worried as I was.

We were in no way prepared for what was to come; we had entered a chapter of our lives that was very unfamiliar. We went through high points and low points. The high points consisted of Molly reaching out to us for help, but by the time we either got to her or returned a message from her, she was on to the phase of being "fine" and not needing help. This continued for several months. I had sleepless nights more times than not at this point. I had gotten into the habit of calling her daily now just to make sure I talked to her. Of course, most days, I couldn't get her, and those times were the hardest to handle. My life had become one of constant worry. There were times that I even had Sam go out to look for her. We knew that she had quit her job. We knew that she had lost touch with just about everyone except for Adam's brother; he seemed to be her lifeline now. To say that we were living in chaos would be an understatement. I never knew from day to day if she was alive. The thought of losing her was too much for me to stand. I was constantly begging Sam to "fix this"; he was truly at a loss most of the time. He was, by nature, a fixer, but this, this was something even he couldn't fix. I spent sleepless nights where I would either pace the floors or cry myself to sleep. I was an emotional mess. But it all culminated with a call from an unexpected person.

It was after midnight when I heard the ringing of my phone. I immediately jumped up to answer it. Nothing good happens after midnight. "Hello!" I shouted. "Molly, is it you?"

After a second, I heard a voice that I hadn't heard in a while. It was Vinny.

"Vinny, are you okay?" I asked.

"No, not really," he answered. "Molly is here, and I think you both need to come over right now."

I hung up and woke Sam up as I was running around trying to get dressed. "Okay, Brenda, try to calm down I know you are upset, but Molly is with Vinny, so I am sure that for right now, things are okay."

"I know, Sam, but please just hurry. I want to get there before she leaves."

"I'm right behind you, honey. Let's go."

We made it to Vinny's house in record time. I practically jumped out of the car before it was stopped. We raced up to his door, where he was waiting for us. He walked us into his room, and there lying on his bed was Molly. At first, I thought she was dead—my heart dropped—but then her eyes fluttered open, and she seemed to be looking at me. "Mom," she said before she closed her eyes again. I looked at Sam and then at Vinny; I didn't know what to say.

"Vinny, why is she here?"

"She called me, Brenda, from a parking lot in a terrible neighborhood. She told me she was in trouble and needed me to come get her, which I did. When I brought her here, she had a needle hanging out of her arm. I had to pull it out and dress the wound it left. I didn't know what else to do, so I called you."

"Thank God you did, Vinny. Thank you for helping her."

Sam reached down and smoothed the hair off her face. "It's okay, Molly. We are here now," he whispered. "We are bringing you home." He lifted her up as if she weighed nothing and took her to the car. I stayed back for a minute longer to thank Vinny again. He looked at me and told me that we needed to get her help right away; he didn't know how much longer she could survive like this.

Sam and I were quiet on the ride home; neither of us knew what to say. When we got home, Sam brought her up to her room and carefully laid her down on her bed. I decided to stay with her that night. I didn't trust that she was okay, and I certainly didn't trust that she would stay at home once she woke up. My fears were correct: once she woke up and realized where she was, she wanted to leave. She was angry at Vinny for calling us. She of course said that she was fine; she didn't know what happened but was sure that it would never happen again.

"How do you know that, Molly? How do you know that next time you are going to be okay?"

"Because I do, Mom. I was stupid this time—I brought drugs from someone I didn't know. Next time, I will be more careful."

"Next time!" I shouted. "How can you even say next time?"

Sam came in to see what all the yelling was about. When he realized that Molly was up and mad, he tried to talk to her. He tried to explain the scene we walked into last night and our fear that we had lost her. Instead of her calming down and listening to him, she got angrier and finally blew up at both us. She was yelling that we needed to leave her alone, get out of her life; she was fine and perfectly in control of her life. As we stood there listening to her, we realized that she truly believed what she was saying; she was so far gone that nothing we could say would get through to her. Not now when she was in this state.

"Molly," I begged, "please stay here, please."

"Are you kidding, Mom? I wouldn't stay here if you paid me to. I am leaving, and there is nothing that you can do to stop me."

Sam and I both knew that she was correct; there was no way to force her to stay. So with heavy hearts, we watched our precious daughter leave once again. I stood there crying in Sam's arms, wondering if this was the last time I would see her alive. This patten went on and on for a year. Each time we saw her, she looked worse than the last time we saw her. Each time I saw her, I begged her to come home, begged her to let us get her help. Her answer was always the same: she was fine; we had the problems.

Her drug addiction at that point had completely taken over her life, so much so that we hardly knew her anymore. We had no idea what she did to survive, but Sam had a feeling he knew. The thought of that was just too gruesome for me to even think about. I can't even count how many times I thought we lost her. I can't even fathom how we hadn't. Our lives, along with hers, had spun out of control. We had no idea how to fix her or, for that matter, fix us. I spoke to Tim several times a day at that point; each call we had ended with him telling us that we needed to get her to treatment. I had run out of ways to try to reach her; she was in no rush to get the help that we knew she desperately needed. At this point, she was a full-blown heroin addict on the fast track to disaster. She still somehow managed to see Adam weekly. He of course fed into her paranoia that we were trying to control her, that we didn't care about her, and he was her only ally. She spent all of her other time with his brother, they had become "druggie buddies," spending what little money they had on drugs to feed their habits. It wasn't till years later that I found out that he was the one who shot her up for the first time.

I will never forget that last call that I got from Molly. I won't ever know what prompted it or why it happened at the time it did. I was sitting in our backyard lost in thought when my phone rang. It was Molly, and she was begging for help. She wanted to go to rehab; she was finally ready. It was a call that I had hoped for but never thought would come. On the slim chance that it would happen, Tim had found a rehab that could take her at a moment's notice. The only thing was that it was clear across the country in Arizona. Tim assured me that it was her best chance for success. Tim and I had become such deep friends that I trusted him totally at this point. I told Molly that we had a place for her. I didn't, however, tell her that it was in Arizona; I didn't want her to get spooked. I told her that she would need to do the intake herself and asked her if she wanted to come home to do it.

"Yes, Mom, I do. I will be there in an hour."

I found Sam sitting in our room doing pretty much what I was doing out back. "Sam, Molly is ready to go to rehab. She is coming over in an hour to do her intake call."

Sam looked at me and asked one simple question: "Does she know it's in Arizona?"

"No, Sam, I didn't tell her that. I thought it would be best to wait until she got here."

"Brenda, I don't want you to get your hopes up that she will go once she finds out it's in Arizona. She may not want to leave Adam."

"I know, Sam, but I am hoping that we can talk some sense into her."

"We can try, honey. That's the best we can do." We both waited in the living room for Molly to get there. As promised, she was there right on time. When she walked in, my heart broke; she was a mere shell of the person we knew. If she weighed ninety pounds, it was a lot; her eyes were sunken into her head. I could see every bone in her body. I tried not to stare or say anything; she was like a frightened deer. I didn't want her to run away from us. Sam led her to the couch and gently told her that the rehab we found for her was in Arizona; we thought that the distance would help her get clean and stay clean. She would have no interruption and could spend all the time she needed on herself. To our surprise, she agreed to go. She made the call to do her intake, and when she was done, she handed me the phone. Her intake counselor told us that they would make flight accommodations for the next day; they felt like the sooner they could get her there, the better it would be. I thanked him and hung up. Molly thanked us for setting this up for her. She wanted to go back to Adam's house for the night and promised to be back home in the morning. I told her that I would call her when I knew what time she would be leaving. She hugged both of us goodbye and left.

Sam and I just sat there, looking at each other, grateful for the gift we just got. The counselor called me back an hour later and told us that her flight left New York the next day at 7:00 p.m. It was the only flight that was a direct one; they found that it was best to have them fly direct. Once she landed there would be someone waiting for her to bring her to the detox facility first. They promised me that we would get a call from them once she landed and was safely in the car. I thanked him again, and we hung up.

I called Molly. She answered right away. She was glad that she was leaving at night the next day; she told us that it would give her time to spend with us before she left. She promised me that she would come home by twelve o'clock. She told me that she loved me before we hung up; it had been so long since I heard her say those words.

I couldn't sleep that night; I kept tossing and turning and worrying. The next morning came quickly, and I was relieved. We were just hours away from getting Molly the help that she needed so desperately. Sam and I were waiting for her at twelve o'clock. By one o'clock, when she still wasn't home, we both began to worry. What if she changed her mind, what it she decided not to go, what if something terrible had happened to her? By three o'clock, we were sure that something had happened. Sam and I had arranged for a driver to take us to the airport. The car would be at the house at four o'clock, so we decided to go to Adam's house, praying the whole way there that she would be there and be ok. Once we got there, Sam jumped out of the car and pounded on the door until someone finally opened it. To our shock and horror, it was Molly, and she, if possible, looked worse than she did the night before. Sam told her to get into the car. We were leaving immediately, he told her. At first, she fought him, but I guess she realized that she had no choice at this point. Back in the car we went. We needed to get home and get her bags, the ones I had packed the night before and be ready for the car to get us.

When we got into the house, Molly immediately went into the bathroom. After a few minutes, I knock to let her know that we were leaving. "I know, Mom," she whispered, "I am almost ready."

When she came out of the bathroom, she looked like death. "Molly, what is going on?"

"Nothing, Mom, I just wanted to make sure that I could make it through this trip."

"What does that mean, Molly?"

"Nothing, just nothing." Sam had to help Molly into the car; she was unsteady on her feet and couldn't seem to keep her eyes open. Once settled in the car, Molly leaned into Sam and put her head on his shoulder. I sat on the other side of her, holding her limp hand. All of a sudden, I had a sickening feeling. Was she going to make this trip? How would she be able to get onto a plane in this condition?

After a few minutes into the ride, Sam leaned over to me and said, "Brenda, is she breathing?"

"Oh my god, I don't think she is breathing." In that moment we both thought we lost her. Sam shook her several times before getting any kind of reaction from her. Before we knew it, we were pulling up to the airport terminal. Once again, Sam had to help her out of the car and into the airport. I saw him pull her aside while I was checking her bags. He was saying to her, begging her to tell him if she had any drugs stashed on her.

"Of course I don't, Sam, I'm not stupid."

It was clear that he didn't believe her; he told her that if she did there wouldn't be anything he could do to help her, this was out of his jurisdiction, smuggling drugs was a federal offense. She again told him that she didn't have anything on her. We both agreed that she was in no condition to make it to her gate on her own. So when she checked in, we asked the ticket agent if one of us could go with her to her gate; we told him that she was a nervous flyer and had taken something to calm her down and needed help to her gate. I could tell that he didn't quite believe us, but he did give me a companion pass to accompany her. She hugged Sam goodbye once again, assuring him that she wasn't stupid enough to bring drugs with her. Molly and I proceeded through security. I was holding my breath the entire time. By some miracle, we made it through. We were through the hardest part was behind us, or so I thought. Little did I know what Molly had in store for me on the other side. Once we made it to her gate, she demanded that I buy her a drink. I just looked at her as if she lost her mind.

"Are you kidding me, Molly? Don't you think you have had enough of whatever it is that you did today."

"Mom," she yelled, "just do it or I won't get on the plane." People were starting to stare at us at this point. Not knowing what else to do, I called Sam and quickly told him what was happening. He demanded to speak with Molly. I put her on the phone, and I could hear him begging her to just get on the plane. He was pleading with her by the end of the call. I tried to walk Molly to the plane, but all she wanted to do was have a drink; she even went up to random strangers asking them to buy one for her. I could not believe what was going on. I finally was able to calm her down; perhaps whatever it was she took in the bathroom at home was finally kicking in. Whatever it was, she became more manageable. Thankfully, it wasn't too long before her flight was called. I grabbed her and hugged her, telling her how proud I was that she was going to get the help that she needed. I told her how much I loved her more than once before she boarded her flight. I stood there watching her until I couldn't see her anymore and then reluctantly walked away. Sam was waiting for me exactly where I left him. As soon as I saw him, I started to cry once again. I told him that I was hoping that we made the right decision. He assured me that it was the only decision that we could make.

Once we got home, I called the facility she was headed to, to let them know that she was on her way to them. They assured me that they would call me once she landed and was safely with them. They thought that it would probably by around midnight their time, which would be 3:00 a.m. our time. Of course neither one of us got any sleep. I kept going over in my mind the events leading up to Molly getting on the plane. She seemed so out of control and so doped up; I hoped that the flight would be uneventful for her. Sam and I paced. We paced for hours that night. By 3:00 a.m., we thought we should have gotten a call; by 4:00 a.m., we were sure something had happened to her. I had started to cry at 4:00 a.m. I thought at that point we had sent her three thousand miles away to die alone. That could be the only reason we hadn't received a call from her or from anyone else yet. Her plane had landed over an hour ago. Of course, we tried to call her, but the call went straight to voice mail. We tried to call the person who was supposed to be picking her up, but that call went to voice mail as well. We continued to pace for another hour. I looked at Sam at 5:00 a.m., sure that my Molly had died, not sure what we were supposed to do now. Sam, who was forever the optimist, had no words of comfort. What I didn't know at that time was he was in agreement with me: our daughter had died on the flight there.

I had worked myself up to such a state by then that I didn't hear the phone ringing at first. I finally heard it and answered it. I sat there listening to the voice on the other end; all I could do was cry, deep, soul-wrenching sobs. After I hung up, I just looked at Sam. I could see the unshed tears in his eyes as he came over to hold me.

About the Author

I am a native New Yorker who has transplanted to Nevada for the time being. My mother instilled in me a love for reading at an early age. This has resulted in a lifelong habit. When I'm not writing or reading, I'm caring for and spending time with my family. This book would not have been possible without them.

CPSIA information can be obtained
at www.ICGtesting.com
Printed in the USA
LVHW112331220422
716780LV00001BA/10

9 781662 436543